THE
TANGLED GARDEN

THE
TANGLED GARDEN

Patricia Lawson

THE
LEISURE
CIRCLE

This edition specially produced for
The Leisure Circle Limited
by Century Publishing Co. Ltd,
Portland House, 12–13 Greek Street,
London W1V 5LE

Printed in Great Britain

To a very special group of friends

PART ONE

Chapter One

The lower stairs were in shadow. The child counted them as she climbed, carrying a mug of hot, strong tea in her hand. 'One, two, three, four, five . . .'

Upon the eighth stair the landing window spilled its light – a cascade of June morning, splashing, bubbling, dribbling its way down the rickety, uneven staircase. She reached for it with her toe, '. . . nine, ten, eleven, twelve . . .' until, at the fourteenth stair, she stood on the landing and lifted her face to the full warmth of the sun.

A pixie of a child, she had red-gold hair and the pale, translucent skin which so often goes with it.

At the landing window she stopped, balancing the mug of tea upon the sill, her fingernails absent-mindedly picking at peeling paintwork as her eyes gazed out across the garden.

It was a large garden – overgrown and untended, like the cottage – with a profusion of wild raspberries and rosebay willowherb, foxglove, mallow, and ox-eye daisies, and with bindweed and old man's beard fighting for prominence amid the elder hedge which marked its boundary.

To one side, cleared of buttercups and couch-grass, lay the vegetable plot, with its bandy rows of whiskered carrot tops and pale green peas twirling taut fingers round lengths of twine.

To the impercipient eye it might appear a tangled waste of unkempt vegetation, but to Barbie it was paradise. For Barbie knew every inch of this garden. She knew of the moist green hidey-hole beneath the elder hedge, where hop vines spread a curtain of secrecy; where she could sit and watch the rabbits at play, and listen to the blackbird chortling his song of territorial rights; could see the flash of the goldfinch's wing as he feasted

1

upon the seed-heads of the thistle, and listen to the hoarse, cracked squeal of the pheasant as he strutted through the barley field.

It was a garden of secrets known only to those who would sit cross-legged and watch the anthill at the foot of the walnut tree, and the beetles which hid beneath the stones. It held pleasures known only to those who had experienced the heady delights of running through shoulder-high cow parsley, or drowning in a great perfumed sea of honeysuckle.

Barbie sighed with a feeling of love and belonging which was almost pain. She never failed to stop and gaze from this window each time she climbed the stairs. It had been her home for all of her ten years and she would never wish to be anywhere else.

A flake of faded, brown paint embedded itself beneath her fingernail. She winced, and studied it for a brief moment, before flicking it towards the shadows at the foot of the stairs. Over the years, the pock-marked paintwork of the sill had given way to her absent-minded probing, until now its centre showed only bare wood, softened by decades of damp and neglect.

Downstairs the clock chimed. 'Oh Lordy.' Barbie lifted the mug of tea from the sill and moved swiftly towards the dim interior of the curtained bedroom.

'Gran . . . ?'

On the high feather bed the old woman slept, her mouth sagging toothless, her breath vibrating from her body in long, snorting blasts.

'Gran, it's a quarter to nine.'

Gran stirred, slapping her lips together in a series of short, sharp clacks, then closed them again folding her face like an old felt hat, and settled back into sleep.

'Come on, Gran.' Barbie placed the mug upon the battered surface of the bedside table and gently stroked the old lady's hair, running her fingers through sparse grey strands. 'It's a quarter to nine. I'll be late for school.'

'Barbie . . . ?' Gran forced open reluctant eyelids. 'What time is it?'

'It's a quarter to nine. Are you ready for your tea?'

'Please. I'll wake meself up when I've had me drop of tea.'

Gran was not old in years, having reached no more than her fifty-seventh birthday, but she was old in spirit. Overweight and slow moving, giving the impression of advanced years, she was considered old by all who knew her. All, except Barbie, who did not give the matter a moment's thought. Like every happy child, she counted her own progress in quarter years and took no note of the passage of time upon her elders. With her inner eye she knew every nook and cranny of this soft, comforting body but with her outer eye she did not see.

Gran had filled her whole life from the moment of her birth and, just as one does not always look at the sun, being content just to know that it is there, so Barbie did not look at Gran. She would have been hard pressed to name the colour of her eyes but she knew instinctively of her moods, her needs, her ups and downs, and she could foretell the thoughts almost before they formed in the old lady's mind.

Barbie held the mug to Gran's lips and she drank noisily, sucking up the strong brown liquid into her parched mouth.

'Have you been at that gin again, our Gran?' She withdrew the mug and peered down into Gran's face.

Gran reached out and took the mug, poured the last of its contents into her mouth, and set it down on the bedside table. 'That's better,' she belched. 'You always make a good cup of tea, my ducky.'

'You have been at that gin.' Barbie sat on the edge of the bed and gently took the old lady's hand in her own. Her voice held a strange mixture of concern and mild reproof far beyond her ten years. 'I can smell it on your breath.'

'And why shouldn't an old woman have a little drop of medicine when there's nothing else as can get her off to sleep?' Gran kept her eyes turned down towards the bed and, with her free hand, fingered the folded edge of the blanket. 'Since when do you begrudge an old woman a little drop of medicine?'

'Was it the pain again, Gran?'

'It was nothing. It was a touch of the screws and a little drop of medicine had me right in no time at all.'

'Come off it, Gran. You don't get screws in your tummy. Even I know that.'

'It's nothing, I tell you. It's only a twinge and a little drop of the medicine puts it right in no time at all.'

'That's three nights you've been out of bed this week. I reckon it's time you went to see the doctor. He'd give you something for it.'

3

'I'll do nothing of the sort. That Dr Martin has killed off more people in this village than he's cured. And as for that young Poulson, I knew him when he was sitting in a pram wearing wet nappies. You don't think I'm going to let him go prodding around my belly, do you?' She withdrew her hand from Barbie's grasp and played a tattoo on the bedclothes. 'That's all they know, these doctors. Come in, sit down, strip off, take this bottle of plonk, next patient please. I'm better off with me little drop of medicine.'

'But you sent me to Dr Poulson when I had a tummy ache.'

'That was different. You're a child and they've got ways of dealing with the young. It's different when you're old. You get twinges when you're old and there's nothing them damned doctors can do about it. I'm better with me little drop of medicine I tell you.' Gran set her lips into a rigid line of obstinacy and stared out of the window. 'There's nothing you can do about the twinges.'

Barbie sighed and dropped to her knees beside the bed searching for the gin bottle. She found it, lying on its side, rolled against the china chamber pot with its painted garlands of pink roses. The cottage did not boast an indoor toilet. It was not a matter to cause them concern but neither Barbie nor Gran had any mind to walk in the chill of the night to the privy at the far end of the garden. It was a journey rendered unnecessary by the strength of Barbie's young stomach muscles and of Gran's good sense to use the poe.

Barbie sprawled on her stomach reaching out to retrieve the bottle, then squatted back on her haunches and held it up towards the light. 'It's empty,' she said accusingly. 'There's nothing left.'

Gran flicked a quick glance towards the bottle then returned her eyes to stare out of the window. 'You must have knocked it over,' she said. 'You've spilled it all over the floor.'

'I have not. You drank the whole lot, Gran. There's nothing left.'

'It's spilled, I tell you. The whole lot has trickled through the floorboards. You look when you go downstairs. There'll be a stain right across the ceiling.'

'What will you do tonight, Gran? What if the pain comes back and you haven't got any gin?'

'And who's to say I'll get the twinges tonight?' Gran sat, her hands clenched above the blanket and her eyes staring through the window. 'Could be I'll be sleeping like a baby. And anyway . . .' she added '. . . there isn't any money.'

'It's Tuesday. I'll go and collect the pension.'

'Well, we've got to find the rent. There'll be the devil to pay if old Bateson turns up and we haven't got the rent.'

'I'll collect the pension at dinner-time and then I'll go and get some gin.'

'We haven't got the rent,' said Gran again.

Barbie moved her position until she was kneeling beside the bed, her elbows resting on the soft feather mattress. 'It's all right,' she said gently. 'He won't be here till the end of the month and we can save it up again by then.' Gran knew as well as Barbie that once the rent money had been spent there was little chance of recouping it. 'And I'll get some sausages while I'm at the shops.' Barbie levered herself to her feet. 'I'm going to be late for school.'

'You're a good girl, Barbie.' Gran passed her hand across the child's red-gold hair. 'I'll have some chips in the pan by the time you get back with the sausages.'

'See you later.' Barbie made to move away. 'I'll get told off if I'm late for school.'

Gran reached out towards her with both arms. 'Give your old Gran a kiss before you go,' she said, and Barbie sank down into the familiar mound of flesh which was her Gran. It was a softness which smelled of gin and sweat but to Barbie it was as sweet as the scent of a thousand lilacs. It was comfort and security, the only luxury she had ever known.

'You're a good girl, Barbie.' Gran held her close.

'Love you, Gran.' Barbie planted a kiss upon the soft, sagging cheek and pulled away.

Gran watched her as she left the room, then listened to her footsteps as she paused for a moment at the landing window before running down the stairs, singing.

Barbie ran all the way to school. She did not go by way of the lane but took the footpath across the barley field and through the copse. It was hot – one of those rare June heatwaves which takes the countryside in its grip – and even at this hour of the morning it was clear that once again the temperature would soar. It was cooler in the copse, a hushed echoing chamber of dappled light and shade, bobbing and weaving about her as she ran.

Even before she made it out of the trees and onto the hard tarmac surface of the lane she heard the clanging of the school

5

bell. 'Oh Lordy.' She threw a quick glance in all directions and made a dash for it across the corner of Mrs Urquhart's orchard, eyes wide for signs of the gardener or for movement behind the tall French windows of the house.

She was out of breath by the time she flung herself through the gap in the hedge and across the school playground towards the classroom door. Miss Beckworth was marking the register as Barbie clicked open the door and stood panting on the threshold.

'Barbie.' Miss Beckworth looked up from the register, her pen poised in mid-air. 'You're late.'

'Yes, Miss.'

'Do you have a reason?' Miss Beckworth was a young woman in her mid-twenties. Her brown hair was short with tight, springy curls which bounced as she moved.

'No, Miss.'

'It's the second time this week.'

'Yes, Miss.'

Miss Beckworth's voice softened and she laid down the pen upon the desk. 'Is everything all right, Barbie?' Barbie liked Miss Beckworth. There was a gentleness and a gaiety about her and she had eyes which held a smile permanently in bud.

'Yes, Miss. Thank you, Miss.'

'Very well, take your seat. But try to be on time in future.'

'Yes, Miss.' Barbie slipped into her desk. For the next three hours she divided her time between listening to Miss Beckworth and staring out of the window. She was not a child to whom learning came easily. She found it difficult to apply her mind to history or the nine-times table when, outside, the skylark was soaring and Mr Smethurst's old, brown dog was nosing his way along the gutter.

With every hour it became hotter. The classroom windows were flung wide to invite the breeze but the air was still, heavy, broken only by the sound of voices in the street outside, a passing car, the call of a songthrush in Mrs Urquhart's orchard.

Miss Beckworth was a good teacher, fresh with the enthusiasm of youth imparting knowledge to the young. She had several times moved Barbie from her seat beside the window but each time had allowed her to return, sensing her need for communication with the world outside. She had tried many ways of capturing Barbie's attention but Barbie smiled her way good-naturedly through every attempt, responding only to tidbits of poetry and painting, coming truly alive when immersed in the subject of nature study.

While other girls in the class spoke excitedly about the prospec of secondary school next year, of smart grey skirts and Burgund blazers and of taking the school bus all the way into town, Barbi viewed it all merely as a separation from the skylark and the olc brown dog. She preferred to close her mind to thoughts of goin to school in town. She did not have to think about it until ne: year and, being ten years old, next year was the other side of . mountain.

When the lunch bell rang Barbie rose from her desk and mac towards the door.

'Barbie. I'm going your way. Would you like to walk with me`

'Yes, Miss.' Barbie obediently waited while Miss Beckwor` collected up her handbag. They walked together through tl playground and out of the gates towards the main street of tl village. The midday temperature had risen to the region twenty-seven degrees and above the nearby hills a heat ha shimmered.

'Do you know where I'm going?'

'No, Miss.'

Miss Beckworth stooped to whisper into Barbie's ear. 'I going down to the stream to eat my lunch, and . . .' she gave he conspiratorial wink '. . . if no one's looking, I'm going foi paddle.'

Barbie giggled.

'Would you like to come?'

'No thank you, Miss. I've got to go and get the pension and some sausages and some . . . something else.'

Miss Beckworth slowed her pace and measured with her eyes the distance to the Post Office. 'Do you always collect the pension and do the shopping?'

'Not always, Miss. If Gran's about, she gets it. If I'm about, I get it. It just depends.' Barbie's eye was following a cabbage white butterfly which vaulted the hedge and cavorted across the street in front of them. 'They only live for a few days, Miss,' she said, pointing towards it. 'There must be an awful lot to see when you've only got a few days.'

Miss Beckworth watched the cabbage white. 'Yes,' she said. 'I suppose it's sad in a way. I never really thought about it that way before.'

7

'Oh no, Miss. They're the happiest, danciest creatures you ever did see. I've never in all my life seen an unhappy butterfly – except when they're injured.'

'Are you happy, Barbie?'

The question took Barbie by surprise. She stopped for a moment pondering on it.

'Are you happy living with your grandmother?'

Barbie looked at her in amazement. 'Yes, Miss. Of course, Miss.'

'That's nice.' Miss Beckworth moved on, dawdling her way slowly down the street. 'I just thought that the other children in the class sometimes get a few more things than you do. You know, ponies to ride, holidays.'

'I don't much care for holidays, Miss.' Barbie was trying to follow Miss Beckworth's logic. 'And I've got Mr Smethurst's pony to talk to any time I want.'

Miss Beckworth smiled and placed a hand on Barbie's shoulder. 'Don't you ever miss having parents?'

'No, Miss. Why should I, Miss? I've got my Gran.'

'Yes, of course.' She gave the shoulder a squeeze. 'We're having nature study this afternoon. Would you like to tell the class about butterflies?'

'Oh yes, Miss. Please, Miss.' Barbie's face lit up. 'There's red admirals, and painted ladies, and peacocks, and clouded yellows, and . . .'

'Good,' laughed Miss Beckworth. They had reached the door of the Post Office. 'I'll look forward to hearing all about them.' She moved off down the street, pausing after a few steps to wave.

'Enjoy your paddle, Miss,' Barbie called in a hoarse stage whisper and returned the wave.

Barbie drew Gran's pension from the Post Office counter then went next door to the butcher. 'Half a pound of sausages, please, Mr Williams,' she said and watched as Mr Williams strung out a skein of sausages.

'Pork and beef,' he said, 'with herbs. Just the way you like them.' He leaned forward to study the dial of the weighing machine, feeding the skein of sausages until the dial registered half a pound then, casting a quick glance round the shop to ensure that no customers were watching, he added an extra sausage, scooping them quickly into a plastic bag before Barbie had a chance to see the extra weight. 'Half a pound of sausages,'

8

he said jovially, handing them to Barbie. 'Big and fat and just waiting to be fried.'

'Thanks, Mr Williams.' Barbie handed him one of the pound notes from the pension money and Mr Williams repaid her the change. 'Gran's got the chips on waiting.'

The church clock struck twelve-fifteen as she passed the lychgate. She took to her heels and ran the last few steps to the village store. It was a long, low, thatched building, stocked from floor to ceiling, and at the far end was a section set aside for off-licence liquor sales.

Mrs Matthews looked up from the piece of cheese she was cutting. She coughed to gain the attention of Mrs Webster on the other side of the counter and jerked her head towards Barbie. 'It's no good, Barbie,' she called across the shop. 'I can't serve you.'

Barbie smiled thinking she was being told to wait.

'I can't serve you,' repeated Mrs Matthews. She clicked her tongue for the benefit of Mrs Webster. 'You're under age.'

'Pardon?'

Mrs Matthews and Mrs Webster exchanged glances. 'I can't serve you,' said Mrs Matthews for the third time. 'I'm not allowed to sell liquor to minors. It's more than my licence is worth.'

Barbie wondered what Mrs Matthews' inability to sell to coal miners had to do with selling her a bottle of gin. 'Can I have a bottle of gin for Gran, please?'

Mrs Matthews heaved a sigh and marched down the length of the counter towards Barbie. 'No, Barbie, no you can't. I've told you three times. If your Gran wants gin she'll have to come in and buy it for herself.'

Barbie flinched.

'I don't know what she's thinking of, sending you in here to buy gin.'

Barbie drew herself up to her full height. 'She didn't send me,' she said. 'I was down here so I came.'

It was not a statement which made much sense to Mrs Matthews. 'Look, Barbie,' she said. 'It's not your fault but I'm not allowed to sell gin to children. You'll have to tell your Gran to come down here and buy it for herself.'

Barbie now at least understood the reason for Mrs Matthews' refusal. 'Sorry, Mrs Matthews,' she said. 'I'll tell her to come down later.'

'There's a good girl.' Mrs Matthews' voice softened. 'Better hurry home with those sausages or you won't have time for dinner.'

'Thanks, Mrs Matthews.' Reminded once more of the time, Barbie ran home. She went by way of the churchyard, through the copse and across the barley field which had become a vast open stretch of shimmering heat.

'It's not right, you know,' said Mrs Matthews returning to the cheese and to Mrs Webster. 'Ma Harding sending that child down here for gin.'

Mrs Webster twitched her head and tightened the features of a face which appeared to be screwed into place. 'Disgusting,' she said. 'Quite disgusting.'

'I know I shouldn't say it.' Mrs Matthews paused once more in the act of cutting the cheese. 'But that's the fifth time in three weeks that Ma Harding's been in here to buy gin.' She made a display of looking round the empty shop then lowered her voice to a whisper. 'I think she's turned to drink.'

Mrs Webster gave the screw of her face another turn.

'She always has been one for a bit of a tipple, but . . .' Mrs Matthews sent her eyes once more round the empty shop '. . . five bottles in three weeks!'

'It shouldn't be allowed.' Mrs Webster gave a sniff through her thin, tight nose. 'I don't know why *They* don't do something about it.'

'I suppose *They* must know what's going on?' Mrs Matthews gave up all thought of cutting cheese and leaned on the counter. 'After all, *They* always know about these things, don't they – the Authorities? They must know about the way they're living down there.'

Mrs Webster's head twitched in agreement.

'She's not a bad kid, you know, young Barbie. It's not right for her to be in that place, all alone with that old woman. She should be in a proper home with someone to look after her. She's never had a chance.'

'It's filthy in that cottage, you know,' put in Mrs Webster. 'I wouldn't go near the place myself, but Mrs Phillips went there when she was collecting for the Red Cross. She said it was quite disgusting. She said . . .' she ran her tongue round her lips and spoke out of the side of her mouth '. . . she said it *smells*.'

'Really?' Mrs Matthews nodded attentively. 'I'm not surprised.

Well, what do you expect really. And old woman like that with a young child. I don't know why the Authorities don't do something about it.'

'Somebody should report it,' said Mrs Webster. 'It's not right. It shouldn't be allowed.'

'Do you really think *They* know about it?'

'Bound to. *They* just don't care. They're quick enough when it comes to increasing the rates. But when there's something to be done, *They* just don't care.'

Mrs Matthews nodded, then altered her expression as she became aware of someone entering the shop. 'Half a pound of cheese was it, Mrs Webster? Nice and fresh. Lovely piece of cheddar, it is.'

Mrs Webster slackened her face by one half turn of the screw. 'Very nice, Mrs Matthews, thank you.'

When Barbie reached the cottage there was no sign of Gran. She looked into the garden towards the vegetable plot then ran up the stairs, calling. Gran was still in bed.

'Barbie?' Gran forced herself through a stupor of sleep. 'What time is it?'

'It's nearly half past twelve. Why are you still in bed?'

'The chips!' She shook her head in an effort to rid herself of the dregs of sleep. 'I must have dropped off.' She began struggling with the blankets, heaving and grunting until she manoeuvred her large body to the edge of the high feather mattress. It was an effort which left her temporarily breathless and she paused, sitting on the edge of the bed with her feet on the floor.

'Have you had them twinges again, Gran?'

'I have not. It's nothing at all. I'm a lazy old woman, lying in bed all morning and now it's half past twelve and no dinner on the stove.'

'And you didn't have any gin.' Barbie slid her arms about Gran's neck.

'And what would I be wanting gin for, in the middle of the morning?' Gran pushed her aside. 'I'm a lazy old woman, I tell you, and I ought to be ashamed of myself.'

'And I still haven't got any. Mrs Matthews says she's not allowed to sell gin to children.'

'And I'm a stupid old fool,' Gran cursed herself. 'I should have thought of that myself. Sorry, my ducky.' She raised a hand and gently cupped Barbie's face. 'Did she make a fuss?'

11

'No. She didn't tell me off. She was quite nice about it really. She just said to tell you to go down and get it for yourself.'

'What would I be wanting gin for anyway?' Gran resumed her efforts to rise from the bed. 'I can do without it.'

Barbie reached out and pressed her back onto the mattress. 'We'll go down after school,' she said. 'You stay there in bed and I'll go and get us some bread and cheese. It's too late anyway to start cooking.'

Gran did not resist. She sank back gratefully into the soft depths of the feather mattress and let out a long, low sigh.

For the first time Barbie became aware of the pallor of Gran's skin, an unhealthy, yellow colour. 'You're not well,' she said. 'You stay there in bed till I get home from school.'

'You're a good girl, Barbie,' smiled Gran. 'You go and get yourself a bite of bread and cheese. We'll have the sausages for tea.'

Barbie went downstairs to the kitchen where Bess lay sprawled across the cool stone floor. An old, brown and white Collie dog, she was as overweight and slow moving as Gran.

'Lazy old thing.' She fell to her knees and buried her face in the dog's soft coat. Bess sighed and rolled over to reveal her underside.

'Do you want a scratch?' Barbie pushed her fingers into the long hair, working her way along the chest, round the base of the right foreleg and up towards the neck, beneath the dog's collar. Bess closed her eyes and gave a soft sigh of ecstasy.

'Silly old thing. Do you want some dinner?'

At the sound of 'dinner' Bess pricked her ears and, with an ungainly struggle, lifted herself to her feet, shaking her coat until the fat folds of flesh rippled across her back.

Barbie searched through the unwashed dishes which were stacked in the cracked, brown sink until she found a can opener. She opened a tin of dog food which she took from the shelf. Bess lollopped to her feeding bowl in the corner and waited.

'There you are.' Barbie spooned out the dark brown contents, topping up the bowl with dog meal and adding, as an after-thought, a piece of stale bread which was lying on the kitchen table. She stood watching the dog while the kettle boiled, then she brewed a pot of tea, poured a good measure into a saucer for Bess, and carried the remainder up to the bedroom. She sat on the

12

bed and nibbled a hunk of cheese until it was time to return to school.

'You stay there,' she said to Gran as she left the room. 'We'll go down for the gin when I get home.'

'You're a good girl, ducky,' sighed Gran. 'Such a good, good girl.'

Gran was up and dressed when Barbie returned at half past three.

'Are you all right, Gran?'

'Of course I'm all right. Right as ninepence.'

Gran had washed the dishes in the sink and they were now stacked upside-down on the wooden draining board. She took two of the mugs and wiped them on her apron before filling them with tea. 'Sit yourself down,' she said. 'We'll have ourselves a nice cup of tea. And there's a couple of biscuits in the tin.'

'I thought we were going for the gin.' Barbie handed one biscuit to Gran who dunked it into her tea before sucking the softened paste through her dentures.

'And why should I be wanting gin this afternoon? Tomorrow will do. Or the next day.'

Barbie ate half of her own biscuit then sneaked the other half to Bess beneath the table. Bess scoffed it in one gulp and licked Barbie's hand in appreciation.

Gran drank two mugs of tea and dithered about the cottage, occupying herself first with one chore, then another. 'Nice afternoon,' she said at last. 'Might as well take a little stroll down to the village. Get ourselves a breath of air.'

Barbie gave a small smile. 'We might as well buy that bottle of gin while we're down there.'

'I suppose we might as well. It'll save us a trip some other time.'

Bess accompanied them down the lane, her tongue lolling from the side of her mouth, but she soon gave up and flopped down upon the grass verge. The heat of the day had not abated and ahead of them the bright sunlight bounced off the tarmac surface of the lane.

'Lazy old thing.' Barbie pulled her to her feet. 'You're too fat.'

Bess allowed herself to be dragged along and the three continued for a further distance – a strange trio, the child, small, will o' the wisp and alive with boundless energy, the old woman and the dog each carrying their own weighty burden with discomfort.

'Let her be,' said Gran at last. 'She'll sit there and wait for us till we get back.' They had reached an area of shade where the tall beech trees on either side of the lane formed an avenue of shade.

'Good girl.' Barbie held up a finger before the dog. 'Sit. Stay.' Bess cocked her head to one side, then settled herself comfortably upon the grass verge, stretching out her muzzle along the line of her forepaws.

'She'll be better there in the shade.'

Gran, too, had need to pause for rest. It was quite usual for her to stop several times along the lane to regain her breath but today the stops were more frequent and when they reached the churchyard she sat on the wall with the obvious intention of taking her time.

Barbie stood before her, hopping first on one leg, then on the other, picking with her fingernails at the broken brickwork of the churchyard wall.

'It's a wonder you've got any nails left, the way you pick,' commented Gran.

Barbie grinned. 'Nancy Potter bites hers. Her Mum puts horrid mauve stuff on them.'

'Quite right too,' retorted Gran. 'Nasty habit.'

Mr Smethurst's old, brown dog snuffled his way down the gutter, offered himself up to a friendly pat from Barbie, and moved on, through the lychgate, and into the churchyard. He picked his way between the gravestones, pausing at one to lift his leg.

'Right on your Grandad,' smirked Gran. 'He never did much take to water.'

Barbie giggled. 'Do you miss Grandad?'

'Been gone a long time. More'n seventeen years past.'

'But don't you sometimes wish that he'd come back?'

'Back,' sniffed Gran. 'He was enough blooming trouble when he was alive without bringing the old bugger back.'

'But you must have missed him when he was gone. Didn't our Grandad love you when he was alive?'

'Aye. Me, and half a dozen others.'

'What was that?' Barbie cocked her ear closer.

'Aye,' she said more distinctly. 'He loved me, I suppose. In his way. I never thought much about it to tell the truth.'

Barbie lapsed into silence and gave her attention to picking at the churchyard wall. She got her fingernail beneath a large piece of loose mortar and began easing it gently from its position beneath the coping-stone. 'People are supposed to love one another,' she said, her full concentration upon lifting out the mortar in one piece. 'I don't know why they don't.'

'Aye,' sighed Gran. 'Pigs might fly.'

'Don't people ever love one another?'

'Aye, they do in fairy stories and the vicar blabs a lot about it from his pulpit.' Gran shifted her position on the wall. 'Trouble is, I'm not much for fairy tales, nor listening to the vicar spouting his mouth off and there's precious little of it anywhere else.'

Barbie gave a little cry of triumph. She scooped the mortar into the palm of her hand and examined it with her finger. 'What about my Mum? I bet she loved you.'

'Aye, she loved me,' said Gran quietly. 'When she was a little girl she loved me.' She reached out and touched Barbie's hair. 'A lot like you she was when she was a little girl.' Barbie turned the mortar with her finger, crumbling it into the palm of her hand. 'She'd have been all right if she hadn't got in with the wrong sort of crowd.' Gran wiped the back of her hand across her eyes.

Barbie looked up. 'She might come back one day.'

'Aye, one day. When she gets tired of the fast life in London.' Gran lowered her head but not before Barbie had seen the tears.

She dropped the mortar and flung her arms about the old lady's neck. 'I love you, Gran,' she said.

'Aye, you love me, ducky.' There was a very special look of love in the old lady's eyes as she enfolded the child in her arms. 'And I love you.'

'I'll always love you, Gran.'

Gran pulled away and stood up. 'We best be getting to them shops.'

Barbie helped her to her feet. 'Are you all right?'

'Of course I'm all right. Right as ninepence.'

Barbie took her hand and together they walked to the village store to buy the gin.

It was still hot when they went to bed that night.

'Are you coming to bed?' asked Gran but Barbie stood at the open window gazing out at the approaching night. At ten o'clock the light was fading, throwing a soft, pearl grey haze across the landscape, but the air was still with hardly a movement in the leaves of the apple tree.

The bedroom window offered up a vista different from that of the window on the landing. It faced south across the corner of the barley field to the copse and beyond to the village, which mushroomed its way up the side of the hill, its rooftops of mellow red brick with lichen grown slates and the occasional thatch.

'Are you coming to bed, Barbie? Or are you going to stand there all night?' Gran threw her weight onto the bed which creaked beneath its familiar burden. She spat her dentures into an old, cracked mug on the bedside table.

'In a minute, Gran.'

If anyone had asked Gran why they slept together in the same bed, she would probably have replied that the other room was damp, that it was on the cold side of the cottage and that the plaster was peeling from the ceiling. On another occasion she might have replied that it started during Barbie's infancy when she was too old to run from one room to another when the baby cried in the night. Barbie would have had no answer. She had never given the matter a moment's thought. She had always slept with Gran and could remember sleeping nowhere else.

From this window Barbie could see only a small section of the garden but on the stretch of green which separated the cottage from the hedge and the barley field she caught sight of movement, a flash of white. She leaned further through the open window and watched the rabbits at play.

'What are you grinning at?' Gran watched the smile flitting across her face.

'Rabbits,' said Barbie. 'Down by the hedge.'

'Bloody rabbits.' Gran hauled herself up on one elbow. 'They're after them lettuce.'

'No, they're not. They're just playing.'

'Throw something at them.' Gran was struggling to raise herself from the bed. 'They'll eat the lot while you stand there looking at them.'

Barbie searched until she found an empty paper bag lying amongst the rubbish piled on top of the chest of drawers.

'Perishing varmints. Got all them weeds out there and they've got to eat the bloody lettuce. Go on. Throw it at 'em.'

Barbie screwed the bag into a ball and tossed it a good distance beyond the rabbits. The movement was sufficient to send them scurrying through the hedge.

'Did you hit them?'

'Yes, Gran.'

16

'Are you sure?'

'I said so.'

'Good.' Gran collapsed back into the mattress. 'Then come to bed.'

Reluctantly, Barbie left the window and climbed onto the bed. 'Haven't you forgotten something?'

'Sorry.' She got off again and sank to her knees beside the bed. 'GentleJesusmeekandmild. Lookuponthislittlechild.'

'Say it properly,' ordered Gran, unusually stern. 'And think about what you're saying.'

'Gentle Jesus,' she started again. 'Meek and mild. Look upon this little child. Help me make it through the night. Keep me always in Your sight.'

'Did you think about it? Really think about it?'

'Yes, Gran,' sighed Barbie and climbed into bed.

'I want you to think about it always, Barbie. I want you to speak nicely to Jesus.' She looked at Barbie long and hard, then reached out and touched her hand. 'You never know when you might need Him.'

For a moment Barbie returned the look, wondering at the change of tone in Gran's voice, but almost immediately she dismissed it from her mind and snuggled down into the softness of the mattress. ''Night, Gran.'

''Night, ducky.' Gran reached out again to touch her. 'Sleep tight.'

In the heat of the bedroom beneath the cottage eaves they had thrown back the blankets and had covered themselves only with a sheet. It was cool to Barbie's skin and she wriggled her toes towards the cool recesses at the foot of the bed. Then, with a sigh, she turned towards the soft, comforting body of her Gran. She lifted her knees beneath Gran's bottom and wound her arms about her waist. As she did so, Gran winced and caught her breath with a sound which was almost a cry.

'Here, Gran.' She lifted herself to look at Gran's face which had become strangely contorted, the lips pulled tight between tooth-less gums. 'What's that lump?'

Gran's hand moved gingerly across her abdomen until she fingered the lump. 'What lump?' she said. 'I can't feel any lump.'

'That lump in your tummy.' She made to touch it again but Gran restrained her.

'There isn't any lump. It's your imagination.'

'That's what's been giving you them twinges.' Barbie kept herself propped up on one elbow. 'You've got something stuck in your tummy.

'Aye,' said Gran slowly. 'Reckon that's what it must be. Something I ate.'

'Peter Sparkes swallowed a toy soldier once. He told me. The doctor gave him some medicine and he had to keep watch until it came out.' She looked over the top of Gran's body to reassure herself that the full bottle of gin was standing on the bedside table. 'I expect yours will come out soon if you keep watch for it.'

'Aye, ducky,' sighed Gran. 'Maybe you're right.'

She settled herself down once more to sleep. 'You tell me when you see it come out,' she said. 'Promise?'

'You go to sleep.'

Barbie buried her face in the soft flesh of Gran's back. 'I wonder what it was? Must have been one of those days when you didn't have your teeth in.'

'Aye,' said Gran quietly. 'Reckon that must be it.' She moved her arm to pat the child's rump and shortly afterwards heard the soft, rhythmic breathing of sleep.

Later, in the darkness of the night, she disentangled herself from Barbie's embrace and sat up in bed. She poured herself a measure of gin and prepared to spend another sleepless night.

Chapter Two

It was cooler by Saturday. The heatwave had broken with a thunderstorm and, as is typical of the British climate, once the awaited rain had arrived it showed a marked reluctance to move on. Gran and Barbie waited for a break in the showers then started out along the lane towards the village.

'Come on, Bess,' Barbie called over her shoulder but the old dog merely blinked her eyes and settled down by the gate to await their return.

'Leave her be,' said Gran. 'She's better staying where she is.'

They had almost reached the village when a car came up behind them. The driver tooted his horn and waved.

'Looks like my Dad's got himself a new car.' Barbie returned the wave.

'Aye. Going down to show it to his folks, no doubt.'

Barbie watched the car until it disappeared round a bend in the lane. 'There's one thing I've never been able to figure out,' she said. 'Why is it that when he's on his own he always waves, yet when he's got his children with him he never sees me?' She looked up at Gran. 'I've been standing right in front of him sometimes but he doesn't seem to see me.'

'That's folk,' said Gran. 'Sometimes they see you. Sometimes they don't.'

Barbie did not often see her father. He lived in Wickhampton with his wife and children and only occasionally returned to the village to visit his parents. She would have liked to have known him better. There had been brief, tantalising moments when he had spoken to her in the street. – 'How was she?' 'How was she getting on at school?' 'Wasn't she growing tall.' 'How old was she now? Could it really be ten?' But always his eyes would be on the street and not upon her. His body would be tense, eager to be on its way. Once he had given her a toffee wrapped in silver paper and several times he had given her money with which to buy sweets, but which she had taken instead to Gran.

'And there's another thing I've never been able to work out,' she said, deciding to press on with the imponderables. 'Why was I born if my Mum and Dad weren't married?'

Gran looked at her out of the corner of her eye. 'It happens, ducky. It happens.'

The reply was no more satisfactory than had been the reply to her first question. 'But he's married now, isn't he. To that lady with blonde hair. I've seen her sometimes in the car.'

Gran nodded. 'Just after you were born. Went to live in Wickhampton.'

'Was that when my Mum left too?'

'No. She stayed around for a while before she took off.' There was the familiar mist across Gran's eyes. Barbie reached out and took her hand. Gran smiled and gripped the fingers tightly.

They were in the main street now just a few paces from the village store. Gran hesitated and looked down at Barbie who squeezed her hand again. 'It's all right, Gran,' she said. 'Just go and ask.'

Gran turned and began to walk off in the opposite direction. 'No. I'll not bother. I can be doing without it for a day or two.'

'Go on, Gran. It won't do any harm to ask.'

Gran hesitated. 'No,' she said. 'I'll not bother.'

Barbie held on to her hand and pulled her back towards the store. 'What if you need it again tonight, Gran?'

'And who's to say that I'll be needing it.' Just the same, Gran retraced her steps. 'Agh, to hell with the old buzzard,' she said. 'She can only say "No".' She swallowed hard, drew back her shoulders and entered the store. She manoeuvred her large body through the main section of the store towards the off-licence counter at the far end.

Mrs Matthews coughed loudly to attract the attention of her husband who was serving another customer. 'Another bottle of gin, was it, Mrs Harding?' she asked, with just the slightest emphasis on 'another'.

Gran's affirmation came with a tightness in her throat. 'And if you'd be so kind, Mrs Matthews . . . if you'd be kind enough to put it on the . . .' she looked around at the customer at the other end of the store and lowered her voice. 'If you'd just put it on the slate.'

Mrs Matthews drew in her breath. 'Well, I don't know. It's not something we like to make a practice of. Especially with drink.'

Gran looked at her but said nothing.

'It's not like you, if I might say so, Mrs Harding. You've always been most particular about paying.'

Gran swallowed the comment with an audible sound. She had always been proud of paying her way.

Mrs Matthews looked pointedly at the bottle of gin. 'Had a few extra expenses lately I expect.'

'You could say that,' said Gran and Barbie was surprised by the strange hoarseness of her voice.

Mrs Matthews looked across at her husband who shrugged his shoulders offering no assistance. 'Well, I really don't know. You place me in a very difficult position.'

'Please, Mrs Matthews.' Barbie stepped forward and offered up her sweetest smile. 'It's only for the weekend. It's Family Allowance Day on Monday and Tuesday's Pension Day. I'll bring it in to you first thing on Monday.'

Mrs Matthews drew the palms of her hands down the front of her apron.

'And Gran needs it,' continued Barbie. 'She's got . . .'

Gran laid a heavy hand upon Barbie's shoulder. 'If it's not convenient,' she said thickly, 'we'll leave it. I'm sorry I asked.' She made to move away from the counter.

'Oh, very well. Just this once, but only until Monday.'

'Thank you.' Gran was almost totally overcome by embarrassment. 'Thank you very much.' She picked up the bottle of gin and blundered from the store.

Mrs Matthews heaved a sigh and walked back along the counter towards her husband. 'I know I shouldn't say it,' she said. 'But that's the sixth bottle of gin in just over three weeks.'

'It's all right, Gran.' Gran was standing in the street, trembling. 'We'll pay her back on Monday.'

Gran nodded, her face totally devoid of colour. 'And this time I'll make it last.'

'The lump might be gone by then,' said Barbie brightening. 'You won't need it once you've got rid of the lump.' Gran forced a smile. 'Or you could go to the doctor. It would be a lot cheaper than buying gin.'

'I've told you before,' said Gran curtly. 'I'm not going to the doctor.'

'All right.' Barbie looked up, pained by the sharpness of the response. 'You don't have to if you don't want to.'

Gran saw the expression and softened her voice. 'You go home and make us a cup of tea,' she said. 'There's something I must do.'

Barbie looked at her.

'I've got to go and see a man about a dog.'

Barbie stood her ground, perplexed, and Gran placed a hand on her shoulder. 'Go on,' she said gently. 'Go and put the kettle on. I'll be home before you know it.'

'Where are you going?'

'Never you mind, nosey.' Gran touched the tip of her nose. 'There's just someone I need to see.' She gave Barbie a gentle push in the direction of home. 'And take this wretched bottle with you before I drop it.'

'Will you be all right?' Barbie hesitated, reluctant to leave.

'Aye. Right as ninepence.'

Barbie made her way down the street, turning repeatedly to watch Gran making slow progress in the opposite direction. She lost sight of her as she reached the end of the main street and turned the corner.

Gran continued walking until she reached a row of small, terraced cottages, each guarding its interior behind spotless, white net curtains, each tiny, pocket handkerchief garden vying with its neighbour. She gave a nod of satisfaction as she saw Ken Radlett's new car parked outside number twenty-three and heaved her bulk onto the low garden wall where she settled down to wait.

Ken Radlett was visibly surprised when he saw her there. 'Ma Harding,' he said. 'What can I do for you?'

'I'd like a word,' said Gran rising from the wall.

'What, now?'

'It won't take long. Unless, of course, you don't want to be seen talking to the likes of Ma Harding.'

'You'd better come in.' His eyes turned to take in the street. 'We can use the parlour.'

Gran followed him through the front door and into a small

room overlooking the street, conscious of necks craning in the back kitchen as Tom and Hetty Radlett strained to see who it was being ushered into their front parlour.

The room was immaculately tidy, smelling of furniture polish and disuse. The light from the window was almost obliterated by an assortment of potted ferns, and, on every square inch of shelf space, mantel and sideboard was a variety of ornaments, photographs and knick-knacks of every shape and size.

Ken gestured with a hand towards the high-backed three piece suite, its back and arms protected by hand-embroidered antimacassars. Gran grunted her acknowledgment and flopped down into the nearest armchair, throwing into disarray its embroidered protection.

'It's about Barbie,' she said without preamble. 'I want you to take her when I'm gone.'

Shock registered on Ken Radlett's face with a draining of colour.

'She's your child. You'll have to take up your responsibility.'

'Why me?' Ken held on to the back of the chair looking as though he might fall. 'Where does your Sandra come into it?'

'She's your child as much as Sandra's. It takes two hands to clap.'

'But Sandra's her mother.'

'Aye, and I don't know where she is. You're the father; and you're here.'

Ken ran his hand through his hair and down the back of his head, passing it repeatedly across the nape of his neck. 'Look, Ma. What's this all about?'

'Just something that needs to be settled.'

'But why now? Out of the blue?'

'Now's as good a time as any. It's time we got things sorted out.'

Ken continued to hold on to the back of the chair, all thoughts of sitting in it removed from his mind. 'But it's not as if I've ever let the kid down. I've paid.'

'Aye, you've paid lad. A few quid here and there.'

'A few quid!' His voice was high-pitched for a man. In anger it was almost feminine. 'I'm not made of bloody money. I've got a wife and kids.'

'That's not what I meant.'

23

'Then what did you mean? Has there ever been a month when I haven't paid?'

'No lad. I didn't say that.'

'You'd better not. Or I'll have the Law on you.'

Gran began to realise that she had set this conversation off on the wrong footing. 'I mean,' she said, 'that's there's more to it than money.'

'I've got a mortgage to pay, bills to meet.'

'And a new car to run.'

'It's a company car. As if it's any of your bloody business. It goes with the job.'

Gran pointed to the sofa set diagonally to her chair. 'Sit yourself down, lad,' she said. 'Take the weight off your feet.'

He sank compliantly onto the sofa and sat staring at the fire screen in the unlit hearth. Gran gave him a few moments and then started again. 'What job are you doing now? Still with the Post Office?'

'I'm a Rep. Have been for two years.'

'Salesman,' nodded Gran. 'Must be a good job.'

'A representative.' He glared at her. 'Industrial freezer units.'

'Good job,' nodded Gran again. 'Good prospects.'

'And that doesn't mean that there's any to spare. I've got a wife and kids.'

'I didn't say it did, lad,' responded Gran reassuringly. 'I didn't say it did.'

She shifted her bulk in the chair and rearranged her feet. 'I'm sorry lad. I don't always think before I speak. It must have been a bit of a shock.'

Ken took in a breath and looked at her out of the corner of his eye. 'Well you certainly don't pull any punches.'

Gran gave a slight smile. 'I have been known to jump in with both feet.'

She watched him as he fumbled through his pockets for cigarettes. 'You don't like me, do you, Ma,' he said. 'You never did.'

'No lad. There's no call for that. If I didn't like you I wouldn't be here now.'

He passed her a small unconvinced glance and looked away, tearing the cellophane wrapping from the pack.

'No lad. You got caught, that's all. You did what most young-sters do but you got caught. That's the difference.'

24

'Silly young buggers.'

'Aye, lad. You're all silly at that age. Most get away with it but some get caught.'

'Your Sandra . . .'

'My Sandra was a good girl. She'd have been all right if she hadn't got mixed up with the wrong sort of company.'

'I didn't say she wasn't. I was only going to say . . .'

'Good. Just so long as you don't.'

Ken extracted a cigarette and lit it, drawing the smoke down into his lungs.

'Does she know about Barbie – your wife?'

'Of course. We don't keep any secrets.'

'And what does she think?'

'She forgave me.' He expelled smoke through pursed lips.

Gran raised one eyebrow. 'Very big of her, I'm sure. And what about the kids?'

'Look Ma.' He turned and looked at her steadily over the top of his cigarette. 'We don't want anyone poking their noses into our affairs.'

'I wouldn't dream of it, lad. Wouldn't dream of it.' She waited until he drew again on his cigarette. 'But you may have to tell them yourself, one of these days.'

'Look Ma, what is all this?'

'I've already told you.'

'You've told me nothing. You just appear on the doorstep after all these years. You've never bothered before. You've been content enough to cash my cheque every month.'

Gran stiffened. 'I've never taken more than Barbie's rights.'

It was Ken's turn to raise his hand in a gesture of conciliation. 'What is it exactly that you want?'

'I just want things settled in case something happens.'

'And what's likely to happen?'

'I might get run over by a bus.'

'Oh, come on, Ma.' He stopped and drew on the cigarette as if a thought were passing through his mind. 'Or . . .' he said, looking up at her '. . . are you getting fed up with looking after her?' The withering look which she returned spoke louder than words. He dropped his eyes and turned away. 'Well, what is going to happen?'

'It's just insurance,' said Gran. 'Don't tell me you haven't heard of insurance.'

Ken reached out for an ash tray, a heavy pottery object, roughly moulded into the shape of a horseshoe, and with the words *'Greetings from Margate'* emblazoned across its centre. He flicked the tip of his cigarette above it and balanced the ash tray on his knee. 'Look Ma, I know how old you are. Your Sandra told me. You've got years ahead of you yet.'

Gran shrugged. 'Who knows. I might be gone next week.'

'Come off it, Ma. You're just making waves. You know you are.' He leaned towards her. 'How old is Barbie now? Ten?' Gran nodded. 'Another seven or eight years maybe and she'll be off. You know what kids are. They grow up before you know it and they're off standing on their own two feet.' He gave her a nervous grin. 'And if you haven't got another few years left in you, then I'm a Dutchman's uncle. You're the tough sort, Ma. Your kind goes on forever.'

'Some do,' said Gran. 'Some don't.' She sat looking at the mantel before her crammed with its ridiculous curios – *'A present from Dorset'*, a china dog, *'To dearest Mother'*, three brass monkeys pretending neither to see, to speak, nor to hear. The whole room was pretending – pretending to be a room which was lived in when, so obviously, it was not. It was a room for being laid out in a coffin for all to pass by and observe. She shivered.

'Sorry. Afraid it's a bit chilly in here.'

She said nothing and Ken observed the expression on her face. 'Look,' he began again. 'I think I know how you feel. It's a big responsibility being landed with a kid, the way you were. I guess I've taken things a bit too much for granted.' He stubbed out his cigarette and reached for another. 'Perhaps I could stretch to a few extra quid. It won't be much but we could pull in the belt a bit tighter. Squeeze out a few extra quid.'

'There's no need for that. I'm not asking for charity.'

'Then what are you asking for?'

'I can't put it much plainer. I want you to have her when I'm gone.'

Ken sighed. 'I thought we'd just discussed that. I really don't see the need to make waves.'

'Yes, or No?'

'Oh, for crying out loud.' He stopped and for a long time sat staring at the tip of his cigarette. When he spoke again the tone of his voice had changed. 'Look, Ma,' he said. 'Don't think I haven't thought about Barbie. I have. Many times. But I've got a wife and two kids.' He looked up at her. 'Things are best left the way they are. I'll find you a few extra quid and you can come to me if she needs something special but there's no sense in upsetting my family – or Barbie.'

'So you don't want her.'

'I didn't say that.'

'Then what is it to be? Yes? Or No?'

Ken sighed. 'You haven't been listening to a word I've said.' Gran continued to look at him steadily. 'I'll think about it. Will that satisfy you?'

'I guess it'll do.' She began the forward swaying movement preparatory to heaving herself from the chair. 'Can't ask for more than you think about it.' With one supreme effort she was up and standing on her feet, knocking the embroidered antimacassar to the floor.

Ken sighed again and shook his head.

'When will you be coming to the village next to see your folks?'

'In a couple of weeks. I usually drop in every two weeks or so.'

'Good,' said Gran. 'I'll see you then. You can give me an answer.'

Ken had reached the parlour door before her and was about to open it. 'Not here,' he said quickly. Gran heard the scuttle of movement outside in the hall. 'I'll come to your place. It's more convenient.'

'Suit yourself. Makes no difference to me.' She put out her hand to delay Ken as he turned the doorknob. 'There is one thing you can do for Barbie. You can drop in and see her sometimes.'

Ken stopped short. 'Damn it, Ma. I've got my own kids to consider.'

'Barbie is your kid. She's as much your kid as the others are. It wouldn't do you any harm to speak to her.'

Ken stood for a long time, his hand on the doorknob, chewing his lip. 'OK,' he said at last. 'I guess you're right. I'll give you a lift home and see her now.'

Gran smiled. 'You won't regret it. She's a nice kid. You'll like her.'

Out in the hallway Hetty Radlett hovered. 'Afternoon, Mrs Harding.'

'Afternoon, Mrs Radlett.'

In the back kitchen Tom Radlett coughed, trying to draw his wife away.

'A bit cooler now the rain's come.' Hetty stood between Gran and the front door. 'The gardens could do with a drop of rain. They were crying out for it.'

'Excuse me, Mum.' Ken pressed past her. 'I'm just giving Ma Harding a lift home.'

'I'd appreciate a word, Ken. If you'd be so kind.'

Ken opened the front door. 'Just wait outside a minute, Ma,' he said. 'I won't be long.' He stepped aside to allow her out onto the street, then closed the door behind her.

'I couldn't help overhearing,' began Hetty, launching straight into the attack.

'I'm not surprised, seeing you were standing outside the door.'

'I'll have you remember, my lad, whose house this is.' Ken turned his eyes to the ceiling. 'I couldn't help overhearing,' began Hetty again. 'And if you don't mind my saying so, you must be a bigger fool than I took you for.'

'And if you overheard,' said Ken, 'you'll know as well as I do that Ma Harding's got a point. The kid is mine. It won't do any harm just to go and see her once in a while.'

'Oh yes. It won't do any harm to see her. And before you know it, you'll be saddled with her. And how's Mary going to feel about that?'

'Mum . . .'

'Ask yourself how's she going to feel about you taking in some bastard kid whose mother was no better than she ought to be.'

'Nobody's taking anyone in.'

'You mark my words,' said Hetty Radlett. 'That kid's going to land you in trouble.'

'Come off it, Mum.' Ken laid a restraining hand on her shoulder. 'You're as bad as the old girl. Getting your knickers in a twist about nothing at all. Ma Harding needs a bit of support and I'm going to call in there just once in a while. Where's the harm in that? It can't have been easy for her all these years.'

Hetty Radlett shook her head. 'Cunning old devil. Coming in here interfering in people's lives. She's got something up her sleeve, you mark my words.'

'Mum. Trust me. I know what I'm doing.'

'Huh. I wish I could believe it. God knows how you let the old devil talk you into it.'

28

'Perhaps she made me feel guilty.'

'Guilty!' exploded Hetty. 'After all these years of paying out hard cash, you find the need to feel guilty.'

Tom Radlett moved quietly down the hall behind them and took his wife's arm. 'Leave the lad alone, dear,' he said. 'Ken knows what he's doing.'

'And you're as bad as he is,' she turned on him. 'Can't see trouble when it's staring you in the face. And there's another thing . . .' She tore her arm from his grasp. 'It's never been proved to my satisfaction that she is your kid. How do you know you haven't been paying all these years for some other man's bastard?'

'Oh, come on, Mum.'

'Don't "come on" me. That kid's got ginger hair.'

Ken sighed again and made for the door. 'She's mine,' he said, opening it. 'You can take my word for it.'

He went outside, where Gran was sitting on the low garden wall. He unlocked the door of the car and helped her into the passenger seat. Gran looked at him out of the corner of her eye but did not interrupt his thoughts.

Barbie had been home for almost an hour. She had brewed the tea which had now grown cold. She had walked back and forth between the back door and the gate, ten times at least, and once as far as the tall beech tree at the turn of the lane. She played with Bess, walked once more to the gate, swinging on it, peering up the lane, straining her eyes for sight of Gran. She went back into the kitchen, threw out the stewed tea and re-set the kettle to boil. Yet again, out to the gate, standing on the cross-strut, her fingernails picking at the soft, rotting, paintbare splinters of wood. Back to the kitchen, pouring boiling water into the teapot, and suddenly there was a car outside, voices, Gran walking down the path.

'What's the matter, Gran? Are you all right?' The great body was soft and warm beneath her hug.

Gran was laughing, holding a hand to Barbie's mouth. 'Goodness, ducky. You'll knock me over.'

Barbie looked past her towards the other figure, to Ken Radlett.

'Have you brewed the tea?' asked Gran. 'I'm parched to croaking.'

Barbie looked at Ken shyly beyond the bulk of her grandmother's body, but did not allow their eyes to meet.

29

'Be a good girl. Another cup for your Dad. He's come to call.'

Barbie busied herself with setting out mugs, running her eye along the shelf for the least chipped mug to give to Ken. She turned it upside-down to let fall the dog hair and fluff which had accumulated within. Ken sat down on a kitchen chair, stiff-backed and uncomfortable, beside the table.

Why had he come? After all these years – sitting in the kitchen, waiting for tea.

Bess lumbered across the floor and pushed her nose beneath the hand resting on his knee. Ken responded hesitantly, stroking his hand down the length of the old dog's back, then withdrew it, wiping it against the leg of his trousers.

Barbie poured his tea, added two heaped spoonsful of sugar without thinking to ask, and placed it on the table before him. 'She's been rolling in the dirt,' she said. 'It makes her coat all dusty.'

'Oh,' said Ken, conscious of the fact that she had seen the movement of his hand upon his trouser leg. 'What's her name?'

'Bess.' Barbie dropped to her knees beside the dog and buried her face in the long, soft coat. 'Silly old thing. She's the same age as me.'

'That's nice.'

Barbie got up, fetched a teaspoon from the draining board, and placed it on the table beside Ken's mug. 'I forgot to stir it.'

Ken twitched a smile and revolved the spoon in the dark brown liquid, surveying the mug as though working out in his mind from which side he intended to drink. Barbie stood watching him intently, fascinated by his actions.

'How are you?' he asked, squirming beneath her gaze.

'All right,' she said. 'Thank you.'

'And how's school?'

'All right.'

They were the same questions he had asked in the street but this time he was here, sitting in the kitchen, drinking tea. He was a small man with pale skin, small features, his hands small, almost feminine, about the mug. He gulped the tea, swilling it down in one long draft, like medicine, as though afraid to pause and drink again. The hair on his face was fair, like his head, showing faintly through the skin, and halfway down his neck, on the right-hand side, was a pimple, white and firm, standing out above a hair follicle. Barbie's fingers tingled at the thought of picking it, feeling it burst, the taut white head giving way beneath her nails.

'And what do you like about school?' he was saying. 'What subjects do you like?'

'Nothing much.' Barbie watched the pimple. 'It's boring.'

'Oh dear. Don't you like reading? Writing? Geography? Playing games?'

Barbie shook her head. 'It's boring.'

If she placed her fingernails on either side of the pimple she would need only to press.

'Well, what do you like?'

'Nothing much. Just looking.'

'Looking at what?'

'Just things. Trees, and grass, and spiders' webs, and pebbles.'

'Oh, I see,' he said, obviously not seeing.

'There's a Jenny Wren's nest in the garden,' she said, warming to her subject. 'Do you want to see it?'

Ken hesitated as if to refuse. He looked across at Gran who nodded her head.

'OK.' He got up from the chair. 'If it doesn't take long.'

She ran ahead of him out into the garden and made her way through the thick vegetation, sure of her tread. Ken followed, uncertain, pushing back the tendrils which sprang about his face, stumbling in the dense undergrowth.

'Shh.' She placed a finger to her lips and slowed her pace, moving quietly towards the tumbledown privy. Russian vine had grown over it, entangling itself within the timbers and covering the dust-encrusted windows. It weighed down the corrugated iron roof so that it bowed inwards.

She waited until Ken was beside her then, slowly, gently, lifted the creeper to reveal the nest, suspended like an upturned pitcher. Its interior was crammed with four naked chicks, grey tufted heads with beaks stretched wide. Barbie looked at Ken, holding her breath, awaiting his reaction.

'Very nice,' he said. 'Aren't they cute.'

She let go her breath. Somehow, she had hoped that he would see but he did not. He was looking at the chicks but he was blind to the wonder.

'What did you say they were? Wrens?'

'Yes,' she said, letting the creeper fall. 'They're wrens.'

31

'They're cute.' He moved away. 'I think I'd better be getting off now.'

Barbie walked with him to the gate.

'We'll see you in a couple of weeks,' said Gran as he got into the car. 'You'll give me an answer?'

'I'll pop in on the way to the village.' He avoided the latter half of her question. 'I'll call in whenever I can.' He dipped into his pocket and flipped a coin towards Barbie. 'Here,' he said. 'Buy yourself some chocolate.' And, with a smile and a wink, he was gone.

Gran let out a long sigh and walked back towards the cottage.

'Gran . . . ?' Gran did not reply. Barbie followed her into the cottage and knelt beside her chair. 'Why was he here?'

Gran smiled and stroked her hand across Barbie's hair. 'He gave me a lift, that's all.'

'But why?'

'What's wrong with giving an old woman a lift? Now stop your questions and pour me another cup of tea, there's a good girl.'

Later, in the evening, they went into the garden. Gran squatted on a stool – an old wooden chair cut down to size – pulling weeds from the vegetable plot, while Barbie lay on her back in the long grass.

'You'll get rheumatism lying in that wet grass,' commented Gran, more from habit than from any request that Barbie should move. 'It gets into the bones.'

Barbie laughed and spread-eagled herself, arms and legs stretched wide in the shape of a St Andrew's cross. She stared up through the tall grass heads to the sky beyond. 'It tickles.'

The showers had cleared, leaving a warm, still evening, heavily laden with the scent of damp earth and honeysuckle.

'Damn rabbits.' Gran threw out a tattered, half-chewed lettuce. 'I'd wring their necks if I got hold of 'em.'

Barbie smiled, content in the knowledge that Gran would do no such thing. 'You'd have to put salt on their tails before you could catch them.' She rolled over, stretching her arms into the damp undergrowth and, as she did so, disturbed the last remaining raindrops, hanging pendulous from the tips of leaves. She wrinkled her nose and giggled, exploring the undergrowth with her fingers – roots, pebbles, the soft cold touch of a slug, until she felt something hard. What was it? Oh yes, the cross. She parted the grass until it was revealed, a tiny cross of bound twigs pushed upright into the soft soil.

'It's the grave I dug,' she announced to Gran. 'Do you remember? The squirrel?'

Gran looked across and nodded.

'I'd forgotten all about it.' She pulled herself up into a sitting position, cross-legged with feet tucked beneath her, and cleared the grass. 'I wonder what it's like to be dead.'

Gran stopped in the action of pulling a weed and for the space of two heartbeats remained immobile. 'Peaceful,' she said. 'I hope.'

Between the roots of the grasses a woodlouse ran, hard and brown, with a ridged back, scurrying on tiny legs. Barbie watched him, then picked him up, holding him in the palm of her hand. Immediately, he rolled into a ball, round like a brown, hard-coated pea.

'We all have to die,' said Gran, her voice cutting across Barbie's thoughts. 'Even me.'

'Of course.' She looked up. It was not the comment which caught her attention but the tone of Gran's voice. 'When you're old.'

'I'm old now.'

Barbie stretched herself tall, surveying her grandmother as if for the first time. 'No,' she said at last. 'You're not old. Not yet.'

Gran smiled in spite of herself. 'You won't be old for ages yet.'

She replaced the woodlouse beside the wooden cross and watched him unroll and run away. 'This is a good place for a grave,' she said. 'Where would you like to be buried when you're dead?'

Again Gran stopped short, her eyes fixed on the patch of soil before her.

Barbie did not notice, 'Do you know where I'd like to be buried?' She watched the progress of the woodlouse but it disappeared and she got to her knees, searching for it. 'In the corner of the churchyard underneath the big yew tree. It's lovely and quiet and peaceful there. You could lie there forever just listening to the birds.'

Gran shuffled the stool a little further along the row of lettuces. 'Sounds like a good place to lie.'

'If you go first, I'll come and visit you and read you stories.'

Gran closed her eyes and swallowed.

'And if I go first, you can do the same for me.'

She gave up the search for the woodlouse and returned to her back, staring up at the sky. In the place of rain clouds, white streaks of cotton were threading their way across the tapestry of blue.

'I wonder where you go when you die,' she said, and stared out into the blue beyond. 'I know you go to Jesus; but, well . . . I wonder *where*?' She did not fancy going up into the sky. The sky was for looking at but Barbie was a child of the earth.

'Barbie; there's something I want you to know.' Barbie continued to stare at the sky. 'Barbie, are you listening?'

'Yes, Gran.'

'I want you to know . . .' There was a terrible, chilling strangeness about Gran's voice. Barbie shot upright, looking at her. 'I want you to know that even after I die, I'll still be out there somewhere, watching over you.'

Barbie shuddered. 'Just listen to that blackbird,' she said. 'You'd think he was trying to deafen you with all that noise.'

'Even when I'm with Jesus, I'll still be with you. I don't know how; but I'm damned if I won't find a way.'

'I wish he'd shut up singing like that. I'm hungry. Is there any bread pudding left over from tea?'

She got up and went into the kitchen. She really was quite starved. She'd feel better with a hunk of bread pudding inside her. And she would put on a cardigan while she was there. The evening had suddenly turned quite chilly.

Gran shuffled her stool along the row of lettuces and quietly pulled the weeds.

Chapter Three

Barbie waited for Gran's health to improve but, instead, she saw only deterioration. As days passed, gathering themselves into weeks, she watched her growing weaker, refusing food.

'That thing will have to come out soon. It must have got itself wedged.' She was quite exasperated by the recalcitrance of the obstruction. Several times she ventured to suggest that the time had come to call in Dr Poulson but each time she shrank from the unaccustomed severity of Gran's response. So, she took to carrying the worry within herself, unable to share it.

There were those in the village who noticed the change in her disposition but few who saw the need to ponder deeply upon the reasons for such a change. The news of Gran's drinking habits had spread and her occasional appearances in the village did nothing to allay the gossip. Her increasing frailty and the faltering of her gait could easily be attributed to the contents of a gin bottle and it was an assumption fed by the fact that her only port of call was to Mrs Matthews' off-licence counter.

There were many who voiced the view that 'someone' should report the matter to the Authorities but only one person considered it their personal responsibility to do so. Miss Beckworth was aware of the change in Barbie. She watched her closely but she, too, had heard of Gran's thirst for gin. Time and again she wrestled with her conscience, arguing that for the sake of Barbie's welfare the Authorities must be informed yet, at the same time, aware of the repercussions which such action could set in motion.

Many times she tried to speak to Barbie, endeavouring to draw out some detail concerning the current situation at the cottage but on each occasion Barbie would prevaricate. 'Everything's fine, Miss. Thank you, Miss.' Or, 'No, Miss. I'm not worried, Miss.

Why should I be worried, Miss?' Yet the lacklustre of her eye denied the assurance. Consequently, Miss Beckworth put off, day by day, the action which she knew she must ultimately take.

Just as the illness sapped Gran's strength, so the gin sapped their financial resources. As each empty gin bottle was discarded into the dustbin, it became increasingly difficult to replace it. Gran ate little and, as she entrusted the shopping to Barbie and spent the greater part of her time dozing in her chair, she did not notice that Barbie, too, had adjusted her eating habits.

When, on the last Thursday in the month, the sour-faced Bateson called to collect the rent, he was taken aback to find that for the first time in thirty years it was not forthcoming. He went upon his way muttering threats about court orders if the full amount were not awaiting him on his return.

Barbie stood behind Gran's skirts watching him retreating down the garden path. She felt her heart palpitating in her chest, sharing Gran's shame. 'It's all right, Gran. The lump will be gone by next month.' Gran squeezed her hand but even in the pressure of her fingers Barbie was aware of the growing weakness.

They did not see Ken Radlett on the appointed Saturday. Gran spent the afternoon dozing in her chair and Barbie was crouched beneath the walnut tree engrossed in the world of a myriad ants. When she returned to the cottage she found a five pound note and a scrawled message lying on the kitchen table. *'Sorry I missed you. Going on holiday next week. Torremolinos. Will pop in when I get back.'*

Gran sniffed. 'There's a knocker on that door. Doesn't take much to wake a sleeping woman and a dog.' Bess opened one eye and went back to sleep. 'No matter. Sooner or later he'll have to give me an aye or a nay.'

'An aye or a nay about what?'

'Never you mind.' Gran reached out and touched Barbie's arm. 'Nothing that you need fret yourself about.' She folded the five pound note and slipped it into her apron pocket. 'Be a good girl and put the kettle on. Then we'll take a little stroll down to the village.'

'You're not well. I don't think you're well enough to walk to the village.'

Gran fingered the money in her pocket. 'You just put the kettle on. I'll be right as ninepence.'

On the sixteenth of July, two days before school broke up for the summer holiday, Gran reluctantly took to her bed. Barbie made one last appeal to call Dr Poulson but when this failed she sat beside the bed stroking her fingers through the sparse grey strands of hair upon the pillow. She carried mugs of tea and poured measures of gin until, at last, Gran's voice became slurred and she fell into a restless sleep.

Barbie did not wake her before she went to school the following morning. She sat at her desk restlessly watching the clock, waiting for the lunch bell to ring.

'Barbie.' Miss Beckworth stopped her as she was running from the classroom. 'Is everything all right?'

'Yes, Miss. Thank you, Miss.' Barbie pranced on her toes, anxious to be off.

'You seem to be having some difficulty in concentrating.'

Barbie lowered her eyes. 'Sorry, Miss.'

'You're sure everything is all right?'

'Yes, Miss. Thank you, Miss.'

'I haven't seen your grandmother recently. Is she well?'

Barbie felt an overwhelming desire to share her worries with Miss Beckworth.

'I normally see her in the village. I thought she might be feeling poorly.'

'She's got . . .' She felt her throat tighten. 'She's got . . .' But she could not go through with it. 'She's got a tummy upset.'

'Oh, I am sorry. Have you called a doctor?'

'No, Miss. Gran doesn't like doctors.'

'Oh, I see,' said Miss Beckworth. 'I understand.'

'I think it's something she ate.' She kicked the toe of her sandal against the desk.

'Would you like me to come round after school to see if there's something I can do?'

'No, Miss. Thank you, Miss. Gran wouldn't like it.'

'But there may be something I can do to help.'

'She wouldn't like it, Miss. She doesn't like people interfering. She wouldn't want anyone to see her when she's took bad.'

'Well, we ought to do something. We can't have you worrying like this, can we.'

Barbie forced a smile. 'I expect she'll get better soon, Miss.'

'I hope so, Barbie.' Miss Beckworth placed an arm about Barbie's shoulders. 'But you will tell me if there's something I can do?'

'Yes, Miss. Thank you, Miss.' Barbie looked up at the clock and pulled away. It was ten minutes past twelve. 'Excuse me, Miss. I've got to go now.'

'Yes, of course.' Miss Beckworth released her hold. 'But let me know how she is as soon as you get back to school this afternoon.'

'Yes, Miss. Thank you, Miss.' Barbie ran all the way home.

Gran was asleep when she arrived. Her mouth was open, a loud, rattling snore echoing from within her throat. Barbie did not wake her. She marked with her eye the level of gin remaining in the bottle and sat on the bed holding Gran's hand.

Gran stirred as she got off the bed to return to school. She opened her eyes, blinking towards the ceiling.

'Are you all right, Gran?'

Gran nodded.

'Sure you're all right?'

'Yes, ducky.' The words were little more than a whisper. 'Right as ninepence.'

'It's time for me to go back to school.'

Gran smiled. 'You go to school. I'll be just fine.'

'I love you, Gran.' Barbie knelt close and kissed the sagging flesh of her cheek.

Gran raised a feeble hand and touched her hair. 'I love you too, Barbie. I love you.'

Barbie left the room but hovered in the doorway. 'You're sure you'll be all right?'

Gran waved her away with a movement of her hand. 'Get a move on, or you'll be late for school.'

'I'll come straight home.' Barbie came back and kissed her again, then turned and left the room.

Gran lay on the bed and listened to her footsteps on the stairs. She noted that they did not pause at the landing window. Barbie always paused at the landing window; today she did not.

Through an alcohol-induced stupor she felt the pain rising within her – a terrible pain, aching, aching, aching, until it was overtaken by greater agonising stabs which drew her knees to her chest and robbed her of the ability to draw breath. She lay there until the pain subsided back to the dull, heavy ache.

She moved her head until she could see the gin bottle and stretched out her hand for it but she could not reach. Again, the griping pain came, drawing up her knees. Pressure was pulsing through her head and singing its awful beat within her ears.

She drew breath again and reached out for the gin bottle, stretching her fingertips. A little further, and she was almost touching it. With one great effort she lifted the heavy body above the bed and the bottle was within her grasp. She took it by the neck, swigging the colourless liquid straight from the bottle, one great, gurgling gulp and then another.

The pain was easing, just a little. She replaced the bottle upon the bedside table and settled back into the pillows, wiping the sweat from her brow. Through the open window the sky was an expanse of blue with clumps of cumulus drifting across it. Was it July? Or was it August? Soon it would be Barbie's birthday. No, how stupid of her. Barbie was born in October. October was the next goal to reach. She must keep going for just a little longer. She must get back on her feet for Barbie.

It came again. Pain. She took another swig of gin. With its easing there came another sensation. She was going to vomit. She must not be sick on the bed. She reached for the chamber pot. Where was the chamber pot? At the bottom of the bed, beyond her reach. Must not be sick on the bed. She tried, tried so hard to reach the chamber pot but it was no good. Too late.

The vomiting brought its own relief but not for long. Soon it came again, unable to stop. Retching. Bright flecks of blood.

More gin. She must have more gin. She reached for the bottle, her arm swinging wildly. She felt for it with her hand and heard it fall, off the table, rolling across the floor. The gin was on the floor.

She lay there, staring at the ceiling, knowing only that she must have the gin. She rolled sideways until she was at the edge of the bed, then fought to free herself of blankets until, at last, she could slide her feet towards the floor. Cold linoleum. Her feet touched cold linoleum. She must stand up. No, she could not stand. She must crawl on hands and knees towards the gin. She eased herself off the bed towards the floor.

The room was spinning. Where was the gin? Her feet were numb. She could no longer feel the floor. Was it July? No, October. Must find the gin. Must have October. There was a rush of noise. It was turning dark. The last thing she saw was the corner of the bedside table rushing up towards her head.

She was lying on the floor when Barbie found her. A thin trickle of blood stained her temple.

'Gran . . . ?' One arm was outstretched towards the gin bottle which had rolled against the wall. She was breathing – a faint movement of rise and fall, and a strange, rattling hiss with each exhalant breath. 'Are you all right?' There was no sound but for the hissing rattle and far away, in the garden, a blackbird sang.

Barbie was on her knees. 'Gran. Wake up. Are you all right?' She moved her fingers and stretched them out towards Gran's head but could not bring herself to touch it. The face was still, pale and yellow, eyes tight closed but with a flicker now and then from yellow eyelids, revealing sightless eyes.

Barbie crouched there paralysed with fear but knowing that this was one moment in Gran's life, and in hers, when she must call for help. Then she was running headlong towards the telephone call-box in the village. Her heart was hammering within her chest and her mouth was stretched wide gasping for air to fill her straining lungs. With trembling fingers she tried to dial nine . . . nine . . . nine.

She expected the ambulance to be there when she returned to the cottage but it was not. Ten minutes stretched into eternity as she knelt beside Gran, straining her ears for sounds of its arrival. At last, there came the wailing of the siren and a blue light flashing reflections upon the ceiling. Heavy footsteps came up the stairs.

'Don't worry, luv. Leave it to us. We'll take care of her.'

Both men were tall, self-confident in their movements. 'Was it you who called us, luv?' One man knelt beside Gran loosening the button of her bedjacket at the neck. He gently moved Barbie to one side in order to make room.

Barbie nodded. 'She's my Gran.'

'Good girl. Your Gran's going to be mighty proud of you when she comes to.' He pressed his fingers into the soft flesh of Gran's wrist, feeling for the pulse. Then he turned her head, looking at the thin trickle of blood. 'Have you moved her?' Barbie shook her head. 'Good girl.' He tipped Barbie's chin and smiled. 'Don't worry, luv. We'll soon get her down to the General. They'll take good care of her there.' Barbie flashed a small grateful smile.

The other man was moving furniture, pushing the bed against the wall to make room for the stretcher. Barbie made herself small, pressed into the corner beside the chest of drawers, as they manoeuvred the stretcher and lifted Gran upon it. They carried her across the landing and down the stairs. Barbie fluttered behind, catching her breath as they negotiated the rickety, uneven staircase.

Once outside, they moved quickly, lifting the stretcher into the ambulance. One man climbed in beside Gran while the other prepared to close the doors. Barbie hovered anxiously, expecting the man to invite her in. 'Don't worry, luv.' The ambulance man blocked her way. 'We'll take good care of her.'

Barbie felt a moment of rising panic. 'But . . .'

Already the doors had closed. 'You go home and tell your Mum and Dad that we've taken your Gran to the General.' The driver gave her a wink and moved off quickly to the front of the vehicle. 'They'll be right proud when they hear what you've done.'

Barbie stood in the centre of the lane and watched the ambulance drive away. She watched it until the blue flashing light disappeared from sight beyond the bend, then continued to listen until the wailing siren could be heard no more. Suddenly, everything seemed very quiet, very still. Even the blackbird chose to remain silent. Far away, a dog barked. There was the sound of a machine cutting silage, a shriek of laughter. Somewhere, children were at play.

Barbie bit her lower lip and sauntered over to the gate. She swung on it, her nails biting into the wood. The empty loneliness was so real, she could feel it upon her skin. A cloud passed over the sun and she shivered.

The gate squeaked back and forth on rusty hinges. Soft footsteps padded up behind her and a cold nose pushed itself against her leg.

'Oh, Bess. It's you.' She dropped on her knees and flung her arms about the old dog's neck. 'It's all right, Bess.' The grip was too tight for the dog's comfort and she struggled so that Barbie was forced to release her, squatting back on her heels upon the path while Bess shook her coat and settled down beside her. 'They've taken Gran to hospital.' She gave Bess a nervous pat on the rump. 'She's going to be real mad when she finds out.' Bess cocked an ear and shifted to a more comfortable position upon the sun-warmed path. 'They'll have that thing out of her in no time at all. They might even cut it out, like Jenny Cutler's appendix.'

A sudden breeze disturbed the dust and ruffled the leaves of the trees, causing one bough of the apple tree to rub against another with a creaking sound. Barbie, her nerves already taut, jumped in fright. She flicked her eyes about her and wrapped her arms once more about the old dog's neck. She sat for a while, her muscles tense but when no further sound came she gradually

41

relaxed. 'We're going to have to look after ourselves while Gran's away.'

The breeze gusted again but this time Barbie's eyes were turned towards the apple tree and she caught sight of its movement. 'You silly old dog. Fancy being afraid of an apple tree. You're not to go doing silly things like that just because Gran's away. I've already told you I'm going to look after you.'

She leaned back against the gate-post. 'And there's another thing. We'd better not let anyone know that Gran's not here. Else someone is bound to come nosing round and Gran wouldn't like it.'

Bess lumbered to her feet and made off towards the cottage, turning repeatedly to look at Barbie over her shoulder.

'What's the matter?' asked Barbie. 'What do you want?'

The dog padded a little further then turned, looking again at Barbie. Barbie got up and followed her as she waddled into the kitchen, plodded across the floor to her feeding bowl, and nosed it with a loud clatter against the wall.

'Oh, poor Bessie.' She planted a kiss between the dog's ears. 'I forgot your dinner.' She ran quickly to fetch a can of dog food from the shelf and spooned it into the feeding bowl. The dog scoffed it as it fell.

'Greedy old thing. It would do you good to miss your dinner. Get rid of some of that fat.'

Bess champed and swallowed, licking the bowl until it was clean, then belched contentedly and settled down to sleep beside the back door.

Barbie sat with her for a while, then climbed the stairs, counting them, as she always did – 'One, two, three . . .' – and stood at the landing window, gazing out across the garden. The elder-flower was over, the saucers of white now turned to ochre, and, beyond, the barley field had turned to gold. Behind her, the cottage was silent, a mixture of inaudible sighs and creaking. Barbie turned to face it, mistrusting the silence at her back, finding it strangely hostile.

She crossed the landing to the bedroom and stood, hands on hips, looking about her. The room was in total disarray. The bed had been pushed back against the wall and upon the high feather mattress lay the foul, soiled bedding. She made to move away but realised that she could not leave it unattended.

She gathered the bedding into the centre of the mattress,

bringing together the four corners of the bottom sheet to form a bundle, and carried it downstairs to the wash-house.

The wash-house was a lean-to extension of the cottage, without windows, and with a corrugated iron roof. Its outer walls were overgrown with ivy and a weathered door was permanently wedged open, hanging upon one hinge. Barbie dumped the pile of soiled linen upon the floor and proceeded to light the fire at the base of the old stone copper which had been built into the corner. She watched it crackle into life then began the trek for water, back and forth, time and time again, from kitchen to wash-house, bucketful after bucketful poured into the copper's gaping mouth, until at last it was full.

She let out an explosion of breath, digging a fisted hand into the small of her back. 'Oh Lordy, that's hard work.'

A long-legged spider ran down the wall and scuttled across the floor. She followed it, smiling at the way in which the small, round body bobbed at the centre-point of the circle of legs. She lost it as it dodged through a crack into the dark recesses behind the copper and waited a while to see if it would reappear but, when it did not, she returned to the linen.

One by one she placed the items into the water – two pillow cases, a bolster case, two sheets and a blanket – prodding them down beneath the surface with a length of water-bleached broom handle which served as a copper stick. Finally, she added a good measure of soap powder which she stirred into the water with a twirl of the copper stick and closed the heavy, wooden lid.

It took a long time for the water to come to the boil. She sat in the doorway of the wash-house upon an upturned zinc bath, picking with her fingernails at the mortar between the brickwork. Occasionally, she got up, moved across to the copper and prodded its contents with the stick, before returning to the doorway and fixing her attention once more on the mortar and on thoughts of Gran.

A red-breasted robin hopped almost to her feet and cocked towards her one bright, shoe-button eye. Barbie sat quietly watching him, her only movement from her fingers which continued to scoop a furrow in the wash-house wall. She watched him but without her usual attentive concentration and when he flew away she barely bothered to follow his flight.

The water in the copper began to bubble – glurp, glurp, glurp, plop . . . glurp. She rose and prodded it again with the stick then

43

left it for a further time. At last, satisfied that she had left it long enough, she turned the zinc bath upright and carried it over to balance it upon the ledge beside the copper.

She screwed her face and pondered for a moment upon the job in hand. Somehow, she had to remove the heavy, sodden contents from the boiling water. It was a task which she and Gran had handled together often enough, a task simplified by their instinctive teamwork, but it was not a job which Barbie had ever tackled alone.

She pushed in the copper stick, stabbing it between folds of linen, and heaved upwards but the weight was too great for her. She tried again, giving out loud, straining grunts and succeeded this time in retrieving first the bolster case, then each of the two pillow cases. Next, she tried the sheet but time and again it fell, flopping back into the boiling water so that she had to jump sharply to one side in order to avoid the scalding splash.

She prodded, heaved, lifted, gasped for breath, until, at last, she found a loose corner and lifted it, streaming with boiling water, into the zinc bath. Little by little, she worked the stick along the sheet, lifting it inch by inch from the copper until its entire length was transferred into the bath. She gave a small grunt of satisfaction and wiped her forehead with the back of her hand. 'One down and two to go.'

She prodded the stick into the water but the remaining sheet and the blanket had become entangled. She would have to lift them both together. The blanket was a mass of matted fibres and it crossed her mind that maybe she should not have boiled it. She vaguely remembered that Gran had said one should not boil wool, that it would shrink. 'Oh Lordy.' But there was no time to think of such things now.

She gritted her teeth and tried again, stopped, paused for breath, and heaved once more. This time she got the sodden mass to the rim of the copper and held it there, as it streamed water and the steam puffed up into her face. She had it almost halfway between the copper and the zinc bath when the bath tipped over. She let out a cry, dropping the weight of the blanket back into the water as she jumped aside, and, with a great, crashing, clanging clatter, the zinc bath fell, spewing the hot, sodden linen across the floor.

Barbie crashed against the wall, the hot water stinging her legs as it splashed upwards from the floor.

Outside, a pheasant, startled by the noise, screeched its way across the barley field.

She stood, her back pressed against the wall, looking at the mess. The heap of steaming linen sent water flowing in runnels towards the door. Slowly, she slid her back down the wall until she was crouched on her haunches upon the floor.

'Well, what do you expect?' she shouted. The sound of her voice bounced off the corrugated iron roof and echoed back at her. 'I'm only a bleeding kid.'

Again the pheasant screeched and flapped its wings.

She bunched her fists and pushed her knuckles into her eyes, running down the garden towards the hidey-hole beneath the elder hedge. She pulled down the hop vine curtain and stayed there until her tears ran dry.

It was getting late when she looked about her, mid-evening at least. She heard sounds of evening percolating through the hop vine curtain. She moved aside the vine and stepped out, feeling shaky upon her legs. The air held a chill and the sky was overcast, threatening rain. She made her way back to the cottage and up the stairs to the bedroom, gazing again upon the chaos of the disordered furniture.

Gran's dentures were in the mug on the bedside table. She stood looking at them and listening to the silence. Then, quietly she took the dentures from the mug, shook off the excess water, and wrapped them in a tissue handkerchief which she placed into the pocket of her dress. She knew now what she would do.

Downstairs the clock in the hall struck seven-thirty. She took some money from a jam jar on the kitchen shelf and put on her cardigan. She would catch the seven forty-five bus into town.

The rabbits were at play as she closed the back door. 'Bloody rabbits.' There was a note of hysteria in her voice. She picked up a stone and threw it at them intending to hit them, but her aim was poor and the stone bounced a good distance away. 'I'll kill you if I catch you on them bloody lettuce.' The rabbits whirled and scurried through the hedge.

It was eight-twenty when she reached the hospital. Visiting hours were over and the building had the air of a busy establishment settling down for the night. The corridors were empty but for a woman with a vacuum cleaner sucking up an accumulation of dust from the carpet and nearby, another woman with a large, black plastic bag was emptying ash trays and waste paper bins.

The administration offices stood silent, some with their doors open, revealing typewriters covered with plastic hoods and cabinets tight closed, guarding secrets. Beyond one open door a woman sprayed furniture polish upon a desk, coughing behind the cigarette which dangled from her lips.

Barbie stood at the plate glass entrance door, uncertain, twisting her finger within the fabric of her dress. She was afraid to launch out along the forbidding expanse of carpet. A man carrying a pot plant and a carrier bag came towards her and passed by without paying her any heed. She took a deep breath, set her eye upon a point in the middle distance, and set off.

Before she had taken more than half a dozen steps she was stopped in her tracks by a porter who stepped from a nearby room.

'Good evening, Missy.' He touched the peak of his cap. 'And what can I do for you?'

Barbie blinked. He was an elderly man, so tall that her eyes were level with the middle button on his jacket. It was a metallic button, gold-coloured, with an emblem stamped in relief. She took a step backwards in order that she might look at his face without stretching her neck. 'I've come to find my Gran.'

'Oh,' he said. 'And where might your Gran be found?' He looked towards the cleaning women as though expecting the answer to lie with them.

'I don't know.'

'Then how do you think you're going to find her?'

Barbie moved her feet. 'The ambulance men told me this was where they were bringing her.'

'Oh, I see.' His voice softened. 'So, your Gran's a patient here; and you want to see her.'

Barbie nodded.

'Well now.' He bent down until their faces were level, his hands supported just above his knees. 'That might prove to be something of a problem.' Barbie felt a flutter of panic. 'Visiting time's over for today. Two till eight, that's visiting time and this is . . .' He looked at the watch on his wrist '. . . getting on for half past.'

Barbie bit her lip and looked at him.

'And anyway,' he went on, 'it's against the rules. We must have rules, you know, and we can't have children coming in here visiting without a grown-up, can we.'

The flutter of panic grew. Barbie fidgeted on her toes. The man before her was a barrier which separated her from Gran – a huge barrier with large hands and gold buttons.

'Now I'll tell you what you do.' The porter removed one hand from his knee and placed it about Barbie's shoulder. It was heavy, restraining. 'You go home and you ask your Mum and Dad to bring you back here tomorrow. You tell them to ask Sister if she'll let you see your Gran. I'm not saying she will, mind. It just depends.'

She set her mouth into a rigid line. 'I want to see her now.'

'Not now. Tomorrow.' The porter's voice was kind but held the impatient note of a man who wished to return to his evening newspaper. 'Come back tomorrow with your Mum or Dad.'

'I haven't got a Mum and Dad.'

The man's eyes took on new interest. 'I'm sorry to hear that,' he said. 'Very sorry.' He straightened up, reaching into his jacket pocket for a bag of toffees which he offered to Barbie. 'Where do you live?'

'With my Gran.' Barbie put out a hand and took a toffee from the bag. It was a black liquorice toffee, wrapped in a band of silver foil, patterned with a design of blue triangles. There was a slight tremor in her fingers as she unwrapped it and popped it into her mouth, rolling the paper between her fingers.

'I see.' The porter nodded. 'And who's looking after you while your Gran's in hospital?'

'No one.'

She was immediately aware of the disbelief across his eyes. 'Now, now. You're not trying to tell me you haven't got anyone to look after you.'

She swallowed, tasting the sweet liquorice toffee on her throat. She took a step backwards but he caught her arm.

'What's your name?'

'Barbie Harding.'

'And what's your Gran's name?'

'Ma Harding.' She considered it a stupid question.

They stood looking at one another, Barbie's gaze wide and steady, while she rolled the toffee paper between her fingers, feeling the sausage shape thinning to a thread.

'I think you'd better come with me.' He increased the pressure on her arm, drawing her away from the main body of the hospital. The panic which had been welling within Barbie

47

suddenly rose to an uncontrollable level. She wheeled round and aimed a sharp kick towards his shins. He let out a cry and released his hold.

'Why, you little . . .' He tottered backwards sucking in his breath.

Barbie made to run but the porter was standing between her and the interior of the hospital, jumping on one foot, the injured shin cupped in his hand. There was nowhere for her to run but back, out of the heavy plate glass door, towards the car park. She glanced over her shoulder and saw him hobble a few steps in pursuit but he stopped when he reached the door and watched her as she increased the distance between them.

She dodged between cars, working her way round to the side of the building. At the far end of the car park stood a prefabricated, single-storeyed structure with a low stone wall skirting its perimeter. Barbie stopped when she reached it and sat on the wall, sucking hard on the toffee and running her tongue round the inside of her mouth, imagining the black, sticky substance discolouring her teeth. Before her, the hospital building towered like a giant ocean liner, five storeys high. The air was cold, with heavy cloud, threatening rain, bringing with it a premature dusk. She shivered and pulled her cardigan closer across her chest.

In the hospital every light had been switched on, pooling themselves into a single blaze. She sat and looked at them. One hundred lights behind one hundred windows and, somewhere, beyond one of those windows, was Gran. She had no idea how she was going to find her.

She ran her eye along the rows of glass. Here and there a curtain was drawn; figures moved about dressed in blue or green, with white caps and aprons; a woman in a dressing gown was staring out across the rooftops of town.

She tried to form a plan but her mind was weary and confused. She knew of only one door and beyond that door was the porter, sitting in his room, lying in wait. There was probably another door on the other side of the building but beyond that would be other porters, other people who would prevent her from finding Gran. Visiting time was over for the day and no one would allow her to enter the building.

She wondered if Gran had woken yet and shivered as her mind flashed back to the scene she had discovered that afternoon –

Gran stretched out upon the floor, yellow skin and sightless eyes, blood across the temple. And yet, what had she said at lunch-time? 'I'll be right as ninepence,' she had said. 'You go to school. I'll be right as ninepence.'

'You didn't have to go off like that, did you, you silly old bleeder.' She choked on the toffee, swallowing the last of it down her throat. 'What about me? You didn't think about *me*, did you, running off like that, without a word.'

She stopped short, feeling pain in her fingernail. She had been digging it into the stone wall beneath her, so hard that her nail had split, torn down to the quick. She put the finger to her mouth, sucking the salty taste of blood to mingle with the remaining flavour of the toffee.

She did not hear the porter coming up behind her and almost choked with fright as he placed his hand upon her shoulder. 'So there you are. I've been looking for you.' She wheeled round, wild-eyed, but he held her fast.

'Now, hold on there.' His voice was gentle, while the pressure of his hand was firm. She did not trust him and thought only of escape. She tried to scratch.

'Enough of that!'

She lashed out with her feet, then tried to bite.

'That's enough,' he shouted. 'I'm taking you to your Gran.'

She stopped short and looked at him.

'That's better,' he said, gentle once more. 'I've had a word with Sister. I'm taking you to your Gran and we'll sort out what this is all about.'

She stopped struggling and he released his hold.

'OK?'

'OK,' nodded Barbie.

'Good girl.' He placed his hand lightly about her shoulders and led her back across the car park towards the door. She noticed that he was limping. 'She's on the third floor,' he said. Together they walked down the corridor towards the lift.

'I'm sorry.' She indicated his leg. 'I'm sorry I kicked you.'

He smiled. 'I should think so, too. Got me right on top of me bit of shrapnel.' He pressed a button and the lift doors closed, depressing Barbie's stomach as it rose swiftly upwards. 'Got it in the last War, out in the desert with Monty. See . . . ?' He lifted his trouser leg, revealing a grey sock and, above it, a large mauve bruise fast appearing above a jagged scar. 'Right there.'

Barbie nodded, feeling ashamed and thinking of the poor man's shrapnel. 'I'm sorry,' she whispered.

'Want another toffee?'

Barbie took the toffee and gave him a smile. He was a nice man really.

'You'd better have another one for later.' She took another and put it into the pocket of her cardigan.

The lift stopped and he led her through another door, past cubicles of beds and handed her over to Sister Thorpe.

Before he left, he shook her hand 'Everything's going to be fine. Just you wait and see.'

Barbie watched him walk away, biting her lip as she observed again his limp.

Sister Thorpe was a kind and sensible woman. She lost no time in taking Barbie to Gran and delayed her only long enough to prepare her for the coming shock.

'Barbie,' she said. 'Your Gran is still unconscious – asleep.' Barbie nodded soberly. 'She has some tubes attached to her but they are not hurting her. They are there to help her feel better.' Barbie nodded again, not understanding.

Sister Thorpe led her to an open door, immediately adjacent to the nurses' station. It was a single room, furnished only with a hard-backed chair, a locker, and there, upon the bed, was Gran, her large body immobile, covered by a light cellular blanket.

'Gran . . .' Barbie rushed forward.

From Gran's nose there protruded a length of plastic tubing, held to her cheek by a strip of adhesive tape. Attached to her right forearm was another tube of clear white plastic, its end obscured beneath layers of bandage wrapped about a splint, and its other end attached to a plastic bag, pot-bellied with clear colourless fluid, hanging from a stand beside the bed. From the bag the fluid dripped into the tube.

'Gran?'

Sister Thorpe did not restrain her as she flung herself upon Gran but stood by only to see that the pressure did no harm.

'Are you all right?'

The body was warm and soft, with still a trace of gin, but now there was the scent of something new – antiseptic, the smell of dentists' and of doctors' waiting rooms. She was on her knees, her head pressed close against the unencumbered hand.

Sister Thorpe turned her back busying herself at the wash-hand basin, offering her a moment of privacy. When she turned again, Barbie had raised her head and was gazing at the unresponsive face.

'Perhaps she'll wake tomorrow, Barbie. She may be able to speak to you then.'

Barbie nodded and stroked the liver-spotted hand. 'You'll be right as ninepence by tomorrow, Gran.'

Sister Thorpe made no attempt to move her but drew up a chair and sat down. 'I'd like you to tell me something about Gran,' she said quietly. 'And about yourself.'

Barbie bit her lip. 'Gran doesn't like me telling people about us.'

'It's very important, Barbie. I wouldn't ask you if it wasn't important to you.'

Still Barbie looked uncertain.

'And important to Gran.'

So, little by little, it all came out. Sister Thorpe listened quietly, prompting sometimes but at pains not to appear inquisitive.

'Yes, I see,' she said at last. 'Thank you for telling me. I think we'd better see what we can do.' She rose from the chair and, patting Barbie lightly upon the head, she left the room and walked down the corridor towards her private office.

She closed the door and lifted the telephone, checking a list of numbers pinned against the wall. She found the home telephone number of the duty social worker and gave it to the operator who came on the line.

'Hello. Daphne Crawley here.'

'Mrs Crawley. This is Sister Thorpe. I think we've got problems.' She outlined the story she had gleaned from Barbie. 'There's nothing we need do tonight,' she concluded. 'The best place for her now is on the ward. She needs to be near her grandmother.'

The voice at the other end of the line confirmed agreement. 'I'll call in to see you first thing tomorrow morning. We'll sort it out then.'

'Thanks. I'll see you then. Sorry to disturb you at this time in the evening.'

'Think nothing of it. That's why I'm on call.' The line clicked off as the receiver was replaced.

Sister Thorpe went to the kitchen to ask the young Pupil Nurse to prepare poached eggs and milk.

'Sister?' Pupil Nurse Fletcher busied herself with the pan on the stove. 'What's the prognosis? For Mrs Harding, I mean.'

'Nothing we can do, I'm afraid. It's merely a matter of time. The old lady has a massive c.a. of the gut. And goodness knows how many secondaries.'

'Isn't there any chance of surgery?'

Sister Thorpe shook her head. 'It's almost certainly inoperable. And, in any case, there's no question of operating with that concussion.'

Nurse Fletcher slid two slices of bread to toast beneath the grill. 'I wonder why she didn't do something about it before it got so bad?'

'Heaven only knows. She must have carried it about with her for ages.'

'Perhaps she was afraid.'

'I'm sure she was. But there's more to fear in not taking action. The proof of that is over there.' She nodded her head towards the open door.

'That poor kid. Whatever is she going to do?'

'I don't know, Nurse. But we have a lot of sad cases. We handle them all in the very best way we can. And we never . . .' she looked at her pointedly '. . . we never get emotionally involved.'

'Yes, Sister.' Nurse Fletcher broke the eggs into the pan. 'But sometimes it's very hard.'

Sister Thorpe smiled. 'I know,' she said and left her to the eggs.

Barbie jumped as Sister Thorpe placed a hand on her back. She had fallen asleep, still kneeling on the floor and with her face pressed against Gran's hand. 'It's time for bed.' Sister Thorpe led her to a room on the opposite side of the corridor. She sat her on her lap and undressed her like a baby.

Barbie did not resist but gave herself up to the gentle hands which unfastened the buttons of her dress and slid it to the floor. 'Oh.' She heard the soft thud as it dropped. 'I forgot the teeth.' She reached down to retrieve Gran's dentures from the pocket and handed them to Sister Thorpe.

'Thank you.' Sister Thorpe accepted the tissue-wrapped offering. 'I'll put them in some water beside Gran's bed.'

She tucked Barbie into bed and handed her the supper tray which Nurse Fletcher had prepared. 'Eat up,' she said. 'I bet you missed your tea.'

Nurse Fletcher had cut the crusts from the toast and set the tray with a pretty cloth. Barbie had never before eaten so regally. She sat up in bed and ate to the last crumb.

When she had finished Sister Thorpe brought medicine in a tiny glass. 'Drink up,' she said. 'It will help you to sleep.'

Barbie took the glass without question and downed the liquid in one gulp. It was thick and sweet, clinging to the roof of her mouth. 'Ugh,' she shuddered and swallowed on the taste.

Sister Thorpe laughed and settled her back into the pillows. She pulled the blankets tight across Barbie's body and tucked them beneath the mattress, giving her a feeling of protection and security. She was very tired. The day had stretched endlessly across a string of traumatic hours and now she was close to sleep. Outside the sky was dark, blanketed with heavy cloud, and rain hammered against the window pane, reinforcing the feeling of safety within her blanket cocoon.

'Sleep well.' Sister Thorpe smoothed back the hair from Barbie's cheek. Barbie smiled in return and listened to the rustle of her apron as she walked away.

She made no attempt to close the door but left it ajar so that, merely by turning her head, Barbie had full view of Gran across the corridor. She lay there watching the rise and fall of Gran's breathing until gradually her eyelids drooped. She had almost drifted into sleep when suddenly she remembered something important.

'GentleJesusmeekandmild . . . Lookuponthislittlechild . . .' She broke off and opened her eyes to look across at Gran. 'Hey, Jesus. Are You there? Because if You are, it's about time You started doing something for our Gran after all that praying she's been doing for You.' She looked again at Gran and remembered her manners. 'Sorry, Jesus. Please. Amen.'

She closed her eyes and watched as coloured swirls of light formed patterns on the dark inside of her eyelids. She knew now what Gran had meant about, 'You never know when you might need Him'.

'And You'd better do it quick. Because she's not going to like it when she wakes up and finds herself in here.'

She was glad that she had thought of it. It was up to Him now. She settled her head more comfortably into the pillow and fell into a deep sleep.

Across the corridor another figure appeared. A white-coated

53

doctor stood with Sister Thorpe looking down at Gran. 'How is she, Sister?'

'Not good I'm afraid, Doctor.'

He took Gran's wrist feeling for the pulse, then leaned over to raise her eyelid, peering into the pupil.

'I was hoping that she might regain consciousness,' said Sister Thorpe. 'Just long enough to speak to her grand-daughter.'

'Very doubtful, I'm afraid. I don't think she's going to last very long.'

'That's a pity.' Sister Thorpe looked across the corridor towards Barbie. 'It's very important to the child.'

'Yes, I know. But I don't think this old lady is likely to speak to anyone again.'

Chapter Four

Daphne Crawley, Hospital Social Worker, found a space in the staff car park and hurried to her office on the ground floor of the hospital complex. It was one of those days when she wished that she could put back the clock and start again. One half of her wanted to put it back to seven o'clock that morning when the family had risen in an aura of combined ill-humour. The other half put it back to a time two years ago when she had decided that, with careful management, it was possible to combine an exacting career with the duties of a wife and mother.

There were others she knew who organised their lives with effortless serenity, but Daphne had a son who clutched his stomach with symptoms of agonising appendicitis when she suspected the 'disease' to be the prospect of a Maths lesson with 'Stinky' Thompson. She had a daughter who was petulant when called upon to take her turn with washing the breakfast dishes, and a husband who did nothing but grunt at her morosely from behind his newspaper.

The children were always at their worst when she and John were at loggerheads and they had been sniping at one another since last evening. It was always the same when she was 'on call' for the Department. John could not accept that the people who made demands upon her could not organise the crises of their lives to fall between the hours of nine and five. He did not understand the complexity of her job, the emotional demands which are made upon those who are asked to juggle with the commodities of life and death.

Sometimes the responsibility frightened her. She wished that she could give up and go back to being a housewife. Maybe then, she would have given Robbie the benefit of the doubt and kept him away from school. She would have been free from the nagging fear that perhaps this time he really did have appendicitis. At the very least, she would have had more time to find out why he should be so strung up about Maths with 'Stinky' Thompson. The irony of storting out other people's problems was that one never had time to deal with one's own.

She had hoped to get to the office early this morning but now she was late. She had a mountain of work to get through in the course of the day and the first problem on the list was the child who was about to lose the only person in her life who cared for her. She was thankful that this one would probably not fall upon her own shoulders. She would pass the case over to the community social workers where it would doubtless prove to be one of their long-term headaches. She was glad that it would not be hers.

There were four new referrals on her desk to add to the backlog of work left over from yesterday. Old Mrs Barnes wanted to go home and live alone in her flat but she was severely disabled and her family were pressing for her to be put into a Home . . . There was a baby in Paediatrics with suspicious contusions of the buttocks and a broken arm; the parents claimed that the injuries were caused by a fall . . . Young Mark Jordan had been diagnosed – leukaemia; his parents had taken it hard . . . Mr James had lost his right arm in an accident; what does a carpenter do without his right arm?

Daphne put on her white coat and took off Daphne Crawley, housewife and mother. Would the school think to contact her if Robbie was in pain? . . .

'Sally.'

The clatter of the typewriter ceased in the adjacent room. 'Morning. There are four new referrals on your desk.'

'I know. Is there any chance of some coffee?'

'I'll get you some from the vending machine.'

'Ugh. Well it's better than nothing.' She flipped a coin across the desk.

'Oh, by the way.' Sally turned as she was leaving the room. 'Dr Jenkins wants you to ring him before ten.'

'I'll do it in a minute.' Daphne pushed aside the pile of referrals. 'There's another call I want to make first.'

She rang the Area Social Work Office on the other side of town and spoke to Veronica Standish, Community Social Worker.

'Veronica. Does the name Barbie Harding mean anything to you?'

'Funny you should ask me that.' Veronica Standish sounded slightly surprised. 'I had a phone call this morning from a teacher at the village school. What's your interest in the case?'

Daphne outlined the story as it had been relayed to her by Sister Thorpe.

'Well, it's not the same version as the one given to me by Miss Beckworth. But it fits.'

'I haven't seen Barbie yet,' said Daphne. 'I was thinking it would be best to hand her straight over to you. She's not a hospital case and it would confuse her to have too many people flitting in and out of her life at the moment.'

Veronica Standish murmured her agreement. 'I can't do anything until mid-afternoon at the earliest. I'm in a Case Conference all morning and I'm up to my eyes in work.'

'Aren't we all,' offered Daphne silently.

'We don't seem to have much to go on,' went on Veronica Standish. 'The mother disappeared years ago and there doesn't seem to be anyone else who's likely to want to take on the child's care.'

'I was hoping that your Department might have some more detailed information about her. I thought you might have been keeping in touch.'

'Well I have dug out an old file.' Daphne heard the rustle of paper at the other end of the line. 'It's not so much on Barbie. It really concerns her mother. According to this, Sandra Harding was a right little tearaway as a teenager. It was long before my time but it seems that getting herself pregnant was only one of a whole string of problems. She ran off to London shortly after the child was born and has never been seen since. The Department did try to trace her but she was eighteen shortly afterwards so no longer under our supervision.'

'What about Barbie? Didn't you keep in touch with her?'

'For a while, but we kept it very loose. Mrs Harding resented the Department's interference. By all accounts she was doing an excellent job in caring for the child. It was a bit rough and ready, but what's a little dirt compared to a whole load of love.'

'Sister Thorpe was very impressed by the obvious bond of affection between them.'

'Exactly. And that's why we kept a low profile. The old lady made it clear that she didn't want us around and we didn't want to do anything which would jeopardise her relationship with the child. We have made a few home visits over the years but each one only served to confirm the strength of the bond between them.'

'Withdraw it,' said Daphne, 'and how does she fill the vacuum?'

'Did she mention any other family? Anything that might possibly give us a lead?'

'Only her father and she doesn't seem to have had much contact with him.'

'Well he's paid maintenance for her all these years. According to this file he's always paid regularly.'

'He'll have to be told.'

'I think I'll have a word with him as soon as possible. I don't suppose he'll be much help but he may be able to tell us something which would indicate a course of action. I expect we shall finish up receiving the child into Care but let's explore all other avenues first. Apart from any other consideration, we haven't got any vacancies locally. We should have to send her some distance away.'

Daphne nodded into the telephone. 'He ought to be informed of the situation.'

'Can you have a quick word with Barbie? See if you can find out where he works. I'd better not contact him at home just in case his wife doesn't know about the child.'

Daphne smiled. 'We've got enough trouble without stirring up another hornets' nest.'

'I'll have a word with the child before I do anything. She may have some ideas of her own. But it would be helpful to speak with the father.'

'I'll pop up to the ward in a minute and ring you back.'

'Thanks.' Daphne heard another rustle of paper. 'There's another name down here – a Mrs Beatrice Russell. She's down here as Mrs Harding's next of kin. I think she must be her sister. Probably about the same age. We'd better arrange an interview with her too.'

Daphne wrote down details on the notepad before her. 'Good. I need that,' she said. 'I'll ring her straight away. She'll have to be informed of Mrs Harding's condition.'

'OK.' Veronica Standish was only too happy to off-load one

58

facet of her task. 'I'll leave it to you to contact her in the first instance. Can you ask her if there are any other members of the family around? See if she can suggest anyone with whom Barbie might have had a good relationship.'

'I'll ask her to come in and sort out Mrs Harding's affairs. And I'll have a word with her then.'

'Look, I've got to go now.' Veronica Standish's voice quickened. 'They're screaming for me because I'm holding up the Case Conference. We'll liaise this afternoon. Any chance of meeting for a quick sandwich at lunchtime?'

Daphne looked at the papers on her desk. 'Not a hope. I'll give you another ring when I've had a word with Barbie and with Mrs Russell.'

She put down the telephone and gave her attention to Sally who was hovering in the doorway.

'Dr Jenkins is on the other line. He's been holding on.'

Daphne put her fingers to her forehead and lifted the receiver. 'Hello, Dr Jenkins. Sorry to have kept you.'

'Oh Mrs Crawley. You remember that young West Indian woman who was brought in unconscious from the street? Well it's much more serious than we thought . . .'

Daphne clicked off her concentration from Barbie Harding and homed it in on an unnamed young woman up on the second floor.

'Can you come up to the ward straight away, please.'

'Yes, of course. I'll be right there.'

It was ten-thirty by the time she was able to give her attention once more to Barbie. She took the lift to the third floor and found her sitting beside Gran's bed, aimlessly picking at the cellular blanket with her fingernails.

'Hello Barbie. I'm Mrs Crawley.'

Barbie looked apprehensive. Since eight o'clock that morning, when the day staff had come on duty, she had been confronted by a succession of people hiding behind the anonymity of white coats.

'I'm the Hospital Social Worker.' In the absence of a second chair Daphne Crawley leaned against the bedside locker. 'Sister tells me that you've got a little problem that you need some help with. Is that right?'

Barbie bit her lip. Gran was not going to be pleased about all these people nosing into their affairs.

'It won't be me who helps you,' Daphne went on. 'It will be a lady named Miss Standish but I just wanted to pop in and say hello.'

'Hello.'

Daphne smiled. 'We seem to have a little problem about who's going to look after you now that your grandmother has been taken ill.'

'It's all right, Miss. She'll get better soon.'

'Isn't there anyone you would like to stay with for a while? An aunty? Or a cousin? A friend?'

Barbie shook her head and clammed up. Daphne did not wish to press her. There was little point in distressing the child when she would be handing over the case to Veronica Standish. She made to move away. 'Just one thing, Barbie. Do you often see your father?'

Barbie shot her a glance. 'Oh, he wouldn't want to come and look after me, Miss.'

'Does he come to see you?'

'He came to tea once. But next time he came we didn't hear him so he left us a five pound note.'

'Do you know where he works?'

Barbie thought for a moment. 'Gran told me he works in a big place where they make freezers.'

'Ah, yes.' Daphne nodded. 'I think I know the place you mean.'

There was movement at the door and both Barbie and Daphne looked up as the day duty Sister joined them. 'Excuse me interrupting, Mrs Crawley. Dr Fleming wants to speak to you. He's waiting by my desk.'

Daphne Crawley sighed and went to speak to Dr Fleming.

'Mrs Crawley.' Dr Fleming was writing notes in a file. 'A Mr Simmons was admitted this morning – cardiac arrest. I'd be grateful if you'd have a word with his wife. She's in a bit of a state about how she's going to cope. She's got four young children.'

'Yes, of course.' Daphne glanced at the clock above his head. 'I'm rather pushed for time this morning but I'll see her as soon as I can.'

'Good.' He looked up from the file and smiled. 'And there's another young girl I'd like you to see when you have a minute to spare.'

'Spare minutes are something in very short supply. Can it wait until the next ward round?'

'Sure.' He finished writing and closed the file. 'No rush. Tomorrow will do.'

Daphne made a mental note to speak to Mrs Simmons during afternoon visiting hours and returned to Barbie. She felt the pressure of work building up about her like a physical weight and she found herself hunching her shoulders as if this would somehow bring her some relief.

The Ward Sister was still in the room when she returned. She was checking the drip but it was obvious that her main intention was to contribute to the conversation.

'I'm not happy about Barbie sitting here all day,' she said. 'I think she's in need of some fresh air, and a little diversion.'

'No.' Barbie clutched at the cellular blanket. 'I want to stay here.'

Daphne thought for a few moments and looked at her watch. The idea she had in mind would eat up another hour of her precious time. 'Supposing I take you to school,' she said. 'You could have some company for the afternoon and then come back here at tea-time.'

Barbie shook her head. 'I don't want to go anywhere.'

The Sister leaned across the bed towards her. 'Gran won't mind if you go off and have a break for a while,' she said. 'I'm sure you really ought to. And I promise that I'll ring the school and send for you straight away if she needs you.'

'It's a lovely day,' said Daphne briskly. She took Barbie's hand and drew her from the chair. 'Who wants to sit in a stuffy old hospital when they can have a ride out into the country.'

She did not know that she had hit on the one means of persuasion. Barbie had the sudden need to suck into her lungs great gulps of fresh, village air.

They were on their way down to the ground floor when the bleep sounded in Daphne's pocket. She made for the nearest telephone and lifted the receiver. 'Hello. Daphne Crawley here. Oh, it's you, John.' She heard her husband's voice at the other end of the line.

'Daphne. Can you slip out to the bank for me? I'm stuck in a meeting all morning and then I've got to go straight out to lunch with a client.'

Daphne hesitated. 'John, I'm sorry. I can't.'

'Well surely you could go at lunch-time. It will only take you fifteen minutes.'

'I don't think I'll have time for lunch today. It's a bit hectic here.'

She heard the intake of breath. 'Good God, Daphne; I don't understand you sometimes. You're *entitled* to a lunch break. Just down tools and go. No one can stop you.'

'It's not a question of entitlement.'

'Honestly, Daphne. You're a fool to yourself. You just see whether anyone at that place cares a damn when you fall sick from overwork.' Daphne removed the receiver a short distance from her ear. 'The day the Local Authority starts paying you a decent salary, that's the day when you can start putting in a few extra hours for them.'

'All right, John.' She had no wish at this moment to embark upon this ever-recurring argument. 'I'll go to the bank.'

'Good.' His voice softened once he thought he had won her over. 'Take an extra long lunch break and go for a walk in the park. It will do you good.'

'I'll see you this evening.' Daphne prepared to break off the conversation.

'Bye. Don't forget I want an early dinner tonight. It's my evening for playing squash.'

Daphne put down the receiver, causing a passer-by to look up as it slammed into the cradle. She held out a hand to Barbie. 'Come on,' she said. 'Let's make a run for it before anyone else can interrupt us. I've got to make a little detour to the bank on the way but you can come with me.'

Barbie entered the village feeling as though she had been away from it for a very long time. She stared from the windows of the car taking in every house, every field, every gateway, the mellow red brick of buildings, the scarlet of roadside poppies, the sight of Mrs Webster walking down the High Street with her shopping basket. It was almost as though she were seeing them for the first time.

'I'll have a word with your teacher,' said Daphne. 'I expect she'll be wondering why you didn't turn up for school this morning.'

Barbie stood at the back of the classroom watching the two women in conversation.

'Come in, Barbie,' said Miss Beckworth at last. 'Come and sit down.' She took Barbie by both hands. 'I'll take you back to the hospital myself straight after school.'

'Thanks. That would be a great help.' Daphne Crawley was in a hurry to leave. 'Goodbye, Barbie.' She walked out of the door. Barbie never saw her again.

'Now, children.' The class was a-bubble with curiosity. 'I want you all to be especially kind to Barbie today. She's just come from the hospital. Her Gran is feeling very poorly.'

A voice came from the back of the room – 'Is she going to die?' – but Miss Beckworth stifled it with a glance. Barbie heard the question but it washed across her unabsorbed.

'We're doing some painting, Barbie.' Miss Beckworth placed a sheet of paper on the desk before her. 'Perhaps you would like to join us. The subject is "seasons".'

Tommy Jenkins self-consciously pushed a bag of crisps towards her across the desk. Barbie accepted it and twitched a smile.

She painted a picture of scarlet poppies against an azure sky. The colours were garish and the brutality of her strokes brought her some measure of relief. She had finished and was in the process of destroying it with brutal zig-zag stripes of black when she suddenly had a thought and turned quickly towards the clock.

Miss Beckworth glanced at the mutilated painting. 'Have you finished, Barbie?'

'Yes, Miss.'

'Would you like to go to the library and fetch me a book?'

'It's nearly lunch-time, Miss. I've got to go and let Bess out. She's been locked up all night. She must be busting.'

Miss Beckworth echoed her concern. 'Go now. Don't wait until twelve o'clock.'

'Oh, and Barbie,' she called as Barbie rushed from the room. 'I'll come down to the cottage and join you later. I'll bring some sandwiches.'

'Yes, Miss. Thank you, Miss.'

As Barbie raced towards the cottage she was puzzled to see Bess stretched out on the back doorstep. The old dog waddled up and made a fuss of her. 'Who let you out?' But, at the same moment, she felt the skin prickle on the back of her neck as she became aware of another person's presence.

She stopped and looked around. Things had been moved. She

was not aware of specific objects which had been tampered with but there was an atmosphere which only she could interpret; she knew that it had been disturbed. She moved cautiously through the kitchen, out into the hall, and stood hesitating at the foot of the stairs.

'Why, you must be little Barbie.' The voice came from above her on the landing. A woman, whom Barbie had never seen before, came down the stairs towards her. She did not know her but the similarity to Gran caught her by the throat.

'I'm Aunty Beattie, dear. Aunty Beattie Russell.'

Barbie recalled the name. Gran had mentioned a sister who lived in Aylesborough. She drew back as the woman enveloped her in a suffocating hug.

'They rang me from the hospital, dear. I came straight away to see what I could do.' Barbie stepped back, instinctively mistrusting. 'Fancy poor old Gerty about to be taken off like that. I couldn't believe it when they told me. Well, she was younger than me, dear; and only the two of us left.'

She took Barbie by the shoulders and held her out for inspection. 'Aren't you getting to be a big girl, dear. How old are you now?'

'Ten,' said Barbie.

'Ten,' repeated Beattie. 'My, how time flies. We were very close, you know, your Granny and me.' She read the look in Barbie's eyes. 'We haven't seen much of one another lately. Not with my Cyril and his bad leg. But we were very close.'

Barbie's mind flashed to the conversation she had had that morning with Daphne Crawley. The thought that Beattie Russell had come to look after her was frightening. She moved away, withdrawing herself from Beattie's grasp. 'I've got to feed Bess,' she said. 'She must be hungry.'

'And I must get on.' Beattie turned and went back to the bedroom. 'There are lots of things to do at times like this.'

Barbie went into the kitchen and reached for a tin of dog food. She listened to the sound of movement from upstairs, identifying the opening of drawers, the squeak of the cupboard door, but refusing to acknowledge the questions which were flooding her mind.

'Barbie, dear.' Beattie Russell came upon her from behind. 'Did your Granny have any special things?' Barbie looked at her puzzled. 'You know . . .' Beattie had a slight twitch of her eye which became exaggerated at this moment. 'Any . . . *special* . . . things?'

Barbie pointed towards Gran's chair in the parlour. 'She likes her chair,' she offered.

'No, dear. Did she have a place for keeping things?' Beattie Russell's eye twitched. 'I remember once she used to have a little cameo brooch.' Barbie knew nothing about a cameo brooch. 'Sometimes people have a special place for keeping things.'

Barbie did not know what she was talking about and she was relieved when she heard Miss Beckworth's voice calling from outside the back door.

'Hello Barbie. Are you there? I brought us some sandwiches . . .' She stopped as she saw Beattie Russell. 'Oh, I'm so sorry,' she said. 'Am I interrupting something?'

Beattie Russell altered the expression on her face. 'Of course not, dear. Come on in.'

'I'm Gloria Beckworth; Barbie's teacher. I've just popped in with some lunch.'

'Isn't that nice.' Beattie turned to Barbie. 'Isn't that nice of your teacher to bring you some lunch, dear.' She held out a hand and took the one offered by Miss Beckworth. 'I'm Beattie Russell. Mrs Harding's sister. They sent for me from the hospital, you know.' She winked heavily towards Miss Beckworth. 'Next of kin.'

'Oh,' said Miss Beckworth. 'I see.'

'I came down as soon as they told me. Well, dear, there's such a lot to do at times like this.'

'Is there anything I can do to help?'

'No thank you, dear.' Beattie Russell adjusted her hat. 'It's very kind of you but I've got to be going now anyway. I told my Cyril I wouldn't be long. He's waiting in the car just down the lane. You know what men are, dear. Said he'd rather wait in the car.'

Miss Beckworth smiled uncertainly. 'Well, if there's anything I can do at any time. You'll find me at the school.'

'That's very kind of you, dear, I'm sure.' They watched her as she walked to the door and down the garden path. 'But I'll come back later.'

Miss Beckworth looked at Barbie enquiringly.

'She's my Aunty Beattie, Miss. I never saw her before.'

Miss Beckworth raised her eyebrows with a look which Barbie did not understand. 'Shall we go and eat our sandwiches? It's too nice to sit indoors. Let's go and eat them in the garden.'

Barbie led her to the bottom of the garden and showed her the hidey-hole beneath the elder hedge. It seemed natural to share the secret with Miss Beckworth.

Miss Beckworth was like a child. 'Oh, isn't this lovely,' she cried. 'I used to have a place just like it when I was a little girl.'

Barbie crawled in beside her.

'We used to live up North in an old house on the edge of town.'

'Was it a big house, Miss?'

'Quite big. It went with my father's job. He was curator of the museum.'

Barbie nodded, impressed.

'We had a lovely old garden with a spinney and, in the centre of the spinney, was a huge rhododendron. You know how they grow when they're old? Very tall and wide, with branches spreading out across the soil.'

Barbie nodded.

'Well, in the centre of that bush, I had the most super hidey-hole.'

Barbie settled herself more comfortably to listen.

'I used to go there to read. I was always reading when I was a little girl. My mother used to call, and call, and call and I'd just sit there reading.' She turned and smiled. 'I was rather naughty when I was young.'

Barbie giggled.

'She never found out where I was hiding. I'd sit there and wait until the coast was clear and then come out in my own good time. And she'd always say, "Didn't you hear me calling?".'

'Whatever did you say, Miss?'

'I had all sorts of ways of getting round it. My brother caught me once but he never split. He was sitting on the wall and I didn't see him.'

Barbie found it difficult to think of Miss Beckworth with brothers and sisters. 'Did you have lots of brothers and sisters, Miss?'

'Only two. They're both married now with families of their own.'

Barbie sat and thought for a while. 'What colour was it?'

'What colour was what?'

'The rhododendron.'

'Oh, mauve. It was just the common type of mauve that you see

66

everywhere. But it was lovely in the spring. I'd sit deep inside the bush and when the sun shone there was a kind of mauve haze in amongst the shadows, like light shining through coloured glass. And there was that lovely fresh scent of newborn leaves and flowers.'

Barbie nodded understandingly.

'And in the autumn there would be that lovely musky, nutty smell which comes just before the leaves begin to fall.'

'It must have been nice.'

'Yes, it was. Just like this.' She handed Barbie a sandwich. 'It brings back memories.'

'Lots of things have smells, Miss.'

'Yes they do, Barbie. We don't always think about smells.'

'Only the bad ones, Miss,' laughed Barbie.

'What are your favourite smells?'

Barbie thought for a moment. 'Damp earth when it's been raining, Miss. And the sap from the big pine tree, and dogs' ears, and the geraniums in Mrs Tarrant's window boxes.'

'Not bad. How about roses, and mignonette, and the smell you get from brown paper when you're wrapping a parcel?'

'And candles,' said Barbie, 'when you've just snuffed them out. And tar when they're mending the road.'

They sat together in the hidey-hole, close together in a space which had been hollowed out for one. They ate the sandwiches and sat back chewing on bars of toffee.

'Did you know, Miss?' Barbie was watching a family of black-birds disturbing a pile of dry leaves in their search for food. 'Some birds hop and some of them walk.'

'Yes. Blackbirds hop.'

'So do robins, and sparrows, and thrushes. Pigeons walk; so do starlings and crows.'

'And gulls,' put in Miss Beckworth.

'Finches hop,' said Barbie. 'I like finches.'

'It's a good way to tell the difference between a blackbird and a starling. Blackbirds hop and starlings walk.'

'Anyone knows the difference between a blackbird and a starling, Miss.'

Miss Beckworth laughed. 'Not everyone, Barbie.'

'Oh, everybody knows that, Miss.'

Miss Beckworth laughed again and took her hand.

'Do you ever go back to the house, Miss?'

'No Barbie. My mother doesn't live there any more. They moved away when my father retired.'

'Didn't you want to live with them any more?'

Miss Beckworth smiled. 'It wasn't that. We all have to grow up and spread our wings.'

'It must get lonely living all on your own.'

'Sometimes. Not often, but sometimes.' She glanced sideways at Barbie. 'Perhaps I ought to find someone to share.'

'It's nice up in the part of the village where you live, Miss. You could easily get someone to live with you up there.'

'Would you like to live up there?'

Barbie sat and thought for a moment. The idea of living anywhere but in the cottage was too alien even to consider. 'If I didn't live here with Gran.'

'You love this place very much.'

'Yes, Miss. Of course, Miss.' Barbie felt a prick of discomfort.

'You'd miss it a lot if you had to move away.'

'Yes, Miss.' Barbie half-looked at her but could not bring herself to find her eye. 'Do you think it's time to go back to school now, Miss?'

'Yes.' Miss Beckworth reached out and touched her arm. 'It is about time we left.' She collected up the remains of their lunch and lifted the hop vine curtain. 'It wouldn't do to be late for school.'

Immediately upon returning to school, Miss Beckworth sought out the headmaster.

'Mr Taylor,' she said, as soon as she was seated across the desk. 'I'm thinking of making a home for Barbie Harding. I'd like to take care of her.'

He tented his fingers and sat looking at her across the top of them. 'That could be a very noble gesture,' he said.

'Could?'

'But may I ask whether you've thought it through?'

'There isn't much to consider. Barbie needs a home; and I'm more than willing to provide one for her.'

'And you're sure,' he enquired gently, 'that it isn't tinged with the emotion of the moment?'

She was surprised by his attitude. 'Of course there's emotion in it. It's a very emotional time.'

'And not the best for making rational decisions.'

'Are you saying that I'm being irrational?'

'Not irrational, just a little . . . subjective? Or perhaps – dare I say it – a little – *unprofessional*?'

'Unprofessional!'

'Teaching is a difficult enough job to do; unless we can maintain our objectivity, it's downright impossible.'

'I've always done my best.'

'I know. And you're an excellent teacher. I'm glad to have you on my staff.

'But . . . ?' she filled in for him.

'But, in this instance, I think you may have momentarily lost that sense of objectivity.'

'I don't know how you can say that.'

He sucked in his cheeks and continued to look at her across his tented fingers. 'You've been giving a great deal of time and attention to Barbie.'

'Of course. She's going through a very difficult time. And I'm fond of her.'

'A fact which hasn't gone unnoticed.'

'By whom?'

'A number of the staff have commented recently that you've been giving her an undue proportion of your time.'

'Because she has special needs.'

'We try to give individual attention,' he said kindly. 'That does not entail an undue emphasis on one child which would inevitably affect the other members of the class.'

'Are you saying that I've been neglecting my class?'

'No; merely that there has been a danger of your doing so.'

She looked at him, shocked. 'I wouldn't dream of it.'

'Not intentionally, I'm sure.' He smiled at her. 'How do you think parents would feel if they knew that you were giving so much attention to this one child? Isn't it possible that they'd suspect that you were not giving sufficient time to their own?'

'I hope they'd be glad,' she said. 'They'd know that I'd do the same for their child in the event of a similar catastrophe.'

'Catastrophe,' he said. 'Isn't that, in itself, a little emotional?'

'Of course it's catastrophic. Barbie's about to lose everything.'

'It's catastrophic for Barbie,' he agreed. 'We, as teachers, would do better to be a little more constructive. She needs our support to see her through it.'

'And isn't that exactly what I'm doing?'

He smiled at her. 'How many rooms do you have in your flat?'

'It's a bedsitter.'

He raised his eyebrows at her.

'I've already thought of that. I was thinking that maybe I could rent Mrs Harding's cottage. I could do it up; and Barbie wouldn't need to move.'

'You have been giving it some thought. And what about the future? Presumably, one day, you'll meet some man and want to marry.'

'Possibly.'

'And what if a child were to prejudice your chances?'

'I don't accept that,' she said. 'If a man couldn't accept my child – natural, or adopted – he wouldn't be the man for me, anyway.'

He smiled at that. 'I'm not sure it's quite as cut and dried as all that.'

'It would be if he couldn't accept my child.'

'All right,' he said, and his face became more serious. 'Let's look at it from another angle.' He spread his left hand, counting off his fingers with the index finger of his right. 'One,' he said. 'I doubt that the Authorities would allow a single woman to adopt a child.'

Gloria Beckworth's face clouded.

'It would be a most exceptional circumstance if they did. And it's not as if there are blood ties, or anything like that.'

'There's always the exception.'

'And, two,' he went on, counting off his second finger. 'It may not be in Barbie's best interests.' He stopped and looked across at her. 'It is Barbie's interests which are of primary importance?'

'Of course.'

'Then, have you thought that it could jeopardise her chances of becoming part of a real family?'

'I thought . . .'

'She needs a mother and father, brothers and sisters; the sort of family relationships she has never known.'

Miss Beckworth bent her head, studying the wood grain on the surface of the desk.

'I doubt that she has ever had any male influence in her life.'

'I hadn't thought of it like that.'

'She needs a man to whom she can relate. If she doesn't get it, she's likely to experience problems a little later on.'

'I've got friends; and two brothers.'

70

'She needs a father, Gloria. And a family.'

'Yes,' she sighed. 'That's one aspect I must admit I hadn't considered.'

'Don't you see,' he said kindly. 'I'm not trying to put you down. But there may be a family out there somewhere who can give her what she really needs – parental and sibling affection. The kind of relationships which are vital to her; and which you could never give.'

'Yes; you're right.' She stood up and straightened her skirt. 'I hadn't thought it through.'

'I hope I haven't upset you.'

'No.' She brushed the tip of her finger across her eye and turned to leave the room. 'She needs a family.'

'Thank you for talking it over with me.'

'I hadn't seen the situation clearly.'

'Oh, and Gloria,' he called her back as she reached the door. 'She is going to need our support to see her through these early stages.'

'Yes. But as soon as a family is found, I'll start to bow out.'

Veronica Standish drove her car down winding country lanes. She was aware that she was driving too fast and that her mind was not fully alert to the dangers but it was three fifteen and she wanted to get to the village school before it closed for the day. The Case Conference had taken all morning and now, at mid-afternoon, she was only just beginning to tackle the problems of the day.

If anything, her case-load was even heavier than that of Daphne Crawley and she had more travelling to do. She was a caring social worker but she was under constant pressure and it worried her that she was never able to give adequate time to the people who presented their problems to her. She was younger than Daphne Crawley, attractive and with a lively mind which clutched at tidbits of interest as she plunged headlong through her life. She liked to keep her hair in shape and spent more than she could afford on clothes but she never quite managed to achieve that well-groomed look for which she strove.

The children were flinging themselves through the school gates as she entered the car park. She found her way to the headmaster's office and sat talking to him for a while before he took her to a classroom where Barbie sat watching Miss

Beckworth writing at her desk. He introduced her to them and left.

'Hello, Barbie.' She held out her hand. 'I'm Veronica Standish.'

Miss Beckworth rose to leave and Miss Standish caught the fleeting reaction of tension which this brought from Barbie.

'Would you like Miss Beckworth to stay?'

Barbie nodded.

Miss Beckworth indicated another chair and Veronica Standish sat down. 'Barbie,' she said. 'I've been asked to try and help you. I want to do everything I can to make you happy and to find you a home where you can settle down and be well looked after.'

Barbie's reaction was immediate. 'Oh, I don't need a home, Miss. Thank you, Miss.'

The two women exchanged glances. 'Barbie,' Miss Standish resisted the need to clear her throat. 'You know that Gran is very ill, don't you.'

'She'll be better soon, Miss.'

'I think we must face the possibility that . . .'

Barbie decided that she did not like Miss Standish. She had red fingernails. Nor did she like the red lipstick which matched the nails.

'. . . we must face the possibility that Gran may not . . .'

Outside, in Mrs Urquhart's orchard, a pigeon called, sounding for all the world as though he were suffering with laryngitis. 'Coo-coo cook. Coo-cook.' Barbie listened and heard another replying a short distance away. There were a pair of them; one on this side of the orchard, the other in a tree to the right.

'Barbie . . . ?'

'Yes, Miss?'

'I think,' said Miss Standish, 'that we must make a few plans just in case we need them.' She recognised that Barbie was going to need time to come to terms with the reality of her situation: she only hoped that Gran would give her that time.

Barbie forced her mind to return to the classroom.

'Is there anyone you are particularly fond of? Anyone who you would like to go and stay with?'

Barbie shook her head.

'No one at all?'

Miss Beckworth opened her mouth as if to speak; then she closed it again.

'Do you have any aunties or uncles?'

Barbie thought of Aunty Beattie and averted her eyes.

'I know that your mother didn't have any brothers or sisters but sometimes we have people whom we call "aunty" or "uncle" who aren't really our uncles and aunties at all.'

Barbie shook her head again.

'What about your father, Barbie?' Barbie's pulse quickened. It was the second time that day her father had been mentioned. 'Do you see him often?'

'Sometimes, Miss.'

'And how do you get on with him? Do you like him?'

'He doesn't understand about wrens, Miss.'

Miss Standish passed Miss Beckworth a puzzled glance. 'What do you mean, Barbie – he doesn't understand wrens?'

'He doesn't understand them, Miss.'

'But you do? You like wrens?'

'Oh yes, Miss.' For the first time a flicker of response leapt into Barbie's eyes. 'They're only small and they're brown but they've got the cutest little stand-up tails.'

Veronica Standish wanted to make contact with Barbie but she was at a disadvantage. She knew little about birds. 'There used to be a wren on one side of the old farthing,' she said, grasping at the first piece of knowledge which came to mind.

'Yes, Miss,' said Barbie uninterestedly. 'I've got one of those at home.'

'Perhaps you could tell me about them some time.' But already the spark of animation was fading. She tried to think of something to say about sparrows but Barbie had slipped away from her. 'I'm going to see your father this evening,' she said. 'I rang him at work this afternoon to make an appointment.'

Barbie was immediately on her guard, suspicious, but she gave no outward sign.

'I think he might like to know that Gran has been taken ill.' She watched closely for Barbie's reaction but Barbie was giving nothing away. 'And I'm going to see Gran's sister tomorrow morning.'

This time Barbie shot a glance towards Miss Beckworth who, in turn, glanced at Miss Standish.

'Do you have much contact with Mrs Russell?'

'She was in the cottage when I went home for dinner, Miss.'

'Does she come often to visit you there?'

'I never saw her before, Miss.'

73

Miss Standish looked across to Miss Beckworth and they exchanged meaningful glances.

'Is there anything else you would like me to do?'

Barbie shook her head.

'Very well. I'll go to see your father and Mrs Russell and I'll make a few other enquiries, then I'll come back and see you again tomorrow.'

Barbie bit her lip uncertainly.

'But there's one other thing we have to sort out now. And that's where you sleep tonight.'

Miss Beckworth spoke for the first time. 'I wonder,' she said, 'whether I might take her home with me. I only have a bedsitter but I'm sure I could make room and I would love to have her.'

Veronica Standish was more than grateful for the suggestion. For Barbie's sake it was much preferable to being taken into Care overnight. For her own, it would save her a good deal of trouble. 'Thank you very much,' she said, then turning to Barbie, 'Would you like to stay with Miss Beckworth?'

Barbie's face lit up. 'Yes, Miss. Please, Miss.'

And so it was arranged.

'I'll see you tomorrow then.' Miss Standish collected up her briefcase and rose to leave. 'I'll tell you then what I've managed to come up with.' Barbie chewed her lip and watched her go. 'And don't worry, Barbie. I'll not make any final arrangements without discussing them with you first.' Barbie nodded dumbly.

'Bye for now.'

'Bye,' said Barbie.

Veronica Standish hurried out to her car. She had four more calls to make before returning to her office. She had hoped to wash her hair this evening but now she must drive to Wickhampton to speak with Ken Radlett. Her hair would have to wait.

'Come on.' Miss Beckworth smiled and held out her hand to Barbie. 'I'll take you to the Wimpy Bar in town and buy you something special for tea before we go to the hospital.' Barbie reached for the hand. It was warm and she held it tightly all the way into town.

She was still holding it when they reached the hospital but she dropped it as soon as she came within sight of Gran. Gran had not moved and there was no flicker of response when she called her name. Miss Beckworth left her and unobtrusively moved off to

74

find a comfortable chair in the day room where she took out a book and began to read.

Barbie resumed her vigil beside the bed. She was still there at eight o'clock when the night staff came on duty.

'Hello Barbie.' Sister Thorpe went through the routine procedure of checking the saline drip. 'I hear you went to school today.'

'She hasn't woken up yet.'

'No Barbie; I'm afraid she hasn't.' Sister Thorpe hesitated as if to speak again but changed her mind. She had a great deal of work to do within the next hour and there was no time to spend with Barbie. She wanted to speak to her about the inevitable outcome of this vigil but it would have to wait. Later, when things had settled down for the night, she would find a suitable opportunity. 'Would you like Nurse Fletcher to get you a cup of tea?'

'She's going to die, isn't she.'

'Yes, Barbie.' She was glad that it had come from Barbie and that it had not been left to her to engineer a way of breaking the news. 'It will be quite soon now, I believe.'

'Will you put her teeth in. She wouldn't like to go without her teeth.'

Sister Thorpe put out her arms in a gesture of comfort but Barbie got up and walked past her out into the corridor.

'Please, Jesus.'

Her limbs had a strange lack of co-ordination as she walked away.

Sister Thorpe did not try to stop her but kept an eye on her as she moved slowly down the corridor.

'Please Jesus; Jesus, please!'

Outside the ward door the porter whom she had met the previous evening was carrying boxes of laundry through the open doors of the lift. 'Hello. Thought I might see you up here.' He put his hand into his pocket and handed her the bag of toffees. 'How's your Gran?'

'She's going to die.' Barbie automatically reached out and took a toffee, unwrapped it and placed it in her mouth.

The porter took the last box of laundry from the lift and, placing it against the wall, he sat on it and drew Barbie down upon his knee. He did not speak but gently massaged her back, communicating with her through the pressure of his hand. She buried her face against his shoulder and they sat for a long time in silence.

75

People came and went. Some looked at them oddly but most passed by with only casual interest. Sister Thorpe went about her duties, pausing every now and then to glance through the door.

'I'm sorry I kicked you.' It occurred to Barbie that he was probably someone's grandad.

They were still there when the lift doors opened and Beattie Russell emerged. 'Oh, why, hello Barbie dear.' Barbie did not look up and Beattie Russell eyed the porter with undisguised suspicion. 'I didn't expect to find you here, dear. It's past visiting.'

Barbie looked at her briefly then returned her head to the porter's shoulder.

Beattie Russell moved her feet uncomfortably then addressed her next comment to the porter. 'I came to check whether she's . . .' her eye twitched '. . . gone yet.'

The porter glared at her and increased the pressure of his hand on Barbie's back. 'Well, she hasn't,' he retorted.

Beattie Russell backed away. 'Oh well, I just wondered. They did say it might be tonight.' The porter glared at her again and made angry signals with his eyebrows above Barbie's head which Beattie Russell chose not to interpret.

'She's going to have a lovely funeral, dear. I've made all the arrangements.'

Barbie sat up and looked at her.

'You leave everything to your Aunty Beattie, dear. We'll see that your Granny has a right royal send-off.'

'She wants to lie in the churchyard,' said Barbie. 'In the corner near the big yew tree.'

Beattie Russell was visibly taken aback. She spent several seconds fingering the clasp of her handbag.

'She told me so,' said Barbie.

'Well, I didn't know you'd want something special, dear.'

'You know now,' said the porter angrily. 'She's just told you.'

Beattie Russell opened the clasp of her handbag and snapped it shut with a loud click. 'Why didn't you tell me earlier, dear. I've arranged a lovely cremation with a big car and the organ.'

The porter slid Barbie to her feet and stood up towering over Beattie Russell. 'Then you'll just have to go and change it, won't you.'

Beattie Russell took three steps backwards. 'I don't know what to say. It's all arranged.'

Sister Thorpe intervened. She placed a hand on the porter's arm but Barbie did not wait to hear more. She took off down the corridor towards Gran's room, colliding with a nurse pushing a trolley, and almost slipped and fell.

She shook Gran as she lay immobile on the bed. 'Gran . . . !' The tube in Gran's arm made a whiplash movement as she pummelled the great unresponsive body. 'Wake up.' There was the slight rise and fall of her chest, the harsh sound of breathing but no sign of response. 'Get up. Get up you lazy devil and tell these people what to do.'

The commotion brought Miss Beckworth running. 'What's the matter, Barbie? Tell me; what is it?' Sister Thorpe appeared and explained what had happened and both women shook their heads at one another behind Barbie's back.

'Barbie,' said Miss Beckworth. She got down on her knees beside Barbie. 'The old corner of the churchyard near the yew tree is no longer in use. It hasn't been used for many years.' Barbie was sobbing uncontrollably and she did not know if she was getting through to her. 'It wouldn't be possible for Gran to lie there. Perhaps she could be put to rest next to your Grandad. She would like that, wouldn't she.'

'They're going to burn her up.'

'I'll have a word with Mrs Russell.' She put her arms around Barbie but Barbie shook her off. 'I'm sure she'll agree to alter the arrangements.'

'How am I going to find her if she's all burned up?'

'Leave it to me. I'm sure we can sort something out.'

But Miss Beckworth was not allowing for the pertinacity of Beattie Russell. She did speak to her and, when she failed, she called upon the assistance of Miss Standish, and later the vicar, but Beattie Russell enjoyed funerals, she enjoyed her role as stage manager and saw no reason to alter her plans.

Meanwhile, the evening settled down. Barbie resumed some sort of calm but it was now a calmness overlaid by an even greater sense of numbness. Outside the hospital dusk gathered, sounds of an urban evening mingling with the sound of a skylark high above a nearby building site. Across the sky there flew a flock of starlings, like tea leaves in a giant, pearl-grey brew, making for their roosting site (. . . *starlings walk and blackbirds hop* . . .). The world revolved, taking no note when, at twenty-six minutes past nine, Gran drew her last breath.

'She's dead, isn't she.'

'Yes, Barbie. She's gone.'

'She didn't even say goodbye.'

There were no tears. Her tears had all been cried out in anger against Beattie Russell and now her eyes hurt by their very dryness. She raised them upwards towards the ceiling in what she considered to be the general direction of heaven.

'And don't ever expect me to speak to You again, You bleeding bastard.'

Sister Thorpe sucked in her breath.

'Because You're no bleeding use.'

Miss Beckworth took her home and put her to bed but, in spite of the medicine which Sister Thorpe had sent with her, sleep would not come. The bed was comfortable but it was not the bed she was used to. She was cold. She thought of her own feather mattress at the cottage, of Gran beside her, large and warm, the smell of sweat and gin.

She remembered how it felt to draw up her knees beneath Gran's buttocks and to wrap her arms around the great mound of her stomach. She remembered the sighs and the creakings of the cottage, the scuttle of a mouse across the floorboards, and the house-martins in their nest beneath the sill. Never again would she hear the rustle of the wind through the barley field, the echoing bark of a dog across the hill.

She thought of Bess all alone. She had gone to the cottage with Miss Beckworth before leaving for town and they had left the door ajar so that Bess could come and go. But now she was all alone and did not know that Gran was dead.

'Barbie.' Miss Beckworth crossed the room and knelt beside the bed. 'Are you asleep?' She was in her night attire, pale pink which shimmered in the dim light of the shaded lamp. She smelled of talcum powder and freshness but it was no substitute for Gran. 'Would you like some milk?'

'No thank you, Miss.'

'Would you like to talk? It's sometimes good to talk.'

But Barbie had no wish to talk. She knew of no words with which to speak out the loneliness and the emptiness and she had not the will to try.

'I remember it so well.' Miss Beckworth reached beneath the bedclothes and found Barbie's hand. 'When my Daddy died . . .' The tears sprang to her own eyes and she brushed

78

them away with the knuckle of her index finger. 'I know how it hurts.'

She saw Barbie shiver and lifted the covers to climb into the bed beside her. It was a narrow bed, scarce room for one yet alone for two, but she wriggled down until they were lying side by side. Barbie shivered again and pressed herself close against the young woman's body.

While Barbie lay dry-eyed, she felt Miss Beckworth's own tears fall upon her hair and listened as she hummed a melody which Barbie would remember for the rest of her days.

Chapter Five

Ken Radlett swung his car into Wansdyke Avenue. He was whistling. He asked himself how he felt and decided that, at last, he was at peace – the kind of peace which follows heart-searching.

He had been at odds with himself ever since that day in June when he and Ma Harding had sat together in his parents' front parlour. What was it that she had sparked off deep within him? Guilt? Remorse? The knowledge that he had a child whom he hardly knew? Whatever it was, she had uncovered something which had lain dormant for years.

He had been on the point of admitting his dilemma the second time he visited the cottage. He had not known what he would say, or what he would do, but he had known that something was about to happen – so certain that his courage had failed him and he had walked away. He had seen the old woman sleeping in her chair and had felt his mouth run dry. It had been easier to leave the five pound note and put off the meeting until his mind was clear.

Now he no longer had time. The old girl was dying. Barbie was without a home and the decision had been made.

He had telephoned Mary from the office immediately following Miss Standish's call. The news had floored him and he had marvelled at Mary's coolness.

He had been surprised, too, by Miss Standish's reaction when he rang her back to inform her of their decision. She had been noncommittal, suggesting that they leave further discussion until the evening. 'We'll talk about it then,' she had said. 'It's a big decision for you both to make.' He had thought she would be pleased.

He changed gear and slid the car into the drive of number fifteen.

'Mary?' He got out and walked round to the back door. She was in the kitchen preparing the evening meal. She had been out at work all day but the house was spotless, the hall carpet beyond the kitchen door showing ripples of upturned tufts newly furrowed by the vacuum cleaner.

He sniffed the air. 'Smells good,' he said.

'Coq au Vin with potatoes and peas.' She glanced up briefly to acknowledge his presence. 'Something new I found at the supermarket.'

'Smells good,' he said again. He kicked off his shoes on the back doorstep and found his slippers. 'Where are the kids?'

'Playing with friends. I thought it best to keep them out of the way for a while.'

'Thanks.' He came up behind her and hugged her tightly about the waist.

'Not now, Ken. I've got a lot to do.' She turned and gave him a quick peck on the cheek. 'What time did you say she was coming . . . ? Miss . . . ?'

'Standish,' offered Ken. 'Seven o'clock.' He sat down at the kitchen table playing with the car keys still in his hand.

'You could lay it instead of sitting at it,' she said. 'It would help.'

'Sorry.' He got up and went to the cutlery drawer taking out knives, forks and spoons.

'Mary,' he said. 'How are we going to tell them?'

She looked up at him across the room.

'The kids. How are we going to tell them about Barbie?'

'Well, we're not the first family to think about taking in a child. The Slocombe's had a Biafran girl.' She was peeling potatoes, her movements quick and efficient as she deftly scraped the mottled brown skin.

'But this one's mine.'

'It makes no difference. We'll tell them that you were married before and that the marriage failed. They'll accept that if we say she's been living with her grandmother.'

'We can't say that. It's not true.' He set out the cutlery, judging precisely the distance and angle of each piece in relation to another.

81

'Ken. There comes a time in everyone's life when a small lie may be preferable to the truth.'

'I suppose you're right. I don't think I could face them with the truth.'

She plopped the potatoes into boiling water and turned to watch him as he reached into another drawer for placemats and napkins folded within chromium-plated rings. He set three of the napkins beside the placemats, carefully aligning the edges, then he stood twirling the remaining napkin in its ring. At times like this his actions irritated her.

'I don't know whether I can go through with it,' he said.

'Don't be silly. Of course you can.' She went to the freezer for peas, steadying herself in the knowledge that two strong-willed partners do not an ideal marriage make. 'We shall have to get the spare room ready this evening. I expect they'll want Barbie to move in straight away.'

'As soon as that?'

'We shall have problems when Mother comes to stay but we'll get a folding bed and put the two girls in together. Thank goodness we've got a decent-sized house.'

He was still standing twirling the napkin in its ring. 'Honestly, Mary; anyone else would have blown their top, thrown a tantrum . . . anything but this. Yet, here you are talking about getting the spare room ready.'

'Oh, for goodness sake, Ken. There are times when things just have to be done. And this is one of them.'

'I still say you're fantastic.' He dropped the napkin into the centre of the table and went over to her. 'I don't know what I would have done if you hadn't stood behind me.'

'We both decided that we want to have Barbie here and that's all there is to it.'

He did not release her and she began to struggle against his hold but then went quiet. 'Ken,' she said. 'Just tell me one thing.'

'What is it?'

'Are you quite, quite certain that she is your child?'

Ken instantly released his hold and raised his eyes towards the ceiling.

'After all,' she went on, 'she does have red hair.'

'Praise the Lord for my mother.'

'I don't see what your mother has to do with it.'

'Oh, come on. Don't tell me you haven't been speaking to my mother.'

'I don't need your mother to tell me that the child has red hair. I'm quite capable of working that out for myself.' She turned her back on him and began opening the packet of peas.

'Then you're also capable of working out that two blondes make a ginger.'

'That's an old wives' tale.' She checked the boiling water before adding the peas. 'And I was merely asking a question.'

'Then I'll answer it. I'll answer it just once. And don't ever ask me again.' He came close and spoke directly at her. 'The kid is mine. Are you receiving me loud and clear? Barbie is my child.'

He slammed from the room and Mary went on with her work. She did not look up when he returned a few minutes later.

'I'm sorry,' he said. 'But that question really gets up my nose.'

'There's no need to lose your temper about it.'

'It's bad enough having to face up to it, without having to spell it out.'

Mary turned to him. 'I'm sorry,' she said. 'But I needed to be told.'

Ken reached out and took her in his arms. 'It all happened a long time ago.'

'I know.' She kissed him and ruffled his hair. 'We'll give her a good home.'

'Thanks. And thanks for standing by me.'

They told the children when they came in to eat and, by the time Veronica Standish arrived, had restored some sort of order to the chaos which the news had set off. It erupted again when they spoke to her of their decision.

'Are we really going to see her?'

Miss Standish sat in the background, watching, listening, missing nothing.

'Yes, we hope so. We hope that she'll come to live here.'

'What, all the time?'

'Forever?'

'Yes; would you like that?'

'So long as she's not a bossy drawers.'

'Mark!'

'Well, it'd be better if she was a boy.'

Tracy chewed her lip. 'They'll all be older than me.'

'Does it matter?'

83

'I'll never get anything.'

'I doubt it,' said Mary. 'Not so long as your father is around to spoil you.'

'You'll all get equal treatment,' said Ken. 'You'll get treated in exactly the same way as you do now.'

'Will she have to be our sister?'

'Your half-sister.'

'And what shall we call her?'

'Barbie, of course. What do you think you would call her.'

'It's a funny name. Why do they call her Barbie?'

'It's short for Barbara. Her mother chose it.'

'Sounds like a barber. She's probably up the pole.'

'Mark!'

'Don't you want her to come here?'

Mark shrugged his shoulders. 'I suppose so.' He sneered towards Tracy. 'Anything's better than her.'

'If you're going to be like that about it . . .'

They were reactions which Veronica Standish considered consistent with the situation but she logged in her mind the possibility of other, quite different, reactions should their parents proceed with their stated intention. Tracy said the least but it seemed likely that her ability to adjust might well call for the greater need of support.

'Go out to play for an hour,' said Mary. 'And come back at eight.'

'We want to hear . . .'

'Out. And stay away from that dreadful Thompson boy.'

Veronica Standish settled back in her chair as the children were dismissed from the room. 'Mr Radlett,' she said, 'are you quite certain that you have really given this sufficient thought?'

'I've thought about nothing else for weeks; ever since Ma Harding came to speak to me.'

'It's a big step that you're proposing.' She looked across at Mary including her in the statement. 'It wouldn't all be plain sailing.'

'Children never are,' said Mary. She poured coffee from a pot which she had set ready on a side table.

'True. But this one is likely to raise a few more difficulties than most.'

'I don't see why.' Ken reached for cigarettes. 'She's a kid just like any other kid.'

'She's shortly going to experience a period of intense grief. She's going to need a great deal of understanding to see her through it.'

Mary handed her a cup of coffee and Veronica Standish nodded her thanks. 'We'll do our best.'

'I'm sure you will. But the relationship which Barbie had with her grandmother was particularly strong. She's going to miss her dreadfully and she's had very few other relationships in her life. It's going to be very difficult for her to adjust.'

'I see that. But surely with time she could be helped to get over it.'

'And,' went on Miss Standish, 'the life you would ask her to live here is quite different from the one she's been used to.' She cast her eyes round the immaculate room. 'You would be asking her to take on a whole new way of life.'

'If you're talking about being brought into a decent home, surely it's about time she was given the chance of a better life.' Ken drew on his cigarette. 'I've worried myself sick about her ever since I saw her in that filthy old hovel.'

'Well, it may not have been very clean but I think you'll find that Barbie was extremely happy.'

'But it wasn't right,' said Ken. 'She needed to be in a proper home with a proper family.'

'I doubt that Barbie would agree with you. But she's certainly in need of a family now.'

'Then there's no problem.' Ken spread his hands in a gesture of finality. 'We're willing to have her and we'll do everything we can to give her a good home. She's my responsibility and I'm willing to shoulder it.'

Veronica Standish watched him closely. 'There's no need,' she said, deliberately brutal, 'to do penance for fathering the child.' She watched his eyes and saw them blaze.

'If I may say so . . .' he spilled his coffee and dashed it off his leg '. . . that's damned offensive.'

'Sorry. But it had to be said.'

'Well, you're wrong.'

'What he means,' cut in Mary, 'is that we want to offer Barbie a home. Ken doesn't always explain himself too well.'

Veronica Standish smiled. 'I know what he means. But I have to make quite certain that you both know exactly what you are proposing to let yourselves in for. It's not easy taking in another

85

woman's child.' She looked closely at Mary. 'It takes a very special kind of woman.'

'Barbie is Ken's child. And she needs a mother.'

'She needs a mother and a father.' Veronica Standish looked back again at Ken. 'She's had very little male influence in her life. She needs a father to whom she can relate.'

'He's very good with the children,' said Mary. 'He's always doing things with them. Even the neighbours' kids adore him.'

'What is this, a mutual admiration society?' Ken looked slightly embarrassed and flicked ash from the tip of his cigarette. 'I enjoy doing things with them. They're good fun.'

'I believe Barbie is fond of birds.'

'I know.' Ken remembered the wrens' nest. 'I don't know much about them myself but perhaps we could take her to one of those bird parks.' He looked across at Mary. 'Do you remember that one in Somerset? It's a pleasant ride down there. We'd all enjoy it.'

'Mr Radlett.' Veronica Standish changed tack. 'Why has it taken you so long to make contact with Barbie?'

Ken sat for a moment and stared at the tip of his cigarette. 'I've never missed a payment.'

'That's not what I asked.'

'No. I know it wasn't.' He sucked in his breath and went on without raising his eyes. 'I've asked myself the same question more than once recently and I'm not very proud of the answer. We were all pretty irresponsible in those days and then when Mark and Tracy came along it all got a bit embarrassing. How do you tell your kids that you've got an illegitimate child? Well, I suppose we've done it now but at the time I kept putting it off. It's one of those things that the longer time passes the more difficult it gets to do anything about it.' He looked up. 'And Ma Harding didn't exactly welcome callers round at that place.'

Miss Standish nodded. 'She did keep herself pretty much to herself.'

'You can say that again. I was staggered when she came and asked me to call round to see Barbie.'

'She must have known that she was dying.'

'I should have seen it myself. But I didn't. I wondered what on earth the old girl was on about.'

'And how did you get on with Barbie when you did go round to see her?'

'It was a bit strained but that's hardly surprising, is it. She was probably as baffled as I was.'

'It will be different now,' said Mary. 'You can get to know her properly and she can get to know us.'

'Yes,' said Ken. 'I think I'm going to enjoy it.'

Veronica Standish sat on, watching, listening, asking questions and observing responses. She had not believed that the problem could be so easily solved and yet, if it worked, it could prove to be the perfect solution – the natural father taking the child into his own family. Perhaps it was all a little too easy. She was not used to easy solutions. They had a way of raising her intuitive suspicions. And yet, at the same time, she was not searching for trouble if no trouble existed.

She glanced at her watch. She needed to be on her way. Since the afternoon she had collected another urgent case which must be followed up before she could go home this evening. In her briefcase she had a crumpled piece of paper upon which had been scribbled the names of two young children whom, it was reported, could be heard crying each night while their parents were away drinking. She must investigate this evening; if she delayed until tomorrow and something happened to them tonight . . . She could see the consequences emblazoned across the headlines. She lifted her hand half-consciously to her hair and felt the slightly oily texture. She wondered whether the newspapers who reported the shortcomings of social workers ever gave any consideration to the problems of washing their hair.

'So, it's all settled then.' Ken cut across her thoughts. 'We all know that it's not going to be easy but she'll settle down, given time. Mary will see to that.'

In her mind Miss Standish set out the facts, weighing them for and against like entries on a balance sheet. The alternatives to the Radletts' offer were not good.

'I'll go and talk to Barbie tomorrow,' she said. 'I'll put your offer to her and see what she says.'

She knew, also, that she ought first to discuss the case with one of her senior colleagues. But one was on leave and, with the other, she did not always see eye to eye. No; she would make her own decision and, if necessary, accept the consequences.

'Surely she doesn't have much choice.'

'Barbie's alternatives may be limited but she's still entitled to have some say in the matter.'

'Yes, of course she does.' Mary rose to see Miss Standish to the door. 'Would you like me to take the day off work tomorrow?'

'No thanks. If Barbie wishes to come it would suit me quite well to bring her at tea-time. It's going to be a busy day.'

She turned as she reached the door. 'I wouldn't normally arrange matters so quickly,' she said. 'I would much prefer to bring her here for a day to see how you all get on together; then perhaps for a weekend.'

'There doesn't seem to be much point in that when there's a secure home waiting for her here.'

'Exactly. We have to weigh the possible damage which would be done to her by receiving her into Care. It would be preferable for you all to adjust to one another in easy stages but, on the other hand, it would probably be less traumatic for her to adjust to one new environment, rather than two.'

It was a gamble and Miss Standish knew it.

'It would be a crime for her to be put into a Home when her family is waiting to welcome her here.'

'Thanks.' Veronica Standish walked towards her car. 'And thanks for the coffee. I'll see you tomorrow at about six o'clock. Or I'll give you a ring.'

Mary watched her go and felt suddenly tired. She went up-stairs and stood at the door of the spare room looking at the bed with its pink quilted cover. She realised that she was about to have a blinding headache. Ken came up behind her and put his arms about her waist. 'Not now, Ken,' she said. 'I've got a lot to do.'

Veronica Standish pulled out of Wansdyke Avenue and made her way through the streets of Wickhampton, back towards her own patch and towards two crying children. Her scalp itched and in the privacy of her car she found herself scratching it.

The next few weeks were going to be crucial for Barbie. She was not going to find it easy to settle and the whole family were going to need a lot of support. She was worried about the decision which she had made and wished again that she had more time to introduce the child more slowly into the home in order that a proper assessment might be made.

Alternatively, she would have liked to have kept a close eye on the situation herself, but Wickhampton was not Miss Standish's territory. She would have to write up her notes and hand over the case to the local social workers with her recommendations. She knew that she could have kept the case for a short time until she could be sure that Barbie had settled, but she did not have the time to make frequent journeys to Wickhampton.

It was a system necessary for the efficient use of her time and for the smooth running of the Department. Just the same, she wished that the child did not have to be confused by so many changing faces.

Barbie awoke to the sound of Miss Beckworth filling the kettle at the sink. Her limbs ached from the unaccustomed cramped conditions of the narrow bed, and her throat was sore. At some time during the night, after Barbie had fallen asleep, Miss Beckworth had left the bed and had curled up on the uncomfortably small settee. Barbie could see the disordered pile of blankets, half slipped to the floor.

'Hello Barbie. Did you sleep well?'

'Yes Miss. Thank you, Miss.'

It seemed strange to see Miss Beckworth tousled-haired from sleep. She watched her making coffee and thought of Gran. She found that she could not remember the colour of her eyes.

Miss Beckworth brought the coffee to the bed and knelt down beside her. 'Here, have some coffee,' she said and held the mug to Barbie's lips. Barbie came close to tears; Miss Beckworth could not know of the times Barbie had thus held the mug for Gran.

'It's a lovely day.' Miss Beckworth inclined her head towards the window. 'The birds are singing.'

Barbie listened and wondered again why the world was still revolving.

Miss Beckworth waited until she had finished her coffee then sat on the bed drinking her own. 'Now,' she said. 'What shall we have for breakfast?'

The thought of food brought an unpleasant taste to Barbie's mouth.

'I have got . . . cereal, or boiled eggs, or toast, or . . .' she hesitated again and turned her eyes towards the ceiling '. . . I have got two large, fresh cream, meringues.'

She went to the refrigerator and took out a box containing the two meringues. She placed one on a plate and handed it to Barbie with a fork. But Barbie chose to eat with her fingers. As she bit into it, the cream oozed and the meringue crumbled into pieces which showered back upon the plate.

Miss Beckworth licked her own lips and giggled. It seemed so extraordinary to be sitting here on Miss Beckworth's bed, eating cream meringues for breakfast, that Barbie giggled too.

She ate the broken shell, piece by piece, then finished off by dabbing her finger upon the plate and scooping the crumbs into her mouth.

Miss Beckworth took the plate and carried it to the sink. 'I've got an idea,' she said. 'Why don't we two go for a bike ride.'

Barbie looked at her in surprise. 'What about school, Miss?'

'It's holiday time, Barbie. Had you forgotten? We broke up yesterday.'

Barbie *had* forgotten.

'Can you ride a bike?' asked Miss Beckworth, and Barbie nodded. 'Then I think I know where I can borrow a couple.'

Barbie thought of fresh air upon her face, blowing through the fuddled cavities of her mind.

'There's just one thing we have to do first,' said Miss Beckworth. She began quickly tidying the room. 'Miss Standish was calling to see us today. We'll have to ride into town and call at her office.'

They were waiting outside the Area Office before nine o'clock. They leaned their bicycles against a wall and sat in the sunshine until Veronica Standish drove into the car park.

'Hello,' she said. 'What's going on?'

On the pretence of sending Barbie to check the bicycles, she spent a moment with Miss Beckworth.

'Mrs Harding died last evening,' Miss Beckworth told her.

'Oh; I hadn't heard. There's probably a message waiting for me on my desk.'

'At least the waiting is over.'

'Now she has to come to terms with her grief.' Miss Standish looked across at Barbie who was approaching from the other end of the car park. 'How has she taken it?'

'She won't cry. And she doesn't want to talk about it.'

Miss Standish pouted her lip and frowned.

She took them into her office and sat them down. 'Barbie,' she said. 'I have some news for you. Your father and his wife, and your half-brother, and your half-sister, have asked you to join them. They want you to go and live with them and be part of their family.'

It took some moments for Barbie to assimilate the reference to her half-brother and half-sister. Her father's children were faces in the back of a car.

'You would have your very own room, with roses on the wallpaper, and a lovely pink quilt on the bed.' She watched closely for Barbie's reaction but Barbie's expression revealed nothing.

It was Miss Beckworth who reeled in an ambivalence of emotion. 'Barbie,' she choked. 'That's marvellous. Your very own family.' Her voice sounded hollow in her own ears.

Barbie clicked on the expression which she thought was expected of her. 'Thank you,' she said.

'Of course, you don't have to accept the invitation if you don't want to,' said Miss Standish. 'It's entirely up to you.'

Miss Beckworth fought to keep herself in check. 'What are the alternatives?'

'They're rather limited, I am afraid.' She smiled across at Barbie. 'We could take Barbie into one of our foster homes.'

Barbie found herself shaking her head.

'Foster parents are very special people, Barbie,' reassured Miss Standish. 'They do everything they can to give you a happy, settled life.'

Barbie was not reassured.

'In time we might be able to find a family who would like to consider adoption. But . . .' she spoke without enthusiasm '. . . I don't want to mislead you, Barbie. It sometimes takes rather a long time to find a suitable adoption placement for older children.'

Miss Beckworth's jaw ached from the strain of sustaining her smile. 'Your own ready-made family,' she said. 'It does seem to be the best option.'

'Perhaps you would like to think it over,' said Miss Standish. 'Would you like to talk about it with Miss Beckworth?'

Barbie nodded.

'Very well. I have a few things to attend to in another room.' She went out and left them. 'Call me when you're ready.'

'What do you think, Barbie?' The smile on Miss Beckworth's face was becoming increasingly painful.

Barbie shrugged her shoulders. She did not know why Miss Beckworth had not mentioned the alternative of going to live with her. Only yesterday she had said that she needed company and was looking for someone to share her flat.

'It does seem a very good idea to go and live with your father. It would probably seem a bit strange at first but you'd soon fit in.'

Barbie said nothing.

'I've seen him driving through the village. He looks a nice man. It would be fun for you to get to know him.'

'Yes, Miss.' She looked down at the toe of her sandal – well-worn with scuff marks across the leather – and sat wriggling her toes, watching the way in which they altered the surface tension.

'What do you think, Barbie?'

'I want to go home.'

'Darling; you can't do that.'

Miss Beckworth came to kneel down before her. She left a moment's silence, then she said, 'Barbie. I wanted . . .'

Barbie looked up at her sharply.

Miss Beckworth swallowed. 'I wanted you to come . . .'

'Yes?'

She stood up and turned her back abruptly as she walked to the window. 'I wanted you to go to a good family where you could settle down and be happy.'

Barbie bit her lip, hope quickly fading.

'Your own ready-made family would seem to be more than we could possibly have hoped for.'

She came back to kneel once more before the chair. 'Why not give it a try?'

Barbie shrugged. She decided that, after all, she did not really care.

Miss Beckworth reached out and took her hand. 'I love you, Barbie; very much. I only want what's best for you.'

Barbie withdrew her hand. 'Yes, Miss.'

'You know that, don't you?'

'Yes, Miss.'

Miss Standish came back into the room and asked what had been decided.

'She'll go,' said Miss Beckworth. There was still a strange hoarseness about her voice.

'Good. I'm sure it's the best thing. Your family are looking forward to meeting you.'

'I'll return the bikes,' said Miss Beckworth, but Miss Standish held up her hand.

'No; please don't,' she said. 'Go for your ride and enjoy your day.' She looked at her watch. 'I'll call at your flat at about four-thirty. That will give me time to take Barbie to the cottage to collect her things and arrive in Wickhampton at about six.'

'I'll collect Bess,' said Barbie.

Miss Standish was taken by surprise. She had overlooked the dog. Both women exchanged glances and Miss Standish looked uncertain. 'Excuse me a moment,' she said. 'I shall have to check.'

She lifted the receiver and dialled a number from her notebook. 'Oh, good morning Mrs Radlett. This is Veronica Standish. Yes, we'll be coming at about six. Barbie's looking forward to meeting you. Mrs Radlett, Barbie has mentioned her dog, an old collie named Bess . . .'

Barbie sat, listening to the one-sided conversation, watching the expression on Miss Standish's face.

There was an awkward silence at the other end of the line. 'I'm sorry, Miss Standish, but it's out of the question.'

'I realise it might prove a little inconvenient but I'm sure you'll appreciate that Barbie's very fond of her.'

'It's not that. Tracy is allergic to dog hair.'

'Oh, I see.'

'It brings her out in nasty swellings.'

'How very unfortunate.'

'It's rather awkward, really, but we've never had pets. It's not really fair on them when I'm out at work.'

'No, of course not.' She looked at Barbie out of the corner of her eye. 'Do you have any suggestions?'

'No, I'm afraid I haven't. Leave it with me and I'll give it some thought. But I can't possibly have a dog here. It wouldn't be right to put Tracy at risk.'

'Perhaps your neighbours . . . ?'

'I'll ask them, but I doubt it. Most of them go out to work.'

'Well, I'd be glad of your help but, in the meantime, we'll see if we can come up with something from this end.'

'I do feel sorry. She's going to miss the dog terribly.'

'Yes, she is; but we'll have to do the best we can.'

'If it weren't for Tracy I would manage somehow.'

'Don't worry. We'll see you this evening at about six.'

She replaced the receiver and looked at Barbie. 'I'm sorry, Barbie,' she said, knowing that she had overheard.

'If I might make a suggestion,' said Miss Beckworth. She leaned over and took Barbie's hand. 'Barbie, you know Mr Smethurst?'

Barbie nodded. She had once again reached the edge of tears.

'He's a very good friend of mine. I know that he would take care of Bess for you. She could retire to the farm, just like every old dog dreams of.'

Barbie said nothing but her lip quivered.

'And you could go back to the village and visit her often.'

'Yes,' said Miss Standish. 'Your father goes to the village to see his parents. We could ask him to take you with him. You could visit Bess whenever your father goes to visit your grandparents.'

The thought of acquiring grandparents diverted a fraction of Barbie's attention. Her mind focussed upon the little-known faces of Tom and Hetty Radlett but refused to accept the identity.

'And I'll look in on her every day,' said Miss Beckworth. 'I pass the farm on my way to school.'

She rose to leave. 'Come on,' she said briskly. 'We'll take Bess to the farm now and see her safely settled in before we go for our bike ride.' She took Barbie firmly by the hand and led her from the room. 'I'll help Barbie to pack while we're at the cottage,' she called over her shoulder to Miss Standish. 'That will save you some time.'

'Thank you very much. That's very kind of you.' Veronica Standish watched them leave. Gloria Beckworth was a good friend to Barbie, she thought.

Miss Beckworth loaned Barbie a suitcase and they filled it with her belongings – a few clothes, a hair brush, a photograph of Gran on Brighton pier. It seemed so little to take her from one way of life into another.

When they were finished, Bess allowed herself to be led away to the farm. They pushed the bicycles, with the suitcase strapped to the carrier, as the old dog waddled behind.

Mr Smethurst took in the situation at once. 'Of course I'll look after her for you, me dear,' he said. 'She'll be good company for my old Rover. Reckon we might even get some pups afore spring.'

The unlikely thought of old Bess with puppies brought a hint of a smile to Barbie's lips. He chucked her under the chin.

'And you just pop in and see her whenever you have a mind to, me dear. You knows you're always welcome around here.'

If she had to leave Bess anywhere, Barbie was glad that it was to be with Mr Smethurst.

'There's a litter of kittens over in the barn,' he said. 'Reckon you might like to run over there and see 'em afore you goes riding off on that there bike.'

The kittens were small and helpless. Barbie spent a long time watching them before she returned to say goodbye to Bess. She hugged the old dog about the neck and kissed her between the ears. Bess yawned lazily and settled down, her muzzle between her forepaws.

'I don't want you to go giving Mr Smethurst any trouble,' she choked. 'And I'll come back to see you as soon as I can.'

She steered an erratic course as they pedalled away. Repeatedly, she looked over her shoulder but images became blurred behind a curtain of unshed tears.

Miss Beckworth endeavoured to distract her attention. 'I'll race you to the top of the hill,' she called.

Barbie had no heart to race but she followed behind, expending her energy upon getting to the top. With every thrust upon the pedals she grunted out her anger and her pain until at last, panting and breathless, she arrived at the top and free-wheeled down the other side.

Miss Beckworth lifted her head to the sky and, removing her feet from the pedals, she held her legs outstretched. 'Look at me,' she cried. 'I can fly.'

Barbie wondered again why Miss Beckworth had not wanted her to share her life.

They pedalled for miles. The sun was hot but the cooling breeze blew at their hair and found its way inside their T-shirts. In the hedgerows rosebay willowherb held pink-purple spikes towards the sky and bees pushed their way into the last of the foxgloves. They did not stop until they reached the river bridge where water flowed deep and smooth beneath the shadows.

They dismounted and pushed the bicycles along the towpath until they came to a thicket of hawthorn, and collapsed exhausted beneath its shade.

Barbie lay on her back and felt the sun upon her face as she panted towards the sky. She was totally spent. She closed her eyes, not realising that she was drifting into sleep and when she awoke the sun had moved a little further across the sky.

'Welcome back, old sleepy head,' Miss Beckworth greeted her with a smile. 'It's lunch-time and I'm starving.'

They pushed the bicycles to a nearby shop where they bought fresh-baked bread with cheese, cans of ginger beer and flaky apple turnovers, then returned to the river bank where they sat dangling their feet in the cooling water.

Barbie watched the acrobatics of a grasshopper as it sprang from blade to blade in the grass beside her. She marvelled at its speed and movement, then, hands cupped and breath inhaled, she pounced. Gently, she held it in her hands, feeling its movement tickling her palms, and gingerly peered between her thumbs. Then she held it out for Miss Beckworth's inspection before carefully uncupping her hands to release it.

'Hoppy old thing,' said Miss Beckworth as she watched it go. In all her life Barbie had never intentionally hurt anyone, or anything.

Together, they paddled in the water, feeling the soft mud oozing up between their toes. They caught tiddlers in a plastic bag and scurried to the safety of the bank when hissed at by a pair of passing swans.

'Thank you, Barbie,' said Miss Beckworth as the afternoon was drawing to a close. 'Thank you for a lovely day.' She held out her arms. 'I shall always remember it.'

But Barbie looked at her and pulled away.

They cycled home through lanes dappled with the light and shade of late afternoon and arrived in time to meet Miss Standish.

Miss Beckworth held out her arms again. 'Goodbye Barbie.' Barbie deliberately misunderstood the gesture and shook her hand.

Miss Beckworth held on to the hand and squeezed the fingers. 'I'll be thinking of you,' she said. 'And we shall see one another when you come to the village.'

Barbie climbed into the car and was driven away. She did not look back.

Miss Beckworth stood in the lane and watched the car until it was out of sight. She wished that Barbie had looked at her.

She knew that she must do nothing which might jeopardise the chances of Barbie's future success. She would not intrude upon this new relationship with her family. Yet, life would never again be quite the same. She brushed a hand across her eyes and went inside to make herself a cup of tea.

Barbie stared through the windows of the car. There was safety in not thinking. She watched the fields as they were replaced by houses and gradually the countryside petered out.

Veronica Standish tried to talk to her but she was in no mood for talking. She answered questions in monosyllables or pretended not to hear. Miss Standish had hoped to use the time in the car to get to know something more of her feelings but eventually she gave up and did not press her further.

They passed an estate of factories. It was almost six o'clock and the roads were crowded with people making their way home, pushing, squeezing, or being limply swept along. Barbie looked at the faces, tense, anonymous, preoccupied, and felt a moment of strangling claustrophobia. She was in town.

They passed through estates of houses, street after street, until they came at last to Wansdyke Avenue. It was a cut above the rest, a road of some twenty houses, each identical in its boxlike appearance, but with four bedrooms instead of the usual three, and with mock-Georgian windows and a double garage at the side. On the pavement, in front of tiny, open-plan lawns, young rowan saplings had been planted in deference to the title 'Avenue'.

Miss Standish halted the car outside number fifteen and turned to Barbie. 'We're home, Barbie,' she smiled. 'What do you think of it?'

'It's posh,' said Barbie flatly.

'It's going to seem strange at first. But you'll very soon get used to it.'

Mary Radlett was at the door. 'Hello Barbie,' she called. 'Welcome home.'

Barbie held back, shyly looking at the two children peering at her from behind their mother's back.

'This is Mark.' Mary reached behind her and drew forward the children. 'And this is Tracy.'

Mark was nine, a year younger than Barbie, and Tracy six. She was a pretty child with long fair hair and pale, delicate features. The three children stared at one another in an awkward silence.

'Well, say hello to Barbie. Where are your manners?'

'Hello.' Mark gave an embarrassed grin.

Barbie caught the glint in Tracy's eye.

The hall carpet was white. Barbie stood looking at it, feeling out of place. 'We always take our shoes off at the door,' said Mary. 'Do you have some slippers?' Barbie shook her head. 'Never mind. I'll buy you some tomorrow.'

She slipped off her sandals and squirmed at the sight of river mud still stuck between her toes. Mary gave an almost inaudible sound, then said, 'I think you had better put them back on. But wipe them on the mat.'

Miss Standish checked her own shoes before entering the house but did not remove them. 'Where's Mr Radlett?' she asked.

'He rang to say he's been delayed.' Even as she spoke Ken's car appeared round the corner and he swung it onto the drive.

'Sorry I'm late. I wanted to be here when you arrived.' He stood looking at Barbie, not knowing what to say, then he dipped into his pocket for three bars of chocolate.

'Oh Ken, I do wish you wouldn't buy them chocolate at mealtimes.'

'Sorry.' Ken winked at Barbie.

'Well, you'd better give it to them now. But don't eat it, please Barbie, until after dinner.'

Miss Standish accepted an offer of coffee and dallied over it, listening, observing, measuring the atmosphere. The children kept their distance, prowling like animals sniffing the air, while Ken was over-voluble in his embarrassment. She wished yet again that she could have given more time to introducing Barbie into the family; but she had used her judgment in Barbie's best interests. It was a pity she would not be around to see it through.

She rose to leave. 'Goodbye Barbie. It's been nice knowing you.' Barbie shook the hand which was offered to her. 'I shall always be interested to know how you're getting on.'

'Yes, Miss.'

'I've arranged for one of the Wickhampton social workers to come and visit you. His name is Mr Ogilvie.' She watched for Barbie's reaction but again there was nothing. 'I'm sure you're going to settle down and be very happy here; but if you're in need of help at any time I know that Mr Ogilvie will do everything he can.'

'Yes, Miss.' Barbie watched Miss Standish leave. Already she had decided that she would not like Mr Ogilvie.

'We're having spaghetti bolognese for dinner, Barbie.' Mary broke into her thoughts. 'Do you like spaghetti bolognese?'

'Yes,' she said, although she did not know what it was. Her diet with Gran had consisted almost entirely of stew, eggs, sausages, and factory-produced meat pies.

She sat at the table and contemplated the plate before her. To Barbie, spaghetti came in tins, complete with tomato sauce. This spaghetti trailed itself round the plate like a nest of worms cradling a thick, brown substance at its centre. She sat, not knowing what to do.

'You can start, dear, whenever you wish.' Mary took the napkin from its chromium-plated ring and placed it upon Barbie's lap.

Barbie was not hungry. She watched Ken twirling the spaghetti round his fork and lifted her own fork in an attempt to copy him but succeeded only in splashing the sauce across the table.

'Here, let me help you.' Mary took the fork from her, demonstrating the technique. 'Now, see if you can manage that.'

The children exchanged glances.

'Just get on with your own dinner.' Mary scowled at them. 'And mind your manners.'

'What's she going to call you, Mum?'

Mary looked again at Mark and frowned.

'Is she going to call you Mrs Radlett?'

'No, of course not. And don't talk about Barbie as if she isn't here. She's a member of our family.' Mary smiled warmly at Barbie who was pushing the food around her mouth and swallowing on its unaccustomed taste. 'And she's very welcome.'

Barbie attempted to return the smile.

'But he has got a point,' said Ken. 'What is she going to call you?'

'As a matter of fact, I've been thinking about that,' said Mary. 'I know a family who call their parents "M" and "D". I thought perhaps Aunty "M" and "D". It has a nice ring to it.'

'Yes; I like that. What do you think, Barbie?'

Barbie looked at him shyly and nodded. She was glad of the suggestion. She could not have called him Daddy.

'"D" it shall be then,' he said. 'I rather like "D".'

'If you don't want your dinner, you can leave it,' said Mary. 'You probably haven't much appetite this evening.'

Barbie put down her fork gratefully.

'Would you like some tinned peaches with icecream?'

'That's not fair,' cut in Tracy. 'We're not allowed to have peaches if we haven't eaten our spaghetti.'

'That's enough,' retorted Mary sharply. 'Barbie doesn't feel like eating.'

It was an innocent comment but it opened a floodgate which caught Barbie by surprise. She needed Gran.

'Would you like some icecream?' asked Mary again.

'No, thank you.' Barbie shook her head and was silent for the remainder of the meal, thinking of Gran.

At eight o'clock Mary announced that it was time for bed. Barbie looked at the clock. With Gran, she had slept at ten, or even twelve. 'I'll run your bath. Do you need any help?'

'No, thank you,' she said indignantly.

Barbie had never had a bath. There had been no bathroom in the cottage but on Saturday evenings she and Gran had washed themselves before the kitchen range. Until this moment it had not occurred to her that she had never had a bath. She found it an interesting thought and pondered on it while Mary took her upstairs.

Mary turned on the taps, swishing the water to a foam with scented bath oil. The air became warm and moist, smelling of pine. 'I'll leave you to it then,' she said, and, after she had gone, Barbie locked the door and removed her clothing.

The water was warm and softly yielding like an old woman's breasts. She lay there, almost totally submerged, staring at the ceiling and her mind became filled with images of fields and trees, of clover, and of butterflies. 'Oh, Gran,' she whispered softly. 'Gran.' She wandered through fields of barley and lingered in the copse. The ceiling became the sky and high above a lark soared, singing its heart out to the world. 'You look after her Jesus. And she likes two spoons of sugar in her tea.'

She did not know how long she lay there but suddenly there was a knock at the door. 'Barbie. Are you all right?' There was a slight edge to the voice which shot her up out of the bath.

'Yes,' she said, dazed. 'Thank you.'

'Then hurry up, please dear.'

She threw on her pyjamas, hardly bothering to dry herself and unlocked the door.

'Oh dear.' Mary's face fell. 'And you've got your hair wet. We shall have to dry it.'

'Sorry.' Barbie touched her dripping hair. 'I didn't know.'

'No; I'm sorry, dear.' Mary's face softened. 'I'm not cross.' She reached for a towel and began rubbing it through Barbie's hair. 'But, you see,' she said gently, 'you're part of a family now. We only get along happily so long as we all remember to think of one another. If one of us spends too long in the bath then the others have to wait and they can't go to bed, even though they're tired.'

'Sorry,' said Barbie.

100

'It doesn't matter, dear. You weren't to know.' Mary bent and kissed her lightly on the temple. 'I'll get the hair dryer. We'll shampoo it tomorrow and one day soon I'll take you to the hairdresser. You've got lovely hair. We'll get it styled and make you pretty.'

Barbie smiled. She had never thought of looking pretty.

'Would you like that?'

'Yes,' nodded Barbie. 'Yes, please.'

She was put to bed in the room with pink roses on the wallpaper and lay in the half-darkness studying unfamiliar shapes – a bookcase and a chair, a dressing table with its mirror reflecting the lights of passing cars. She had never been alone at night. Last night there had been Miss Beckworth and the night before, Gran across the hospital corridor.

She turned her head towards the open door and saw a teddy bear lying on the landing – a soft honey brown in the shadows cast by the downstairs light – one leg pushed backwards beneath its body. For a long time she lay watching it, then tiptoed out of bed. As she picked it up she felt the texture, soft to the touch with hard, smooth eyes like buttons.

Her action had not passed unobserved. From a nearby room Tracy screamed. 'Mummy! Come quick!'

Mary ran up the stairs, alarmed. 'What's the matter? What's going on?'

'I want my teddy.'

'Well, where is your teddy?'

Barbie threw the teddy bear beneath her bed and held her breath.

'He's over there. She took him.'

'What do you mean – took him?'

'She took him, I tell you. I saw her.'

By this time Ken, too, was on the scene. He walked into Barbie's room. 'I think she wants her teddy back,' he said kindly and Barbie pointed wordlessly beneath the bed. He got to his knees and found it. 'She's rather fond of this old thing. She's had it since she was a baby.' In the half-light she could see the outline of his hair but not his features. 'I'll get you one of your own tomorrow,' he said, 'if you'd like it.'

Barbie nodded but she had gone off the desire for teddy bears.

In the ensuing silence she lay again watching shadows and jumped as another figure slipped into the room. It was Mark. He came in furtively and pushed towards her something soft. 'Here,' he said. 'I don't need this.' He thrust it into her hands and left. 'And don't take any notice of her,' he said. 'She's horrible.'

She held out the object towards the light, studying it. It was a toy gorilla, ginger brown, with long arms and a squat, grinning face. She smiled and drew it to her, holding it close throughout the long hours when sleep refused to come.

Downstairs Ken sat watching television. Mary brought in coffee and flopped down beside him, exhausted at the end of the day. Her eyes settled upon the television screen but her mind was preoccupied.

Upstairs, Barbie lay still staring at the shadows. She hugged the gorilla and studied the outline of the framed photograph on the table beside her bed. In the half-darkness she could not see Gran's face but she knew that it was there. She thought of home, and of Bess. The rabbits were probably eating the lettuces right now. 'Bloody rabbits,' she said out loud. 'I'll kill 'em if I catch 'em on them bloody lettuce.'

As she lay staring, her fingers strayed to the wallpaper beside the bed. She ran them across the surface, feeling for bumps and indentations like a blind man reading Braille. She came to a join and slowly ran her fingers down the straight line between two strips of paper until she found a spot where it was loose. Absentmindedly, she slotted her fingernail beneath the paper, and began to pick.

Chapter Six

'Barbie, do you often wet your bed at night?'

'No.' Never before had Barbie wet her bed, yet here she was, wet and stinking.

'Well, don't worry about it, dear.' Mary began stripping the sheets from the bed. 'Go and have a bath, then hurry down to breakfast.'

As Barbie left the room Mary remarked, 'You've moved the poster.'

Barbie turned and looked at the large picture of galloping horses which she had moved from the wardrobe door to the wall beside her bed. 'I wanted to look at it,' she said. 'I like it.'

'That's nice. I'm glad you like it.'

Barbie hooked her finger into the sodden fabric of her pyjamas and held her breath waiting for Mary to lift the poster to reveal the torn wallpaper beneath.

Instead she smiled. 'I like it myself. It's got a marvellous sense of freedom.'

'Yes,' said Barbie. The colour rose across her cheeks and she fled.

On the landing, Tracy was standing listening. She looked pointedly at Barbie's wet pyjamas and sniffed.

Although Barbie's school term had ended on the eighteenth of July, the schools in Wickhampton had another day to go before they broke up for the summer holiday.

Mary faced a dilemma. 'I have to go to work,' she said. 'I tried to take the day off but we've got people away sick.'

'I don't mind,' said Barbie. 'I like being on my own.'

'It's only for today. I don't work during the school holidays.'

Barbie sensed the struggle which Mary was having within

herself. 'I really don't mind,' she said again. She would be glad of the solitude.

'Well, if you're sure you don't mind.' Mary began collecting up her car keys and her handbag. 'I've asked Mrs Cosgrove next door to give you your lunch. You can go and sit with her if you like.'

Barbie did not want to sit with Mrs Cosgrove and Mary had known that she would not.

'Then you may do whatever you please. Go out if you like but don't wander too far and don't forget to lock the door and give the key to Mrs Cosgrove.'

Barbie nodded in agreement.

There was some money lying on the kitchen table. Mary looked at it as though weighing something in her mind, then she picked it up and put it in her handbag. 'There are biscuits in the cupboard and you can help yourself to orange squash or milk.'

She hovered in the doorway. 'You're quite certain you'll be all right alone?'

'Quite sure,' said Barbie.

'Very well; but don't forget to go to Mrs Cosgrove if you need anything. Mark and Tracy will be home at half past three and I'll be back at four.'

The house was claustrophobic in its silence. Barbie wandered about for a while and then went out. There were petrol fumes in the air and a slight smell of sulphur from a nearby factory but she sucked it deeply into her lungs. She had no idea where she would go. The pavement felt hard beneath her feet and everywhere she turned there were houses.

On one street she found an arcade of shops and stopped to gaze into the windows. There was a butcher's shop with a halved pig's head lying on a slab which made her stomach churn. Then a fruiterer's and, next door, a newsagent. She stood reading the notices pinned to the door. 'LOST . . . Black and white kitten. Answers to Joe.' 'FOR SALE . . . dressing table with oval mirrors. Cheap for quick sale.' 'WANTED . . . domestic help three days a week.' She read them all then went inside, thumbing through a magazine from a rack beside the door. 'Yes, dear?' said the assistant. 'Can I help?' Barbie smiled and left. She had no money.

It was by luck that she found the park. She came upon it behind a tall fence and smiled her delight. It was small and it was formal but it was green. Narrow paths threaded past lawns and beds of antirrhinums with salvias, heliotrope and blue lobelia. Here and there were benches and, in the corner, a weeping willow tree, its pale green fronds hanging to the ground.

She hid herself beneath the curtain of leaves and lay upon her stomach, chin in hands, to watch the birds. One by one they came towards her, unafraid of her silent presence – sparrows, pigeons, a robin, a large black and white magpie. At one time an old stray cat appeared and frightened off the birds. She called him to her and stroked his fur as he arched his back, offering a tag-eared head.

She stayed beneath the tree all day and forgot to go home for lunch. She became suddenly aware of the time and wondered if Mrs Cosgrove would be cross.

The schoolchildren were going home as she returned. She saw Tracy with a group of friends and hung back, not wanting to pass them.

'She belongs to my Dad,' she heard Tracy say. 'She's staying with us because her Gran's dead.' They huddled together whispering, then Tracy stood up. 'And . . .' she said, raising her voice, '. . . she wets the bed.'

Barbie stood for a moment on her toes, then turned and walked quickly away. As she increased the distance between them she could hear their laughter.

She turned off the street and found herself in a culdesac of garages. Too late, she realised there was no way out and, standing before her, was a group of boys, some aged about ten, like herself, and some a year or so older.

She made to retreat but a boy blocked her way. 'You know you're not allowed round here,' he said.

Another boy, bigger than the rest, came up and stared at her, uncomfortably close. 'Show us your knickers then.' An air of excitement swept through the gang.

'Yeah. Show us your knickers.'

Barbie clutched instinctively at her skirt and backed away, but the group moved in, pinning her against the wall.

'You're new round here.'

The big boy moved his hand towards her skirt and Barbie lashed out, prepared to fight. More by accident than design, she hit him, full and hard, upon the groin and he sank to his knees, howling.

'Get her!' he yelled and before Barbie had time to draw breath they were upon her. She felt the weight of one boy upon the small of her back while another gave her wrist a 'Chinese burn', twisting the skin until she felt that it must break. There were gravel chippings in her mouth and she spat on it as she struggled.

Suddenly – 'Scatter!' – a cry went up and they were gone. A car was approaching. She picked herself up and walked away not wishing the driver to see her plight.

She almost bumped into Mark as she stepped out onto the street. 'What's the matter?' he asked.

'Nothing,' she said but her hands were pitted with gravel chippings and her nose was bleeding.

'You haven't been tangling with old Thomo and his gang?' Mark stepped back and looked at her with new respect, but she walked off and left him standing. 'I saw them come haring out of here just now.' He caught up with her and tried to look at her hands but she brushed him off.

'You must be mad.'

'I fell over,' she said, but they fell into step and walked home together.

Later, when Mary came home, she questioned Barbie at length. 'Tell me exactly how you fell, dear. You don't get hurt like that by tripping on the kerb.'

'I caught my toe.'

'I'd better take you to the doctor.'

'No.' Barbie was immediately alarmed. 'It doesn't hurt.'

Mary eyed the bloodstained dress and the angry graze across her cheek. 'Have you been fighting?'

'No,' said Barbie indignantly.

'Well, I still don't see how you can get hurt like that by falling over.' She held the throbbing wrist in her hand examining the bruise. 'Just look at that bruise,' she said. 'It's a wonder you didn't break your wrist.'

'I just fell over,' she said again but Mary looked at her, quite clearly unconvinced.

'You had better go upstairs and change your clothes,' said Mary. 'I'll attend to your face and bathe it with antiseptic.'

Mark looked at Barbie across the room and winked.

As they stood before the bathroom basin Mary carefully picked the chippings from Barbie's hands and face.

'Mrs Cosgrove tells me you didn't come home for lunch,' she said.

106

Barbie bit her lip. 'I'm sorry. I forgot.'

'Where were you, dear?'

'I went for a walk.'

'But Mrs Cosgrove was very worried.'

As Mary turned towards Barbie's face she suddenly saw it – that something almost indefinable but definitely there. She caught her breath. There was that certain, unmistakable spectre of Sandra Harding. But that was not all; there was something there also of Ken. She stood and stared. Barbie was a mixture of Ken and Sandra Harding.

'I'm sorry,' said Barbie, afraid of her mood.

She forced herself to look away. 'Sorry isn't good enough, Barbie,' she said sharply. 'You've got to learn to consider other people's feelings.'

She felt Barbie tremble beneath her hands and, ashamed, she softened her voice. 'We'll forget about it this time, dear. But try to remember in future.'

'I'm sorry,' whispered Barbie again.

'I've made an appointment with the hairdresser,' she said gently. 'She's going to cut your hair for you and style it.'

Barbie looked at her, not knowing what to say.

'We've got to try very hard, Barbie; you and I. It's not going to be easy, but we've got to try.'

When Ken came home later that evening he was carrying a parcel wrapped in brown paper. He held it out to Barbie. 'Go on, open it,' he said. 'It's for you.'

Barbie turned the parcel in her hands.

'I bought it for you.'

Tracy appeared as if from nowhere. 'Why?'

He glanced at Mary, aware of a potentially difficult situation. 'Well . . . it's her birthday soon.'

Mary took in a breath and let it go slowly. It was a stupid lie which he could not hope to perpetuate. 'When is your birthday, Barbie?' she asked, hoping that by some miracle it would be in the not too distant future.

'Eighth of October,' said Barbie, and Mary let go her breath again.

'Oh,' said Ken limply. 'I thought it was soon.'

'Then she can't have her present, can she.'

'Of course she can,' said Mary. 'You get more than your share of surprises.'

Barbie handed back the parcel. She did not want to be party to contention.

'No; you keep it,' said Ken. 'And I'll buy another one for Tracy tomorrow.' He gestured towards Tracy with his hands. 'A *great big* one,' he said, indicating the enormity of its potential size.

Mary shook her head. They must face the next six weeks of the school holiday without her salary and bills were pouring in from every side.

Barbie took the parcel to the kitchen table and unwrapped it. Inside was the largest doll she had ever seen, dressed in a froth of white tulle with a bridal veil. She viewed it without enthusiasm, for its body was of hard unyielding plastic, with stiff limbs, and, as she lifted it, the long lashed eyelids swung open to reveal cold glittering eyes.

'Thank you,' she said flatly.

She carried it to her bedroom and sat it upon the dressing table, carefully spreading the dress and arranging the veil over the ashe blonde hair. At last she stepped back, satisfied that she had arranged it to the very best of her ability, and never touched it again.

A few hours later she noticed that the dress had been deliberately cut with scissors. She gave it a casual glance and shrugged; then went to fetch the toy gorilla which she kept beneath her pillow. She took it to bed and ignored the doll.

That evening Ken and Mary sat together in the lounge. 'I'm worried,' said Mary. 'I don't think she's going to fit in.'

'Oh, come on, luv.' Ken was watching television, only half-attending to what she had said. 'She's only been here a couple of days.'

'It's not a matter of time, Ken. I can feel it in my bones.'

'You haven't given her a chance.'

'It's strange. I thought I knew exactly how to handle it; but now she's here, it's different.'

'Miss Standish told us that it wasn't going to be easy.'

'This is something different.'

'She told us to give her time. She's bound to miss the old girl.'

'I could have handled the grieving; and the settling in. It's well . . .' She picked up her knitting and did not continue.

'Well, what?' he asked but she did not reply.

He waited for a moment but when she was not forthcoming he went on to say, 'She'll be all right, luv. You'll sort her out.'

'Why always me?'

'You're better at it than I am.'

She sighed. 'She's your child.'

'I know.'

'Then do your bit.'

He looked at her with a mixture of hurt and bafflement. 'Perhaps we ought to have a word with the social worker if you're worried.'

'I'll do nothing of the sort. I have no intention of airing my problems with any social worker.'

'But you told Miss Standish . . .'

'I know what I told Miss Standish. I could hardly say anything else. But I have no intention of discussing my private affairs with anybody outside this family. Whatever problems we may have we'll sort them out by ourselves.'

'That's what social workers are there for.'

'Then let them go and sort out the problems of someone who really needs them. I'm not having them in here.'

Ken shrugged. 'Shouldn't you have made that clear to Miss Standish?'

'And would she have let us take Barbie if I had?'

He sat and thought for a time. 'I didn't know you felt like that.'

'Well, I do, Ken. I've never yet had to seek outside help in order to run my family and I don't intend to start now.'

They sat in silence for some time. 'Have you noticed,' she asked casually, 'how much she's like her mother?'

'Oh, come on, luv. She's nothing at all like Sandra.'

'There's something about her.'

'Sandra was tall and fair.' He got up and switched channels on the television.

'It's not her looks. It's something else.'

'I've no idea what you're talking about.'

'You're either blind, or you don't want to see.'

'See what?'

'Perhaps it's because I'm a woman.'

Ken shook his head with amused impatience and switched channels again. 'There's never anything worth watching on telly these days.'

'We shall have to keep an eye on Mark.'

'Why Mark?'

'They're going to be in such close contact.'

'What on earth do you mean?'

'Don't be dim, Ken. You know exactly what I mean. That child is like her mother.'

'Good God, woman.' He slapped the arm of the chair. 'She's a ten year old child.'

'She'll grow soon enough.'

'You're talking rot.'

'Am I? I just hope that I'm proved wrong.'

'Anyway, Sandra wasn't that bad. She was just a bit wild.'

Mary clacked her knitting needles and dropped a stitch. 'Why!' she demanded. 'Why, for heaven's sake, does everyone have to stick up for that girl? What did she have that made her any different from any other slut?'

Ken shrugged. 'I don't know. There was just something about her.'

That made Mary even more angry. She continued her knitting in a thick silence, jabbing the needle into the stitches, missing more often than not.

Several minutes had passed before Ken suddenly exclaimed. 'Good God, woman. You're talking about incest.'

Mary stopped abruptly. The thought was as shocking to her as it was to Ken. She put down her knitting and went to sit alone in the kitchen.

Barbie had been at Wansdyke Avenue for three days when the social worker called. She was crouching on the drive with Mark, fitting a new two-tone horn to his bicycle. On each of the three days she had taken an opportunity to slip away to the park, but she had also spent some time with Mark. He had accepted her with an easygoing casualness and they had sat together, quietly constructing model cranes from his Meccano set or pacing toy cars around a track.

A car pulled up and Mark went to investigate. Barbie remained where she was. It was none of her business.

'Hi. I'm Larry Ogilvie.' The young man wore a T-shirt with jeans and open sandals, revealing bare feet. He looked across at Barbie. 'I expect Miss Standish told you I'd be calling.'

Mark pointed to the back door. 'Mum's in the kitchen.'

Larry Ogilvie bent to inspect the horn. He tried it and grimaced at the noise. 'Don't you think it would be better fitted up here?' he suggested. 'It wouldn't interfere with the brake cable.'

Mark accepted the suggestion with enthusiasm. 'Yeah,' he said. 'I hadn't thought about that.'

'You two seem to be getting on quite well.'

Mark and Barbie looked at one another. Neither had given the matter much thought.

'She's not bad,' said Mark. 'For a girl.'

Larry Ogilvie laughed. 'Watch it, mate, or she'll start saying things about male chauvinist pigs.' He gave another blast on the horn and went to knock at the open back door.

Mary was making pastry and felt at a disadvantage caught with dough clinging to her hands. She went to wash it off.

The young man sat down, uninvited, on one of the kitchen chairs and crossed his legs. 'Don't worry about me,' he said. 'Just carry on with what you're doing.'

Mary took in the T-shirt and the sandals. She could visualize him marching with a banner outside one of the redbrick universities. 'Would you like some coffee?'

'Please.'

She had already told herself that she could manage without social workers but, now that she saw him, she asked herself why anyone should send a man so young.

'How's Barbie getting on?' he asked. 'Is she settling in?'

Mary had her back to him filling the kettle. 'Yes; very well.'

'Good. But don't be too surprised if you get a few teething troubles before much longer.'

'Oh, I expect that we shall cope.' She realised that her sarcasm had shown through. 'I'm not anticipating anything I can't handle.'

Larry Ogilvie smiled. 'We all run into problems occasionally which are difficult to handle.'

'There are bound to be a few settling-in problems,' she said more reasonably. 'It's a totally new way of life.'

'They tell me it was a bit rough and ready with her grandmother.'

'I'm sure Mrs Harding did her best.'

'Barbie seemed to think so.'

'Yes, I know. She's going to miss her.'

'But she's showing no signs of grief?'

'She hasn't cried, if that's what you mean. Not everyone shows their grief by crying about it.'

'It would be a lot healthier if she did.'

111

'It will probably hit her all of a sudden.'

Larry Ogilvie accepted the cup of coffee which she handed to him. 'Or it may come out in other ways,' he said. 'Don't be too surprised if you start getting some difficult behaviour to cope with.'

'I expect we'll cope. I have had two children of my own for practice.' He flicked her another glance and she quickly offered him sugar.

He helped himself to three heaped spoonsful. 'What about the children?' he asked. 'How are they adjusting to her?'

'Very well.'

'Mark seems to enjoy her company.'

Mary felt her fingers tighten slightly around her cup. 'They spend a lot of time together.'

He sat on for some time, chatting apparently aimlessly but Mary felt uncomfortable. She suspected that this young man took in more than she wished him to know.

'May I have a word with Barbie?' He got up and went to the window where he could see the children playing on the drive.

'Yes, of course. I'll call her in.' Mary offered up a silent prayer that Barbie would not let them down. She called her to the door and Barbie stood uncertainly, looking at Larry Ogilvie.

'May I see your room?' he asked, seeking an opportunity to speak to her alone.

Barbie led the way, glancing down at the bare feet and sandals which walked across the white hall carpet without comment from Mary. Mary offered up another prayer that Larry Ogilvie did not possess a keen sense of smell for Barbie had wet the bed again last night.

'Nice poster,' he said. He flopped down on the bed beside it. 'Do you like horses?'

Barbie squirmed and turned away.

'How are you, Barbie?' He turned to face her. 'Are you settling in?'

'Yes, thank you.'

'I expect it seems strange after living with your Gran.'

The comment brought a pain to her throat but she swallowed on it without altering the expression on her face.

'But everybody's helping you to settle in?'

'Yes, thank you.'

He chatted with her, trying to draw her out, but she did not respond. He spoke about the contents of her room, her likes and dislikes, her love of nature. She answered the questions politely but made no attempt to expand upon them.

'I hear that you left your dog in the village.' He watched her as Barbie swallowed again. 'When are you going to visit her?'

'When "D" goes to visit his folks.'

'I expect you miss her.'

Barbie nodded but was afraid to speak.

'What's her name?'

She bit her lip and silently begged that he would not ask her any more questions.

He watched the tremor and held out his hand. 'There's no harm in crying about it, Barbie.'

She stepped away from him and made a physical effort to compose her face.

'I know it hurts. But one day soon you'll begin to find it a little easier to bear.'

She sneered inwardly at his foolishness. Security would never catch her out again.

'Is there anything else you would like to tell me?'

She looked at him blankly.

'I'm always here if ever you want someone to talk to.' He got up from the bed and smiled at her. 'It sometimes helps to talk.'

She thought of the night she had spent in Miss Beckworth's bed and felt something twist painfully within her.

'I'll come and see you again soon.'

She watched him leave and sat down on the bed, squeezing her eyes tight shut.

Mary walked with Larry Ogilvie to his car. 'I understand that the funeral is to be held tomorrow,' he said. 'It's going to be a big ordeal for her.'

'I'll be glad when it's over.'

'How do you think she'll take it?'

'I don't know but we shall be with her all the time.'

He got into his car. 'It could be that she'll feel easier once it's over.'

'I hope so.' She smiled with what she hoped was an assurance of confidence. 'I'm sure everything's going to turn out just fine.'

The following morning dawned overcast with heavy cloud and rain. Barbie perched on the back seat of the car behind Ken and Mary as they drove back towards familiar countryside. Her mind was blank. It was like watching a moving screen on which she was involved yet not involved. Every now and again Mary would glance over her shoulder with some comment concerning the passing scenery and several times she caught Ken's glance as he winked at her in the rear view mirror, but each time she turned away and pretended not to see.

In the crematorium car park Beattie Russell stood waiting. Barbie saw her and drew tighter the curtains of her mind.

'Why, Barbie, dear. Aren't you looking smart.' Beattie Russell took in the make, the size, and the registration plate of Ken's car, followed by Barbie's new dress and coat bought specially for the occasion. 'It's a pity the weather turned out so wet.'

Barbie felt Mary nudge her from behind. 'Say hello, Barbie.'

'Hello.'

Beattie Russell turned her attention to Mary. 'It's very nice of you to come, dear.'

Barbie thought it was like being welcomed to a party.

'I said to my Cyril when I heard, "Barbie's a lucky girl", I said. "Going to a family and being taken in like that". Well, I mean to say . . .' she lowered her voice '. . . it's better than being sent into a Home, isn't it, dear.'

Barbie felt the pressure of Mary's hand upon her arm and heard the cough of embarrassment. 'Perhaps we had better be getting inside. It's rather damp out here and I think it must be almost time.'

'Yes dear. Oh . . . by the way . . . I just wanted Barbie to know . . .' Beattie Russell leaned towards Barbie. 'I just wanted you to know, dear, that I've arranged to keep the ashes. I've ordered a lovely little urn and I'm going to take her home, all nice and cosy-like.' She turned again to Ken and Mary. 'Well, it's better than scattering them, isn't it, dear. It's more . . . caring . . . it you know what I mean.'

The enormity of the unfairness swamped Barbie's mind. Gran belonged to her; Beattie Russell had no right to take her home.

A whistling noise rose in her ears, accompanied by the sensation of pins and needles, and for a moment she thought she would be sick.

'We really must be getting in.' She felt herself propelled along the gravel path.

'I told you that you could safely leave it to your Aunty Beattie,' she heard Beattie Russell say as they walked away.

She sat between Ken and Mary on a hard-backed chair. The organ was playing and she looked around at a scattering of people whom she hardly knew. They smiled at her when they caught her eye and made little nods with their heads.

The curtains opened and Barbie saw the coffin piled high with flowers. She fought an overwhelming desire to run towards it, for this was the first time since Gran had died that she had been close; yet she knew that she dare not move. Her hands clutched the sides of her chair so that the knuckles showed white.

The vicar spoke, his voice trailing on in unintelligible words; then they all stood and sang, a smattering of uncertain voices lost in the emptiness of unoccupied space.

And, all the time, Gran lay there, doing nothing.

Here and there, words filtered through – 'Jesus Christ, our Saviour . . . He died that we might live . . .' Empty words, yet no one shouted, 'No. That's not correct.' Gran was dead and Jesus had done nothing; yet no one shouted, 'No'.

Barbie's mind was building pictures – the furnace crackling, waiting to devour; the smell of burning wood.

'Jesus!'

The curtains fell but, just as they did so, the coffin began to move, carried along by a conveyor belt towards its destination.

She screamed, stuffing her fist into her mouth to stifle the sound.

'Jesus! Get off Your bleeding arse!'

There was a moment of deathly silence and all eyes turned. She felt Mary's hand take hold of her arm and she was taken outside, her feet hardly touching the floor.

She was taken home and put to bed. The doctor was called and he gave her a sedative which made her sleep a deep dreamless sleep which lasted for hours, and when she awoke her mind refused to focus.

For a time she could not make out where she was but gradually it all came back. She saw, beside the bed, the poster with its galloping horses; she turned away her head. She saw wallpaper with pink roses and, on the dressing table, a doll in bridal white.

Gran had gone; taken away by Beattie Russell.

She closed her eyes and blotted out the room. It all seemed too much to bear, but, even as it swamped her senses, one small thought filtered through. She remembered the garden on a warm

June evening after rain, lying on her back in damp grass, while Gran sat on a stool, weeding.

'I'll never leave you, Barbie,' Gran had said. 'Even when I'm with Jesus, I'll still be there, somewhere, watching over you. I'll find a way.'

'Gran?' she whispered and listened for a response. 'Gran?'

She tried several times but somehow it did not seem right. The atmosphere was wrong. Gran would not come here. She lay and thought for a while until she knew what she must do. At the very first opportunity, she would go to the old yew tree in the churchyard. There, she would speak to Gran.

She asked Ken about it the next time she saw him. '"D"', she asked. 'When are you taking me to visit Bess?'

He was pleased. She did not often call him by name. 'Let's say Saturday. I'm due to go to the village then. I'll drop you off at the farm.'

It seemed a long time to wait. She filled the days, not knowing how she could endure the greater part of a week until Saturday. But, as it happened, events took a different turn for Mary found the torn wallpaper.

'Barbie,' she said. 'How could you?' She took her to the room and confronted her with the damage. 'After all that we have done for you.'

Barbie held her eyes to the floor and felt her stomach contract.

'I hung this wallpaper myself, less than two months ago. I spent hours and hours of work on it.'

Barbie raised her eyes and, as she did so, Mary saw it again – Sandra Harding – and Ken.

'It's bad enough that you tore it,' she said. 'But it's the deceit which really hurts. You must have known that I would find it.'

'I'm sorry.'

'You're always saying sorry but it doesn't seem to mean much. When you do something wrong you own up. You do not lie and deceive.'

'I'm sorry,' whispered Barbie again.

'It's the sort of thing which your Moth . . .' She stopped herself in time and realised again that she had gone too far.

She softened her voice. 'You've been given a nice room, Barbie, with nice things. Now, it's up to you to show me that you can appreciate it, and that you deserve it.'

'I'm sorry.'

'Oh, for goodness sake.' She put a hand to her forehead. The tension of the past days had got to her more than she had been aware. She felt guilty, yet unwilling to withdraw her words. 'You'd better go outside and play.'

Barbie ran outside and sucked the street air into her lungs. She was ashamed and genuinely sorry that Mary was upset. She wondered how she could make amends.

She kicked her way along the street making in the direction of the park, unaware that Tracy was tagging along behind. She did not make her presence known until they reached a privet hedge beyond which stood a large redbrick house.

'You know what that place is?'

Barbie jumped.

'That's Holly Lodge and that's where they put children who haven't got any fathers and mothers.'

Over the hedge three children were happily at play beside a paddling pool but Barbie did not see them.

'Especially . . .' Tracy let the word hang in the air '. . . especially if they're vandals.'

Barbie turned on her heels and ran, leaving Tracy to stand and watch as she disappeared round the corner.

She ran to the park and dived for cover beneath the weeping willow tree. She lay there for a while, panting, and by the time she sat up, had blanked from her mind all thoughts of Holly Lodge. She was becoming increasingly adept at rapidly drawing down the curtains of her mind.

She pondered on a gift for Mary. In her purse she had the pocket money which Ken had given her last weekend but it did not occur to her to buy a present. Instead, she looked for inspiration from her surroundings.

In a nearby flowerbed salvias blazed with heliotrope and blue lobelia; further back, against the fence, was a border of sweetly scented nicotianas. But she had no thoughts of picking them. Barbie had never gathered flowers, neither from garden nor from hedgerow. To her, plants had life, with rights to their existence as great as any other living creature. They were not there to be plundered simply because they had no voice, and allowed themselves to be torn apart with no protest except to wilt and die.

Beyond the flowerbeds, in a far corner, a pile of coarse gravel had been dumped by a now departed lorry. It was waiting for the workmen to come and make concrete in order to patch the crumbled foundations upon which stood the benches and the litter bins. It was the perfect gift. Barbie went to the pile and squatted beside it, sifting the gravel through her fingers. From it she selected pebbles, some large, some small, some flat in shape, or round, some with jagged indentations. She set them out before her. From a nearby litter bin she took an empty biscuit packet and extracted a flat plastic tray. Slowly, meticulously, she arranged the pebbles in the tray.

It took her a long time but when she had finished she carried it home, carefully balancing the tray across the upturned palms of her hands.

Mary was ironing, her back towards the door. 'Aunty "M".' She turned in surprise. Barbie held out the tray of pebbles. 'I brought you a present.'

Mary looked at the gift and her face softened. 'Thank you, Barbie,' she said. 'That's very kind of you.'

'I arranged them. There are small ones down this end, and dark brown ones over there, and jaggedy ones in the middle.'

'They're very nice. I'll put them over here by the window.' Mary moved a potted tradescantia plant along the windowsill to make room. 'Would you like a drink of milk?'

'Yes, please. And can I have a chocolate biscuit?'

Mary poured the milk and placed two chocolate biscuits on a plate.

'I'm sorry, Aunty "M".'

Mary bent and kissed her lightly on the cheek. 'I'm sorry, too, Barbie. We must both try very hard.'

Barbie took the milk and biscuits to her room but the torn wallpaper stared at her, uncovered, like a huge gaping wound. She went instead to sit on the stairs. She sat there for a long time, methodically screwing nuts and bolts into a half-finished Meccano model. The model was of nothing in particular. She did not care about the finished product, only about the therapeutic effect of screwing nuts and bolts. She did not have to dwell on memories when screwing nuts and bolts.

Ken came home. He had been speaking to Mary for some time before Barbie became aware of their conversation. She homed in on it only then because she heard Mary mention wallpaper. Her ears pricked up.

'I don't know how she did it. She must have been picking at it

118

with something, probably with her fingernails. She's always picking at things with her nails. It's a dirty habit.'

Barbie wanted to cry out. All was not forgiven and forgotten. Mary was recounting the details, adding to her shame.

'Why should she do a thing like that?'

'How should I know why she did it.' Mary was clattering saucepans as she spoke. 'Who knows why she does half the things she does. I doubt that anyone knows what goes on in that head of hers.'

'She must have had a reason. You don't just tear wallpaper without a reason.'

'She's so secretive, Ken. She goes off for hours without telling me where she's going. Goodness knows what she's getting up to. Let's only hope she's not doing anything which is going to reflect on the family.'

'But why tear wallpaper?'

'Honestly Ken, I could have wept when I saw it. After all the work I put into decorating that room. It's bad enough the way she's ruined the mattress. The room stinks after she's wet the bed every night.'

Barbie bit her lip and swallowed.

'Well, she can't help that. You said yourself that she wets the bed because she's missing the old girl.'

'It's one thing to know why she does it. It's another thing to have to cope with the stench. I feel so embarrassed about it every time someone comes into the house.'

'Come on, luv. It's not that bad. I can't smell it.'

'Well, I can. And did you know that she has destroyed that doll you gave her?'

'What?'

'She cut the dress, quite deliberately, with scissors.'

Barbie shook her head. It was not fair.

'But I paid good money for that doll.'

'It must have been her. Neither Mark nor Tracy would do a thing like that.'

'What are you going to do about it? Punish her?'

'No.' Mary stopped and spoke more quietly. 'It's not her fault. I keep telling myself over and over again that it's not her fault.'

'She's never been used to a decent home,' said Ken. 'Perhaps we ought to remember that she's never been taught how she ought to behave.'

'It's that old woman who should be blamed,' said Mary.

'Oh, come on, luv. She did her best.'

'Well I hope she rots in hell.'

Barbie stood up and walked slowly down the stairs. In her hand she still held the small, sharp screwdriver. As she walked down the stairs she dragged it, quite deliberately, across the wall, gouging out a long, shallow trough in the plaster beneath. She opened the front door and began the long walk back to the village.

She did not know the way but she had the homing instinct of an animal. She walked, street after street, out into the country until, at last, she saw a bus which was going to the village. She got on it trusting that the money in her pocket was sufficient to cover the fare.

There were few people on the bus at this time in the evening. The village, too, was deserted and no one saw her as she alighted and made her way to the churchyard. The evening had taken on the pearl grey light of approaching dusk and the air was still, heavy with the scents of the village – night-scented stock and mignonette, woodsmoke from a bonfire, fresh cut grass and horse manure, the sharp, heady scent of the mock orange shrub on the vicarage lawn. Somewhere a blackbird sang and a lawn-mower whirred its way along the opposite side of a hedge. Barbie took a deep breath and her senses reeled. Slowly, her muscles relaxed and the tension of her body drained away. She was home. She walked confidently into the churchyard where she was to meet Gran.

It was deserted, her only companion a speckle-throated thrush rooting through the dry needles beneath the yew tree, reluctant to sleep without first finishing his supper. It was almost dark beneath the shadows. Barbie climbed onto a large, stone sar-cophagus and arranged her skirt.

She cleared her throat. 'Gran . . . ?'

The thrush froze at the sound of her voice then, satisfied that she intended him no harm, resumed his search for grubs.

'Gran . . . ?'

There was silence.

'Are you there?'

The church clock chimed and she jumped in fright. The thrush, too, abandoned his search and flew away.

'Are you there?'

She waited but when no reply was forthcoming she went on, tentatively at first but gaining momentum. 'They made me go to Wickhampton . . . and it's full of houses and the people don't speak to you . . . and they go rushing about all over the place . . . and you wouldn't like it; I know you wouldn't. And I didn't steal her teddy, Gran. I didn't want her stupid old teddy . . . and I wet the bed . . . and I didn't mean to . . . about the wallpaper.' Her voice began to rise. 'And I didn't cut that stupid old dress. Why should I want to cut a stupid old dress . . .'

She stopped again, listening for a response which was not forthcoming.

'And there's a place called Holly Lodge,' she went on again. 'And Bess has gone to live with Mr Smethurst . . . and that girl, Tracy . . .'

Her voice had risen to a cry. 'And . . . and . . . and you're not even there, you silly old bleeder.'

'Who's not there?'

She reeled round at the sound of the voice, her first defensive instinct to attack. In the dim light she made out the vacant, moon-shaped face of the youth, the pale features, almost totally colourless in the shadows. 'None of your business, Mad Billy Watkins. You come near me and I'll punch you right on top of your stupid nose.'

'Who's not here?' he asked again, undeterred.

'None of your business.' But her shock was abating. Mad Billy was no stranger to her. She had seen him lounging about the streets of the village for as long as she could remember. She sat looking at him, defiant.

'What you doing here anyway? It's nigh on dark.'

'I've got as much right to be in this churchyard as you have. So you can just buzz off and mind your own business.'

'I've never seen you in here before.' He was standing in front of her now, a gangling youth of about seventeen, with hands stuffed into the pockets of a jacket which he had long outgrown. 'I'd have seen you if you had been in here. I come in here all the time. Whenever I feel like it.'

'Well I'm here now. And I've got as much right to be here as you have.'

'She's not here . . . your Gran. She's dead.'

'I know.'

'I come here all the time and I've never seen her here. She's not even buried in here. I know everyone who's buried in here and your Gran's not buried in here.'

'Then why ask who I'm talking to, when you already know.'

'What's the use of talking to someone who's not here?'

'Because,' said Barbie.

'Because what?'

'Just because.'

Mad Billy stood, scuffing the dry yew needles with his feet. 'Did your Gran say she was going to be in here?'

'Yes,' said Barbie uncertainly.

'Well if she said she was going to be in here, I expect she'll turn up sooner or later.'

Barbie's sense of reasoning was taking over. 'She's dead,' she said.

'Yeah. I reckon that's what's holding her up.'

'You're mad, Mad Billy Watkins. How can she be here when she's dead?'

'Don't know.' Mad Billy shrugged his shoulders. 'But if your Gran said she was going to be here, I reckon she'll work something out. She was a good old girl, your Gran.' He lost himself in thought for a moment. 'She gave me a lump of bread pudding once. Told me not to tell me Mum.'

He took his hands from his pockets and, placing them on top of the sarcophagus, he vaulted up beside Barbie. Barbie moved over to make room. 'I haven't seen you round the village lately.'

'No,' said Barbie.

'Where you been then?'

'Wickhampton,' said Barbie.

'Oh. Big place, Wickhampton.'

Barbie heaved a sigh.

'You like it there?'

'No.'

'Wouldn't mind going to Wickhampton myself. Big place, Wickhampton. Might come and look you up one of these days.'

Barbie turned on him. 'You wouldn't dare.'

'You'd never guess the places I've been to. I've been all over the place and no one knows where I go.' Barbie looked at him disbelievingly. 'I went to London last week. Hitched a lift on a lorry all the way to London. There's lots of things in London. I went to a place and saw some ladies with big tits.'

'Mad Billy Watkins!'

'What part of Wickhampton you live then?'

'None of your business.'

'You live with your Dad. There's lots of people in this village who know where your Dad lives.'

'You mind your own business, Mad Billy Watkins.' She jumped down from the sarcophagus and turned her back on him. 'You mind your own business and leave me alone.'

'I might come next week. Have they got any places with ladies with big tits?'

'You wash your mouth out, Mad Billy Watkins.' She began to walk away from him but Mad Billy jumped down and caught up with her.

'I'd only come and say hello. Don't you want me to come and say hello?'

'No, I don't.' But even as she said it she realised that she would have welcomed the sight of someone from the village. 'I'm not going back there, anyway. Never again.'

'Where you going then?'

'I don't know. But I'm not going back there.' She walked off, making in the direction of the cottage.

'I went and had a look at your cottage the other day,' said Mad Billy. 'The door was open. Anyone could get in and look around.' Barbie quickened her pace. 'Some of the things were missing but a lot of it's just left lying about all higgledy-piggledy. Old Beattie Russell's been going in and out of there. I've seen her.' Barbie stiffened. 'She's a right old bat, that Beattie Russell. I've seen her going in and out carrying things.'

They had reached the boundary wall of the churchyard. Beyond was the lane and, opposite, the barley field and home.

'You can't stay in the cottage on your own. They don't let kids live on their own without Mums and Dads.'

Barbie began to run. Suddenly she wanted to reach the cottage, to climb into her bed and pull the sheets above her head. She was over the wall and halfway across the lane when the headlights of an approaching car fell upon her. For a moment she stood dazzled. The car squealed to a halt and she heard someone get out but she could see nothing.

'So, there you are, young lady.' The car door slammed and Mary came towards her. 'I believe that you have some explaining to do.'

Barbie turned and looked round for Mad Billy but Mad Billy Watkins was nowhere to be seen.

Chapter Seven

'I don't know what to say. I just don't know what to say.' Mary was slumped in an armchair, her face drawn and tired.

'Well she must have had a reason. Can't you think of a reason why she did it?'

'You think of a damned reason. She's your kid.'

'Well it just seems odd to me.' Ken reached for cigarettes. 'First she tears the bedroom wallpaper, then she gouges a hole in the wall.'

'You tell me why she goes round gouging damned great holes in people's walls.'

'There seems to be a pattern to it.'

'Oh, there's a pattern to it all right. The systematic destruction of my home. I must be mad. I spend years working my fingers to the bone making a decent place for the family to live and along comes some snotty-nosed kid who tears it all apart.'

'That's a bit strong, luv.' Ken held the lighted match until it burned his fingers.

'No. It's not strong. It was thanks to me that we got out of that poky little terraced house. I worked to get a decent place like this. I decorated it and I furnished it and I'm damned if I'm going to let some kid come along and treat it like a pigsty.'

Ken was out of his depth. He was beginning to regret taking Barbie in but he had had no choice. He had not reckoned with this behaviour and, even less, with Mary's reaction. Without Mary standing firm the whole family would rock and that was unthinkable. 'You'll think of some way of handling her, luv. You always do.'

'You think of a way. It's your turn.'

'Perhaps we ought to speak to that social worker.'

'No. We shall not speak to that social worker. I've told you before. If you as much as breathe one word of this to him, Ken, I shall never speak to you again.'

'Well, what are we going to do then?'

Mary picked up her knitting. 'For a start she can stay in that room for the next couple of days. If that doesn't teach her not to gouge holes in people's walls, at least it will keep her out of my sight until I've had a chance to cool off. If she crosses my path now I swear I'll strangle her.'

'She must have known she had done wrong, or she wouldn't have run away.'

'Wouldn't you run away, if you had just gouged a damned great hole in someone's wall?'

'I still don't see why she did it. Why do it on the same day that you took her to task about the bedroom wall. It doesn't make sense.' Ken shook his head and sat staring at his slippered feet.

'And have you thought what she was doing in that churchyard?'

'I don't know. How should I know what she had been doing in the churchyard.'

'In the churchyard,' repeated Mary. 'In the dark. Hasn't it occurred to you that no ordinary child would dream of going into a churchyard in the dark?'

'I don't know.' Ken shrugged and turned the thought over in his mind. 'If the old girl had been buried there . . . but she isn't. Perhaps she was just taking a short cut.'

'Through the churchyard? In the dark?'

Upstairs, Barbie lay staring at the torn wallpaper. Trapped here beside it in her bed, it had taken on a strange fascination. In the half-light she discovered patterns and shapes in its irregular outline – a witch's nose, a chimney puffing smoke, and, just out of reach, a puppy's tail. Downstairs she could hear the drone of voices. She could not hear what they said and she did not care. Her fingers wandered across the wall, searching the torn outline until they came upon a corner under which she could slide her fingernail. She lifted it, probing until she was able to peel a long, thin strip of paper from the wall. Little by little, she formed new shapes, new patterns, feeling the sensation or ripping paper tingling through her fingertips and up her arm. Inch by inch the area of destruction grew until, at last, she fell into a troubled sleep, her fingernails embedded with dry paste and powdered plaster.

Next morning, when Mary found it, she was hard pressed not to lift Barbie bodily from the bed and thrash her bottom. The fact that Barbie had again wet the bed only added to her feelings of anger and frustration.

'Go and have a bath,' she said shakily. 'I'll strip your bed.'

Barbie walked to the bathroom without a word, passing Tracy who stood listening, swinging her teddy bear by the leg.

When she returned to her room she found her bed stripped, the window flung wide, and her breakfast on the bedside table. She chewed and swallowed on the food without tasting it, while, through the dense fog of her mind, she pondered on the possibility that she would be sent to Holly Lodge. The fog cushioned the dread but still the sharp corners of fear pricked at her consciousness. It was enough to send her down the stairs to Mary.

'Aunty "M".'

Mary turned sharply, about to order her back to her room.

'I'm sorry, Aunty "M".'

Mary sucked in her breath and stood looking at her.

'I'm very, very sorry. I'll never do it again.'

She expelled the indrawn breath. 'Oh Barbie,' she said. 'What am I going to do with you?'

Barbie looked at her, dull-eyed. 'I'm sorry,' she whispered again.

Mary lowered herself to her knees and held Barbie's face between her hands. 'Oh Barbie, Barbie,' she said. 'Can you *please* just try.'

She dropped her hands and looked away as the now familiar taunt impressed itself upon her mind – the chin, the nose; and it was something about the way she moved.

'I'll try, Aunty "M". I'll try.'

Mary summoned up all her resources of control. 'I'll try too, Barbie,' she said. 'God help me, I'll try.'

Barbie gave her a wan smile and stepped away.

She was not sent back to her room but wandered instead into the garden. She sat for a while on the front lawn, then sauntered aimlessly down the street.

By the time she reached the corner, she was not looking where she was going. She was concentrating instead upon the cracks between the paving stones. Once or twice she misjudged her step, wobbled and almost overbalanced onto a crack, which was no longer a crack, but instead a cobra, black, sinister, lying in wait for her misguided feet.

'What you doing then?'

She looked up and her stomach appeared both to rise and to fall at the same moment. Mad Billy was leaning against the lamp-post.

'What you doing here, Mad Billy Watkins?' She raked her eyes up and down the street and across the windows of number fifteen but there was no sign of Mary, nor of Mark nor Tracy. 'You've got no business coming round here.'

'Came to see you, didn't I.' Mad Billy leaned nonchalantly against the lamp-post, hands in pockets. 'Told you I'd come.'

'Well you've got no right.' Barbie was in a panic, her eyes looking this way and that, the fingers of both hands opening and closing over the palms. 'You just go away and leave me alone.'

'OK. If that's what you want.' He shrugged his shoulders and moved off.

'No – wait.' Barbie watched him go and changed her mind. 'This way,' she called, and began to run for the park.

Mad Billy turned to join her, tailing on behind, breathless and complaining. Several times she looked over her shoulder for him but she did not slow her pace. She was a good distance ahead of him by the time she reached the park and crawled beneath the weeping willow tree, leaning back against the trunk waiting for him.

'What you run for?' He crawled in beside her and sprawled out on the grass, panting and holding his ribs.

'Because.'

'You're mad.'

'No I'm not.'

'What you run for, then?'

'I told you. Because.'

He gave up talking and wheezed in silence.

'Why do cows wear bells round their necks?' he asked suddenly.

'I don't know.' She looked at him bewildered.

'Because their horns don't work.'

'You're mad, Mad Billy Watkins. And, anyway, I heard it before.'

'Want to hear another one?'

She nodded.

'What do you get if you drop a piano down a mine shaft?'

'I don't know. What do you get if you drop a piano down a mine shaft?'

'A flat miner.'

She laughed at that and sat waiting for the next.

'What's white and blue, and falls out of trees?'

'I don't know. What is white and blue, and falls out of trees?'

'A fridge in a denim jacket.'

'That doesn't make sense.'

'I lied about it falling out of a tree.'

She laughed again, but, this time, to her surprise, she found that she could not stop. She giggled and squirmed, rolling about holding her sides in a paroxysm of laughter, as tension transformed itself into an explosion of hysteria.

Mad Billy was pleased. He was not used to such a response. 'Do you want to hear another one?'

But Barbie was not listening. There were tears mixed with the laughter and she had forgotten the joke.

'I heard this good one on the telly.'

She did not respond. The tears had taken over now and she was sobbing uncontrollably.

He waited until she lay drained and panting into the soil and then began again. 'Why can't a bike stand up by itself?'

He looked towards her and waited in vain.

'Because it's two tyred,' he finished.

But still Barbie lay on her stomach, her face pressed into the soil.

'Knock, knock . . . This is Justin . . .'

He gave up and sat staring at the sparse patches of grass beneath the umbrella of the tree.

Barbie jumped as he touched her on the shoulder and flinched as he thrust a worm before her face.

'You stop that, Mad Billy Watkins,' she responded. 'You leave that poor little worm alone.' She took it from him, cradling it in her hands, before releasing it onto the moist turf. 'And you can't frighten me with worms. I've played with more worms than you've had hot dinners.'

He grinned, admitting that his jape had failed, and settled back against the trunk of the tree. 'Shove over.' With an easy, unthinking gesture he placed his arm about her. She moved and, with an equally unthinking gesture, made herself comfortable against him.

'There was this bloke who worked in a factory with my Dad.'

'Your Dad doesn't work in a factory,' she responded easily.

'Don't be daft. It's part of the story.'

'Oh,' said Barbie.

'Well, this bloke was working on a machine and he cut all his fingers off, see.' Barbie screwed her nose in distaste. 'So he rushes off to the hospital and told the doctor. And the doctor said, "Why didn't you bring your fingers with you 'cause then I could have sewed them back on." And the bloke, he says, "Well I tried to, Doctor, but I couldn't pick them up!"'

'Ugh! You're disgusting, Mad Billy Watkins.' But this time the laughter came easily and naturally. 'You shouldn't tell stories about people hurting themselves. It's not nice.'

'Then why are you laughing, if it's not nice?'

'If you didn't tell it, then I wouldn't have to laugh,' she bickered amiably.

The air was warm but fresh from recent rain and the scent of nicotianas hung in the air.

'Have you seen your Gran?' Barbie stiffened slightly and he increased the pressure of his arm.

'No,' she said dully. 'She's dead.'

'But she said she'd come.'

Barbie sighed heavily and closed her eyes. 'She's dead,' she said again.

'I've been thinking. If your Gran's not buried in the church-yard, where is she?'

'Aunty Beattie's got her. In an urn.'

Mad Billy turned sharply and looked at her. 'What's she got her for? What's it got to do with her?'

'I don't know. She's just got her.'

'Maybe that's why she didn't turn up. Because that old bat's got her.'

'I don't know,' sighed Barbie. 'But she belongs to me.' The tears welled and began to fall. Mad Billy put his other arm about her and cuddled her close. He made no comment on the tears, merely offering comfort without demand for words. Barbie buried her face in his shoulder and wept. It seemed the natural thing to do.

'I'll have to go now,' she said at last, pulling away. 'Aunty "M" will be cross.' She overcame his slight reluctance to release her and stood up. 'I don't like it when she gets cross.'

'I'll see you,' said Mad Billy. 'I'll meet you here next Saturday.'

Barbie walked off without acknowledging the arrangement but then retraced her steps. 'I can't,' she said. 'Not Saturday. I'm going to the village to see Bess.'

Mad Billy shrugged. 'OK. I'll see you in the churchyard.'

As she turned the corner into Wansdyke Avenue Barbie's heart faltered. Larry Ogilvie's car was parked outside number fifteen. She went in by the back door and moved quietly through the kitchen. The sound of voices drifted out from the lounge.

'She was upset by the funeral, of course.' It was Mary's voice, an unnatural, crackling quality about it. 'But apart from that, everything's fine.'

Barbie stopped and listened. Any moment now Mary was going to mention wallpaper . . . stairs . . . running away . . . wet beds . . .

'No signs of disturbance? Difficult behaviour?'

'No.'

There was the sound of rattling teacups followed by Larry Ogilvie's voice. 'I'd feel a lot easier if she showed some outward sign of grief.'

'Well of course she's upset about her grandmother. It's only natural, isn't it?'

'But she hasn't given you any reason to think that she's unduly upset? No unusual behaviour?'

'No. She's settling down very well, given time.'

Barbie did not understand and she did not want to. She began to climb the stairs to her room.

'Is that you, Barbie?' Barbie stopped, her fingers tracing the line of the scar on the wall. 'Would you come down here, please.'

'I'll go up and see her in her room.' The nearing of Larry Ogilvie's voice indicated that he was approaching the door into the hall.

'No.' Mary's response was a little too quick and sharp. 'I'll call her down.'

But Larry Ogilvie had already opened the door. 'Hello Barbie.' At the same moment his eyes were level with the wall. 'Oh dear,' he said. 'Somebody had an accident?'

'Afraid so.' A slight colour rose across Mary's neck but Larry Ogilvie's back was turned towards her. 'We were carrying something up the stairs.'

Barbie inwardly shook herself.

'Oh dear. I bet the air turned blue.'

Mary laughed an unnatural laugh. 'I nearly murdered Ken. He's always so clumsy.'

'Shall we go to your room, Barbie?'

'No.' Again Mary's response was a little too quick. 'I haven't tidied it yet.'

'That doesn't matter. I don't mind.' He took a step into the hall.

'No. Take Mr Ogilvie into the lounge, Barbie. It's more comfortable. I'll be in the kitchen if you need me.' She shot Barbie a glance which Barbie did not understand.

'How's things, Barbie?' Larry Ogilvie settled back into his chair and crossed his legs. His jeans were faded and his T-shirt carried an anti-nuclear slogan. Barbie perched on the edge of the chair. 'What have you been getting up to recently? Anything interesting?'

'Not much.'

'Well, how do you spend your time? Who do you play with?'

'Just mucking about.'

'Where?'

'Down in the park . . .' She regretted mentioning the park, it was her private place. She did not wish to share it with Larry Ogilvie.

'That's nice. You mean the park in Fenton Street – the one with lots of swings and slides?'

'No,' said Barbie quietly. 'The one with flowers.'

'Oh, the garden. What do you do with yourself in there?'

'Nothing much,' said Barbie. 'Just sit.'

Larry Ogilvie looked at her for a moment. 'Have you made any friends yet, Barbie?'

Barbie looked at him flatly. 'Yes,' she lied. 'Hundreds of them.' And Larry Ogilvie smiled.

'I hear that your father is taking you back to the village on Saturday to see Bess.'

Barbie nodded and for the first time her face showed some animation. 'I can't wait for Saturday.'

'What will you do? Take her for a walk?'

'Yes.' Barbie chewed her lip and thought. 'We'll go through the

131

copse and across the barley field. And I've got to go and see how the lambs are getting on.'

'You're missing home, Barbie.'

Barbie said nothing and Larry Ogilvie watched her drawing down the curtains of her mind.

On Saturday morning a letter lay beside Barbie's plate at the breakfast table. 'There's a letter for you, Barbie,' said Mary, obviously curious. 'It's from Derbyshire.' Barbie did not know anyone in Derbyshire but the handwriting was familiar. She opened it and read it. It was from Miss Beckworth.

Dear Barbie,

How are you? I think of you often and hope that you are settling in with your family.

I am writing this letter from Derbyshire. My mother is ill and she needs me here to look after her. She is going to need me for a long time so I have to give up my job and my room in the village so that I can be with her.

Barbie, I cannot keep my promise to meet you when you go to the village to visit Bess but I should like to keep in touch. We could write to one another and perhaps you could come and stay with me for holidays sometimes. Wouldn't that be fun? The countryside is lovely around here – just right for bike rides. There is a skylark singing at this very moment and the buddleia shrub is festooned with butterflies. I should love you to see it.

Just before I left the village Mrs Matthews' cat had kittens – such cute little things with tight shut eyes and squeaky voices. Tommy Jenkins fell off his bike and broke his leg. Poor Tommy. His leg is in plaster but he is asking everyone to autograph it.

How are you, Barbie? I do hope you are well. If you want to keep in touch with me just reply to this letter, then I shall know. Just a few short lines will tell me that you are well and that you wish to keep in touch.

Until then Barbie I remain, your friend,

Gloria Beckworth

Barbie took the letter to her room and re-read it three times before she tore it into shreds and threw it into the dustbin.

'Who was it from?' asked Mary.

'Miss Beckworth.'

'Oh,' said Mary. 'Who's Miss Beckworth?'

'My teacher.'

'Oh,' said Mary again. She looked across at Barbie, realising she was going to get nothing more from her, then she looked at Ken and shook her head despairingly. The child was so secretive; she shared nothing. She pondered for a moment on the advisability of opening future letters before handing them to Barbie. She was uncomfortable with the thought and put it off until the occasion arose.

Barbie said nothing more until she was in the car with Ken on their way to the village. 'How far is Derbyshire?'

Ken pursed his lips. 'Don't know,' he said. 'It must be about a hundred and thirty miles, at least.' He turned and looked at her. 'Why? Are you thinking of taking a trip?'

'No,' said Barbie. 'It's not important.'

Ken dropped her off at Mr Smethurst's farm gate. 'I'll be back in an hour,' he called. 'Wait for me here.'

She walked the first few steps then took to her heels and ran. In the distance, in the shade of the barn, she could make out the outline of Bess lying in the grass. 'Bessy!' Bess looked up from where she lay, clambered heavily into a sitting position, and cocked her ear. 'Bessy, it's me.' Tears ran salty into her mouth as she raced along the rutted track. The old dog rose heavily to her feet and waddled towards Barbie, her tail wagging as rapidly as the folds of fat flesh would allow.

'Oh, Bessy.' Barbie fell to her knees and buried her face within the soft, warm coat. As she did so, Bess turned and licked her ear. 'I don't need a wash.' The tears were mixed with laughter. The old dog licked enthusiastically and quivered with joy.

Mr Smethurst looked on and smiled. 'Reckon she be right pleased to see you,' he said. 'Her's been looking forward to this day.'

Barbie hugged Bess tight about the neck. 'Have you been a good girl?'

'Good as gold, she been, Miss Barbie. Reckon you be right proud to know how good she been.'

'Oh Bess, you're a good girl. Such a good, good girl.'

'Missus is doing some baking up in the kitchen,' commented Mr Smethurst. 'Reckon she got some jam tarts waiting to be eaten.'

But Barbie had need to be alone with Bess. She stood up and

took Bess lightly by the collar. 'Can I go for a walk, please,' she said. 'With Bess.'

'Course you can, me dear. Jam tarts'll still be here when you get back.'

She made off through the south pasture sending sheep scattering in all direction. 'Scaredy custards,' she called. 'Scared of your own shadows.' She reached out for a lamb as it fled from her path but she missed and it ran bleating to its mother. 'Scaredy old thing,' she laughed. 'I'm not going to hurt you.'

High up in the sky a lark was singing. Barbie turned her eyes towards the heavens, tracing the sound across the tattered wisps of cloud until she found it, a tiny speck against a vast backcloth of blue. For a fleeting moment she wondered if Gran were up there somewhere far beyond the blue expanse but, almost before the thought had formed, she had blanked it from her mind.

There was a lightness to her step as she skipped across the meadow. 'Come on, Bess. Let's go to the cottage.' The sun was high with a stiff breeze which sent the wisps of cloud scudding across the sky. She did not think about Mad Billy until she passed the churchyard wall. She thought of him only then because she caught sight of movement beneath the yew tree. She joined him as he stood beside the sarcophagus, grinning broadly, with his hands held behind his back.

'What have you got there?' she asked, for he was obviously hiding something.

'A surprise.'

'What sort of surprise?' She leaned to one side, trying to peer round behind him, but he dodged away, enjoying the game.

'A special surprise.'

Barbie shrugged, feigning indifference. 'I don't care. If you don't want to show me I'll go and do something else.'

Mad Billy stopped retreating and took a step towards her. 'Close your eyes,' he said. 'And don't open them until I tell you.'

Barbie closed her eyes and waited.

'Now,' he said and when Barbie opened her eyes he was holding out before him . . . an urn.

'Oh! Mad Billy!'

'I told you it was a surprise.'

She clutched out towards the urn but immediately drew back. 'Where d'you get it?'

'I found it.'

'Oh Mad Billy, you stole it.'

'No, I didn't.'

'Yes you did. You stole it.'

Mad Billy shuffled his feet. 'Well, it wasn't hers, silly old bat.'

'Oh, Mad Billy.'

'Besides, she shouldn't go leaving it lying about where people can find it.'

Barbie's fingers ached to take hold of it.

'Don't you want it then?' He held it out towards her but still she held back. 'I got it for you, special.'

'Yes,' whispered Barbie. She took it from him and held it cradled against her chest. 'Thank you.'

'Are you pleased? It's a surprise.'

'Thank you,' she said again. 'Thank you very much.'

Mad Billy grinned, well pleased. He sauntered over to lean against the sarcophagus. 'I got this good story,' he said. 'It's about an Englishman, a Scotsman and an Irishman . . .'

'I've got to go now.'

She saw the look of disappointment on his face. 'I thought you'd be pleased.'

'I am.' She looked at his crestfallen face but longed to be alone with the urn. 'But I've got to go.'

'It was a surprise.'

She walked up to him and kissed him lightly on the cheek. 'Thank you,' she said. 'Thank you very much.' Then she turned and ran, calling Bess to accompany her. Mad Billy watched her go then turned and kicked the stone sarcophagus.

Barbie ran all the way to the cottage but she was hampered by Bess' lack of speed and was impatient when she had to stop and watch the slow progress of the old dog as she waddled behind. Eventually, knowing that Bess would find her own way to the cottage, she left her behind and did not stop until she had threaded her way through the tangled vegetation to the hidey-hole at the bottom of the garden. She drew down the hop vine curtain and sat with the urn resting on her knee.

'Gran . . . ?' She ran her fingers lightly across the lid of the urn. 'Is that you?'

In the walnut tree a blackbird sang and across the barley field she heard the squawk of a pheasant signalling the approach of Bess. The stiff breeze ruffled the seed heads of the thistles, bearing them away on minute parachutes.

'I love you, Gran.'

The urn was made of unvarnished beechwood, oblong in shape, some six inches by three and it was undecorated except for the slightly bevelled edge of the lid.

'Are you there?' There was no sound but for the sounds of the garden, no presence but the presence of its living inhabitants. The breeze disturbed the hop vine curtain and a beetle scuttled across the dry soil at her feet.

'I need you, Gran.'

Through the tangle of vegetation she could see the vegetable patch, the remaining lettuces going to seed, and, lying on its side, was Gran's weeding stool.

'I'm here, Gran, I'm over here.'

Bess arrived and flopped down at Barbie's feet, her tongue lolling from the side of her mouth. Barbie held out the urn before her nose inviting her to smell it but Bess gave it a perfunctory sniff and settled down to sleep.

The lid was secured by four small screws. Barbie slotted her fingernail into one of the screws, attempting to turn it but succeeded only in hurting her nail. She put it to her mouth and sucked. Then she thought of the coins which she carried in her pocket and selected one which she used to remove all four screws, setting them down carefully at her side.

Slowly and carefully, she removed the lid, setting it down beside the screws. Inside was a plastic bag filled with ash. She looked at it and her stomach contracted with an undefined disappointment. She had known that it would contain ash yet when she saw it she knew only disappointment. She opened the bag and touched the ash with the tip of her finger.

'Gran . . . ? Is that you?'

She emptied the contents into the body of the urn and picked up a pinch of it, rubbing it between her fingertips, feeling it disintegrate to powder.

This was not Gran.

She picked up another handful, letting it trickle back into the urn, then turned her hand, palm uppermost, studying the grey dust on her skin.

'Oh, Gran; you liar.'

Gran was not here. She never would be here.

'You liar. You bleeding, stinking, filthy liar.'

She took the urn and hurled it from her, sending it hurtling through the hop vine curtain, scattering its contents across the garden. She launched herself after it, stamping the ash into the soil where it lay.

'You liar. You bleeding, bleeding, bleeding liar.'

The breeze whipped through the undergrowth, sending the remaining ash to whirl across the garden, dissipating it into a mist of fine particles.

'You bleeding liar.' She watched it as the ash cloud spread and, too late, realised what she had done.

'Oh, God!'

She clutched at it as it was whirled away, grabbing frantically at pale grey flakes which disintegrated to dust within her hands, clutched madly, vainly, retrieving nothing as the last flakes fluttered down, filtering through the tall grasses to be dissolved in dense undergrowth still damp from an early shower.

'Oh God. What have I done?'

One last flake fluttered to settle upon the nose of Bess who shook her head and snorted it away. There was nothing left but a discoloration of the soil beneath her feet.

'Oh Gran, oh Gran. What have I done?' She sank to the ground and held the empty urn in her hands.

'Barbie! Barbie, where are you?' She shot to her feet as Ken's voice echoed out across the garden. In a daze she scrabbled in the dry soil beneath the hedge and hid the urn in a shallow grave.

Ken was thrashing his way through the undergrowth. 'Where have you been? I told you to meet me in an hour.' He stopped short when he saw her face. 'What's the matter? You look as if you've seen a ghost.'

'No,' she said quietly. 'There was no one there.'

He looked at her puzzled. 'Come on,' he said. 'We're late for lunch.'

She sat in silence in the car and as they turned the corner into Wansdyke Avenue saw a police car draw away from number fifteen. Mary stood ashen-faced at the door and Barbie overheard snatches of the ensuing conversation. 'Stolen . . . Mrs Russell . . . Friday evening'. She lowered her eyes and slipped quietly to her room.

'What did you tell them?' Ken paced the kitchen floor rattling his car keys.

'The truth. What else could I tell them.' Mary was visibly

unnerved. 'She was here all Friday evening. She couldn't possibly have gone to Aylesborough.'

'What an awful thing.'

'It's positively ghoulish. I've never heard of anything so awful in my life.'

'But who on earth would do a thing like that? Why steal the ashes of a dead woman?'

'I don't know. I just thank God it couldn't have been Barbie.'

'Christ! I wonder about the mentality of some people.'

'We'd better make sure that Barbie doesn't get to hear about it. I can just imagine the trouble we'll have with her if she finds out.'

'I don't see how we can. It's bound to be reported in the newspapers. It's just the kind of thing they like.'

'Then we shall have to keep them away from her for a while. I'm not taking the risk of having even more trouble from her.'

Ken paced in silence and Mary returned to the salad she had been preparing.

'Ken . . . ?'

'What?'

'You don't think she could have had anything to do with it?'

'Of course she couldn't. You said yourself she was here all evening.'

'I know; but . . .'

'But what? Come on, luv; Barbie wouldn't do a terrible thing like that. She's not the sort.'

'I just wish that I could be so sure.'

Ken sat down at the kitchen table and ran his hand through his hair. 'I know she does things which are hard to figure out . . .' He thought of her face in the garden. She was, indeed, a strange, unfathomable child. 'But she would never do a thing like that.'

Upstairs, Barbie fingered the photograph of Gran on the bedside table. She was truly gone now, the last of her blown away by the wind, but at least it was the wind which blew across the garden.

Later, when she undressed at night, she found one flake of ash caught in a fold of her sock. She took it carefully in the palm of her hand and transferred it to a piece of tissue paper which she folded neatly and placed at the back of a drawer.

The next time Barbie went to the park she found Mad Billy waiting for her beneath the weeping willow tree. He was there again a few days later and in the ensuing weeks they spent a good deal of time together. Barbie took it for granted that at least two or three times each week she would find him sitting there, waiting. They rarely left the park together but would sit for hours beneath the tree telling jokes or drifting off into long companionable silences. As the weeks passed they became firm friends and together they passed away the days of August which, in turn, were replaced by the sharp clear days of early September. Mad Billy was good for her. He asked no questions, made no demands, and by his very presence he soothed the pain. It was no less evident, but the edges were slowly planed down to settle like a heavy weight beneath the laughter.

Barbie knew that within a week she must face the ordeal of settling into a new school but for the moment she closed her mind to thoughts of tomorrow and thought only of today. As she entered the park she was met by the scent of dahlias, the musky smells which come with autumn. Autumn had always been a favourite season for Barbie, with beech trees turning to every shade of amber and brown, gardens filled with chrysanthemums and michaelmas daisies, golden rod, and the elder hedge hanging low with berries. Yet, this year, as she entered the park she caught that faint foretaste of oncoming decay, vibrations of approaching winter, trapped here within the confines of the town.

A gardener was hoeing the flowerbed just inside the gate. He watched her as she made her way across the park and disappeared beneath the curtain of leaves. He saw, too, Mad Billy enter the park half an hour later and make his way in the same direction. The gardener leaned on his hoe and watched Mad Billy as he glanced in all directions before diving beneath the cover of the tree.

Mad Billy flopped down and settled himself comfortably against Barbie. 'Knock, knock.'

'Who's there?'

'Arthur.'

'Arthur who?'

''alf a minute and I'll go and find out.'

'That's one's as old as the hills, Mad Billy Watkins.'

Mad Billy grinned. 'That's only for starters. I heard this good one on the telly last night . . .' And so began his patter of the day.

Barbie felt relaxed, protected from the world by the curtain of leaves. She eased herself forward to allow Mad Billy to place his arm about her and she leaned against him, a warm, conforting presence.

'There was this bloke who wanted to go to America, see; but he didn't have any money.'

'What did he want to go to America for?'

'I don't know. That's not part of the joke.'

'Oh.'

'Well, this bloke; he decided to stow away on a big ship. So he bought himself a long, green overcoat . . .'

As Barbie listened an ant crossed the dry soil beside her and travelled along the hem of her dress.

'. . . He put on the long, green overcoat and went down to the place where they keep the ships . . .'

Barbie was not aware of the ant until it left her dress and transferred itself to her leg. She twitched as she felt movement across the bare flesh of her thigh and moved, inadvertantly trapping it beneath her.

'. . . He put his suitcase on his head and he went to see the bloke who was in charge . . .'

'Ouch!'

'What's the matter?'

'An ant. It bit my leg.'

'Where?' He leaned across her. 'Let me have a look.'

Barbie raised her skirt to her thigh. 'Here,' she said. 'Under my knicker elastic.'

A small red spot was visible on the pale flesh. Mad Billy stroked it with his finger. 'Does it hurt?'

It was at this moment that the willow curtain parted and both looked up into the faces of the gardener and a policeman.

There followed a sequence of events which Barbie found totally confusing. Accusations were made which she did not under-stand. Mad Billy was truculent, aggressive, as she had never seen him before.

They were taken eventually to the police station, Mad Billy to one room, she to another. Mary was summoned and she sat tight-lipped beside Barbie as they waited to be interviewed.

Barbie sat on the edge of her chair, her senses reeling, and looked into the face of the policewoman before her.

'Did he interfere with you, Barbie?'

140

The policewoman's expression was kindly but Barbie did not trust her. She did not reply.

'Do you understand what I mean?'

Barbie looked at her blankly.

'Did he touch your private parts?'

Barbie turned on her, shocked.

'He was seen to be handling your knickers.'

She shook her head in stunned disbelief. 'He didn't.'

Mary moved suddenly in her chair, causing Barbie to jump. 'They saw you,' she said.

'Would you leave it to me, please, Mrs Radlett.'

Mary gave an uncomfortable swallowing sound in her throat and fell silent.

'You say he didn't interfere with you in any way?'

'No.'

The two women exchanged glances and Mary made as if to speak again but the policewoman silenced her with a gesture of her hand. 'Have you met him before, Barbie? On other occasions, before today?'

Barbie bit her lip. The policewoman waited for what seemed an interminable time.

'Well; did you?' demanded Mary.

Barbie closed her eyes.

'How many times?' The policewoman's voice was in marked contrast to Mary's.

Barbie shrugged.

'Three times? Four times?' She waited again for Barbie, then said, 'More than that?'

Barbie shrugged again.

'Oh, God!' Mary placed a hand to her forehead. Her fears for the future had been realised today.

'Please, Mrs Radlett.' She turned again to Barbie. 'Has he ever done this sort of thing to you before?'

'What sort of thing?'

Mary made a choking sound in her throat and brought down her hand against her chair. 'Damn it, Barbie; you were seen. How the hell can you deny it?'

'Please, Mrs Radlett.' The policewoman's voice rose sharply, then resumed its pitch. 'This is not going to help.'

'Well, she was not exactly fighting him off.'

'Look, I know how difficult this must be for you. But this sort of

141

attitude is not going to get us anywhere.' She left a moment of silence. 'Would you like to go and have a cup of tea, or something?'

'No.' Mary fought for composure. 'I'm sorry.' She folded her hands in her lap and swallowed. At all costs she must keep control.

'Now, Barbie. Listen to me very carefully. There's no need for you to be afraid. We know all about Billy Watkins. He has done this sort of thing before, several times.'

'Oh God!'

'All you have to do is tell us what he did and leave the rest to us.'

Mary thought that she might faint. She gripped her hands together and took three long, deep breaths. She thought again of Mark.

'Are you all right, Mrs Radlett?'

'Yes, I'm quite all right.'

'Do you understand, Barbie?'

On the shelf above the policewoman's right shoulder was a sheaf of papers which fluttered slightly in the breeze from an open window. Barbie fixed her eyes on them, watching as the corners lifted, and wondered how long it would take before they all came fluttering to the floor. If the breeze were to blow just a little stronger they would all come cascading down about their feet.

'Barbie . . . ?'

'Pay attention when you're being spoken to.'

'What . . . ?'

'Are you listening?'

'She never listens.'

'Barbie, I was just saying . . .'

The door opened and a young policeman stepped inside. 'Doctor's here,' he said and closed it again.

'Oh, right. We'll come straight away.' The policewoman turned to Mary. 'We need to have her examined,' she said. 'You understand?'

Mary nodded, tight-lipped. 'Do what you have to.'

'We'll come back and finish our talk later, Barbie. There's no need to be afraid of Dr Griffiths.' She explained what was about to happen but Barbie did not take it in.

She was taken to another room where the doctor waited. He

was a tall man with dark, partly greying hair. He had been called from the golf course and wore an open-necked shirt and slacks.

'Hello Barbie. I'm Dr Griffiths.'

In the corner of the room was a small handbasin and, against the wall, a hard examination couch, unholstered in brown vinyl.

'Have they explained to you what I am going to do?'

Barbie bit her lip.

'It's nothing to worry about. I just want to take a look at you.'

Barbie allowed herself to be led to the examination couch and submitted to the preliminary examination. Dr Griffiths handled her gently but Barbie was confused. She had no need to be examined. She was not ill. To one side Mary sat on a hard-backed chair, her nerves stretched taut. Barbie was aware of her every movement and jumped each time she made the strange clicking sound in her throat as she swallowed.

Dr Griffiths spoke to her all the time, reassuring her, but Barbie's tension mounted and when he came to the lower parts of her body, control snapped. 'You leave my bum alone.'

'Barbie!' Mary jumped from her chair.

'It's all right, Mrs Radlett.' Dr Griffiths laid a gentle hand on Barbie's leg but Barbie threw him off.

'There's nothing wrong with my bum.'

'I just want to take a look at it.'

'Well, you're not going to.' She hit out and caught him a blow across the side of his face. He let out a slight exclamation of surprise and Barbie went for him like an animal. She kicked, and bit, and clawed her way to the corner of the room, holding all at bay.

'Barbie!' shrieked Mary. 'Behave yourself.' But Dr Griffiths signalled her to be quiet. He drew a chair across the room and set it down a short distance from the corner in which Barbie was crouching. He sat down and crossed his legs.

'Our Gran was right.'

'How's that?'

'You're all the same, you doctors. There's nothing wrong with my bum.'

'I'm afraid her grandmother didn't approve of doctors,' put in Mary, embarrassed.

'So I see.' He settled himself more comfortably in the chair. 'He's a friend of mine, Dr Poulson,' he said.

143

Barbie eyed him warily, responding slightly to the mention of a familiar name.

'You must have been a patient of his before you came to Wickhampton.'

She nodded almost imperceptibly.

'He's got a little donkey, I remember. Keeps it in the orchard behind his house. Nice little thing. Brown and white with a touch of grey on his belly. Ever seen it?' Barbie had, often. 'Likes to stand at the gate and beg for food. Particularly fond of currant cake if I remember rightly. Can't think of his name. Now, what was it . . . ?'

'Dinky.'

'Oh, that's right. Dinky. Nice little fellow but much too fat.' He smiled at her. 'Comes from eating too much currant cake.'

He talked to her for twenty minutes, gradually bringing round the conversation to the purpose of the examination, explaining again what he intended to do.

'But he didn't do anything.'

'Good. I'm very glad to hear it. You let me have a look at you and I'll be the first to say that I can't find anything, if there's nothing to be seen.'

'It wasn't his fault the ant bit me.'

'Oh? What ant was that?'

'The flying sort, with wings.'

'Mm,' he said. 'Nasty things, ants.'

'No, they're not. The ant didn't know.'

'Better let me have a look at it just the same. Ant bites can cause a bit of a problem sometimes.'

Little by little, Barbie relinquished her defensive posture. 'Come on. Then you can have a nice warm drink and something to make you feel better.' Gradually she unravelled her limbs and gave herself up to persuasion.

Much later that afternoon after Barbie had been put to bed in her room, she heard the murmur of voices in the hall below as Larry Ogilvie was ushered into the lounge. Ken was home, having been summoned from his office.

'Unpleasant business.' Larry Ogilvie settled himself into the chair. 'Have you any idea why Billy Watkins followed Barbie here?'

Ken shook his head. 'We had no idea she was seeing him.'

Mary remained unusually quiet. Larry Ogilvie noted the fact

but did not comment upon it. 'I understand that it's been going on for weeks,' he said and saw her stiffen.

Ken fumbled for cigarettes. 'My wife tells me this lad is well known to the police. That he's done this kind of thing before.'

'So I believe.' Larry Ogilvie was immediately on his guard. He was under obligation at all times to safeguard the confidentiality of the Department's clients.

'And under the supervision of the Local Authority,' pursued Ken.

'So I believe.'

'Well, is he? Or isn't he?'

'He's known to Miss Standish. I confirmed it with her this afternoon.'

'Then why the hell is he allowed to come round here molesting children?'

'I said he was under supervision. I didn't say he was under constant surveillance twenty-four hours a day.'

Ken's hackles rose. 'That's no bloody answer. He ought to have been locked up.'

'I'm sure we should need to know all the facts before we could come to a conclusion like that.'

Ken looked at him sideways. 'Well, it's not good enough. Something's got to be done now.'

'It's difficult to know what we can do under the circumstances. Barbie denies that she was assaulted.'

'They were seen,' countered Mary. 'By a policeman.'

'He was seen touching her leg. Barbie says she was bitten by an ant. That hardly constitutes an indecent assault.'

'What do you want?' she said. 'To catch them in the very act?' She stopped short, embarrassed by her own words.

'It has been a heavy day,' he sympathised and let the comment pass. 'There's no medical evidence and Barbie denies assault. You can't take someone to Court without evidence.'

'Well, surely you're not going to take her word for it,' said Mary. 'She's hardly likely to own up.'

Larry Ogilvie raised one eyebrow. 'There's no reason whatever to suspect that Barbie had any intention of indulging in indecent behaviour. Everything points to the fact that she is totally confused by the whole affair.'

'It still remains that they were seen.'

'Tell me, Mrs Radlett,' he said quietly. 'Would you take that same line if it were Tracy who had been seen?'

'Tracy,' she said, turning on him, 'would not have been found, hiding under a tree with some mentally deficient youth.'

'But you think Barbie's different?'

'She's her mother's child.' Mary bit her lip and wished that she could retract the comment.

Larry Ogilvie hesitated and looked at her for a moment. 'I think we ought to have a talk when this is all over.'

'I'm sorry.' She pulled herself together with a visible effort. 'I didn't mean that. I'm a bit overwrought. It's the tension of the day.'

'I still think we should have a talk.'

'You still haven't told us what you're going to do,' interrupted Ken. 'If you're not going to lock him up out of harm's way, what are you going to do?'

'There's no question of locking him up; but we can see to it that he doesn't come near Barbie again.'

The assurance brought an audible break to the tension. 'Well, that's something,' acknowledged Ken. 'At least we can all sleep more easily in our beds.'

'We can make it clear to him that he's not to come to Wickhampton.'

'I shall expect you to guarantee that.' Mary drew herself up and leaned forward in her chair towards Larry Ogilvie. 'You will see to it that he never comes near this area again. If I so much as lay eyes on him, I shall ring the police and complain.'

Ken nodded in agreement.

'And, as an added precaution,' she went on, 'from this moment, the park is out of bounds to Barbie. She can play in the house, or on the street where I can see her, but she will never, *never*, go near that park again.'

Upstairs, Barbie lay sedated into a state where she did not know whether she was sleeping or awake. Disjointed thoughts passed like dreams across her mind and faded so that she could not reach out to grasp them.

. . . Bess lying sleeping in the sun beside the cottage door, eyes twitching as she dreamed of rabbits.

'Bloody rabbits!'

The curtains were drawn across the window, throwing the room into dim pools of shadow. Downstairs she could still hear the murmur of voices. Beside her, she could make out the outline of the torn wallpaper – a clown's boot, a teapot, a dog's hind leg. 'Oh, Bessy.'

The cottage. The broken tread on the seventh stair. Sights and sounds and smells of home. Mrs Matthews at the corner shop. 'Half a pound of cheddar, was it dear? Lovely piece of cheddar. Nice and fresh.'

Mr Smethurst's old brown dog.

'Oh Bessy, Bessy. I miss you Bess.'

Miss Beckworth. Cream meringues and bike rides by the river. Dear Miss Beckworth. But Barbie had torn up the letter.

She didn't care. She didn't care that Miss Beckworth had gone away.

'Knock, knock.'

'Who's there?'

'Mad Billy's here.'

But he's not here. Mad Billy, too, had gone away.

They all had gone away.

What did she care.

'Gran; oh, Gran. Why did you go away, with no goodbye?'

She reached for the gorilla and lay staring at the torn wallpaper – torn pink roses. It would have been easier if she could cry.

PART TWO

Five Years Later

Chapter Eight

'Please, Barbie, be a sport.' Mark put on his most appealing smile. 'I'm only asking you to a party. Girls are supposed to enjoy parties.'

'If they're all so keen to go, why not ask one of them.' Barbie shrugged him off but Mark was persistent.

'Because I promised Simon that I'd take you.'

At fifteen, Barbie had become something of an enigma. Aloof, always on the edge of the crowd, allowing no one to enter the inner sanctum of her real self, she was a mystery which many a young man would have paid dearly to solve.

'I don't like parties. I wouldn't know what to say.'

The child had blossomed into a young woman of outstanding beauty, her fine features framed by the halo of red-gold hair. Her beauty, coupled with her inaccessibility, acted like a magnet.

'You don't have to say anything. The way Simon turns up the volume on his hi-fi they'd never hear you anyway.' He looked at her knowing that his efforts at persuasion were falling on deaf ears. 'Come on, Barbie. You know all the guys down there fancy you like crazy.'

He knew at once that it was the wrong thing to say. He had put paid to any chances of success.

'Take Tracy. She'd jump at the chance.'

She walked off but he dodged to the door, barring her way.

'You must be kidding. She'd spoil the whole party. Look Barbie . . .' He hesitated and lowered his eyes. 'I owe Simon a favour.'

'What sort of favour?'

'He got me out of a spot of bother and now I owe him.'

'And . . . ?'

'He said I'd got to get you there tonight, or else. Come on, Barb. If you don't go I shall be welshing.'

'You rotten pig.' She hit him over the head with a newspaper which was lying on the table beside her. 'Using me to pay off your debts.'

'It's only a party.' He held up his arm to protect himself from the blows. 'Anyone would think I was selling you into slavery.'

'You're a rotten pig.' She gave one last blow across his raised forearm then threw the newspaper at him. 'Don't you ever do that to me again.'

'Does that mean you're going?'

'It seems like I haven't got much choice.'

'Good old Barb. I knew I could rely on you.'

'Pig!'

He laughed. 'We leave at seven o'clock.' And scuttled up the stairs. 'You won't regret it.'

'Won't I?' said Barbie. 'And I'm coming home early!'

At seven o'clock Mary stood at the bedroom window. It was late March and darkness had already fallen. A strong wind whipped the dust along the pavement beneath the street lights. 'I can't think why Mark asked Barbie to that party tonight. I don't know why she can't make friends of her own.'

'What's wrong with taking his sister to a party?' Ken came up behind and stood at her shoulder. 'It's better than quarrelling like some families do.'

'She's been here five years and she still acts like a lodger.'

'Oh, come on, luv. She's settled down pretty well on the whole.' Ken watched Barbie walking down the street and felt a faint stirring which was immediately replaced by acute shame and embarrassment. It was something about the way she walked.

'She's too damned attractive.' Mary glanced at him out of the corner of her eye and he squirmed, fearing that his thoughts lay naked before her. 'And she flaunts it. I always said she was too much like her mother. Perhaps you'll believe me now.'

'Is she?' He shrugged. 'I still can't see it myself.' And Mary glanced at him again.

'I do hope Simon's parents are going to be at that party. I don't like to think of all those youngsters left unsupervised.' She moved away from the window and sat at the dressing table, applying make-up in preparation for an evening with friends.

149

'Come on, luv. They'll be all right. Anyway, Mark's got to start sowing his wild oats sooner or later.'

'Really, Ken. You do say the most stupid things. He's a fourteen year old child.'

Ken smirked to himself as he buttoned his shirt. 'I'd hate to tell you at what age I started to sow mine.'

'Yes. And we all know who with.'

The smirk faded. 'It wasn't, as a matter of fact. Sandra wasn't the only girl in the village.'

Mary turned on him as if to make issue out of his comment but changed her mind. 'It's not Mark we need worry about. You'd do better to concern yourself with Barbie.'

'Don't be stupid.' He was surprised by the sharpness of his own reaction. 'She's not like that.'

'Really? She was already giving us good cause for concern when she was ten years old.'

'God, Mary.' He was tying the knot of his tie but he was not satisfied with it and pulled it apart again. 'I do wish you'd let that drop. She didn't do anything.'

'So she said.'

'So the social worker said, and the police.'

'Maybe.'

'She didn't do anything, I tell you.' He was still having difficulty with his tie. 'It was that boy, Billy Watkins.'

'It takes two to tango.'

'You've never let it rest, have you. Not even after five years.'

Mary studied his reflection in the mirror. 'And you will continue to close your eyes until one day you will be forced to face the facts.'

'You have absolutely no right to say things like that.'

'Let's just bide our time. Sooner or later you'll have to admit it.'

'God, woman. I wish you'd just shut up about it.' Ken tore apart the knot of his tie and knew in that moment what he would do to the man who sullied his daughter.

The party was in full swing when Mark and Barbie arrived. Music was blaring from the dark recesses of the dimly-lit house. Barbie had difficulty in adjusting her vision to the gloom but, as she peered at moving shapes and shadows, she became aware that the youths standing about the room were all several years older than Mark. The girls were of her own age, some younger, but the boys she placed at around seventeen.

150

'You know Simon.' She heard Mark shouting above the din and turned to find Simon Turner at her elbow. At the same moment she caught the jerk of Simon's head to indicate Mark's dismissal. 'I'll leave you then. You'll be all right?'

'Of course she'll be all right.' Simon stepped beside Barbie and took her arm.

'She doesn't like parties.'

Simon mouthed a thinly disguised instruction to 'Shove off' and steered Barbie into the room from which emanated the rock music.

'Do you want a drink?'

Barbie hesitated.

'There's plenty of Coke.'

'Yes, please.' She allowed him to steer her towards a pile of cushions stacked against the wall.

She could only dimly make out his movements as he went to the corner of the room and sorted through the rows of bottles set out on an improvised bar.

'Cheers.' He handed her the glass and flopped down beside her. 'Drink up. Then you can show me how you dance.'

'I haven't had much practice.' She took a gulp from the liquid in the glass and grimaced. 'Ugh. This isn't Coke.'

'Yes it is. I put a little something in it.'

'What?' She held the glass to her nose and sniffed.

'A Simon Special.' He laughed and jogged her arm. 'Go on. It's not going to do you any harm.'

'I'd rather not.'

'Christ! Anyone would think I was trying to get you drunk or something. There's hardly anything in it.'

'Sorry.' She took another sip and found that, taken in a more restrained manner, it was really quite pleasant. 'I didn't mean that.'

He smiled at her. 'I wouldn't do that to you. I'm not like that, honest.'

'You're sure it's not strong?'

'It's almost drowned in Coke.'

'Sorry,' she said again. 'It's quite nice really.'

'I told you it was. Now drink up and show me how you dance.'

It was hot in the room and when they stood to dance they found themselves hemmed in by other gyrating bodies but she had a natural sense of rhythm and found herself more

151

than usually well disposed to offer herself up to the pulsating beat.

'You're not bad,' he said.

She leaned forward trying to catch his words. 'Aren't you afraid that the neighbours are going to complain?'

He laughed. 'Too noisy. We'd never hear them if they came banging on the door.'

It got hotter and when the music paused while discs were changed she asked for another drink. 'Plain this time.'

'The last one didn't hurt you, did it?'

'No. But I don't normally drink.'

'I'd hardly call that drinking.' He gave her a look which came close to boredom and she wondered how Mark would fare if she did not come up to expectations.

'I'd rather just have it plain.'

She was feeling slightly embarrassed and out of place and when she found that the drink had been lightly laced she thought better than to complain. She drank it and went back to the dance floor. It was becoming unbearably hot and as she danced she found that she was very slightly light-headed. She shook her head and blinked but she was enjoying the music and found that the dizziness made her all the more disposed to throw herself into the rhythm.

'Why don't you come here more often?'

'I don't like it much.'

'You seem to be enjoying yourself all right now.'

'The music's good.'

'And the company?' She smiled at him, thinking him rather silly. 'Do you want another drink?'

'Yes please. This is thirsty work.'

The music changed to a particularly hectic tempo and as they danced she was surprised and pleasantly confused to find that the walls were pulsating in a steady beat, beat, beat in time with the music. She watched fascinated as the blurred shapes of walls and ceiling throbbed with a movement in unison with her own, yet strangely independent. She wondered vaguely why she could not feel the floor beneath her feet but resolved the matter, fully reassured that she was dancing on the air. When he handed her another drink she did not question it but drank it on the dance floor, holding it in her hand as she danced. She spilled some of it and found herself giggling in a manner quite unlike her usual self.

By the time she had finished her fifth drink the whole universe was vibrating to the same crazy beat, which emanated from the stars for the sole purpose of formulating itself into a language which her body must shout. And all around there were other bodies, also shouting, and which she touched in the close confines of the room. Each time they touched she felt the same unmistakable, pulsating thrill. At any other time she would have avoided the physical contact of other people. She did not like to be touched but tonight her senses were crying out for it.

Suddenly the music changed again, this time to a slow number and each couple automatically drew together and moved in a dreamy embrace. Simon placed his arms about Barbie and it was as though every nerve-ending in her body had been stimulated at the same moment. She gritted her teeth to check the tremor which passed through her and felt the steady warmth of his breath on her neck.

'You really ought to come here more often. We could make good music together.' At any other time she would have laughed at the hackneyed line but tonight it sent a further thrill through her. She clung to him and felt each movement of his body as they danced.

Again the music changed tempo and couples groaned as they drew apart. He held on to her, reluctant to release her, and when at last they drew apart she held out her hand to him. He took it, and when he led her to the cushions piled against the wall, she did not resist. Nor did she resist when he pushed her back against the wall and kissed her on the neck. Encouraged, he kissed her again, this time on the mouth, inexpert and inconsiderately demanding but his lips were warm and she answered to them as he fumbled with the buttons of her blouse and slid his hand across her skin. He explored her neck, her shoulders, and found her breast.

'Shall we go upstairs?'

She knew what he intended and asked herself why she did not refuse, but it was as if she questioned a stranger. She took his hand and meekly followed as he led the way upstairs. She wondered again why her feet did not touch the floor and why the walls, which had been pulsating, were now revolving, turning slowly to confuse her sense of direction.

There were other people in the bedrooms. Low muffled

whispers were interspersed with laughter. He led her by the hand from room to room until he found the privacy he sought.

'On here.' He pushed her down on the bed, still wearing her shoes, and wrenched at the zip of her jeans. She made to help him but the walls were spinning and she had need to concentrate in order to prevent herself from falling, even though she was lying down.

'Lift yourself up.' There was an excited hoarseness about his voice as he tore at her undergarments but she needed all her powers of concentration to focus upon the revolving darkness.

He went straight into her, fumbling only for a means of entry, and, as she felt his flesh upon her own, she felt the darkness dip and sway. She fought for closer contact and wrapped her legs about his body but he struggled against her for greater freedom of movement.

He worked himself vigorously so that she knew not whether to cry out in pain or in need of some inner feeling which longed to be aroused but which was refusing to awaken. His flesh was there, thumping against her own, but it failed to stimulate her and only made her all the more aware that she was in need. She found herself oddly detached, as if she were a casual observer, aware of his movements but unaffected by them. She let herself go limp and cried out inside for her failure to respond.

She watched him as he reached a state of frenzy, thinking him ridiculous, and, as he arched his back in one last contortion, there flashed before her a brief, unaccountable image of Gran, followed by an equally brief stirring in her loins, before he fell upon her, a dead weight, spent and exhausted. She knew it was all over and she had experienced nothing but a brief, flickering moment which was already fading beyond recall.

'Oh God; that was great.'

She grew repulsed by his gasping in her ear, and threw him off. She was aware of the feel of sweat, and stickiness, and of the indignity of her dishevelled clothing.

'Sorry.' He jumped up. 'You didn't object. I thought you wanted it.'

She did not answer but turned her back on him, zipping her jeans.

'Are you angry with me?'

'I think I'd better go home.'

'Do you want me to come with you?' He was fumbling with his own clothing.

'No. I'll be all right.' She pushed him aside and stumbled to the stairs, heading blindly for the front door.

The cold night air struck her like a douche of iced water and she stumbled against a wall, vomiting helplessly into a flowerbed. She staggered through the streets, blinded by the glare of passing traffic and collided with objects which unaccountably stepped into her path, until she came at last to the corner of Wansdyke Avenue. She found the front door of number fifteen and, eventually, her bed.

The house was in darkness, for Ken and Mary had not yet returned from visiting friends. When, a short time later, they let themselves in through the front door, Mary saw the shoes kicked off upon the mat and felt a moment of satisfaction that Barbie had become quickly bored and had left Mark to the company of more suitable friends.

Next morning, Barbie was awakened by Mark sitting on her bed. 'I'm sorry, Barbie. I really am.' He was close to tears.

It took a moment for her mind to focus. Her head ached and a feeling of nausea permeated her whole body.

'I had no idea he was going to go all the way; honest. I wouldn't have taken you there if I'd known.'

She forced open her eyes then closed them again.

'He only said he wanted to meet you.'

'It's all right,' she lied. 'He didn't do anything.'

'Really?' The relief was self-evident. 'God; you gave me a fright.' The exclamation vibrated through her head and she put out a hand to hold him still. 'When they told me he'd taken you upstairs . . . I thought he'd . . .'

'We only talked.'

'God; I thought I'd really let you in for it. I had my eye on you all evening, and then you suddenly disappeared. I looked for you everywhere, and someone said he'd taken you upstairs. I thought . . . God; I'm not saying what I thought. Then someone said you'd gone home.'

'I didn't feel well.' She put out her hand again to steady his movement. 'He put something in my Coke.'

'Rotten bastard! You wait until I get hold of him. I'll . . .'

'Just leave it. It was my fault for drinking it. I should have known better.'

'I'll ram that bloody bottle down his bloody throat.'

'Just leave it. Please. And, anyway, he's a lot bigger than you.'

Mark fell suddenly quiet, revealing that she had touched an exposed nerve. 'You might as well know,' he said, 'they only let me into that party because I promised to take you.'

'I thought it was a bit strange they were all so much older than you.'

'I'm sorry, Barb. I didn't know . . .'

'It's all right.' She opened her eyes and gave him an affectionate pat on the arm. 'Forget it. There's no harm done beyond a blinding headache.'

'I've always wanted to get drunk.'

'You wouldn't, once you'd tried it.'

'Mum says to tell you to come downstairs. You're late for breakfast.'

The thought of food made Barbie's stomach lurch. 'Tell her I don't want to eat.'

'She's going to come up here to find out why.'

Barbie nodded and held a hand to her forehead. 'Look, I've got to go out. Can you think up an excuse?'

'Sure. I'll tell her you had to go back to Simon's house. I'll say you left something there last night.'

'OK. But what's so urgent I have to skip breakfast?'

'I don't know. Just leave it to me. I'll come up with something.'

'Thanks Mark.' She put out a hand. 'You're a pal.'

'Christ, it's the least I can do.'

He left her to get dressed and when she slipped downstairs she could hear voices in the kitchen but no one challenged her as she quietly opened the front door.

She went to the park and made straight for the weeping willow tree, leaning back to rest her head against its trunk. The tree had not yet put forth new leaf so cover was minimal but the park was deserted and no one came to disturb her privacy. She closed her eyes and felt the steady throb in her temples as each pulsebeat sent a fresh wave of nausea and pain.

Like Barbie, the tree was five years older. It was a little taller and more sweeping in circumference but otherwise little changed. It was still the haven under which she frequently sought sanctuary.

For a long time after the incident with Mad Billy Watkins the park had been banned to her, but time and again she had slipped

156

back to it unnoticed, and, after a period of several months, Mary had grown lax in her scrutiny of Barbie's movements. Eventually the ban had been forgotten. With each following year of Barbie's growth the tree too had grown to accommodate her beneath its concealing branches and today, as always, it encompassed her like the arms of an intimate friend.

She drifted into a world of familiar daydreams which mingled with the throbbing in her head – soft summer sunshine, barley fields, the smell of damp earth and bluebells beneath the beech trees in the copse, Bess . . .

Bess was no longer there. Gone were the days of visits to Mr Smethurst's farm for Bess had outlived Gran by less than a year. She had grown old during that winter and increasingly lame. With the coming of spring she had shown new heart but no one was surprised when, one day in late May, she had failed to waken from sleep. Mr Smethurst had gone with Barbie to a quiet corner behind the barn where the sun could penetrate for the greater part of each day and there they had dug a grave. She had planted it with wild flowers but when Mr Smethurst had suggested she should erect a cross she had refused. She would never again erect a cross.

She squeezed her eyes tight shut and with the increased pain blanked from her mind all thoughts of Bess. She thought of the village street, of the post office and the horse chestnut tree which overshadowed it, candles of blossom and hard, brightly polished conkers; Mrs Trimmings shouting at the boys who annually threw stones to harvest the conkers and invariably smashed at least one window. She thought of Mad Billy and wondered what Mary would say today if she knew of Simon Turner.

She had seen Mad Billy but once in the distance as she walked Bess through the back lanes of the village. She had watched him walk away, for she was under strict orders not to speak to him. The penalty was an end of her visits to Bess. As he retreated she called to him but he did not turn.

A short time later there circulated rumours in the village that he had been caught 'up to no good' and had been 'sent away'. Mrs Matthews at the village store was heard to voice the opinion that 'a lot of people would sleep more easily in their beds knowing that he was safely put away'.

I say, I say, I say. Why do giraffes have such long necks?
I don't know. Why do giraffes have such long necks?

157

Because they can't stand the smell of their feet.

'Oh, Mad Billy; I do hope that you're still joking.'

She eased herself upon the dry soil. Apart from a slight soreness, there was nothing but a fuddled memory to mark the fact that last night she had stepped through the barrier between child and woman. There was no elation, no wild ringing of bells, such as she had read in magazines. Simon Turner, a boy whom she hardly knew, had, for a few brief moments, offered her a promise which had come to naught.

She asked herself where she had failed but, then again, she knew. It was the price which must be paid.

Five years ago, Barbie had learned a valuable lesson. She had learned to conform. To conform was to survive. So, she had learned to simulate an enjoyment in things she was required to enjoy, and to denounce the things which would not find favour with those who pulled the strings of her vulnerable young life. But the price was high. She had forged a path to co-existence but steadfastly she had refused to feel. To feel emotion was to lay oneself open to the danger of pain and Barbie had known pain enough. Pliable though she might be to the manipulations of others, her emotions had become irrevocably sealed.

It was a condition not dissimilar to the plight of the short-sighted man whose eyes can discern the substance and the colour of objects before him but cannot focus upon their shape and form. In such a way did Barbie grope her way myopically through a labyrinth of feeling, aware of joy and pain, laughter and sadness but always through a mist which blurred the edges. She had made use of the self-inflicted disability with such skill that now it had passed beyond control. It was no longer open to her to make the choice. She could not feel.

Until this moment it had not worried her. What puzzled her today, was why it should matter now. Last night she had become aware of a need and she had failed to respond. It mattered to her desperately. She had almost found the key to something which was locked away and lost.

A cold wind cut across the park and disturbed the branches of the weeping willow tree. She shivered. Her limbs had become numbed and as she moved, stretching her taut muscles, the movement brought a renewed throbbing to her head. She got up and began to walk towards the gate. She had already decided what she must do.

As she walked, Barbie stooped to touch a drift of yellow crocuses which were blooming beside the path. The next time she was invited to a party she would accept: and she would go upstairs. Then, if she failed, she would try again. She would keep on trying until such time as she found the key.

Over the next seven months Barbie went to many parties. She tried many times to capture the elusive experience which she sought, but each time she failed and each time she tried again – always with a different partner. There were times when she thought she had almost found it, just one more moment and all would be fulfilled, but always in that very moment her hopes would fade and she would open her eyes to gaze upon another bedroom ceiling, yet another heaving body pressed on hers.

She became a joke. The young men passed her round and placed their bets upon her. The once inaccessible Miss Harding had become the property of all. She did not care. Standing in a bus shelter one day, she saw, scrawled amid the graffiti *B. H. is the easiest lay in town*. She wondered what Mary would say if she should read it but Mary rarely travelled by bus. She took a pen from her bag and scribbled over it, erasing the comment from view and, at the same time, she blanked it from her mind.

In mid-November Mark was approaching his fifteenth birthday. Barbie was just sixteen.

'Please, Mum,' he said. 'All the other guys have parties. Why can't I?'

Mary was reluctant to comply. 'Let's do something really nice for your birthday treat this year. Theatre . . . ? Dinner . . . ? Anything you choose.'

'Oh Mum. I'm past all that stuff about birthday treats. I want a party like all the other guys.'

'But you're only fifteen.'

'Yes, *fifteen*, Mum. I'm a big boy now.'

'Well, I really don't know. Perhaps the other boys have parents who don't mind a horde of youngsters rampaging all over their houses.'

'We don't rampage, Mum. We play records, or we sit around and talk.'

'Yes, and I can just imagine the mess you would make.'

'We wouldn't, Mum. And I'd clear up afterwards, honest.'

'You mean *I* would clear up afterwards.'

'Please, Mum.'

'I still say you would do better to go to the theatre.'

'I don't want to go to the theatre. I want to have a party.'

'Oh, very well.' Mary spread her hands in a gesture of reluctant capitulation. 'But I'll show the door to anyone who steps out of line.'

'We don't have parents there, Mum. They always go out.'

'What do you mean?'

'The guys would laugh at me.'

'You mean to say that you wish to hold a party in this house in my absence?'

'Yeah.' Mark chewed his lip. 'All the other parents do it.'

'Well this parent does not.'

He slipped his hand through her arm with a childish appeal which he knew to be unfailing. 'You wouldn't want to make me look a fool in front of all my mates, would you?'

She looked down at him and he offered her a smile for added appeal. 'You could go and visit Aunt Lucy.'

'Are you trying to get round me?'

'I'm just saying it's about time you started to trust me.'

Mary stroked the hand slotted through her arm. 'Well, I don't know.'

'Please, Mum.'

'You're sure I could trust you?'

'Promise. I give you my word.'

'And what about all the other boys? Can I trust them?'

'Of course you can. They're my mates.'

'Oh, very well.' She reached out to kiss his forehead and he allowed her to do so. 'If it's what you really want.'

'Thanks, Mum. And you can take Tracy with you. She's just a kid.'

On the appointed day Mary took Barbie to one side. 'Barbie, I want you to keep an eye on this party while I'm away. You're older than Mark and I hold you responsible to see that things don't get out of hand.'

Barbie had no wish to shoulder such responsibility but neither did she wish to cause problems for Mark. 'I'll try but it's difficult when there are a lot of people here.'

'I expect you to do more than try. I have no intention of coming back here and finding my home in a shambles.' Mary put on her coat and took one last look round the house. 'Aunt Lucy's number is on the pad. Call me immediately if there are signs of trouble.'

Ken winked at her behind Mary's back. 'Have a good time.'

'Really, Ken. I don't think you have any idea of the trouble we could be letting ourselves in for.'

'Oh, come on, luv. What harm can they do holding a party?'

'Honestly, Ken. I sometimes wonder about you.' They went out and Mary came back for yet another last look round. 'I'm beginning to regret that I ever allowed myself to get talked into it.'

The party began at eight o'clock but the atmosphere was slow to build. The guests were ill at ease and Barbie was uncomfortable with her repeated requests to 'mind the carpet' and 'don't lean on the wall'. They laughed at the iced cake, complete with birthday candles, but they ate the food and brought out bottles of liquor to supplement the cans of lemonade and Coca-Cola. By ten o'clock the atmosphere was more relaxed and people were dancing or lounging on the floor.

Barbie watched the clock, uncomfortable in her role, and when things appeared to be going smoothly, decided to slip to her room for a while to escape the noise. She picked her way through people sitting on the stairs and crossed the landing. When she came to the door of Ken and Mary's room she stopped abruptly and listened. She held her ear close and heard muffled sounds of giggling. Her heart stopped. She tapped on the door and the giggling subsided.

'Would you please come out.' She turned the handle. The door was not locked but she thought better than to interrupt. 'I'll give you five minutes then I want you to come out.'

A girl's voice, which she recognised, called back, 'Go on, Barbie. Don't be a spoilsport.'

'My aunt wouldn't like it.'

'Just give us a short while and then we'll clear up after us. She won't even know we've been here.'

Barbie turned reluctantly. 'Another ten minutes then I'm coming in.'

She went to her room and sat on the bed listening for the sound of retreating footsteps. She intended to go in after them and eliminate any trace of their presence. The footsteps which she heard were not the ones for which she was listening. They came up the stairs and advanced towards her room. When she looked up Simon Turner was standing at the door.

'Hello. I thought I saw you come up here.'

She did nothing to acknowledge his presence and he stood for a moment, uncertain.

'Can I sit down?'

She shrugged indifferently.

'I won't, if you don't want me to.'

'Suit yourself. I shall be leaving in a minute.'

He came and sat down beside her and for a full minute neither spoke. 'I wanted to have a word,' he said at last. 'It's about that night.'

'What night?'

'You know what night. I've been feeling bad about it ever since.'

'I don't know why. There's no reason.'

'Yes there is.' He turned to her. 'I'm sorry, Barbie. I didn't treat you very well.'

She shrugged again. 'I didn't notice.'

'Yes you did. It was the drink. Oh hell, Barbie; no it wasn't.' He hesitated, and then went on in a rush. 'It was you. You know darned well that there's something about you that drives a man crazy.'

'Don't be silly.' She said it with genuine scorn.

'I lost my head. It was my first time. I'd never done it before.'

She turned slightly, half-looking at him. 'I didn't realise it was your first time.'

'I know. Before that it was all talk. You know how all the guys try to make out they've done more than everyone else. I'd never gone all the way.' He stopped and looked at her. 'You won't tell anyone, will you.'

'It was my first time, too.'

'I know. And that's what makes it worse. I didn't treat you well.'

'It doesn't matter. Forget it.'

'It does matter, Barbie. I've thought about it ever since.' He reached out and placed his hand over hers. 'I'm very sorry.'

'It doesn't matter,' she said again, but this time with a smile. 'We all have to start somewhere.'

'Thanks. Has anyone ever told you you're a really nice girl?' He stroked his thumb across the back of her hand.

'Not often.'

162

'And beautiful?'

She withdrew her hand. 'I told you not to be so silly.'

He sat rebuffed and for a while neither spoke.

'You've done it plenty of times since.' He half-turned to her again. Barbie shrugged. 'You've done it with nearly all the guys.' She did not respond. 'But never with me.'

'There's not much point.'

'Was it because I wasn't any good?'

'You're about the same as anyone else.'

'But I've learned a lot since then.'

'About what?'

'About women. About how to please them.'

'Good for you. I hope it brings you luck.'

'Please, Barbie. Don't be like that.' He reached out to her again. 'You know what I'm asking. Let's try again. Please.'

She shook her head. 'I can't. I've got to keep an eye on the party.'

'Hang the party. What difference is it going to make if you're not around for a while. Nothing's going to happen.'

'I promised. I'll get into trouble if anything goes wrong.'

'What's going to go wrong? Come on, Barbie. It won't take long.' He pressed her back onto the bed and kissed her. 'I want to show you just how sorry I am.'

He had, indeed, learned a great deal since their first meeting. He was gentle and considerate and she put up but minimal resistance before giving in to his caresses. His hands explored the crevices of her body and she was once again aware of the now familiar need. She pressed herself against him, willing herself to respond to the need, willing the tension to rise through her body and to culminate in some, as yet unexperienced, explosion. Half-formed fantasies filled her mind. Maybe this time . . . maybe this time . . .

Suddenly, the door was flung wide. She crashed back to reality as Simon gave out a strangled cry of surprise and his body was torn from her. He appeared to hurtle across the room and gave out another yelp as a foot was aimed at his groin.

Ken was standing beside the bed, his eyes blazing.

'You little slut. You dirty little slut.'

His hand crashed down and Barbie squealed in fright.

'You filthy, dirty little slut.'

Mary was standing in the doorway but it was Ken who rained

163

down the blows. She edged away from him, clutching at the blankets to shield herself from the blows and from the shame of her own nakedness, but she was trapped against the wall and there was no escape from his hands and from the obscenities which he flung at her. It was the first time he had ever chastised her and it was the shock which bruised her even more than the blows.

From the corner of her eye she saw Mary leave the room and it was a brief moment later that she returned.

'Ken.' Her face was masked with a shock which had turned it grey. 'It's Mark.'

Her voice was but a whisper but there was something about it which caused Ken to stop and look round.

'I think you should come at once. He's in our room.'

An hour later, Barbie sat in the lounge. She was dressed but, despite the bulky sweater and jeans, she felt naked. Mark had been sent to bed and the guests all ordered away. Tracy was in the kitchen but hovered within earshot.

Barbie sat and looked at the debris of the party. A chair was tipped on its side and half-eaten food lay on paper plates scattered about the floor. On the far side of the room, stretching its tentacles across the carpet, was a large stain where something had been spilled. She huddled into the corner of the settee and, despite the fact that at no time did Ken look at her, she felt the discomfort of his eyes boring into her.

Mary came and sat on the opposite chair. The grey pallor had not left her face and when she spoke it was as someone recovering from a long illness. 'I suppose I must blame myself.' She picked up her knitting and automatically began slotting the needle through the stitches. 'I've always known that it would happen and yet I did nothing to prevent it.'

Barbie was aware of a slight movement from Ken but she did not look at him and he did not speak.

'I brought you into this house, Barbie, knowing that sooner or later you would give me cause to regret it. It was born into you as surely as the colour of your hair.' Barbie felt, not for the first time, that the colour of her hair had been inflicted upon her like the mark of Cain.

'But I never expected . . .' Mary stopped and there was a hollow silence broken only by the sound of the knitting needles and of Ken's breathing which came to Barbie from across the room. 'You are not content with bringing yourself down. You have to teach Mark your sordid, dirty little ways.'

Barbie was unmoved by the accusation. She was long past the days of stinging from the blows of injustice.

'I took you into this house, and I gave you a home. I fed you and I clothed you. And what do I get in return? I find my son . . . I regret the day I brought you into this house, Barbie. I want you to know that. It was the biggest mistake of my life.'

Barbie raised her eyes and her steady gaze locked with Mary's. She held it there, not wavering, and knew in that moment that the time had come for her to move on.

'Go to your room and get out of my sight. Maybe tomorrow I'll decide what I'll do with you.'

In the early hours of the morning Barbie slipped quietly through the darkness of the house and out beneath the street lights of Wansdyke Avenue. She had with her only the belongings which could easily be packed into two carrier bags and beneath her arm, as an afterthought, she held an old, worn, and slightly faded, toy gorilla. She set off towards the railway station without once looking back.

Chapter Nine

In the early hours of the morning Paddington Station slouched morosely in the damp November air. Barbie shivered as she felt the dampness touch her skin, and hitched one carrier bag beneath her arm to ease the weight.

The train had disgorged its early morning commuters who now were hurrying away, their shoulders hunched against a world which called them off to work whilst the city slept. There were others scattered about – night people – who no longer scurried for there was nowhere left to go. They huddled, drawing down inside grubby overcoats, beneath the spurious warmth of neon lights and the fellowship of men who did not see them as they passed.

Barbie looked about her and felt lonelier than she had felt in all her life. An old man with a tattered beard and clothing built up in layers over many years, held out his hand to her. She shied away, half in pity, half in fear, and made for the nearest blaze of light which was the station buffet.

She ordered tea and a piece of cake, hard and dry with specks of currants, more to occupy her hands than because she was hungry. She took it to a table in the more distant corner, as far as possible from her fellow occupants who sat dejectedly staring at their cups, or at the walls, or dozing, chin on chest.

The tea was hot and strong, in direct contrast to the anaemic woman who had brewed it. The woman looked across at Barbie but paid her scant attention. She had seen many young girls on many mornings and one looked much like any other.

Barbie drank the tea but it did little to warm her spirits. Some sense of purpose would have warmed her but Barbie had no plans. She had merely packed her bags and left without thought of where she should go.

She glanced up at the sound of movement at the door and saw a man, not down-at-heel like her companions, but cheerful, whistling through his teeth, his hands thrust deep into the pockets of a heavy overcoat. She watched him abstractedly as he ordered tea, then became alarmed as he caught her eye and made a beeline for her table, sitting down beside her. She made to move but he smiled at her, with such a friendly smile, that she responded.

'Cor blimey. It's perishing cold out there today.'

She lowered her eyes and remained silent.

'You been here long?'

'I've only just arrived.'

'Oh,' he said. 'It's perishing cold.'

He was short and stocky, in early middle age, with a thatch of dark, tightly curling hair. They sat for some time without speaking and when she raised her eyes she found him studying her. She could see from the badge pinned to his coat that he was a taxi driver.

'I've got my cab outside. Do you want me to drop you anywhere?'

She shook her head.

'Haven't you got anywhere to go?'

'I'm going to stay with my uncle.' It was an unconvincing lie which he ignored.

'Reckon you'd better start making yourself a few plans.'

Barbie felt uncomfortable. She had no wish to discuss her situation with a total stranger. 'I think I'd better be going now,' she said and made to stand, but he was in the way.

'Don't you know anyone at all in London?' He made no effort to let her pass.

'I told you I'm going to my uncle.'

'You're not the first girl to run away, Sunshine,' he said. 'There are other daft young kids doing it all the time.'

'I'm not running away. My uncle's expecting me.'

'You'd better find yourself somewhere decent to stay.'

She looked at him, not knowing how to cope.

'I know a place,' he said. 'Over Clapham way. You can go there if you like.'

'No thanks.'

'What's the matter? Don't you trust me?'

167

'No; it's not that . . .'

'Then what? It's not every day you get offered a nice warm flat.'

'I'm sorry; it's just . . .'

'You're just wondering why a bloke like me should come in here, offering a girl like you a flat, when he's never so much as clapped eyes on her before.'

'Well . . .' Barbie gave a small embarrassed smile.

'Look, Sunshine . . .' He dropped six cubes of sugar into his tea and stirred them with a spoon. 'I'm not one to beat about the bush. And I'm not one to get you into something without first telling you what you're letting yourself in for.' He looked her in the eye. 'I'm looking for a nice young girl to join my other two. They work for me. They . . . entertain . . . You know what I mean?'

Barbie lowered her eyes.

'I see that you do.' He tapped the spoon against the rim of the cup before replacing it in the saucer. 'And it's not what you had in mind when you came to London.'

'No. Of course not.'

'No; you young girls never do. But it's the way that you always finish up.'

'I have no intention . . .'

'I don't suppose you have.' He looked at her long and hard, then said, 'OK. What's the first thing you're going to do today, when you walk out of this station?'

Barbie shrugged. 'I don't know. Find a job, I suppose; and a place to live.'

'Cor blimey, Sunshine. Do you know how many other young kids come into this city every day thinking they're going to find a job and a place to live? There aren't any jobs, luv; and there aren't any places to live. Not unless you've got the money to pay for them. Have you got money?'

Barbie shook her head. 'I'll earn it.'

'Oh yeah?' His tone was firm but not unkind. 'And just what are you qualified to do? Secretary – librarian – hairdresser – telephonist? Or . . .' he looked at her closely '. . . or are you more at home in a school blazer?'

Barbie bit her lip.

'Just as I thought. No, my Sunshine; you've got as much hope of finding a job and somewhere to live as I've got of sprouting wings and flying right out of this station.'

'I'll manage somehow.'

'Look, Sunshine.' He reached out to touch her hand but she withdrew it quickly. 'I don't want to make you feel bad. But I've seen it all a hundred times before. As sure as God made little green apples, you're going to finish up on the street. And there's no knowing what company you'll likely get mixed up with out there.' He reached again for her hand and this time held it so that she could not move. 'You're a nice kid and if you're going to finish up that way I'd rather you did it where I'm around to look out for you.'

She looked up at him shakily.

'You're not to know it,' he said. 'But there are worse blokes than me to work for, and I'd see you right.'

Barbie shook her head. Dispirited as she was, she had no intention of taking up his offer.

'All right, my Sunshine.' He released her hand. 'You wait till a few days time when you're hungry, and it's pissing down with rain, and you've got nowhere to go. You'll think of old Curly, and you'll think of that nice warm flat over in Clapham, and you'll be sorry you're not there, in a nice cushy little number that'll set you up for life with money in your pocket.'

Barbie was oddly drawn to him despite the nature of his offer. 'Thanks,' she said. 'But, no.'

'Look . . .' He smiled at her kindly and slipped his hand into his pocket for a scrap of paper. 'What's your name, by the way?'

'Barbie.'

'Right, Barbie. I'll write the address down here. Then, if you change your mind, you can go and see the girls. Tell them Curly sent you.' He scribbled an address and passed it to her. 'You've got . . . experience, I take it?' The colour rose across her face. 'Yes,' he said. 'I thought you had. Haven't been in the game all these years without being able to recognise it.'

He downed his tea and stood up. 'I'd better be getting back to my cab.' He took a step away then turned. 'And as soon as I've gone, you're going to start asking yourself, "what's a pimp doing driving a taxi cab?"' He winked and walked away. 'Well, I'll tell you if you come and work for me.'

At the door he turned again and raised his hand. 'See you.'

'See you,' said Barbie, though she had no intention of doing so.

The city was waking when she left the station. Cars and buses plied the streets and pedestrians jostled, their collars turned up against the mist-laden air. She had been to London several times before, to the theatre and to museums on family outings but she had no liking for city streets. If she hated Wickhampton, she hated London more.

She wandered along pavements hoping to find her bearings and, on turning a corner, came upon an accommodation agency with details of furnished apartments neatly set out in its windows. She stopped and looked, setting down the weight of the two carrier bags.

> *Luxury flat. 2 bedrooms, sitting room*
> *kitchen and bathroom . . .*

She scanned the details and gulped when she came to the rental. It was more than she had possessed in her entire lifetime.

She moved on, dismissing the feeling of despondency which the notices had given her. After all, she had no need of grand apartments. She needed little more than a roof under which to lay her head. Just the same, she would have given a great deal at this moment to know just which roof it was to be.

A little further on, in a tobacconist's shop window, were other cards, more in keeping with her needs. Among the articles for sale she saw a card which caught her eye.

> *Girl to share with two others. Own room*
> *. . . rent and rates . . . plus gas and*
> *electricity . . . payment in advance . . .*

The figure was much more reasonable but she had no money. She decided that the first thing she must do was to find a job. The promise of a pay packet to come might possibly suffice.

By nine o'clock, when offices opened for business, she was waiting outside an employment agency door.

The woman who unbolted it was middle-aged, wearing a knitted cardigan and with traces of grey in the hair swept back from her forehead. 'Good morning,' she said. 'You're off to an early start.'

'Yes, please.' Barbie felt nervous. She sat down in the chair indicated by the woman. 'I need a job.'

'And what sort of job did you have in mind?'

'It doesn't matter. Any sort of job would do.'

The woman looked at her closely and at the two carrier bags at her side. 'What did you do in your last job?'

Barbie mumbled something, unprepared for the question.

'And how old are you?' she went on without waiting for an answer.

Barbie chose to lie. 'Eighteen.'

'And have you worked since you left school?'

She tried to control the flush which was rising across her cheeks.

'Now look, dear.' The woman put down her pen and leaned across the desk. 'It's none of my business, but why not take a little advice from someone who has a daughter of about your age.' She smiled at her kindly. 'Go home. I bet there's a Mum and Dad back there who are worried sick about you.'

For the first time Barbie thought of Ken and Mary and wondered whether they had started to look for her yet. 'They know where I am. I've come to London to find a job.'

The woman sighed. 'It's none of my business,' she said again. 'But the London streets aren't paved with gold.'

'I know,' said Barbie dispiritedly. 'I need a job.'

'With the best will in the world, dear, I don't think I can offer you a suitable job.' The woman picked up her pen and began flicking through a card index on her desk. 'Do you have any special skills? Any training?'

Barbie shook her head. Her uninterested progress through school had led to little achievement on her part.

The woman continued to look through the card index and clicked her tongue. 'There's nothing here today,' she said. 'Come back tomorrow; and every day, until something suitable comes in.'

Barbie rose and smiled her thanks.

'I'm sorry, dear. I'd help you if I could.'

'Thank you.' Barbie picked up her bags and trudged towards the door.

'Think about what I told you, dear. There's no shame in giving up and going home.'

It had been warm in the office and the chill of the street struck her as she walked away along the pavement. She was hungry and the effort of fighting down her anxiety was exhausting her. She decided to stop at a coffee bar and buy something to eat. With little money in her pocket she could not be sure when next she would have a meal.

It was warm in the coffee bar. Her spirits lifted slightly, and then they soared as she saw a notice on the counter.

WANTED. Waitress. Experience preferred.
Apply to Manager.

'Please,' she said. 'I want to see the Manager.'

He was a tall, good-looking man with a swarthy complexion and black, thickly waving hair. 'What experience have you got?'

'None, but I can learn.'

He eyed her up and down, causing her acute discomfort, but it was obvious that he liked what he saw. 'I need someone straight away.'

'How about now?' She began to peel off her coat.

He looked her over again, minus her coat, and nodded. 'You'll do.'

'Thanks,' she said. 'Just tell me what to do and leave me to it. I won't let you down.'

'You'd better not,' he said. 'There's always someone else who can take your place.'

The work was hard and exhausting. She was not used to standing on her feet for long hours and by mid-afternoon her back was aching, she had a pain across her forehead, and she was feeling the effects of going without sleep the previous night.

She began to question the wisdom of her decision to find a job before looking for a room, for now she was trapped in the coffee bar until six o'clock and she grew more anxious by the hour that she had not secured a bed for the night.

During her meal-break she was entitled to help herself to any of the sandwiches stacked on the counter and she was aware that she ought to eat, for she had no money with which to buy a meal later in the evening, but she was without appetite and could bring herself to do no more than peck at the food.

At six o'clock she collected her two carrier bags and walked stiffly to the back room where the Manager sat in an old armchair, feet on table.

'It's six o'clock,' she said.

He looked her up and down as he had done when he had first seen her. 'What hours have you worked?'

'Nine-thirty until six.'

'Tomorrow you can do a two till ten.'

Barbie was pleased that she would have the morning free.

'Do you wanna come back to my place?'

She was taken aback by the suggestion but she had no wish to offend him. 'No thanks. I've got to go and get myself fixed up with a flat.'

'I live upstairs.' He nodded his head towards the ceiling.

'Oh.' There was an awkward silence. 'Thanks, but I know where I can find a flat. I saw it advertised this morning.'

'Suit yourself.' He shrugged indifferently and turned away from her.

'Well, I'll see you tomorrow, then. Two o'clock.'

He did not look at her but began to pick his teeth. 'Don't be late.'

She hurried out of the coffee bar and back to the tobacconist's shop. It was already closed but the card was still clearly displayed in the window.

She weighed the rental against the wage she had been offered at the coffee bar. There would be very little left for food. She had been in no position to bargain over her pay and the Manager had been ill-disposed to generosity.

She found a scrap of paper in her pocket and bit her lip when she found it was the paper on which Curly had written the address in Clapham. She turned it over and jotted down the telephone number of the flat to let, then looked around for a public callbox.

She had to walk back to Paddington Station before she found one, only to discover that it was engaged. There were eight callboxes on the station concourse and all were occupied. Rush-hour was in full swing and she was jostled by the crowd as she stood waiting. One carrier bag, which she had placed at her feet, was knocked over and trampled upon. She heard the sound of breaking glass and knew at once that it was the framed photograph of Gran on Brighton pier.

Someone emerged from one of the callboxes but, before she could collect up her bags, someone else had already beaten her to it. The same thing happened again, three times in all, before she found herself at last squeezed into the tiny cubicle. It was stuffy and retained the musty smell of sweat and the damp clothing of its previous occupants. She set down her bags, with very little room to move, aware of people waiting impatiently outside.

'Hello, who's that?' The girl's voice at the other end of the line sounded bored.

Barbie swallowed, nervous. 'I called about the flat.'

'Oh God, not another one.' The remark was passed for the benefit of someone else at the other end of the line. Then to Barbie, 'Sorry, it went first thing this morning.'

'Oh.' Barbie did not know what to say. There was an empty silence and she sensed that the receiver was about to be replaced at the other end. 'Are you sure?'

'Of course I'm sure. Christ, the bloody phone hasn't stopped ringing all day.'

'But I haven't anywhere to go.'

'You, and half of London, ducky. What do you expect me to do about it – bring 'em all in here?'

The receiver slammed down and Barbie heard the whirring sound of the disengaged line. Slowly she replaced her own receiver and stood staring blankly at the wall. Someone began banging on the glass of the door. She turned, picked up her bags, and fought her way back through the crowds of people.

Darkness had fallen more than an hour ago and now a steady drizzling rain began to wet the pavements, causing the harsh street lights to reflect off its surface. Shops and offices were closed for the night and everywhere people hurried towards their own particular destination. Barbie trudged away from the station, fighting down her fear and feeling that never had the world been more inhospitable.

For three hours she walked the streets, searching for any notice, any card, in any shop window, which might lead her to the comfort of a room but she achieved nothing beyond another three fruitless telephone calls. Her legs and her back ached and the carrier bags felt like two leaden weights. She was chilled to the bone. Several times men called to her and whistled as she passed, causing her to hurry off down side streets where she had no wish to go.

At last, having nowhere else to turn, she crept into Hyde Park and sat on a bench, huddled against the damp night air. Her coat was not waterproof and the rain had soaked through, causing her clothing to stick to her skin. She badly needed a warming drink but she dared not spend her few remaining coins. At Wansdyke

Avenue now they would be drinking hot chocolate, with steaming mugs cupped in their hands as they sat watching television. She wondered if they were thinking of her. She pictured Mark and Tracy, Ken and Mary, then thought of her room, her warm bed. She longed for comfort but, at the same time, knew that she would never return.

The cold forced her to move on. The pain in her feet begged her to rest but the numbness, brought on by cold, called for movement to increase the circulation. Paddington Station was the place to go. She had seen people there last night, sheltering from the cold. She quickened her pace, anxious for the shelter of its roof, and arrived a little after ten o'clock. She had been there for no more than half an hour when she saw two figures approaching. They were making their way slowly, shaking each bundle of sleeping humanity, asking them to move along. Barbie got up and hurried away. She had no wish to be confronted by the police.

Back on the street she found a shop doorway, deeply recessed and free from the driving rain. She sought sanctuary within its dark interior and, in a far corner, crouched down upon her haunches on the cold concrete floor. She arranged her bags about her and waited for the dawn.

She emerged as soon as it was light and began once more to walk the streets. The rain had stopped but she was bitterly cold and lightheaded after two nights without sleep. She wished that she could seek the warmth of the coffee bar but she was not due to start work until two o'clock and, somehow, she must find accommodation before that time. She scoured the streets, willing to accept anything which could serve as a temporary roof but her search was in vain and, at last, exhausted, she sought shelter in an amusement arcade, wandering among the slot machines and breathing in the smell of fish and chips from a nearby cafe. She would have no choice but to accept the invitation of the coffee bar Manager. She did not like the idea of sharing his flat but anything was better than the plight she faced.

She sat out the time until two o'clock then made her way back to the coffee bar. A girl, whom she had not seen before, was leaning against the counter studying her long, manicured nails.

'Are you Barbie?' The girl eyed her with a look of distaste. 'Chris asked me to give you this.' She handed Barbie a ten pound note.

Barbie looked around. There was no sign of the Manager.

'He said to tell you that you're not needed any more.' Barbie's numbed senses reeled. 'You're fired.'

'But why?'

'I decided to come back.' The girl went back to studying her nails. 'We had a row but now I'm back.'

'But he gave the job to me.'

'Correction, ducky. He gave the job to you when he thought I wasn't coming back. But now I have. And there's no room around here for two of us.' She nodded her head towards the ceiling. 'Especially when I'm shacked up with him upstairs.'

'Oh,' said Barbie, not knowing what to say.

'So; off you go then. You've got your money, so get on your bike and shift.'

There was nothing Barbie could think of to say. She turned and walked away.

With the ten pound note she bought herself a meal and afterwards, in the warmth of the restaurant, sat contemplating her fate. Her damp clothing was still sticking to her back and in the warmer atmosphere she was uncomfortably aware of goose-flesh and clay-cold steam. She had no home, no job, and very little money.

The scrap of paper seemed to be burning a hole in her pocket. She took it out, read it, replaced it, then took it out again. The paper was damp and the ink had smudged but it was still possible to decipher the address, on Clapham Common, South Side. It had an inviting ring to it. It offered the warmth of a flat, a job – of sorts – and money in her pocket. She ordered another cup of coffee and sat for a long time deliberating upon her possibilities. She could go home, but there was no question of that. She could get another job and find a flat; slender hope. Or, she could go . . . for just a short while . . .

One of the lessons which Barbie had learned in life was that people use one another. Without compunction, they use and then discard. So, why not she? She need not stay for long. She could use the flat as a stepping stone to something new. She would have to work, to . . . entertain. But, what did it matter? It was a job and nothing more. She would use it as a breathing space while she made plans. She paid her bill and caught the tube to Clapham.

It was raining again when she emerged from the underground

176

but she found the flat without difficulty and rang the bell. She rang three times and her heart began to drop from fear of another wasted journey. As she waited she repeated over and again her prepared speech of explanation but when the door eventually opened she merely blurted, 'Curly told me.'

'You must be Barbie.' The girl before her was wearing a blue silk negligée, hastily draped about her. Her eyelids were heavy with sleep and it was obvious that she had just risen from her bed. 'Sorry, luv. I just got up.' She smiled and yawned. 'Curly told us you'd be coming.'

'But I told him no.'

The girl laughed. 'Old Curly's never wrong, luv. I bet his old Granny had a crystal ball.' As she spoke she stepped to one side in a gesture of welcome and Barbie went inside. The flat was spacious with a comfortable, lived-in atmosphere and the air temperature was warm, making her all the more aware of the sticky discomfort of her damp clothing.

'Sit yourself down. I'll get you a cup of coffee.' As she passed, she tapped on a door which was immediately opened by another girl wearing a towel wrapped round her head. 'Sue. This is Barbie.'

'Hi.' The second girl flashed Barbie a smile. 'Glad to see you've made it.'

'Barbie; this is Sue. Oh, and by the way, I'm Debbie.'

'Hello.' Barbie was half-shy, half-overwhelmed by the warmth of the reception. After the cold hostility of city streets she found it difficult to adjust. She dropped the weight of the two carrier bags and sank gratefully into the comfort of the settee.

'Here; drink this up.' Debbie handed her the mug of hot coffee. 'You look as if you need it.'

Barbie wrapped her hands about the steaming mug. 'Thank you,' she said. 'You're very kind. I don't know why you should.'

'We were all new in London once, luv. Someone helped us out.'

Sue unwrapped the towel from her head, letting fall a heavy mane of thick, waist-length hair. 'London's a great place when you've got friends,' she said. 'When you're on your own it can be hell.'

'It is lonely,' said Barbie with feeling. She downed the coffee but its effect was to make her shiver.

'Here, come on, luv. You'd best be getting out of those wet

clothes.' Debbie placed her hand on Barbie's damp coat. 'You'll catch your death of cold. Hey, Sue; run her a bath, and make it nice and hot.'

At any other time Barbie would have put up some kind of resistance but at this moment she was totally exhausted. She meekly allowed herself to be led to the bathroom which was filled with hot steam and the perfume of expensive bath oil.

'There's a robe behind the door,' said Sue. She laid out a pile of clean towels. 'You can wrap yourself in it when you're ready.'

She left Barbie alone and Barbie sank down beneath the surface of the hot, perfumed water. Only minutes before she had been out on the cold, inhospitable streets and now here she was, in surroundings of luxury, feeling the chill being driven from her body. She closed her eyes and sighed, feeling herself unwind, the tension and the fear, the aching muscles and the cold, all giving way to a feeling of relief. Beyond the door she could hear the sound of voices, the clatter of plates, a short burst of laughter, and she allowed herself to sink deeper into a state of relaxation. The flat was warm and welcoming, the girls were kind. It was a haven and she would accept their hospitality for a while until she was ready to move on.

The girls were cooking eggs and bacon when she emerged and there was a smell of freshly-percolating coffee and toast. 'Sit yourself down,' called Debbie. 'One egg, or two?'

'One, please.' Barbie sat down at the breakfast table which was laid ready for her. 'I've already eaten lunch.'

Sue laughed. 'You'll soon get used to us. We always eat breakfast when everyone else has tea.' Barbie looked at her watch. It was almost four o'clock.

'Help yourself to anything you need.' Debbie broke eggs into a pan, then carried over a plate which she placed before Barbie. 'We have a Mrs Andrews who comes in to clean for us and she always stocks us up with piles of food.'

'It's very nice here.' Barbie looked about her. 'It's a lovely flat.'

'Real home from home. Old Curly does us proud.' Debbie looked across at Barbie and the smile was replaced by a more serious expression. 'He's a good chap, Barbie. You're lucky that he found you.'

'I don't know how he knew. I told him I wouldn't come.'

'Curly knows how to choose his girls, luv. He has a knack for it.' Debbie brought two more plates to the table and sat down to join them.

Sue poured coffee then went to a cupboard for a bottle of mayonnaise. 'Would you like some?' She offered the bottle to Barbie who squirmed at the thought of mayonnaise on bacon and eggs.

'Don't take any notice of her,' laughed Debbie. 'She has some very strange eating habits.'

Sue grinned and unscrewed the cap from the bottle. 'There's nothing wrong with me just because I happen to like mayonnaise.'

'I've just remembered.' Debbie leaned backwards in her chair and took an envelope from the shelf behind her. 'Curly said to give you this.' She handed it to Barbie. 'He said to give it to you and tell you that you needn't start work until you feel you're ready.'

Barbie slit open the envelope and gasped. It contained ten, five pound notes. 'I can't take that. It wouldn't be right.'

Debbie shrugged. 'That's up to you. He just told me to give it to you. He said you might need it.'

Barbie pushed the envelope to one side. She was feeling confused and her need for sleep was overlaying the situation with an even greater sense of unreality.

'Does he live here?' She looked around for signs of male habitation.

'No. He's got a house over in Putney. He's got a wife and three kids. Thinks the world of them.'

'Do they know?' Barbie found it impossible to correlate the family man with the purpose for which she knew he had recruited her.

'Know what?'

'What he does in this flat?'

'No.' Debbie was once again serious. 'It's the one thing which Curly insists on. For all they know, he's just a cabbie.'

'Oh,' said Barbie. 'I see,' although she most certainly did not see.

'Whatever you do, Barbie, you must always make sure that you do nothing to let his family know about this place. It's the one thing which would make him really angry. We never go near Putney and if we go out with Curly in his cab we act like we're paying passengers. Agreed?'

'Agreed,' said Barbie.

'Apart from that, there aren't many restrictions. This is a high-class establishment and we're lucky to have Curly as the Boss.'

'It's a service really,' put in Sue. 'Just think of all those women out there who'd get raped if it wasn't for us. They'd soon miss us if we weren't around.'

Barbie bit her lip, apprehensive when faced with the role to which she had submitted herself.

'Don't tell her that. You'll frighten her half to death. Anyway, we're not hookers. We don't stand around on street corners.' Debbie smiled encouragingly at Barbie. 'We have a very exclusive clientèle,' she said. 'We only take them on personal recommendation.'

'Oh, we're very exclusive,' mimicked Sue, good-naturedly. 'We must never call ourselves "hookers"; we're "escorts".'

'We *are* escorts,' said Debbie. 'You'd soon know the difference if you were standing on some street corner.'

'A rose by any other name,' said Sue, still grinning.

Debbie threw her an affectionate but reproving glance. 'Our clients pay for our company,' she said to Barbie. 'They take us out and we perform any other service they require.'

'They take you out?'

'To all kinds of places. Wives are all right at home but there are some places where a man wants to be seen with someone young and trendy, someone who knows how to enjoy themselves and have a good time.'

'Oh,' said Barbie again.

'They're more like friends really,' said Debbie reassuringly. 'We very rarely get any trouble.'

'And Curly will soon come running if we need him,' said Sue. 'He's got a phone in his cab.'

'We've never had to call him yet. Curly vets the clients. He's as good at choosing clients as he is at choosing his girls.'

'One of the girls in Wandsworth once had a psycho,' put in Sue. 'You should have seen old Curly sort him out.'

'So he's got other girls, then?' queried Barbie. 'In other places?'

'Three flats, not counting this one. They're all nice girls. You'll like them. We all get together sometimes and have a party.'

'Oh,' said Barbie for the umpteenth time. She looked down at the envelope on the table. 'He must be a rich man with all those girls.'

'I don't know. It doesn't matter very much so long as he pays us well.'

'I didn't mean . . .'

'He's a good boss, Barbie, as far as pimps go, and if he takes a liking to you then you're on to a good thing.'

'And he likes you,' cut in Sue.

'Oh, I shouldn't think . . .'

'He took a real liking to you; you can always tell.'

'Oh,' said Barbie limply.

'Did you sleep last night?' Debbie began clearing the plates from the table.

'No.'

'I thought not. You'd better get some rest now.' She piled the dishes in the sink and left them for Mrs Andrews to wash. 'I'll show you to your room and you can go to bed.'

Barbie ran her knuckles across eyelids which were heavy and sore. 'I am rather tired,' she admitted. 'It was a bit scary last night in that shop doorway.'

'Jeez! I remember my first week.' Sue was testing the dampness of her hair. 'Three nights in a hostel, then down on the Embankment with the junkies. God knows what would have happened if Curly hadn't turned up.' She took out a brush and began to draw it through the mane of hair. 'I'm going up West later. There's this fab outfit I saw last week. All slinky black with a neckline down to your boots.'

'With your bust,' smiled Debbie 'there isn't anything to cover anyway.'

Sue squared up a figure which was lithe and boyish but which would have seen her through any of the top London fashion houses. 'Jealous,' she said good-naturedly.

Debbie smiled and led Barbie down the hall to her room. She was a girl with sufficient attributes of her own. She had no need of jealousy. 'We shan't disturb you,' she said. 'We start work at about eight and we don't get back here until the early hours.'

Barbie looked about the room and smiled her thanks. 'Debbie . . .' she said, as Debbie was leaving. 'I'm not sure . . .' Debbie turned in response '. . . if I'll be any good.'

'Don't worry, luv.' Debbie smiled and closed the door. 'It's only a job.'

The room was large and comfortable, with heavily-curtained windows facing out onto the Common. The air was misty and already it was almost dark but she could just see the outline of trees. It would be pleasant in the summer – if she stayed that long. She could go for walks and feel the grass beneath her feet. She slipped between satin sheets and fell immediately into a deep sleep.

It was morning when she woke. The girls were sleeping and she tiptoed about the flat, tidying up, washing the dishes which had been left in the sink for Mrs Andrews. It was a pleasant feeling, a feeling of belonging, of self-assurance such as she had never known in Wickhampton.

At ten o'clock Mrs Andrews arrived. She was a happy, bustling little woman, her shopping basket crammed with food to supplement the already well-stocked larder. She accepted Barbie with a ready smile, asking no questions.

She took out her apron and a polishing cloth, setting about the furniture with a zest which Barbie found infectious. She offered to help but, when this was refused, she went out onto the Common, walking away her own excess energy beneath the dripping plane trees. She did not return until midday.

When she let herself into the flat she found Curly sitting waiting for her. 'Wotcha, Sunshine,' he said. 'Feeling good?'

'Yes, thank you.' Barbie stopped, surprised to find him there. He was sitting at the kitchen table reading a newspaper.

'Any chance of a sandwich?'

'Yes, of course.' She stood looking at him for a moment, sharply aware that it was entirely due to this man that she had reason to feel good. It brought a sensation of unease and she wondered again what she had let herself in for. He looked up at her, aware of her hesitation, and she moved quickly to the refrigerator. 'Ham? or cheese?'

'Cheese,' he said. 'And don't spare the pickle.'

She handed him the sandwich then went to her room for the envelope containing the fifty pounds. 'You had better have this back,' she said. 'I haven't earned it.'

He smiled without looking up from his newspaper and pushed it back towards her. 'Keep it. There's plenty more where that came from.'

'But that's not fair.'

'Fair? Who's talking about fair?'

'I can't take money I haven't earned.'

He laid down his newspaper and looked at her. 'You don't need to work until you feel you're ready.'

She shook her head. 'That's not right.'

'Look, Sunshine. You'll work a lot better if you start when you're ready. That way you'll be happy and relaxed. That's what the clients like. It's what they pay for.'

Barbie lowered her eyes. 'I don't know if I can.'

'Of course you can. I wouldn't have brought you here if you couldn't.' He waited until she raised her eyes. 'If you weren't here,' he said, 'you'd be out there somewhere on the streets. There are some bad people out on those streets, Sunshine. I wouldn't like to think of you mixed up with them.' Barbie nodded. She felt grateful to him without trying to unravel the logic of his reasoning. 'Watch the girls and take your time. You're young yet but you'll soon learn.' He pushed the envelope a little nearer to her. 'And enjoy yourself while you're learning.'

She did not pick it up but said instead, 'Would you like another sandwich?'

'No thanks, but I'll have a cup of coffee.' He leaned back, crossing his legs as he watched her. 'What colour do you call that hair?'

She touched her hair self-consciously. 'I don't know. I suppose it's ginger.'

'No. That's not ginger.'

He sat looking at her for a further moment. 'I had an old dog once who was just your colour. Lovely old thing, he was. Do you like dogs?'

Barbie nodded. It was a long time since she had thought of Bess. 'I had one once.'

'What breed?'

'Collie.'

'Collie, eh,' he said. 'Nice dogs, collies.'

'Yes; she was a lovely dog.'

'What happened to it?'

'She died.'

She felt uncomfortable beneath his gaze but sensed that it was not ill-intentioned. She handed him the cup of coffee.

'Do you want to tell me something about yourself?'

Immediately she felt herself stiffen, on her guard. 'There's nothing to tell.'

183

'There's always something to tell.'

'No,' she said sharply. 'There's nothing very interesting about me.'

'Then I'd better get back to work.' He smiled at her kindly and downed the coffee in one gulp without pausing for breath. 'I've got a cab to run.' He rolled the newspaper and tucked it beneath his arm. 'I'll see you around. Thanks for the coffee and the sandwich.'

'See you,' she replied and watched him walk out of the door.

She did not see him for three days but when he next appeared at the door there was a broad grin upon his face and his arms were folded across the front of his overcoat. 'I've brought you a present,' he said. 'Close your eyes and hold out your arms.' Barbie looked at him intrigued as she saw movement inside his coat. 'Close your eyes,' he said again. She closed her eyes but thought immediately of the churchyard and Mad Billy. She opened them in time to see him removing a puppy from his coat. 'Here you are. His name's Sam.'

Sam was an Irish Setter puppy, with a coat of mahogany red and with long silken ears and eyes the colour of marmalade. He flopped into Barbie's arms and licked her face.

'Oh, he's lovely, Curly.' She held the puppy which wriggled and kicked against her. 'But I couldn't possibly take him. It wouldn't be right.'

'What's all this about right? According to you, nothing's right.'

'But, why?'

'You mean, what's the catch.' She flushed and smiled. 'You're a suspicious little wench. How about "because I like you"?'

She shook her head. 'I couldn't.'

'For crying out loud! I bought him for you because I thought you might be in need of a friend. What's wrong with that?'

She hesitated and half turned away. It shocked her to know that Curly had interpreted her need but she sensed again that his interest was not intrusive. 'I don't know what to say.'

'Then don't say anything. There's no need.'

'Thank you, Curly. Thank you very much.'

Curly laughed. 'He'll be a big dog when he's grown. He'll run you off your feet.'

'Oh no he won't.' She ruffled Sam's ears. 'We're going to run across the Common together, aren't we, Sam. Just you and me.'

She released the wriggling puppy, setting him down on the

184

floor and laughed at his antics as he ran about sniffing the legs of the furniture and then slipped and fell, rolling over in a silken ball. 'He's lovely, Curly. I think he's the nicest present I ever had.'

'I'm glad you like him, Sunshine. You're a proper smasher when you smile.' She gave him a quick self-conscious glance but he grinned and turned away. 'I've got another one just like him in the cab. I'm taking him home for the kids.'

Barbie looked at him again. She had great difficulty in coming to terms with his dual role. At this moment he was a typical family man. 'How old are your children?'

'I've got two boys of nine; they're twins. And then there's Katy. She was six last month.'

'You must be very proud of them.'

'Don't know about proud.' Curly pouted his lower lip. 'They're right little tearaways, those boys. Reckon they're worse than I was at their age, and that's saying something.' He grinned again. 'There's no harm in them, though. Tough as nails on the outside but their hearts are in the right place.'

'And what about Katy?'

'Katy? Right little smasher, our Katy is. The Missus reckons I'm proper soft with all of them. Says I spoil them shocking.'

'I'd like to meet them.'

'Yeah, it's a pity that you can't. You'd like the Missus. Not much to look at but she's a good girl, my Eileen.'

'It must be nice to have a family.'

'I expect you'll have one of your own, one of these days. Most people do.'

'Maybe,' said Barbie, but without enthusiasm.

'You wait, some day you'll meet some big, handsome bloke and finish up with half a dozen kids.' He bent down and patted Sam in a gesture of farewell. 'Well, I must be off and earn some money. Else the wife will starve.'

Barbie wished that he did not confuse her so. 'Thank you, Curly. He's a lovely present.'

'See you, Sunshine.' He gave her a broad grin and walked out of the door.

Sam proved himself to be a demanding charge. He puddled the floors and chewed the furniture until very little remained which did not bear his toothmarks. Debbie and Sue loved him and, although they all tried to divert his attention to more acceptable habits, no one minded when he was found chewing a slipper or a pair of jeans. Barbie devoted every moment of her time to him, feeding him only the very best food and lavishing upon him all the love and affection for which, for so many years, she had had no other outlet.

She was so preoccupied with her new-found interest that, before she stopped to count the days, a month had passed. It was mid-December and the shops in Clapham High Street were alive with the activity of Christmas. She bought presents for Sam and for Debbie and Sue, then looked round for something special for Curly. It had to be something which would please him but which he would not need to take home. The solution defeated her and she returned to the flat with the intention of leaving Sam and venturing, for the first time, to the West End stores.

Sue was in the kitchen, having got up early in order to do her own Christmas shopping. 'Curly left you this,' she called as soon as Barbie entered the room. She handed her an envelope. It was heavy and Barbie could tell at a glance that it contained a large sum of money. She had refused other envelopes over the past month, insisting that she had not yet spent the money in the first, but now Curly had left it in her absence. 'He said you'd need it for Christmas.'

Barbie turned the envelope in her hand. 'I've been here a whole month and I've done absolutely nothing.'

'Yes, you have. You're always cleaning the place up. You're doing Mrs Andrews out of a job.'

'You know what I mean.'

'Jeez, I don't know what you're worried about. Curly told you that you needn't work till you're ready.'

'But I've been here a month.'

'So what? Maybe it will take you three, or even six.'

'No, I can't do that. It wouldn't be right.' She drew back her shoulders and swallowed on the decision which she knew she must make. 'I think it's time now that I started to earn it.'

Chapter Ten

Barbie was quick to learn in her newly-acquired profession. Debbie and Sue took her in hand and set about transforming the image of a sixteen year old girl into a trendy sophistication which belied her tender years. 'Men are funny creatures,' said Debbie. 'They like their girls young, yet they don't like to be accused of cradle snatching.' It was a remark which made Barbie look again at the two girls, realising that it was impossible for her to assess their ages.

They took her to the West End stores and taught her how to buy her clothes, keeping abreast of fashion but with always an eye to clothes which would enhance her natural grace and beauty. With make-up she learned to highlight her delicate features, and her hair was re-styled to fall about her face with a soft casualness, enhanced by its natural curl and rich colouring. The final image surprised her and delighted the men who flocked to seek her company.

The girls took her to restaurants and taught her poise and etiquette. They taught her to have fun and, above all, to be a good companion. To this end, they also taught her to spend money with an attitude of 'easy come, easy go' – which filled her wardrobe with expensive clothes to be worn once and then discarded for something new.

It was a style of life which could have turned the heads of many girls but not of Barbie. She played her role and she had fun but a certain part of her remained at all times private, never shared, except with Sam. To her clients there was something particularly alluring about the girl who appeared to give so much and yet retained a certain secret place which no man could ever enter.

She did her work well and learned to please. No one ever

guessed the secret feelings of frustration, the longing for fulfilment which never came. There were the times when she thought she would succeed – the rising tide, the quivering expectancy that any moment it would surge – but always it would come to naught, fading away beyond recall, and once again she was the actress playing her part of make-believe so that no man ever suspected her desire to rise up from the bed and crash her head against the wall in sheer frustration.

She did not dwell upon her sense of failure but tried to keep it locked away, burying it beneath a zest for life and for her new-found freedom. Yet, repeatedly, it overflowed and trickled through her joy in icy runnels which would not be stemmed.

She awoke each day before noon, long before the other girls stirred, and shared her day with Sam. They would walk across the Common, she throwing sticks, while Sam leapt and charged across the grass, a streak of mahogany red in hot pursuit. Then he would tease her with the stick, refuse to give it up, growl and shake it between his teeth, and she would laugh and bowl him over in a boisterous game of youthful spirit, until each was spent and they lay together in the grass.

Together they made voyages of discovery to every park and open space in London and often ventured further afield to Richmond, or to Runnymede, or Windsor. The nights were for dressing up, for glamour and pretence, but the days belonged to Sam.

It was on one such day that she happened by chance to see Curly as she crossed the Common. An early spring had given way to high summer and she and Sam were revelling in the warmth of the sun. 'You're an early riser, Sunshine.' Curly drew over to the kerb and opened the door of his cab as an invitation for her to get in.

'It's much too good to lie in bed.' She called to Sam who bounded up beside her on the seat. 'Poor old Curly, to be working. Today's a day when everyone should take a holiday.'

Curly laughed. 'And where would Madame like to take her holiday?'

She thought for a moment. 'To the sea, I think. I'd like to feel the wind blowing on my face.'

Curly pulled away from the kerb to join the stream of traffic. 'Your wish, my Sunshine,' he said, 'is my command.'

'Hey, Curly. I didn't mean it. I was joking.'

But Curly only smiled. 'It's much too good for working. You said so yourself.'

He drove the cab to Southend while she sat in the back with the windows opened wide to the wind which blew her hair and ruffled the long, silken coat of Sam beside her.

'And what now, Madame?' asked Curly as he parked the cab. 'Would Madame like to dip her toes?'

'Oh, yes, please, Curly.'

The water shimmered in the mid-afternoon sunshine and all about was the sound of children's laughter. The beach was crowded and they had to thread their way across the shingle, their feet sinking and sliding upon the pebbles, to reach the water's edge.

'Come on, Curly, off with your shoes!' Barbie flung off her own sandals and hobbled towards the water. 'Ow! I wish this beach was sand.'

Curly laughed. 'You go. I'm staying here.'

'Oh, come on, Curly. Be a sport.'

'I'm past the age for paddling.'

'I don't believe you.' She smiled the smile which he could never resist. He took off his shoes and tied the laces round his neck. They rolled their trousers above their knees and jumped the waves like children, running and laughing as they stamped and splashed, while Sam, rollicking in his first experience of the sea, swam, and barked, and shook himself all over them.

They lunched on jellied eels and chips which tasted more delicious than all the cordon bleu delights to which Barbie had become accustomed. They washed it down with cans of lager and finished off with ice cream cones topped with strawberry sauce and sticks of flaked chocolate, standing up like ears.

'I warrant you'll be sick,' said Curly but Barbie laughed and took his arm.

'Will you take me to the fair?'

'The fair? On top of jellied eels and ice cream?'

'Oh, please, Curly. I've only been to the fair once. And I wanted so much to ride on the big dipper and Aunty "M" wouldn't let me.'

Curly glanced at her out of the corner of his eye. 'Who's Aunty "M"?'

Barbie clammed up but, when he did not pursue the subject,

she gradually let go her pent-up breath and smiled at him knowingly. 'I don't believe I've told you about Aunty "M".'

'I can't recall you mentioning her.' He cupped his hand over her own which rested through his arm. 'And you don't have to now if you don't want to.'

They had begun to walk along the promenade at a slow, leisurely stride, as Sam dashed back and forth about their heels. 'No, I don't mind. She was my father's wife.'

'Was?'

'Still is, I suppose. I haven't thought about them for a long time.'

'Perhaps they think of you.'

'I doubt it.'

'They may wonder where you are.'

She shrugged. 'Maybe.'

They walked on for a while without speaking then Curly said, 'Sometimes people do their best even though it's not good enough.' She looked at him, not understanding. 'Just because they fail, it doesn't mean they didn't try.'

She thought about it for a moment. '"D" was quite nice really. I think he was afraid of Aunty "M".'

Curly laughed. 'A mouse, was he?'

'You could say that, I suppose.'

'Sometimes a mouse can become a lion in the right circumstances.'

Barbie laughed with him. 'I can't imagine "D" ever being a lion. But . . .' She hesitated and the laughter faded. 'I remember once he got very angry with me.'

She had become tense and he squeezed her hand. 'People get angry when they really care. If he didn't care about you he wouldn't have bothered to get angry.'

'I never thought of it like that.'

'Perhaps you should. Things sometimes look different when you understand the reasons behind them.'

'I doubt that Aunty "M" ever really cared.'

Curly fingered his ear with his free hand and looked out to sea. 'Sometimes people have a funny way of showing that they care. They've got so much trouble coping with their own hang-ups, there isn't much energy left for other people.'

Barbie coughed out a small, bitter laugh. 'She had plenty of time for cleaning the house and going out to work!'

190

'That type often work their butts off so there's no time left to face themselves.'

Barbie stopped walking and turned to look Curly full in the face. 'Curly, you never stop surprising me. You know so much about people.'

Curly stuck out his lip, amused. 'I don't know about that,' he said. 'But I've done my share of reading.'

'You're always coming out with things I don't expect.'

'So, you don't expect me to be able to read? You think that pimps don't read?'

'Oh, please don't, Curly.' He had spoiled the moment. Curly looked at her sideways but said nothing. 'What sort of books do you read?'

'All kinds of books. Freud, Jung, Adler. I like to know what makes people tick. Plato . . .'

'Plato!' exclaimed Barbie.

'Plato,' he repeated. 'What's wrong with Plato?'

'Nothing,' she laughed. 'I just can't imagine you . . .' She tailed off knowing that she had no need to finish. He patted her hand and both knew that they had formed another, closer bond to their affection.

'I wish you'd been my Dad.'

'You've got ice cream stuck on your chin.'

She wiped it off with the back of her hand. 'I still don't think you're right about my Aunty "M". She could cope with anything.'

He shrugged. 'Maybe. How should I know. I never met her.' They were passing a stall selling picture postcards. He took one from a rack and flipped a coin towards an assistant who was standing nearby. 'There is one thing I do know, though – about your Dad. He'd like to know that you're OK.'

Barbie felt her muscles go tense, and he responded with a slight pressure on her arm. 'You need only write a couple of words.'

'But I don't want them to know, Curly.'

'What's wrong with letting them know that you're OK?'

'They wouldn't like what I'm doing.'

'How could they know? A few words on a postcard from Southend. They couldn't even trace you.'

'Oh, I don't know, Curly.' She drew away from him but he kept hold of her arm. 'They've probably forgotten all about me by now.'

'You don't really mean that.' He led her to a nearby bench and

191

sat her down. 'You're not telling me that your Dad never stops to wonder what's happened to you.'

'I guess he does.'

He reached into his pocket for a pen and handed it to her with the postcard. 'Then write a couple of lines and put his mind at rest.'

She balanced the postcard on her knee and let the pen hover for a moment, then she wrote quickly.

Dear Aunty M and D,
   Everything's OK. Please don't worry.
   Love,
   Barbie.
   PS I hope you all are well.

Curly fished into his wallet and produced a stamp. 'Here,' he said. 'Stick that on and we'll drop it into the nearest postbox.'

As she dropped it into the box she turned to him and smiled. 'I've got a sort of good feeling for doing that.'

He laughed. 'Come on, Sunshine. I'll take you to the fair.'

They walked on along the promenade in a comfortable, companionable silence.

'Curly? Why do you do it?'

'Do what?'

'You know . . . the flat.'

'It's a good source of income.'

'Come off it, Curly. It's not the money.'

He grinned self-consciously. 'Now who's the philosopher?'

She tightened her arm upon his. 'Why, Curly?'

'Perhaps it's got something to do with memories.'

'Memories of what?'

'Of watching my Mum get beaten up by some sod of a pimp who took all her money.'

'I'm sorry, Curly.' She turned to him and smiled. 'I would have thought it would have put you off the game altogether.'

He gave a wry smile. 'That's what you call burying your head in the sand. There'll always be daft young kids finding their way into it.'

'But there's no need for you to be involved.'

'Reckon they're better off with me than with some of the others.'

'But why . . . ?' She was still not fully in tune with his logic. 'I don't understand . . .'

'I thought we were supposed to be going to the fair.' He increased his pace and she knew at once that he had finished with the conversation.

'Can I go on the big dipper?'

'You can go on anything you like so long as I get home in time to see the kids before they go to bed.'

Later, in the cool of the evening, he dropped her off outside the flat. As he leaned back from the driving seat in order to open the passenger door he gave her a long, searching look. 'Are you happy here?'

'Happier than I've been for years.'

'When you feel the need to move on, there's nothing here to hold you.'

She looked at him, surprised. 'I like being here.'

'There are lots of other things to do in life.'

'But there's nothing else I want to do.' She reached out for his hand and he took it and squeezed the fingers.

'Some day you'll think of something. Or some man will come along.'

'Who knows? Maybe I shall never meet anyone who will want me.'

'Don't hang about to say goodbye. Just leave a note and go.'

'You know I'd never do a thing like that.'

'Why not? You don't owe me anything.'

'You've been too good to me.'

'You'll see.' He smiled and raised her hand to his lips. 'And I hope he'll be good to you.'

He released her hand and she stood watching after him as he drove away. She kept him in sight until he disappeared amid the heavy stream of traffic, then she turned on her heel and went into the flat to prepare for the client of the evening.

Almost two years passed and nothing happened to change Barbie's mind. She entertained a hundred men but no one ever touched her heart and never once, in all that time, did she achieve that satisfaction for which her body craved. At eighteen, she had matured to even greater beauty. She had money and expensive clothes; everything, she told herself, that any girl could ever hope to have.

The day on which she met the fat man started out much like any other, except that it was a day on which her spirits were particularly high. It was early May and the Common had burst forth into new leaf. The horse chestnuts were preparing to unsheath their candles and, over dingy backyard walls, almond and cherry trees were wantonly scattering petals before the feet of passers-by. She had taken Sam to Richmond Park and now she returned happy and refreshed, ready for the evening.

Her client was a man whom she had not met before and she rushed to get ready, aware that she was short of time. He arrived by taxi and it was Sue who opened the door to him. 'Your client's here.' She put her head round the door of Barbie's room. 'He's not the most handsome man I've ever seen.'

'Do you want to swap?'

'You must be joking. I've got that tall one with the gorgeous legs.'

Barbie kept him waiting for a few minutes, then stepped out to greet him. 'Hello. I'm Barbie.'

He was grossly overweight, breathing heavily through a bulbous nose. 'I'm charmed to meet you.'

She noticed that there were beads of perspiration on his brow and that the flesh of his neck hung in folds across a too-tight collar. She was almost tempted to feign some illness which would incapacitate her for the night; but Barbie was a professional. She swallowed down her feelings of repugnance and held out her hand in welcome.

'You're very beautiful,' he said, and she smiled as if it were the first time anyone had ever told her so. He took the hand to his mouth and she could feel the breath from his nostrils.

'You're very kind.' She pulled gently to make him release her fingers and handed him a long, embroidered evening coat which he took and placed about her shoulders.

'What would you like to do tonight?' he asked.

She turned and smiled. 'That's up to you. I'm here to please you.'

She heard him swallow and fancied that the beads of perspiration stood out more prominently across his brow.

'I suggest we eat,' he said. 'And then . . .' he swallowed again '. . . we'll think of something else to do.'

He wined and dined her, then took her on to the Casino where they played the tables. As he cast his bets she stood behind his chair with her hand on his shoulder. Several times he looked up at her and the beads of perspiration stood out so that he had need to take out his handkerchief and wipe them away. He gambled heavily, passing to her all the chips he won and shrugging elaborately at his losses. By the early hours of the morning she was one hundred pounds richer and, with a fixed professional smile, she took his arm and led him back to the flat.

Debbie and Sue were both in their rooms, having returned earlier than she. She heard the sound of music and of a man's voice raised in delighted laughter.

'Do come this way.' She took the fat man's coat and ducked provocatively as he reached out a clammy hand to touch her. 'Just help yourself to a drink in there and I'll go and freshen up.'

She went into the kitchen where Sam stirred in his basket and wagged his tail. 'Goodnight, Sam.' She knelt down on the floor beside him. 'I've really got to earn my money tonight. He's like a big, fat pig.' She lifted Sam's ear and snorted into it, while Sam turned lazily and licked her face. 'It's all right for you, lying there asleep. I've got to go in there and do my bit.' Sam let out a long sigh and settled back to sleep.

She left him and went to the bathroom where she showered and wrapped herself in a pale lilac-coloured negligée. The silk felt good against her skin and she shivered at the thought of the fat man's hands.

He was in his underpants when she entered the room – baggy boxer shorts, with the elastic biting into the pale, anaemic flesh of his flabby belly. His erect penis protruded like an undersized finger.

'What took you so long?' He beckoned and she walked towards him.

The skin of his chest and shoulders was pale and hairless, mottled with blue veins. She put her lips to a slightly jutting nipple and kissed it, stroking her hands across his body as she did so. She felt him shudder and he tugged at her negligée, tearing it away from her shoulders and flinging it across the room.

'I want it at least three times,' he breathed heavily. He kissed her, full and wet, upon the mouth, his breath laden with the smell of gin.

'Of course. Let's make it four.' She doubted that this man could make it even once but it was her task to see that he did, and she was highly skilled for the purpose.

195

'I want to do it other ways.' His heavy breathing had become a harsh, rasping sound and his body was quivering.

She led him to the bed, his hands and mouth all over her, groping, kissing in an all-pervading smell of sweat and gin.

As she sank down upon the bed she thought of Gran. She knew not why, for the connection was not evident in her mind, but it was the smell of sweat and gin. It was also something about the feel of his flesh, the soft folds of excess fat enveloping her as he pressed down, suffocating her with the smell of sweat, and gin, and fat.

'Gran . . . ?' The cry was silent first as her hands reached out for the long familiar touch of something which was now but a hazy memory. Her mind became filled with thoughts of home, the sights, sounds and smells of home, – the memory of Gran's dentures in the old cracked mug on the bedside table.

'Gran . . . ?'

Her hands began to grope towards some half-formed recollection and her body struggled frantically as memories rose like a nebulous picture show, building ever stronger until they screamed for recognition. She struggled, and writhed, and fought towards a greater understanding until she heard her own voice crying out.

'Oh, Gran! Oh, Gran! I love you, Gran.' With a great explosion her body rocked, convulsing in a never-ending series of tremors which left her weak and gasping.

'My God, you're good.' The fat man fell back and gasped against the pillow. She turned and looked at him, the pale flesh now almost grey, and his mouth open to emit the gasping breath. His jaw hung slack, sagging into the folds of his fat neck.

She thought she would be sick. Her body heaved and she struggled to her feet. 'I don't feel well,' she whispered and stumbled from the room. As she went, he held out a flabby hand to restrain her but she pulled away and, exhausted, he let it flop back on the bed. She took one last look at him and felt her stomach heave again. This was the man who had brought her orgasmic fulfilment and she found the sight of him utterly repulsive.

She emptied her stomach then threw herself beneath the shower, scrubbing her body until the skin was red and painful. She sat on the floor and rocked back and forth, banging her head softly against the wall. The self-loathing heaved and lurched inside her.

It took a long time to gain some measure of control over her shivering limbs but eventually she picked herself up and dressed herself in a sweater and a pair of jeans. She went back to her room, intending to tell the man that he must leave, but he was sleeping, snoring through a gaping mouth. She left him there and called to Sam, taking him with her as she let herself out of the front door and onto the streets of Clapham.

The early morning air felt soft against her face and the pale glow of dawn was breaking up the eastern sky. A silence hung in the air as though the city were holding its breath waiting for the dawn chorus of the birds. She walked on the Common, avoiding the trees which stood darkly forboding in skirts of shadow, and kept instead to the perimeter. She knew that it was unwise to walk the streets at this hour of the morning but she did not care and, in any event, she had Sam close by to protect her.

She took great gulps of cool air, drawing it down into her lungs through parted lips in some vain hope that it would cleanse her of the self-disgust which sickened her. Instead, it had the effect of making her dizzy and she was forced to rest for a while upon a bench.

'Oh, Gran. Oh, Gran. I miss you, Gran.' The thoughts mingled with the self-loathing and the dizziness until her mind reeled in confusion. 'Why did you go away with no goodbye?' Her head slumped forward into her cupped hands. 'The only man who ever made me come and he was so . . . Oh, God, he was so . . .' The thought of the fat man made her stomach lurch again. 'Why did you go away with no goodbye?'

She did not know how long she stayed thus upon the bench but in time she lifted her head and parted her hands from her eyes. On the opposite side of the road which skirted the Common there was a poster. She could see it quite clearly, for it carried a simple message printed in large red letters upon a plain white background.'

'JESUS LOVES YOU'

'Oh, Gran. You bleeding liar.'

'*Gentle Jesus, meek and mild . . .*'

'Oh, Gran, you liar. You bleeding, stinking, filthy liar.'

Near her feet, an animal had earlier deposited its excrement. She picked it up and walked with ferocious stride towards the

197

poster. She stood looking at it for a moment, then she lifted her hands and daubed the filth across the clean, white surface.

'You liar. You bleeding, bleeding, bleeding liar.'

She smashed her hands, first with her fists then with the flat of her palms, against the wooden board.

'You bleeding, bleeding, bleeding liar.'

A car approached and slowed down as it passed. The driver craned his neck to watch her actions. It brought her to her senses and suddenly she stopped, looking down at the filth upon her hands, appalled. 'Oh, God!' She spread her fingers and gazed at them in horror.

'*GentleJesusmeekandmild. Lookuponthislittlechild . . .*' she gabbled in some effort to assuage her profanity, and ran to Long Pond, sluicing her hands through the cold, muddy water in the hope of washing away her feeling of degradation. Sam bounded on ahead, barking in the belief that this was some new game. She was crying; hard, long, bitter tears which blinded her and trickled down her cheeks until they gathered on her jaw, pasting tiny wisps of hair against her skin.

She cried as she had never cried before. Sam came creeping back and pushed his nose beneath her arm so that she enfolded him and cried into his coat. 'Oh, Sam. Why can't I be like other girls? The only man who made me . . .' She gulped and felt her stomach rise again. 'Where have I gone wrong?'

Sam turned soulful eyes and licked her face. His body was warm and comforting in her embrace. 'I love you, Sam,' she said. 'I really love you.'

Eventually, her tears were spent and slowly she composed herself. She looked about her then rose shakily to her feet. 'Come on Sam,' she said. 'Let's take a walk.'

The sun was rising quickly now, promising a fine, warm day. The city stirred and came to life. Curtains were drawn back and people stepped out of front doors, yawning as they set off towards their destination. She walked to Clapham Junction, then on, pausing a while in Battersea Park, then on again over Albert Bridge. She simply walked, not caring where she went but making vaguely in the direction of Hyde Park which was the largest open expanse of grass and trees to come to mind. On the Embankment she sat for a while gazing out across the Thames, seeing nothing even though her eyes were on the passing craft. Her mind was blank, cried-out and weary.

Sam jumped up beside her on the seat and, as he did so, knocked aside a small, red notebook which had been left lying there. She picked it up and looked at it, casually at first but then with growing interest. It was well-thumbed, with some of the pages torn at the corner, but the quality of the paper was good. The pages were handwritten in a scrawl which looked like hasty jottings – a sentence here, a few brief words. In another section there were pages of neater script which looked as though they might have been copied from some other book with a more careful hand, for later contemplation. She did not understand the content. It was a mixture of philosophy and science which left her baffled.

She turned the pages. A poem had been scrawled in haste.

> 'I met you once, a fragrant flower,
> And I, a raindrop, kissed your face
> In such sweet ecstasy of love
> That when our next rejoining came
> We knew at once that we were one,
> And we came running, building lives
> Which intertwined, then thrice and
> Four times came again,
> Touching lips in joyous recognition.'

Barbie knew little of poetry. She guessed that this was not good but there was something about it which appealed to her. She could imagine the hand quickly jotting down a fleeting moment of thought and passing on to something new.

She read it again.

> 'I met you once, a fragrant flower,
> And I, a raindrop, kissed your face . . .'

She liked it. She read a few more pages then put down the notebook where it could easily be found.

Sam was eager to be on his way and she got up and walked on but the notebook played upon her mind. Whoever had lost it, would by now be missing it. She knew it to be of importance to them. It was an extension of their mind, captured at random and encapsulated into scrawling ink lines across the page. She went back and picked it up again. On the front, inside cover, dog-eared and faded, she could just make out a name – David FitzGibbon – and the address – 5, Bishops Walk, Chelsea. It was but a few minutes' walk and Barbie had no pressing destination. She called Sam to heel and altered course for Bishops Walk.

She found it within ten minutes and turned in at the entrance gate, wondering who Mr FitzGibbon could be in order to live in such a large, imposing house. It was tall and square, rendered white, but now turning grey from need of redecoration. On the ground floor two large casement windows, one either side of the door, were flanked by shutters secured against the wall, their paintwork showing signs of peeling. Above, a black wrought-iron balustrade ran the width of the house with three large French windows opening on to a balcony. Virginia creeper straggled unkempt through the wrought-ironwork, and reached almost to the small, square attic windows of the upper floor. The drive swept in a circle, bordered on its outer side by lilacs, fighting for space with overgrown laurel, and in the centre was an untended lawn with beds of unpruned roses. She imagined it to be the home of an old man who spent the evening of his days contemplating philosophy and jotting lines of poetry, while a white-haired wife looked out upon the garden which she once had tended.

There were four steps leading to the heavy door. Barbie mounted them, keeping Sam close at heel, and pressed the bell. The sound reverberated through a seemingly cavernous interior but no one came to answer it. She rang again and this time the door was immediately opened, not by the old man she had pictured in her mind, but by a man in his mid-thirties, with dark brown hair prematurely streaked with grey. He wore a pair of faded jeans and a baggy, looseknit sweater.

'Oh, hello. I didn't expect you until this afternoon.'

Barbie was taken aback, half by the fact that he was not as she had imagined him, and half by his response. 'Mr FitzGibbon?'

'Yes. Do please come in.'

She stepped into a hall which had once been magnificent but was now urgently in need of redecoration. To one side a wide staircase swept upwards, drawing the eye towards a high, moulded ceiling. She found herself gazing up towards it.

'I'm afraid it's a big, draughty old place.'

'Oh, no.' She was embarrassed to be found staring. 'I was thinking how beautiful it is.'

'It was once. I'm afraid I've let it go to rack and ruin.'

There was something about the house which grasped Barbie's attention in a way she could not define. It had an ambience which she found irresistible.

'It needs to have a lot of work done on it but somehow I never seem to get round to organising it.'

'It needs to have the light brought in with lots of colour.' She would not normally have been so forthright but there was something about the house which had her unaccountably picturing ways of restoring it to its former splendour.

He raised one eyebrow, amused but impressed. 'And what else would you suggest?'

'I'm sorry. It's none of my business what colour you paint your walls.'

'On the contrary, I'm most interested.'

'No. I'm sorry. I came to . . .'

'Please. Go ahead. I'd like to hear.'

'Well, if the walls were painted in a soft, pastel shade, and with velvet curtains at the windows – a rich, ruby red, I think, or maybe gold. And, if you had lots of lovely, brightly-coloured pictures instead of those dull old paintings . . .' She stopped again, realising that this time she had been more than impertinent, but he laughed.

'Go ahead and throw them all out. They're no great friends of mine.'

His laughter went some way to overcoming her embarrassment. She smiled diffidently and went on. 'And there . . .' indicating the centre of the hall '. . . I would have a huge trough of ferns with lots of different textures and shades of green.'

'And I suppose you would fill the house with bowls of fresh-cut flowers.'

'No. I'd leave them in the soil where they belong.'

He looked at her again with an expression of amused respect. 'That's just as well. I, too, wouldn't approve of cutting flowers.'

'I'm terribly sorry. I don't know what came over me. It's something about this house . . .'

'There's no reason to apologise, I'm only too pleased you like it. As soon as you've got me sorted out you can have a free hand to do anything with it that you choose.' Barbie's embarrassment increased. 'That is what you came here for?' A slight inflection of doubt rose in his voice. 'About the job?'

'No,' she stammered. 'I brought you this.'

'Oh, I'm most terribly sorry.' He threw back his head and roared with laughter. 'How stupid of me. I thought you were someone else.'

She held out the notebook.

'Where on earth did you find that? He took the notebook and she could see at once by the way with which he handled it that it was, indeed, of special value to him. 'I searched the house upside down this morning.'

'You left it on a seat on the Embankment. I picked it up.'

'Good Lord, now I remember.' He struck his forehead with the heel of his hand. 'I'll mislay my head one of these days.'

'I thought you might need it.'

'I do indeed.' He smiled a sincere, grateful smile. 'I really am extremely grateful to you.'

'I'm glad I happened to see it there.' She called Sam to her side and turned for the door. 'It's lucky that it didn't rain.' She put her hand on the door handle to see herself out.

'Won't you join me for some breakfast? I'm just having mine.'

'No thanks. It's very kind, but no.'

'Some coffee, at least. I really am very grateful to you for returning my notebook.'

Barbie's throat was dry and sore. The offer of coffee was tempting. 'I really can't.'

'Please.'

'Just coffee then. It's very kind of you.'

He took her through a room which led off the hall. It was sombre and dusty, the walls lined from floor to ceiling with books. 'The library,' he said with a wave of his hand, and led her on, via a back hall, into the kitchen. The kitchen was a large room, its surfaces cluttered with books and newspapers, each with their pages opened in disarray. On the large oak table were the unwashed dishes of the previous evening's meal, complete with frying pan in which it had been cooked. Across the back of a chair hung a crumpled shirt and, on the corner of the table, an iron with its flex dangling to the floor.

'You can see why I'm in need of a housekeeper,' he said unselfconsciously. 'I'm an untidy brute.' He cleared a chair for Barbie to sit down and selected one of the unwashed cups from the pile before taking it to the sink to rinse it. It stirred memories

202

of Gran rinsing out a mug in the old, cracked, brown sink and wiping it on her apron.

'I get caught up in my work and then I forget to do the washing up. Sometimes I even forget to eat, but that's just as well because eating only makes more washing up.' He spooned instant coffee into the cup. 'Black, or white?'

'White, please. No sugar.'

He handed it to her and cleared a small space on the table. 'Perhaps I'd better clear this place before she comes along. The agency have sent three people round this week. One smelled of Guinness and the other two just took one look in here and ran away.' Barbie laughed and took a sip of her coffee. It was hot and strong. 'You're sure you won't join me for a slice of toast? I burn toast rather well.'

'No thanks. The coffee suits me fine.'

'Please yourself.' He searched through the items on the table until he found a loaf of wholemeal bread and a knife with which to cut it. 'I'm sorry about mistaking you just now. I thought for one moment that my luck had changed.'

Barbie flushed slightly. 'Sorry. I hope you'll have more luck this afternoon.'

'If she's anything like the last woman who worked for me, she'll be tall and bony, with her hair tied back in a bun.' He placed two slices of bread into the toaster. 'And she'll spend half her time tidying everything away so that I can't find it, and the other half telling me off because I've pulled it all apart again.' Almost immediately the bread popped up, uncooked. 'And this damned toaster doesn't work. It either burns it black or throws it out before it's done.'

'Perhaps it needs the dial adjusted on the side.'

'To tell the truth, I think it's got bunged up with crumbs.' He replaced the bread and tried again.

Barbie looked around the kitchen. 'I would have thought people would have been glad to work in this house. It's so beautiful.'

'It's not the house they object to. It's me.'

'You can't be that bad.'

'The woman I had before the tall bony one was fifty-five and as fat as the other one was thin.' Barbie smiled, feeling that he was stringing her a story. 'She insisted on pushing stewed prunes into me each morning and telling me they were good for my bowels.'

Barbie laughed and choked on her coffee. 'She left here to work in an old people's home and when she'd gone I found eight packs of the stuff in the larder. I've often thought of those poor old folk sitting there eating their prunes and then dashing off down the corridors in their wheelchairs.'

'You're having me on.'

'No, I'm not. I've had all sorts in here and all I really want is to be left alone to get on with my work.'

The toast popped up again, well-browned this time. He took one slice upon his own plate and threw the other to Sam. 'Here, Sam. I'm sure you won't say no to a slice of toast even though your mistress does.' Sam scrunched the toast and licked his jowls, looking round for more.

'She used to get upset because I work at night. Said if I didn't get my sleep, I'd get bags under my eyes and my hair would all fall out.' He grinned and ploughed his hand through his hair. 'Perhaps that's why I'm turning grey. She used to get up in the middle of the night and bring me cups of tea. Then I'd feel bad and think I was keeping her awake.'

'Do you always work at night?'

'Not always. It depends on the mood.' He reached for a slab of butter, still in its shop wrapper, and spread it thickly on his toast. 'I'm a journalist, you know, and there's always some deadline to meet. If the mood takes me I tend to keep writing and forget the time.'

She looked at him more closely, feeling that perhaps she should have recognised his name. 'I'm afraid I don't read much.'

He smiled. 'I write mainly for the scientific journals but sometimes I get round to doing something for the glossies and just occasionally they call me to do something on television.' He held his face in mock profile so that she could study it. There was something vaguely familiar about him but she could not place it. 'Every now and again I get round to writing a book.'

'I should have known you were a writer. I liked the poem about the raindrop and the flower.'

'You read it then?'

'I'm sorry.' Suddenly she realised that she should not have done so. 'I didn't mean to pry.'

'It doesn't matter. But I'm not much of a poet. It wasn't meant for any eyes but mine.'

'I'm sorry, but it caught my eye. I didn't think . . .'

'Don't worry about it.' He waved away the apology with a movement of his hand. 'It's a habit of mine. I write down all sorts of bits and pieces that come to mind. There's always something flitting about up there and if I don't write it down I've got a memory like a sieve. Then, I'm always reading things in books and thinking "I wish I'd thought of that" so I write it all down for reference. It probably sounds crazy to you but every now and again I get round to putting it all together in an article or in a book.'

'It sounds much too clever for me.'

'Don't you believe it. Anyone can sit down and think about something until they've got enough information to write about it. It's a question of pooling ideas.'

'I do have a friend who likes to read and think a lot. He likes to read about people and figure out what makes them tick.'

'There's a lot of us about.'

'Except he doesn't look much like a philosopher; and you do.' She finished her coffee and looked at him over the top of her cup. 'You're much more the type.'

'Why? Because I haven't combed my hair?'

She looked away, refusing to be drawn by his gentle teasing. 'Can I have another cup of coffee?'

'Of course. Help yourself.' He chuckled at the way she had backed down. 'The kettle's over there.'

She got up and refilled the kettle at the sink while he cut himself another slice of bread and placed it in the toaster. 'There's no end to learn about people,' he said. 'But what fascinates me most of all is life.'

'I thought life and people were one and the same thing.'

'Oh no. The more one thinks about life, the more there is to learn.'

'I've never really thought about it.'

'There's much more to it than people.'

It was her turn to tease. 'You mean raindrops and flowers.'

'Raindrops and flowers,' he conceded. 'And can I have another cup of coffee while you're pouring yours.'

She took the coffee to the table and placed it before him. 'Would you like me to clear these things before I go? I've got the time.'

He looked surprised. 'There's no need. I'll do it myself later, or I'll leave it till the woman comes this afternoon.'

'What if she's unsatisfactory like the rest?'

'Then I'll have to do it myself.'

She took a deep breath and turned to face him. 'I was thinking of applying for the job.'

'What?'

'I've been thinking about it all the time I've been sitting here.'

'But this isn't a job for you. There's nothing very glamorous about washing my dishes.'

'Perhaps it's not glamour that I need.'

He eyed her knowingly. 'Then there are better places where you could go to catch your breath.'

'Perhaps. But I think this might suit me rather well.'

He sat looking at her for some time with a serious, searching expression which made her lower her eyes. 'I think perhaps you would soon be driven mad by my untidiness.'

'I doubt it. A long time ago I lived in a cottage which was far more untidy than this.'

'Were you happy there?'

'Yes.'

'And you wouldn't run behind me clearing up the mess?'

'Not if you didn't want me to. But I could cook and sweep the floors.'

He glanced at her manicured nails. 'And don't forget that you're going to paint the walls and hang up velvet curtains.' She coloured and looked away. 'And when you've grown tired of running away from the world you can return to it and find something more in keeping with your style.'

'Who said I was running away from the world?'

He did not answer but said instead, 'You're welcome to stay but you need not work.'

'Thank you, but no. I should like to stay and I should like to work.'

'So . . .' He reached out and shook her hand. 'I have a new housekeeper. And a housekeeper's dog.'

'You don't object to Sam?' she asked quickly.

'Not at all. He's more than welcome. It's a long time since I had pleasant company in the house.'

She began stacking plates. 'I'll just wash these dishes, then I'll go and collect my things.'

'You don't need a little time to sort out your affairs?'

'No.' She did not look at him. 'I only need to leave a note and go.'

He watched her with a slight frown across his brow but he did not ask her more.

Later, when he opened the front door for her to leave, he shook her hand again. 'It would help to know my housekeeper's name.'

'I'm sorry. Didn't I tell you? It's Barbie. Barbie Harding.'

'Well, Miss Barbie Harding, if you change your mind as soon as you've had a chance to think it over, just let me know and I'll engage the woman who calls this afternoon.'

'She might try to make you eat stewed prunes.'

'I'll take that chance. But if you do decide to come back, you're welcome to stay until such time as you grow tired of it.'

She smiled and shook her head. 'I'll be back within the hour.'

She took a taxi and asked the driver to wait for her outside the flat. The rooms were curtained and quiet, for the girls were sleeping. She tiptoed to her own room and peered round the door, fearful that the fat man might still be there upon her bed, but he was gone. There was no sign of him but for the crumpled sheets and a glass on the table. She averted her eyes and, with a deep breath, began to throw the contents of her wardrobe into a suitcase.

Before leaving, she wrote a note to Debbie and Sue, and another to Curly.

Dear Curly,

You told me once that I would write a note. I didn't believe you then but something happened last night which means that I must go. Please don't think badly of me but remember me sometimes as I shall think of you. Thank you for everything you have done for me.

Barbie

PS I love you.

There was a sense of irony about this postscript. She, who could not love, had used these words three times today – to Gran, to Sam, and now to Curly. Perhaps there was some hope for her even yet.

She got into the taxi and was driven away, leaving as she had left Wansdyke Avenue, without a backward glance. Her life was forming itself into a set pattern, dividing off into sealed compartments.

Chapter Eleven

When Barbie returned to Bishops Walk the house appeared to be deserted. She rang the bell three times but there was no reply. There was no sign of David FitzGibbon and it seemed almost that the breakfast-time encounter had been a figment of her imagination. She stood on the doorstep, surrounded by suitcases, and began to wonder if she had made a foolish mistake.

Sam became bored and wandered off, nosing his way round to the side of the house. Barbie followed him and, in doing so, came upon an unlocked door. She opened it gingerly and found herself in the back hall from which she recognised the doors of the library and the kitchen. She called out but there was no reply and, as she stood for a moment straining her ears, she caught the clacking of a typewriter in the distance. She let go a small sigh of relief and made towards it, passing through the silent rooms like an intruder.

The sound of the typewriter came from the far end of the house, towards the back, and when she at last located it she paused and tapped at the door. Immediately the clacking stopped and the door was flung wide. 'I'm so sorry. I didn't know you were back.'

'I rang the bell but you didn't hear.'

'Sorry, I got carried away. Lost track of the time.'

He stepped aside for her to enter the room but she declined. 'I didn't mean to intrude. If you'll just show me where to put my things, I'll go and get myself sorted out.'

He gestured with a hand towards the stairs. 'There are plenty of rooms upstairs. Take any one you fancy.' He walked past her and out of the front door, bringing her suitcases into the hall. 'Let me know which room you choose and I'll carry up your luggage.'

'Thanks, but I'll manage.'

'Well, let me know if there's anything you need. Don't be afraid to shout.' He went back to his study and almost immediately the clacking of the typewriter began again. Barbie turned and climbed the stairs.

There were several doors opening off the first floor landing. The first opened onto a spacious chamber which had once been an elegant drawing room but which had obviously not been in use for a number of years. Faded floor-length curtains were half-drawn across the large French windows – most probably by the previous housekeeper in an effort to protect the elegant furniture which graced the room. Through the gap between the curtains she could see the balcony with its wrought-iron balustrade looking down upon the front drive and the purple haze of lilacs breaking into bloom.

There were four bedrooms standing empty except for furniture and for beds draped with faded counterpanes. A fifth was strewn with discarded clothing and books, and was obviously the room used by David FitzGibbon. She chose a room to the left of the stairhead, facing to the rear of the house, having been drawn to it by the sunlight which streamed across it, spilling out onto the landing.

She walked to the window and, to her delight, found that it looked out over a walled garden, a riot of colour and tangled vegetation. Beneath her a magnolia climbed the wall holding ivory, pink-flushed chalices towards the sun. She stood there for a long time pondering on the connection in her mind between this elegant London house and an old, dilapidated cottage in the gentle hills of her memory.

When she went downstairs into the hall the typewriter could still be heard. She did not disturb David FitzGibbon but carried her suitcases to her room and unpacked them into cupboards and drawers which smelled musty from disuse. Last of all she placed the photograph of Gran upon a chest, facing it towards the garden and towards the sun.

On the attic landing she found cupboards stocked with fine linen, hand-embroidered tablecloths, sheets and pillow cases. Each bore a monogram – two 'D's entwined. She took out bed-linen and towels, hanging them across her arm as she ventured further to peep through other doors. Most of the attic rooms were empty but some were stacked with dust-covered furniture and pictures leaning against the walls, and one contained toys. A huge, black spotted rocking horse stood in a corner, near a farmyard complete with animals, and a train set, its engine tumbled on one side, gathering dust. She wondered if these could have been the playthings of a young David FitzGibbon of many years ago. She walked over to stroke the blonde mane of the horse and gave it a push on the rump so that it rocked obediently, creaking back and forth on unoiled leather. Whoever had been the owner of these toys had wanted for nothing. She hitched the linen across her arm and went downstairs to make her bed.

By the time she had finished, it was almost lunch-time. She went down to the kitchen and searched through the refrigerator. Some of the contents she threw into the bin but there were eggs and some fresh salad. She prepared an omelette and set it on a tray with a pot of coffee which she carried to the study. David FitzGibbon stopped work immediately she entered and looked up with a smile. 'Is it lunch-time already?'

'I hope you like omelette and salad.'

He sniffed the air appreciatively. 'It's better than stewed prunes, any day.'

Barbie set it down on the desk before him and turned to leave but he caught her arm. 'Won't you join me? It's not much fun to eat alone.'

She shook her head. 'I don't want to disturb you. And I never bother to eat at midday.'

But he increased the pressure on her arm and drew her down onto a chair beside the desk. 'Housekeepers need to eat.' He got up and left the room and when he returned he was carrying another cup and a plate. He divided his lunch into two equal portions and passed one half to her, then poured her a cup of coffee. 'I happen to remember that you refused breakfast this morning.'

She took the plate wondering what he would say if he knew of the routine to which she had become accustomed – rising at midday to walk with Sam and then returning for breakfast with Debbie and Sue at four o'clock. It brought the recollection that she had not slept last night and then the surging memory of the man – sweat and gin and excess fat. She swallowed and became aware that David FitzGibbon was looking at her.

'Don't you want to eat?'

'I'm sorry.' She composed her face and smiled. 'I'm really quite hungry.' She ate a little of the omelette and found that it tasted good.

The desk was situated immediately in front of French windows which were flung wide onto a mellow red-brick terrace where thyme and other sweetly-scented herbs grew in profusion. Overhanging it was the same magnolia which climbed the wall beneath her window. 'It's a lovely garden.' It brought her a sense of peace.

'I'm glad you like it. I'm rather fond of it myself but it's got rather overgrown since the gardener retired.'

'I like it that way. It reminds me of somewhere else.'

On the terrace a house sparrow hopped, brown and sooty grey, pecking at the soil between the cracks, and nearby a starling strutted, cocky, as though he owned the garden, his black plumage glowing iridescent in the sunlight.

Starlings walk and blackbirds hop. Oh, dear Miss Beckworth. Everyone knows the difference between a blackbird and a starling.

'Starlings walk and blackbirds hop,' she whispered.

'I remember my nanny taught me that when I was just a boy. It brings back memories.'

Barbie smiled her own secret smile, for her memories too had been stirred. *Dear Miss Beckworth. Where are you now?*

The walls of the study were lined with books and piles of magazines. Placed about the room were a number of potted plants and Barbie's eye was drawn to a rubber plant, one of its leaves clamped between electrodes from which wires led off to recording equipment, producing a steady zig-zagging graph. David FitzGibbon followed the direction of her eye. 'It's an experiment,' he said. 'I'm registering the emotional responses of the plant.' He gave her a quizzical look, awaiting her reaction but she responded only with interest. 'You don't think it slightly extraordinary that your employer should hold conversations with his rubber plant?'

'Tell me more.'

He walked over and threw the switch on a loudspeaker and immediately there came a strange singing, ringing sound similar to the hum of high voltage cables. 'There,' he said. 'Now you can listen to it yourself.' He returned to his desk and tented his fingers, resting his chin upon their apex. 'Every living thing is interconnected. There's a life signal which passes between them all, if only we have the ability and the inclination to tune in to it. It's easy with plants. A small piece of apparatus and we have instant communication.'

'What's it saying?' Barbie walked over and studied the pen recorder, tracing its uneven path across the paper.

He laughed. 'It doesn't actually talk, any more than animals do. But just like them it has responses.' She looked at him, not understanding. 'It responds to my emotions and it's aware of my thoughts towards it. If I threatened it, it would show alarm. And, in the same way, if I burned my finger it would know. It would respond to the death of the burnt cells.' He picked up a large pair of scissors. 'See what happens if I cut its leaf.'

Immediately the pen recorder skidded across the page.

'Why did it do that?'

'It knew what I was about to do.'

'You wouldn't really?'

'No. I was just showing you what would happen.'

'Sorry, plant.' Barbie put out a finger and stroked its leaf.

He smiled. 'It understands me very well. It knows when I am depressed, or when I'm happy. It likes music – but it hates heavy rock.'

'You're kidding.'

'No, really. It simply hates it. Perhaps it's trying to tell us something that we older generation have been saying for years.'

'I don't much like it anyway.'

'That's just as well. You'll be its friend for life.'

'What else does it do?'

'Well; it's in tune with the whole of the universe – the sun, the moon, the seasons, the magnetic fields. It's like I say; there's a fine web of connection between all things.' He paused and looked at her for a moment. 'Are you surprised to learn that plants have emotions?'

'No. I've always known it. I knew it as a child. I didn't know why. I just knew it.'

He nodded. 'Most children sense their natural affinity with other living things. It's a pity that we tend to lose it as we grow up. We might all act differently if we knew of the effect we're having on our own environment.'

'People would never listen.'

'More's the pity. We wouldn't be here at all if it weren't for the plants providing oxygen and turning solar energy into food.'

212

'I never thought of it like that before.'

'Our ancestors did. They knew a lot of things that we've forgotten. We laugh at them for prancing around doing fertility dances; yet, now it's been proved that crops do respond to certain rhythms. We think ourselves clever; yet we've lost touch with the very essence of life itself.'

Barbie returned to her chair and drank the remains of her coffee. 'I see what you mean about there being more to life than people.'

'The more one learns, the more there is to know. There are scientists all over the world who are searching for the answers. When they come up with them it will be the breakthrough to a whole new era of understanding.'

'Is that what you write about?'

'Yes. And I must get back to work. This piece has to be finished by this afternoon.'

'I'm sorry. I've been delaying you.' She jumped up and began putting the plates back on the tray.

'It's nice to have company. I worked well this morning hearing you moving about the house.'

She flushed slightly realising that he had been listening to her. 'I didn't realise you could hear me.'

'You've taken the room above this one. It's a good choice, especially for those who love gardens and the sun.'

She left him to work and busied herself about the house, tidying but taking care not to disturb his personal belongings which were scattered about the places he most frequented. By their position she could tell that he spent most of his time in the kitchen or in his study and rarely used the other rooms. She ironed the crumpled shirt hanging on the back of the kitchen chair and threw a number of items into the washing machine before going out to buy food. She returned with fresh fruit and vegetables, and a chicken which she cooked with mushrooms and green peppers in a white cream sauce. In a storeroom off the back hall she found bottles of wine and selected one which she set aside to chill.

Earlier she had opened the window of the library to let in air and had polished the furniture. The air had brought with it the scent of lilacs and now she set a fire in the large open fireplace and laid the meal on a low table before it. She had heard David FitzGibbon leave his study and go whistling by on the stairs, so

213

now she called him, and when he entered the room she could tell at once by the expression on his face that he was pleased. 'Thank you, Barbie,' he said. 'It's very nice to find a little homeliness about the place. It's been missing for a long time.'

She smiled in return and sat down at the table, for she too had a sense of being at home.

When they had finished eating he leaned back in an armchair beside the fire while she sat cross-legged on the hearth-rug, with Sam sprawled between them, twitching occasionally and giving out soft whinnies as dreams invaded his sleep. Barbie had taken a book from the shelf and was fully engrossed in the story which unfolded before her. Presently she felt his eyes upon her and looked up.

'Do you like to read?'

'I've hardly ever opened a book. I need to feel at ease with myself and my surroundings before I get the urge.'

'I must take that as a compliment to myself and to my house.'

She had not intended to throw a compliment but acknowledged that it was. 'There's something about this house. I felt the atmosphere the moment I stepped in.'

'It's been half-empty too long. It's needed someone young and energetic.'

'Did you really mean it when you said that I could re-decorate it and bring it back to life?'

'Do you really want to?'

'Oh, yes please. I'd really enjoy it.'

'Then go ahead. Decide what you want to do and I'll call in the decorators.'

'Can't I do it all myself? That's half the fun.'

He looked surprised. 'What, you? Climbing ladders? Are you sure?'

'Yes, of course. I know I could do it. I used to help my Aunty "M" to re-decorate her house. It wasn't fun then because it was a chore but it would be different now. I'd be doing it because I want to.'

He shrugged his shoulders and laughed at her enthusiasm. 'Go ahead. But don't blame me when you fall off a ladder and break your leg.'

'Can I start tomorrow?'

'Tomorrow? Don't you want to get settled in first?'

'Oh, I'm sorry. You've got other things you want me to do.'

'Not at all. I told you that you can have a free hand to do whatever you wish.'

'Then you don't mind if I start tomorrow?'

He laughed again. 'Not if it makes you happy.'

'Thanks. I'll go out first thing tomorrow morning and choose the materials.'

'I bet you'll grow tired of it before you're halfway through.'

'Do you want to bet?'

'No,' he said. 'I don't think I'd want to bet with you.'

He went back to reading his book and she tried to return to hers but her thoughts were on the house.

'What are you reading?'

'*Great Expectations*,' she said. 'I always thought Dickens was stuffy but this is good.'

'He was a very great writer.'

'It's about real people. I didn't realise that you could actually see them the way he describes.'

'Dickens had something in common with your friend. He liked to observe people and he knew what made them tick.'

'Why did he call it *Great Expectations*?'

He stopped and thought for a moment, summing up the plot in his mind. 'Pip had great expectations of becoming a rich man, but it didn't turn out quite the way he expected.' He laid down his book on his lap and smoothed the pages with the flat of his hand. 'Money doesn't provide everything.'

Barbie glanced down at her Italian pure silk blouse and took the remark upon herself; but when she looked up she could see that he had been alluding to himself. She watched him, puzzled, but when he looked at her the expression changed. 'I suspect that you're very tired,' he said. 'You've had a long, busy day.'

It was thirty-four hours since she had slept. 'Yes,' she said. 'I am rather tired.'

He called to Sam who instantly snapped out of his doze and raised his head, alert. 'I'll walk Sam for you if you'd like to turn in.'

Barbie rose from her position on the floor, aware now of her overwhelming tiredness, feeling her limbs heavy and clumsy. 'Do you want me to sleep with you?'

He turned, surprised. 'It's not a prerequisite for housekeepers, you know.'

She became embarrassed that her assumption might not be correct.

'Why do you think that I should expect you to sleep with me?'

'You're a man.'

He studied her for a moment. 'You must have had a very bad experience of men.' She avoided his eyes for fear that her life story might be read there like a book. 'What's more important is whether you wish to sleep with me.'

Barbie shook her head. After her experience of the previous night she doubted that she would ever want to sleep with any man ever again. 'No,' she said simply.

'Then it's not a matter which we need discuss.' He whistled to Sam and turned to leave the room.

Barbie went upstairs and fell exhausted into bed. She slept soundly until she heard movement beside her and woke to find that it was morning. The sun was high in the sky and David FitzGibbon had brought her a tray of tea and toast. She shot up in bed, alarmed that she had overslept but he was totally unconcerned by the fact. 'Did you sleep well?'

She ran her fingers self-consciously through her tousled hair. 'It must be late.'

He placed the tray on the bed before her. 'Take your time. There's no hurry.' He walked out of the room but just as he was leaving he paused and put his head round the door. 'And eat up your toast. People who intend to paint walls are in need of breakfast.'

She looked up at him and smiled. 'You're very kind.'

'Don't push your luck. Once I get involved in work I can be a pig.'

She ate her breakfast and when she went downstairs she could hear the tapping of the typewriter keys behind the study door. She did not disturb him but let herself out of the house and went to order paint and decorating materials.

When she returned she changed into her oldest clothes and, tying a scarf around her hair, began to strip wallpaper from the hall. She had a bucket of water and a sponge which she used to moisten the old paper and then, once it had softened, prised up one corner, before ripping it vertically up the wall. It was an exhilarating sensation, feeling the paper tearing beneath her fingers with a loud ripping sound as it parted from the wall. It reminded her of the satisfaction she had received as a child in picking, probing with her fingernails – the joy of tearing paper.

She worked with vigour; damping, soaking, pulling, tearing, and did not notice that David FitzGibbon had entered the hall and was standing behind her, watching with amusement.

'May I have a go? It looks fun.'

She jumped at the sound of his voice but moved to one side in order that he might join her. She showed him what he should do and carried on with her work, oblivious to the chipped varnish and the broken nails of her own hands.

'I thought you were busy working,' she said.

'I was, but I felt like taking a day off. I didn't fancy working while you were out here having fun.' He prised up a small section of paper and then tore a long, thin strip which travelled upwards towards the ceiling. 'You've broken your fingernails.'

'It doesn't matter. They'll soon grow.' She carried on unconcerned. 'It reminds me of when I was a child. I had a terrible habit of picking everything I could get my fingers to.'

'Horrible child,' he said.

'I used to like to make patterns from tearing wallpaper. Look . .' she pointed to the area she had just torn '. . . there's a clown with a tall, pointed hat.'

He inclined his head towards it and stuck out his lip. 'I can't see a clown. It looks more like a mountain peak with a flag on top. Look, there's the top of the mountain and there's the flag.'

'No, it isn't. That's the clown's head and there's his face. He's even got eyes . . .' She stopped short, realising that he was teasing her.

'I do believe that you're a child still.'

She bridled. 'I'm eighteen.'

'Eighteen. It's a long time since I was eighteen.' She looked at him re-calculating his years. 'I'm thirty-three,' he supplied and she was embarrassed that he had read her thoughts so easily. 'Give me a few more years and I could almost be your father.'

'You're not that old.' But it was a comfortable thought. She was at ease with him in a way which would not have been possible with a youth of her own age. 'My father's name was Curly.' She had not intended to lie but the comment slipped out unthinkingly.

'And what about your mother?'

'Sandra.' She hesitated, realising that the lie was likely to lead her into difficulties. 'I lived with my Gran.'

217

'And where does Aunty "M" fit in?'

'She was my . . .' She floundered, for there was no way to extricate herself. 'She was my father's wife.' There was urgent need to turn the conversation. 'Look,' she said. 'There's a church with a steeple.'

He looked at her for a moment and then turned towards the high ceiling above the stairs. 'How do you propose getting to work up there?'

She was grateful to him for releasing her from her self-imposed impasse. 'The people who are supplying the paint are going to loan me some scaffolding. They'll come round and set it up when I'm ready.'

'You are not going to balance on a plank up near the ceiling?'

'I'll be all right. I'm not afraid of heights and it will be fun.'

'What do I do when you fall down and break your neck?'

'You call an ambulance.'

'I was thinking more of the fact that I would have no one to cook my dinner.'

She smiled at his teasing. 'In that case, I'll grit my teeth and cook it before they carry me off.'

He laughed and they lapsed into quiet concentrated work until eventually he said, 'I'm hungry. It must be time for lunch.'

'I'm so sorry.' She dropped the sponge hurriedly into the bucket of water and rubbed her hands on the seat of her jeans. 'I should have prepared it for you. I lost track of the time.'

'I'm glad I'm not the only one who loses track of the time.' He walked off towards the kitchen. 'You stay and play. I'll go and get the lunch.'

'No, it's my job. I'll go.'

'You stay. I think I'm better at preparing lunch than stripping wallpaper.'

She watched him go, feeling that perhaps she should have insisted upon carrying out her duties as housekeeper, but it was lame resistance and she was happy to go back to the task which she preferred.

When he called her it was from the garden, for he had carried the tray onto the terrace where he had set out two chairs, with the tray on a table between them. Two bowls of soup steamed beside hunks of fresh bread, with cheese and a bowl of fruit. The May sunshine was warm, trapped by the south-facing wall of the house with its magnificent magnolia. At its base were polyanthuses, jewel-coloured like scraps of velvet on a cutting room floor, and beneath the wall of the terrace a bed of wallflowers filled the air with a heady perfume.

Barbie crossed the terrace and walked down the steps into the garden. The flowerbeds were thick with weeds but the late spring flowers pushed their way towards the surface. To one side an azalea shrub tossed flowers of orange and apricot and, beyond, the spikes of a lavender-blue lilac vied with the perfume of the wallflowers. Daffodils had been in bloom but were long over, their seedheads lying turgid amid overgrown leaves which sprawled across the soil. She passed through a trellis against which had been trained an apple tree and above her head a clematis was heavy with bud. Beyond was a pond, its banks lined with irises, their buds not yet ready to open emerging between the crossed swords of their leaves. Goldfish floated lazily beneath the surface of the water or hid themselves under tussocks of floating waterweed, while nearby a rock garden was ablaze with yellow alyssum, hummocks of pink thrift, and pink and purple heathers. Beyond the walls of the garden were other houses. They could be seen clearly but they did nothing to intrude upon the peace of the garden. Here, in the centre of London, was an oasis of sheer beauty.

'Your soup's getting cold.' She jumped as David FitzGibbon came up behind her. 'You've been down here for ages.'

'I'm sorry. It's a long time since I was in a garden.'

'You're very fond of gardens.'

'There's something particularly special about this one. It reminds me of another one.'

'The one "somewhere else"?'

She turned and walked back to the terrace, not wanting to share her memories. She sat down and tasted her soup. 'This is good. What is it?'

'I don't know. It came out of a can. You were going to tell me why you like gardens.'

She shook her head and clammed up. 'It's not very interesting.'

'Try me.'

It was an unfamiliar and uncomfortable rôle. 'There's nothing very exciting about it.'

'I wasn't asking for the sake of excitement.'

'I don't really know why you want to know.'

'Then don't tell me. I wasn't intending to pry.'

219

He cut her a piece of cheese and she sat nibbling on it.

'It all happened such a long time ago.'

'I've got plenty of time.'

He could not know how difficult it was for her. She sat for a long time gazing out across the garden, trying to find words. 'It reminds me,' she said at last, 'of a time when I was very happy. I used to live in an old cottage with my Gran. It was a broken-down old place and it wasn't anything to write home about but it had a garden.' She stopped again, looking at the flowerbeds. 'It wasn't anything like this one. You'd hardly call it a garden at all but it had wild honeysuckle and bindweed, and there were big, tall thistles, and the hedges were covered with elderflower and berries.'

She looked at him and he nodded to her to go on. 'We had a vegetable patch and the rabbits used to come and steal the lettuces. Gran used to shout and swear at them, and then she'd make me throw things at them and I'd pretend to, but I'd always miss.'

He laughed. 'Go on, tell me more.'

'There were all sorts of creatures which lived beneath the weeds. I used to sit for hours and just watch them – spiders, ants, beetles – and on the other side of the hedge there was a barley field with pheasants which squawked at you when you disturbed them. And then there was a copse full of pigeons and bluebells. I used to go there every day with Bess . . .' She stopped and reached out for Sam who lay beside her chair. She drew his ear through her fingers. 'I used to go that way to the village and to school.'

'I'd like to see it.'

'Yes,' she said, awash with nostalgia. 'So should I.'

'How about next Sunday? If you've nothing else to do.'

She looked up startled. 'Oh no. I'd rather not.'

'Just as you wish.'

It was seven years since she had seen the cottage. She had not been back since Bess died.

'Memories are sometimes best left undisturbed.'

'I understand.'

But the thought of the cottage brought a yearning to her. After a time she said, 'I think I *would* like to see it, please. If you can spare the time.'

'Sunday it shall be then.' He reached over to the fruit bowl and threw her an apple. 'It would do us both good to have a day out in the country.'

On Sunday they took the motorway out of London. Barbie sat quietly, gazing from the car window, but as they approached Wickhampton she felt her senses recoil. She sank down into her seat, fearing that in some way she would be recognised and brought back to face the consequences of her actions. He sensed her tension and threw her a reassuring glance, mistaking it for strain of another kind.

Beyond the town, on quieter country roads, she let go her breath and ran her tongue across her upper lip. He looked at her again and smiled.

There were bluebells carpeting the soil beneath the fresh green of new beech leaves. Barbie pointed out familiar landmarks as they approached the village.

'I wonder who's living at the cottage now,' he said. 'Perhaps they'll let us in to look around.'

The remark was deeply disturbing. Barbie had not reckoned on anyone living in the cottage. She had counted on it remaining empty as it had been when she had last seen it and as it had remained ever since in her mind. She had a sudden urge to order him to stop the car, to turn round and drive away at top speed. But she knew that she had come too close. She had no choice but to look and to come to terms with the lingering memories.

She need not have feared, for the cottage was derelict, its windows broken and encrusted with dirt. A hole in its roof laid it open to the sky. He drew the car to a halt in the lane and for a full minute she sat, her eyes upon the cottage, while he sat watching her.

Eventually he got out and went round to her side, opening the door and helping her to her feet. 'Come on,' he said. 'Let's go and take a closer look.'

A rabbit broke through the hedge and shot off along the grass verge beside the lane. 'Look,' he said. 'There's one of your rabbits.' Sam caught sight of it and took off in pursuit.

'Sam! Come here!' Her nerves were taut and he responded to the unusually sharp command. Reluctantly he came back to her, his tail hanging low.

'Poor old chap.' David FitzGibbon laughed and patted him on the flank. 'Won't she let you chase rabbits?'

It was sufficient to break the tension of the moment and Barbie laughed too. She picked up a stick and threw it into the garden. 'Here,' she said. 'Chase that instead.' Sam gave a sharp bark of delight and bounded off into the thick undergrowth.

The old gate had long ago rotted off its hinges and lay on the ground almost totally hidden by weeds. The path, too, was overgrown and their feet became entangled as they picked their way round to the side of the cottage. At the back door they stopped, for a plank of wood had been roughly nailed across it. David FitzGibbon studied it for a moment and then, grasping the plank between both hands, began to pull it away from the frame.

'Do you think we should?'

He put his foot against the wall to afford better leverage then heaved on the plank. 'Don't worry,' he said. 'We'll put it back when we leave. It will be easy enough to hammer in the nails with a flat stone.' The nails gave way with the sound of splintering wood and he stumbled backwards, the plank in his hand.

'After you,' he said and opened the door for her.

It was dark in the cottage after the sunlight of the garden and it took a moment for their eyes to adjust. Barbie looked about her and felt her heart give an irregular beat. It was just as she had left it. The old, heavy, wooden table was covered with a thick layer of dust but it was still cluttered with objects which she recognised. The biscuit tin lay on its side, empty but for mouse droppings, and beside it an open can of dog food, its contents eaten away.

She ran her hand across the dust then turned her palm up-wards studying the blackened fingertips.

'Someone should have cleared the place before they boarded it up,' said David FitzGibbon. Barbie thought of Aunty Beattie and felt her mind go blank.

On the floor, pushed into a corner, was Bess' feeding bowl and in the sink two unwashed mugs. Barbie caught her breath. One was hers, the other Gran's. She picked up Gran's mug and the bowl, tearing away a mesh of cobwebs, and placed them on the corner of the table. 'I should like to take them with me,' she said, 'when we leave.'

David FitzGibbon nodded and cupped her elbow in his hand to draw her into the hall.

The clock stood there still, silent now, and Barbie touched it with her hand. In the parlour Gran's chair was missing as was the sideboard and the mirror above the fireplace. They left gaping spaces which were worse than the uncleared mess. Barbie did not want to stay; she turned to climb the stairs.

At the landing window she stopped, as always, and looked out across the garden. The elder hedge was in full leaf but not yet in bloom, while, growing in its midst, a crab-apple tree was showing pink and white. The vegetation, which had always been thick, now seemed impenetrable and the old privy was almost hidden beneath Russian vine. In the far corner, a bough of the walnut tree had snapped but not fallen, hanging limply like a broken arm. Beyond the hedge the barley field was already a lush emerald green and in the still air she caught the squawk of a pheasant as it swooped across her line of vision, long tail outstretched and its plumage gaudy in the sunlight.

She stood there for a long time and would have remained so had David FitzGibbon not altered his position behind her with a slight movement which attracted her attention. 'I'm sorry,' she said. 'I got carried away.'

He smiled and took her arm again. 'Do you want to stay a little longer?'

'I just want to see the bedroom.'

She went across the landing to the open door. The room was as she had left it, with the bed pushed back against the wall. The mattress had turned grey with mould beneath the leaking roof and large areas of it had been nibbled by mice. She looked at the space which had been cleared on the floor and remembered the day when the ambulancemen had come to carry Gran away. She swallowed hard and turned. 'I'd like to go now,' she said and walked down the stairs towards the door.

Outside, the sunlight brought instant relief. She felt her pent-up muscles give way and held her face to the sun, breathing the air deep down into her lungs. 'It's just as I remember it,' she said. 'But more overgrown.'

Sam had been dozing on the doorstep and sprang up as they appeared, bounding off into the undergrowth, one moment lost from sight, the next moment appearing as he bounded upwards, forging his path.

David FitzGibbon laughed. 'He enjoys the countryside as much as you.' He parted the vegetation, breaking a path for Barbie to follow.

Out here, Barbie was happy. She threw herself against the jungle of tall weeds, battling her way through the garden, and shrieked with laughter when she stumbled and had to haul herself back upon her feet.

Halfway down she stopped, knowing she was in the region of the vegetable plot. There was no sign of it now for it was totally overgrown but Barbie stooped and fumbled through the undergrowth until she found Gran's weeding stool, still lying where it had been abandoned. She ran her fingers across its surface and for a moment she felt a tightness in her throat.

'Don't.' David FitzGibbon came up beside her. 'This place holds happy memories. Don't dwell on unhappy ones.'

She blinked at him through unshed tears and knew that he was right. 'I had ten years of happiness in this garden,' she said.

He was standing close, his hands on her shoulders. 'Barbie . . .' he said. There was a look in his eyes which she was not prepared to acknowledge.

'Look,' she countered brightly. 'Look over there. I'll show you something really special.' She made off towards the far end of the garden. 'Just wait until you see it.'

He let her go without resistance and followed her as she fought her way to the far corner of the garden.

'There!' She turned triumphant. 'I knew that I would find it here.'

Entwined within the hedge and sweeping down to the ground, was a tangle of honeysuckle. Its sheltered position, coupled with the warmth of the sun, had brought it into early bloom and the air was filled with fragrance.

'Just look at that,' she said. 'Have you ever seen anything quite so beautiful?'

'No,' he said. 'I never have.'

He was looking at her again and she turned abruptly. 'Have you seen Sam?'

'He's over there,' he said and pointed towards a ripple of movement amid the tall grass.

She called out and, at the sound of his name, Sam came bounding towards her, barking delight. She began to play with him, totally ignoring the presence of David FitzGibbon.

He watched her for a while and then said, 'I'll go and fetch the picnic from the car.'

When he returned she was lying in the grass with strands of honeysuckle drawn down across her face.

'You're beautiful,' he said.

She was annoyed. 'That's a pretty stupid thing to say.'

'It's the colour of your hair, against the honeysuckle.'

She got up and began rummaging through the picnic basket.

'It never occurred to me before,' he said, 'that I should like to become an artist.'

'I should have thought you had enough to do,' she said tartly, 'solving the mysteries of life.'

He smiled at that. 'There's a little time left for other things.'

'You don't have to waste your time on me. I shan't rob you. I'm more than grateful that you've given up a whole day to waste in the country.'

'Do you want to leave?'

'Yes.'

But he pulled her down beside him. 'Barbie; whether you like it, or whether you don't, I have to admit that I've fallen in love with you.'

'Don't talk such rot,' she said.

'It's true.'

'After one week?'

'No. After little more than a day.'

'You're out of your mind.'

'And you're out of your depth.'

'What on earth do you mean?'

'What I mean is that I am asking you to drop your defences, Barbie; and you can't do it, can you.'

'I'm not staying here . . .' She rose again to leave but he pulled her down once more beside him.

'You've got to trust; and for some reason it's beyond you.'

'You've got no right . . .'

'. . . to ask for love?' He kissed her but she turned her face.

'You said you wouldn't.'

'This is for love.'

'Well, I don't want it.'

'You just come here, Barbie, and look me in the eye.' He turned her face and held it so that she could not move. She closed her eyes and would not look.

'I love you, Barbie,' he said gently. 'I really do.'

She opened them then and met a look from which, this time, there was no escaping. The old yearning rose and she held out her arms to him. He came to her with a tenderness, the like of which she had never known.

225

He kissed her, filling the empty, aching void until she gasped and gaped for more, struggling and greedy with unquenchable thirst.

She was almost drowning in the perfume from the honeysuckle. Her body swayed in unison with him and with the rhythms of the earth and sky until she rose and fell as in the waves of a restless sea; rising gently, ever higher, and then to fall, crashing down as if to drown and then to rise again; until, at last, the earth, the sea, the sky, became one, and in that long shuddering sigh of enlightenment, she knew the purpose of it all.

She lay there, her body seemingly molten into the soil, and when at last she opened her eyes, she reached out her fingers to touch the contours of his face.

'I feel alive,' she whispered.

He smiled. 'That's because you're in your garden.'

'No,' she said. 'It's because of you.'

Chapter Twelve

Barbie opened her eyes. For a moment she lay staring at the ceiling but almost immediately she turned towards the face which lay beside her on the pillow. David was sleeping, almost childlike in the way he sprawled across the bed. For almost a month now she had found him each morning lying there beside her but each morning still she sought reassurance and found herself turning in the instant of awakening to touch his face. They were lying in her bed at the back of the house for he had joined her there, not asking her to go to him, joking that he could not deprive her of the garden and the sun.

She moved carefully so as not to waken him and lay there searching his face. The curtains were drawn back from the window allowing the sun, high in the east sky, to slant across the corner of the room glinting upon the coat of Sam who, learning of the path of the sun, had chosen this as his corner for sleep. The magnolia beneath the window had dropped its petals and had given way to the first June roses which climbed the wall.

David stirred, his eyelids flickering as he rose towards the surface of consciousness. She had counted the days – twenty-eight in all – that she had watched him thus and today, as always, the same thin stab of fear invaded her thoughts. 'How long?' 'How long before he goes away?' In all her life, Barbie had never possessed anything which she treasured and which had not, in time, been taken from her.

He opened his eyes and, as always, his first action was to draw her to him, nuzzling his mouth against her breast. She encircled him with her arms, twisting her fingers through his hair. 'Hello,' she said. 'It's another lovely day.'

'You smell good.'

'You always say that.'

'I know; I shan't ever get used to waking up and finding you still here.'

'I was just thinking the same thing myself before you woke.' She ran her other hand across the bare flesh of his back, familiar now with every contour of his body.

'I love you,' he said. 'My whole life has been slow-pedalling just waiting for you to show up.'

'I thought your life was pretty full before I put in an appearance.'

'But with what? It's different now.'

'And for how long?' she said, and even to her own ears the sound rang hollow.

'What do you mean by that?'

'Nothing.'

'What's wrong, Barbie?'

'There's nothing wrong.'

He took her chin and turned it gently towards him. 'There's always something which is not quite right. You're never totally here with me.'

She closed her eyes. 'I'm here right now.'

'But it's as though you've got your suitcase packed and ready in the hall.'

'Perhaps it's just as well to be prepared.'

'You can't go on running away for ever.'

She said nothing for a moment, then replied, 'It isn't I who'll run away.'

'Then who?'

'We'll see.'

'Not me.'

She did not reply.

'Look Barbie; I'm thirty-three and you're eighteen. If either of us is to be concerned that the other will be leaving, it should be me. There's every possibility that you'll tire of me . . .'

'No,' she countered quickly. 'No; I won't.'

'. . . but I don't spend my time worrying that it might happen today.'

'No,' she said again. 'Oh, darling; don't you understand.' She turned and hugged him tightly about the neck. 'I shan't ever stop loving you.'

'Then why?'

'It's just . . .' But she could not bring herself to voice her fears.

'What happened to you, Barbie? What happened to make you so very insecure?'

She shook her head.

'Come on; it's best that I should know.'

'I can't.'

'Why not?'

'It's not safe to meddle with fate. And there's no point in dragging up the past.'

'Where did you go after your Gran died?'

'What's that got to do with it?'

'Just tell me.'

She sighed. 'To live with my father and his wife.'

'Oh yes; Curly and Aunty "M".'

She flushed and turned away, recalling the lie she had told him while standing in the hall.

'What happened next?'

'Nothing happened next,' she said. 'I grew up and I came to London. There's nothing else to tell.'

'Were you happy with them?'

'Yes,' she lied. 'I've had a very happy life.'

He was not convinced. 'What's the matter? Don't you trust me?'

'You know it's not that.'

'Then what?'

'I told you just now. It's not wise to play with fate.'

'Perhaps later on . . . when you trust me more.'

'I trust you now.'

'But not enough to share your past.'

'I didn't know I had to submit to an inquisition.'

'That's deliberately misunderstanding me.'

'Perhaps; but I don't see the need . . .'

'What work did you do when you came to London?'

She swallowed hard. 'I . . . I worked in a café . . . near Paddington Station.'

The conversation had gone too far. 'Look, David,' she said. 'I don't want to talk about my past life. It's not very interesting and it's not at all relevant to my relationship with you. I've told you quite clearly that I don't want to talk about it and I'd be very grateful if you would respect my feelings.'

'Very well,' he said quietly. 'If that's how you feel.'

'I do, darling.' She turned and kissed him gently on the cheek. 'I don't mean to sound hurtful or ungrateful. But I just don't want to talk about it.'

He returned the kiss. 'I promise I won't ask you again until you're ready.'

'David!'

'I promise I won't ask you.'

'Thanks,' she said and they lapsed into silence.

She lay staring out of the window watching the sky. 'Barbie . . .' he said and brought her back to him. 'There's something I have to tell you. I should have told you right from the start . . .'

He said no more for, at that moment, there was a sound downstairs as the postman delivered the morning mail. Sam shot from his recumbent position upon the floor and raced for the door in a paroxysm of barking which, having satisfied himself was sufficient to accredit his functions as a guard dog, he then bestowed upon them, leaping upon the bed and lapping his tongue about their ears.

'Get him off,' yelled David. 'There's no lying peacefully in bed with this brute of yours about.'

'There's no lying in bed anyway,' she laughed. 'We've both got work to do.' She brought Sam under control so that he lay beside them on the bed.

'I'd rather stay here with you.' He reached for her again but she held him off before he could kiss her.

'Well, you can't. You've got a deadline to meet.'

'Slave driver.'

'I can remember a time when you thought about nothing but work.'

'That was before you came along and started putting distractions in my way. Who wants to write about Czechoslovakian research into psychotronic energy and bioplasma when there's a gorgeous hunk of a woman lying here beside them.'

'Research into what?'

'The fifth physical interaction. What the Chinese call Ch'i; variously known as N-Rays, X-Force, et cetera, et cetera.'

'What on earth is that?'

'Give us a kiss.'

She rolled away from him. 'I've got to start stripping wallpaper in the drawing room.'

'Hang the wallpaper.'

'Is that a pun, or a statement?'

'You've already done the hall, and the library, and two of the bedrooms.'

'You wait; one of these days I'm going to turn you out of the study so that I can do in there.'

'Over my dead body. How much longer are you going to keep this up?'

'Until the house is finished.'

'It would do you good to take a day off.'

'I don't need a day off, and you've got a deadline to meet. You wait until you see the wallpaper I've chosen. You'll love it.'

'What I should love,' he said, 'is a cup of hot, strong coffee.' He leaned over and slapped her on the bottom. 'You're the house-keeper. Get up and do your duty.'

'Yes, sir.' She slipped out of bed and stood to attention before him. 'Is there anything else that my master desires?'

'You know very well what I desire.' He grabbed her about the waist and kissed her navel which was level with his face.

'Well you're not getting it. There's work to be done.'

She wrapped herself in a silk negligée and went downstairs where she flung wide the kitchen window to let in the morning. She set the coffee to percolate and prepared grapefruit, then began to cut slices of bread for toast. Before she had finished David was behind her, his arms about her waist, kissing her neck.

'I thought you wanted breakfast in bed.' She squirmed as he found the area of skin where she was most vulnerable.

'Conscience. I couldn't lie there and leave you to get on with it.'

'Well, I am the housekeeper.'

'No, you're not,' he said. He swung her round to face him. 'You're the woman I love.'

She kissed him lightly on the chin. 'And I'm also the woman who's trying to prepare breakfast. You can make the toast, seeing you're so good at it.'

He took the bread which she had sliced and slotted it into the toaster. 'It works better now that you've cleaned out the crumbs.'

'I don't know how you managed before I arrived on the scene.'

'Nor do I,' he said. 'But we won't go into that or you'll tell me again that it's time for work.'

She smiled and reached out with her hand to touch him. 'Do you want eggs, or will toast be enough?'

231

'Toast is fine.' He caught her hand and kissed it. 'I'll go and see what the postman brought.'

She had her back to him when he returned and did not see his expression until she sensed a change in the atmosphere and turned to face him. He was sitting at the table.

'David . . . ?'

'Coincidence is a funny thing,' he said quietly. 'I tried to tell you this morning.'

'Tell me what?'

He held up a pale blue envelope and waved it limply. 'It's from my wife.'

'Your wife?'

'I should have told you weeks ago.'

'Why, David?' She became aware that she was holding the coffee percolator in mid-air and put it down on the table.

'I'm sorry,' he said and tossed the letter onto the table. 'I couldn't bring myself to cast a shadow.'

'Where is she?'

'In Sussex.'

'Oh, I see,' she said, inconsequentially.

'She's been there since the accident. Her spine was damaged.'

'What accident, David?'

'And our little boy . . .'

She realised he was crying and went to stand beside his chair.

'Oh, Barbie; he was such a lovely little boy.' He pulled her to him, burying his face against her waist.

'How did it happen?'

'I was driving too fast.'

'You . . . ?'

'The roads were wet and there were leaves . . . He didn't stand a chance.'

She dropped to her knees, using her hands to smear the tears across his face. 'Don't David; you can't blame yourself.'

'Why not?'

'It was an accident.'

'That doesn't alter the effect.'

'I'm sure your wife doesn't blame you.'

He coughed out a small bitter laugh. 'What difference would it make.'

Barbie pulled away and reached for the coffee pot. She poured

232

a cup of coffee and blew on it before holding it to his lips. 'Here,' she said. 'Drink this.'

He sipped it and, after a while, she said, 'Surely she didn't leave you?'

'Not exactly. She went to stay with her sister when she left hospital and she never came back.'

'But surely . . . ?'

'The marriage was floundering long before the accident. It just brought things to a head.'

'I see.'

'Diana thought it best . . .'

'Diana,' said Barbie, testing the sound.

'Don't, Barbie.' He turned and looked at her. 'It was over long ago. I've hardly seen her for the past seven years. It's just that I feel . . . responsible.'

'There's no need to explain.'

'Yes, Barbie, there is. I'm sorry; I should have told you sooner.'

'It doesn't matter,' she said, but she knew now that her fear of fate had taken on physical shape.

'You had a right to know.'

'I don't see why,' she said without bitterness. 'Who am I to demand the details of anyone's past.'

'It's not that I didn't want to tell you.'

'Not like me, you mean.'

'It's just that I never seemed to find the right moment. I kept putting it off.'

'I told you there's no need.'

'I didn't want to spoil things between us.'

'You haven't spoiled it,' she said quietly. 'Just take happiness where you can find it . . . and for as long as it lasts.'

She stood up and went to pour herself a cup of coffee. David watched her for a moment and then slit open the envelope with a knife which lay beside him on the table. 'Good old Angela,' he said and twisted the corner of his mouth. 'She's got herself a man.'

Barbie looked across at him.

'Diana's sister,' he said. 'The eternal spinster, or so it seemed. She's going off to America for a couple of months and Diana needs some extra money for someone to go in and look after her.'

'Oh,' said Barbie lamely. She felt suddenly like an intruder in a family circle.

233

He sensed the feeling and reached out for her. 'It's seven years, Barbie.'

'Seven years,' she said. 'No wonder this place has gone downhill.'

He began collecting up the coffee cups and placing them on a tray. 'Let's not work today,' he said. 'Let's take our breakfast out onto the terrace and spend the day together.'

She nodded. 'I'll make some more toast. This has gone like leather.'

She made the toast then carried it out onto the terrace to join him. They sat together, their chairs touching.

'I'm sorry I cried,' he said after a while. 'Talking about my son always breaks me up.'

'There's no shame in tears,' she said. 'It's those who can't cry who are torn apart.'

He turned and looked at her but she leaned away from him, pouring coffee.

'What was his name?'

'David. We called him Davie.'

'David, Davie, and Diana,' she said. She remembered the toys in the attic and the monogrammed linen – two 'Ds' entwined.

'It was a family tradition. My father's name was David, and his father's before him.'

She handed him the coffee and he sat drinking it for a while. 'Would you like me to tell you about her?' he asked.

'Only if you want to.'

He went on drinking for a further time before he formed his thoughts into order.

'Diana's parents were friends of my mother's,' he said. 'She was a good catch; highly eligible and all set to inherit a tidy sum from her father. And my mother thought it would be an absolutely splendid idea if we "two young people were to hit it off together".' He had let slip a note of bitterness into his own voice.

Barbie looked across at him and he smiled. 'Don't ever let anyone organise your life, Barbie,' he said. 'It doesn't work.'

'Go on.'

'I suppose I was flattered at first to have a girl like Diana hanging on my arm.'

'That doesn't sound like you.'

He looked up and smiled. 'She was also strikingly beautiful.'

'Oh, I see.'

234

'Whatever it was, we were both too young and foolish to know what we were letting ourselves in for.'

'Was she younger than me?'

'No; but some are more young and foolish than others.'

She gestured with her hand for him to continue.

'It worked quite well for a while. Diana's career as a top fashion model was taking off and I hadn't done too badly at Oxford. I was all set to become a whizz-kid of physics.'

'Sounds very glamorous.'

'I suppose it was in a way. Diana used to travel the world showing the haute couture Collections. We were both too busy seeking our own particular horizons to give much thought to where we were going *together*. But it suited us well enough.'

'So; what went wrong?'

'Diana found she was pregnant.'

'And it wasn't intended.'

'What you might call a "monumental slip-up". From that moment it all began to fall apart.'

'It interfered with her career?'

'It wasn't exactly that. Having Davie set up a tremendous ambivalence within her. She wanted to be a mother, but she also wanted her independence.'

'A lot of women have to cope with that. They usually find a way of getting round it.'

'I know, but Diana never did resolve it. She worked her way through a whole succession of nannies but none of them could ever please her. She was never there to look after him herself but no one else was ever good enough, in her eyes, to do the job for her.'

'So what happened?'

'They came and went so often, he never had a chance to build up a stable relationship with anyone. I began to get annoyed when I could see that he was obviously becoming disturbed.'

Barbie looked at him pointedly. 'And how much time did you spend with him?'

'God, Barbie.' He averted his eyes and spread his hand, studying the palm. 'Don't think I haven't asked myself that same question – a million times.'

He went quiet and she waited for him to continue. 'When I think of it now, there's no reason why my career should have been any more important than Diana's. But my work was everything to me. I just felt that she was his mother and it was her place to give him what he needed.'

'Poor Davie,' said Barbie.

'If we'd spent more time thinking about him, and less about ourselves,' he said, 'perhaps things might have turned out differently.'

He sighed deeply then went on. 'Well, anyway, we started by quarrelling about Davie and gradually the rows spilled over into other areas. It wasn't long before we realised that we didn't have a thing in common apart from our careers.'

Barbie looked across at him.

'I was a selfish, arrogant young bastard.'

'Go on.'

'Diana started to talk about divorce. She would probably have gone through with it, if it hadn't been for the accident . . .' He stopped and reached out for Barbie's hand before he continued. 'After she left hospital she went to live with her sister and the question of divorce was just left hanging in the air.'

'And what about her career?'

'There's not much call for a fashion model in a wheelchair.'

'Poor girl.'

'She took it hard, and there wasn't a damned thing I could do.'

'She could have taken up a new career. People do all sorts of things from wheelchairs.'

'If they have the incentive.' He stroked his thumb across Barbie's wrist. 'But Diana didn't seem to have the will to persevere. She did make half-hearted attempts at more than a dozen things but they were all five-minute wonders.'

'Didn't you help?'

'I tried. God, I tried. I suppose that's another reason why I feel guilty. I used to go down to Sussex quite often but I could never get through to her. Perhaps it was because I was still standing up and she was in the chair.'

'Perhaps that was more in your mind than in hers.'

'Perhaps. Anyway, I arranged for her to go to one of the top couturiers to study design. She wanted to create clothes rather than model them. But she grew tired of it after a while and wanted a boutique.'

'What happened to that?'

'It did quite well for a time but then she handed it over to a manageress and went into interior design. She had ideas about advising the owners of stately homes.'

Barbie thought about her own efforts in redecorating 5, Bishops Walk and wondered what Diana would say if she saw it now.

'And all the time I felt more and more guilty.'

'And she never re-considered divorce?'

'She never mentioned it, and I had no reason to. I felt guilty enough without talking about divorce.' He sat for a while looking at Barbie, then he said, 'But it's different now.'

'Why different?'

'Now there's you.'

Barbie shot upright. 'No,' she said. 'I thought we agreed.'

'Agreed to what?'

'Why can't you just leave things the way they are?'

'But I can't leave Diana now to drift along.'

'Why not?'

'Because things have changed.'

'I don't see why.'

'There's every reason why. I suppose you're referring again to "meddling with fate".'

'Look, David,' she said. 'Fate has a way of jumping up and hitting me in the face. It's all very well for you to put me down and call me stupid. You don't understand. But I prefer to leave it alone.'

'I didn't call you stupid. And wouldn't it be better to grasp fate and use it, rather than waiting around for it to rebound?'

'No; it wouldn't.' Her voice had risen sharply. 'I'd rather we just shut up about it and left the subject alone.'

'Sorry.'

She had hurt him and an awkward silence ensued.

'So.' She broke it by turning and saying brightly, 'You were a whizz-kid of science.'

He looked at her, long and hard, then decided to let the moment pass. 'Or thought I was.'

'What changed your mind?'

'Davie,' he said. 'After he died I began to ask myself what it was all about.'

'You're not the first to do that,' she said, thinking of Gran.

'He was just a child and it all seemed such a dreadful waste. It made me sit down and re-think everything I had ever learned.'

She remembered the days when she had blanked out her own

237

mind and had refused to allow herself to think. 'Well, that's one way of coping with it, I suppose.'

'I began to read, and to ask questions. And, eventually, I began to come up with some answers.'

'What sort of answers?'

'Answers which surprised me more than anyone.'

'Is that when you started to write?'

'No; not straight away. It took me a long time to get my thoughts into some sort of perspective. But then someone asked me to write a couple of articles for a magazine. After that it was a gradual process; little by little the writing took over until it was a relief to give up my work in the lab and to sit here instead, doing my own research and collating the results of others who are working along the same lines.'

'Didn't you miss the high-powered life?'

'Not really. There are still deadlines to meet.'

'And, talking of deadlines,' she said. 'I heard you promise your agent that you'd have that article in the post by this afternoon.'

'Yes, I did.'

'Then don't you think you had better go and finish it?'

He smiled at her through a scowl. 'I've already told you once today that you're a slave driver.'

'But he'll only be on the phone shouting for it if you don't.'

He heaved himself from his chair. 'You're right, of course. I'll go and keep company with my typewriter while you go and attend to your wallpaper.'

She caught his hand as he left. 'Are you feeling better now?'

'Yes,' he said. 'I'm glad I told you.'

'I don't think I'm much help to you.'

'You'll do,' he said and bent to kiss her hair.

An hour later she went to the study. She did not usually interrupt him when he was working and she knocked hesitantly before entering.

'How's it going?' she asked as he looked up.

'It's coming together,' he conceded. 'Just.'

'I just wanted you to know . . .'

She paused and he sat waiting for her to go on.

'. . . that I love you.'

'I love you, too.' He smiled and drew her towards him. 'And I'd rather be out there, spending the day with you.'

238

'Well you can't,' she laughed. 'I'll cook you something special for dinner. And I'll make it up to you tonight.'

'Promises, promises. Oh, by the way . . .' He caught her as she began to move away. 'I've been thinking up a little plan. I've got enough material for another book. And I know of a little place that we could rent. What do you say that we get out of London for a while and have ourselves a little country air?'

'Oh, David, could we really?'

'I don't see why not. It's a quiet little village in North Wales. Plenty of sky and mountains; it's even near the sea.'

'When, David – *when*?' She flung her arms about his neck and plastered his face with kisses, making it impossible for him to speak.

'Soon,' he laughed. 'I've got a few more assignments to complete but I don't see why we can't get away by the end of the month.'

'I can't wait.'

'Neither can I. Imagine; just you and me, and all that fresh air. If the book ever gets written it'll be a miracle.'

'It'll get written.' She took his face between her hands and kissed him. 'And there'll still be time for us.'

It was early July when they locked up the house in Bishops Walk and set off for the mountains of North Wales. It was a day of bright sunshine broken by heavy showers. At one moment the rain would fall, streaming down the windows of the car so that the windscreen wipers were hard pressed to clear an area of vision, and the next moment the sun would shine, sucking clouds of steam from the road surface and off the backs of ruminating cattle.

It was early evening as they entered the village. It was raining again and a pall of mist hung across the mountain peaks, obscuring the view.

'It's beautiful, David.' Barbie had hardly spoken for many miles. 'It has a grandeur all its own.'

He reached over and squeezed her hand. 'You wait until you see the village.'

It was a scattering of cottages, grey stone and slate, hidden away in a tiny valley between mountains. Through its centre a mountain stream tossed noisily over a rocky bed and, on all four sides, the mountains towered, their peaks shrouded now, but revealing to one side the dark green mass of a pine forest, and on the other the scattered dots of sheep.

They passed through the village and, at the far end, David turned the car onto a narrow track, rocking along its uneven surface until they were out of sight of neighbouring dwellings and came at last to the cottage. It was of stone and slate like the others, its boundary marked by a low slate wall, and nearby flowed the same stream which passed through the village.

Barbie opened the door for Sam who had been cooped too long within the confines of the car. He careered across the wet grass, darting first in one direction and then another, showering them each time he passed.

'That dog's a maniac,' laughed David. 'I swear that one of these days he'll end up turning somersaults.'

The cottage was tiny. The front door opened directly onto a parlour, its low chairs upholstered in chintz, and with an ingle-nook fireplace taking up the greater part of one wall. At the back there was a tiny kitchen, hardly room for one to move, and a bathroom added on in recent years. The stairs opened directly onto the only bedroom, squatting beneath a low ceiling, with a large, square bed almost filling it from wall to wall.

David lit a fire to drive out the dampness from the air and they ate their supper of ham and salad, with fresh bread rolls which they had bought along the way. Outside, the rain brought on an early dusk but they did not bother to switch on the lights, content to sit in the glow of the fire. Everywhere was quiet and still, carrying only the sound of the rushing water from the stream.

'It's peaceful here,' said Barbie. She was sitting on the floor beside David's chair. 'Anyone could sit and write a book in these surroundings.'

'Except for the ever-constant distractions.'

'There aren't any distractions.'

'I was looking at you.'

'You're always looking at me.'

He raised one eyebrow at her and smiled. 'You wouldn't like it if I wasn't.'

He got out of his chair and bent to pick her up.

'What are you doing?'

'Thinking of distractions.'

'David . . . !' He was making towards the stairs. 'You're not going to carry me up those stairs?'

240

'You watch me.'

'You can't!' She squealed as he hoisted her more securely into his arms. 'You'll drop me.'

'That's not very gallant.'

'Well, you'll fall down and break your neck.'

'Then you can give me the kiss of life.'

The stairs were steep and narrow. By the time they reached the top David was breathless and she was helpless with laughter. He staggered across the floor and together they collapsed in a heap upon the bed.

'You're a fool,' she giggled. 'And I love you.'

'Show me.'

He took the warm feather quilt and pulled it across them, pulling it up over their heads and drawing her down beneath its darkness.

'How?' she whispered.

'Come here and you'll see.'

Next morning, Barbie awoke to find him gone. She stretched out her hand and for a brief instant tasted the old familiar fear, but almost immediately she heard the sound of the typewriter from the room below. She dressed and went downstairs.

'Morning, darling.'

He looked up briefly as she kissed him on the cheek but he was deeply engrossed. She ruffled his hair and planted another kiss behind his ear but left him undisturbed.

She went into the kitchen to prepare breakfast which she placed beside him on the table and went outside to eat her own.

She sat on the bank of the stream, dangling her feet in the ice-cold water, while Sam dashed madly through the shallows, returning every now and then to share her toast. The showers of the previous day had cleared, giving her full view of the mountain peaks, while the air was so clear and fresh it made her almost light-headed.

She did not return to the cottage but walked instead with Sam towards the mountain, hardly pausing until she broke into the shadowy depths of the pine forest. All was quiet and still in here, the sound of her footsteps heightened by the cathedral of trees and every now and then the scuttle of an unseen animal fleeing from the curiosity of Sam. She walked for miles, not returning to the cottage until the noonday sun was directly overhead and then she slipped in by the back entrance, cocking her ear for the continued clacking of the typewriter.

David stretched as she set down his lunch. 'I've worked enough,' he said. He yawned and grabbed her by the waist. 'What shall we do this afternoon?'

'Has it gone well?'

'Not bad. But the afternoons I share with you. Nothing shall intrude upon the afternoons.'

She sat down beside him, flicking her eye across the type-written pages which lay upon the table. 'You choose,' she said. 'I've already climbed a mountain.'

They drove to the coast and spent the afternoon lazing on the sand of a little rocky cove. Sam, at last tired out by his morning walk, stretched out beside them and Barbie cushioned her head against his back.

'Are you happy?' David rolled over and nuzzled his mouth against her ear.

'Mmm, very.'

'It seems too good to be true. Just you and me, and this raving dog of yours.'

'Whatever happens, David, you've given me the happiest months of my life.'

'Nothing's going to happen.'

She did not reply.

'Marry me, Barbie.'

'Don't, David.' She got up, causing Sam to stir. 'You promised.'

'It doesn't stop me wanting you.'

'One day at a time,' she said. 'I can only cope with one day at a time.'

'I'm sorry.' He reached out and stroked her hair. 'But I can't help loving you.'

'I love you too,' she said. She picked up her bag and began to walk away. 'Now can we go and eat?'

They returned to the cottage and in the evening David worked again while Barbie read and later slipped away to bed.

And so was set the pattern for the coming weeks. During the morning and evening David worked, and each afternoon they played. They walked or lazed, or drove the car, or rode upon the backs of sturdy ponies; and in the early hours of each morning, Barbie would be roused from sleep as he slipped in beside her on

242

the bed. There, she would ease away the strain of his working hours and together they slept into another day.

The summer passed and it was late September when David finally stretched himself before the typewriter and announced that the work was done.

Barbie sat down beside him, collecting up the pages and setting them in order. 'I must read this book,' she said.

'It's about time. You've never read any of my previous stuff.'

'I don't think I could understand it.'

'Nonsense.' He laughed at her gently. 'It's the basic simplicity which proves to be so mind-bending.'

'I can't say that I've ever found life very simple.'

'It's people who make it complex. The basic concept is simplicity itself. All of life is inter-connected. We are at one with everything, and everything is part of us.'

'I thought you said it was simple.'

He laughed and started again. 'We tend to think that our lives are restricted to a span of seventy-odd years, or so, and then we die. In reality, those seventy years are a mere microcosm of our total existence. Life stretches into infinity.'

'I wouldn't have thought that you would believe in Heaven.'

'I don't, as such. But "Heaven" is one word for it; it's just not the word that I would choose. We return to the dimension from whence we came and later we come back again.'

'Good Lord; reincarnation?' She was shocked.

'Why not?'

'Only people in India and the Far East believe in things like that.'

'Once maybe, but not any more. There are a great many scientists who are more than interested in the subject.'

'I thought it was a religion.'

'The scientists are taking over. They're asking questions.'

'About what?'

'Well, for instance – with the use of hypnosis it's quite common for people to recall a number of past lives. We've known about it for a long time. What puzzled us was why the same people kept reappearing in different guises in consecutive lives. It was almost like a repertory company where the same set of actors swap rôles for each new production.'

'So, we're only playing, after all,' she said and there was a note of sarcasm in her voice. 'And all this time I thought it was for real.'

243

'Come on,' he said. 'Don't deliberately misunderstand what I'm saying.'

'Sorry.'

'What I'm saying is that your brother in this life might have been your wife in the last, or your father, or your sister.'

'That sounds a bit far-fetched to me.'

'It's really quite simple when you think it through. We all have the opportunity over and over again to work through our relationships with one another.'

'I still say it seems far-fetched.'

He leaned forward and kissed her lightly on the cheek. 'I wonder where we met before.'

She looked at him and smiled.

> *'I met you once, a fragrant flower,*
> *And I, a raindrop, kissed your face*
> *In such sweet ecstasy of love*
> *That when our next rejoining came*
> *We knew at once that we were one,*
> *And we came running, building lives*
> *Which intertwined, then thrice and*
> *four times came again,*
> *Touching lips in joyous recognition.'*

'You remembered the poem.'

'I liked it.'

He smiled. 'I didn't know I was waiting for you when I wrote it.'

'You're nothing but an old romantic.'

He laughed. 'Scientists aren't noted for their sense of romance.'

'Well I think you are.'

He laughed again and tapped her on the nose. 'I suppose even we can have our whimsical moments.'

'I still don't understand what you're trying to say about this other dimension – this place you say we go to. If it isn't Heaven, then what is it?'

He poured himself a cup of coffee from the pot set beside him on the table. 'We've learned a lot in the past few years,' he said. 'We've made vast improvements in medicine with the result that we're far more successful in methods of resuscitation.'

He took a sip of the coffee and pulled a face, for it was almost

244

cold. 'People are dying and being brought back to life. And some are telling the strangest tales of where they've been.'

Barbie shuddered. 'That's downright creepy.'

'No it isn't. At first, no one took much notice – or put it down to hallucination. But, little by little, a few astute listeners began to realise that there was too much similarity between the stories to ignore. That's when the researchers came in and began to question patients who had just suffered a heart attack, or a serious accident. They caught them in those few minutes after they had been resuscitated – before memory faded and before reasoning had a chance to deny the experience.'

Barbie shuddered again.

'Their stories fitted together with remarkable accuracy.'

'Ugh. It still sounds creepy.'

He tried his coffee again but gave up and replaced the cup on the tray. 'They spoke of an existence not dissimilar to our own – except that they weren't shackled by the limitations which we experience here. And, almost without exception, they reported that they had been met by someone – someone from their family, or a friend. Some of the more religious reported that they had been met by Jesus, or an angel, or some other deity, according to their own particular beliefs. But it was all a variation on the same theme; they were met by someone they were pleased to see.'

Barbie felt a catch in her throat and swallowed on it with an audible sound.

'What's the matter?'

'I was thinking of my Gran.'

'Wherever she is, you can bet she's happy.'

She nodded and bit her lip. 'I've always been afraid of death. It's so final.'

He took her hand and squeezed it. 'There's no reason to be afraid of dying. It's like stepping out of one door and through another. Those who've experienced it are never afraid to die again. The only ones who appear to have problems are those who attempt suicide. I suppose it's like copping out before the job's been done.'

She sat and thought for a moment. 'What you're saying is that we're going round in circles.'

'No; not quite. It's more like a spiral. We're going round and round, but we're always moving upwards. We're working our way steadily through every facet of existence.' He pointed towards the sky. 'Any scientist will tell you that everything is made from the same basic building blocks. You see that bird flying up there . . . or a flower . . . or a cow . . . the clouds . . . you . . . me . . . the moon . . . If you break them down, they're all composed of the same basic elements.'

'I didn't know that.'

'I believe that they're all interconnected and interchangeable. We are at one with all things because we have been all things, or will become so as we work our way steadily along the spiral.'

'*I met you once,*' she recited again, '*a fragrant flower, And I, a raindrop, kissed your face.*'

'Now you've got it.'

'But I still don't go along with it.'

'Good for you. Everyone should be entitled to work out their own philosophy. I only ask you to remember one thing – always keep an open mind.'

She sat and thought on that for a while but he went on, 'I used to think that the answers to everything could be found in ever more powerful telescopes and microscopes. Until I realised that the answers lie within ourselves.'

'I don't understand.'

'We have the answers to all things locked up within that part of us which is infinite.'

'That's as clear as mud,' she countered.

'Well, if we've experienced everything, then we must have that experience locked away somewhere within us. We've all got abilities far beyond those we normally use. Sometimes people discover them by accident, and are frightened by them – like teenagers who trigger off poltergeists.'

'Good God! You're even into ghosts as well.'

'Others set out deliberately to cultivate them – like precognition or telekinesis.'

'Is there no end to the weird things you're dabbling in?'

'Not dabbling,' he smiled. 'There's a lot of serious research going on by very reputable scientists.'

'I wouldn't have thought that they would have involved themselves in such things.'

'There are scientists in America, in Russia, in Britain, all over the world, working on this. And everything we learn is ever more intricate and miraculous. It's turning conventional science on its head.'

She began collecting up the pages of the manuscript. 'Well, I think I'll leave it all to you,' she said. 'It's all far too clever for me.'

He laughed. 'You underestimate yourself.'

'No,' she said and slipped the pages into a folder. 'I'll stick to things I understand, like – what are we going to do with the next few days? We've only got until Sunday.'

'What would you like to do?'

She stooped so that she could see clearly through the window. 'You see that mountain out there?' she asked. 'I'll race you to that line of trees.'

'Pity. I thought I was going to get some reward for being a good boy and finishing my work.'

'Race me to those trees and I'll give you your reward.'

'You're on.' He slapped her on the bottom and she ran squealing from the cottage.

They returned to Bishops Walk a few days before Barbie's nineteenth birthday. She moved about the house, touching objects to reassure herself of their presence for, although she had been happy in North Wales, she was glad to be home. She went into the garden exclaiming at the sight of Michaelmas daisies, the faded pink footballs of hydrangeas, and touched the seedhead of each midsummer flower, regretting that she had not been there at the time of its blooming.

David laughed at her. 'The trouble with you,' he said, 'is that you want to be in two places at the same time.'

She linked her arm through his and laughed with him. 'If I had been there,' she said, 'I wouldn't have seen the rivers, and the mountains, and the pine forests in high summer.'

He patted her hand and led her back into the house. 'What would you like for your birthday? I want to buy you something really special.'

She thought for a moment and frowned. 'There's nothing I need.'

'There must be something.'

'No; I'm very happy with what I've got.'

'How about some jewellery? A ring?' He raised his eyebrow at her.

Immediately her muscles snapped taut and she drew away from him.

'Sorry,' he said. 'Forget I said it.'

247

She made an effort to relax. 'No thanks. I don't want anything like that.'

They were passing through the hall and, as she looked up at the wall, an idea came to her at once. 'I know what I'd like,' she said. 'You remember when we took down those dull old paintings from the hall? You said that we could replace them with something more colourful.'

He nodded.

'Let's not wait until we've finished the house. Let's buy one now.'

'But that's a present for the house. I want to buy something for you.'

'But it would be,' she insisted. 'The house is part of me. It's what I'd really like, David; please.'

He laughed. 'All right. If it's what you really want. I'll take you round the galleries on your birthday and you can choose.'

'Thank you, David.' She reached up and kissed him on the cheek. 'And I love you.'

By twelve o'clock on the appointed day they had viewed the collections of three galleries but Barbie had seen nothing which appealed to her sufficiently to buy.

'I know what I want,' she said doggedly. 'I shall recognise it the moment I see it.'

David trailed behind her with good-humoured patience, pointing out his own particular favourites, but Barbie was adamant in her refusal to consider anything but the painting which she carried in her mind's eye.

As they walked into the fourth gallery she looked about her with an air of disapproval. 'This place is too expensive. Look at that painting over there. It's exorbitant.'

David passed her an amused smile. 'I don't mind paying a decent price if it's a good painting.'

'But look at the price.'

'I told you I wanted to buy you something special.'

Barbie turned to him with disarming candour. 'Are you very rich?'

He laughed at that, loudly enough to cause a woman to look up at him from across the room. 'Let's just say that we're not likely to go bankrupt unless we do something silly.'

She would have been satisfied with that but he went on to explain. 'My grandfather did rather well for himself as an inventor. He developed several, basically simple, ideas which proved to be immensely important to industry. Most of the proceeds passed to my father but part of it came straight to me as the only grandson. Then, when my father died last year, I received a share of his estate.'

'I'm sorry about your father.'

He smiled and squeezed her hand. 'He was a lot older than my mother. They say I'm a lot like him; I suppose I'm proving it all over again.'

She returned the squeeze of his hand. 'I don't like this place,' she said. 'They're charging a fortune for paintings which any child could do.'

'Don't let the artist hear you say that, or he'll tell you that you don't understand art.' He led her to the door. 'Come on; I'll take you to lunch; then afterwards we'll go and visit a friend of mine who owns a gallery in Belgravia.'

He hailed a taxi which was approaching from behind and took her arm as it pulled into the kerb a short distance ahead, restricting the flow of following traffic. He opened the door for her to dive inside and it was not until she was seated that she had an opportunity to look up and observe the driver. It was Curly.

She saw him glance into his rear-view mirror, and watched the flash of recognition on his face, followed by the closing of one eyelid in greeting; but, immediately, it was wiped away and he did not look at her again until they arrived at their destination.

David reached out to pay him. Curly's eye passed across Barbie as it might have passed across any attractive stranger but he gave no hint of their previous association.

Barbie was caught up in an ambivalence of feeling. On the one hand she was grateful for his diplomacy but, at the same time, she could not bring herself to walk away without speaking.

'Hello, Curly,' she said. 'How are you?'

'I'm very well, thank you . . .' he looked down at her left hand . . . Miss. And how are you?'

'I'm fine, thank you, Curly. How's your wife?'

'Very well.'

'And the children?'

'Blooming, Miss. Growing faster than you can wink an eye.'

'It's nice to see you.' She held out her hand and he shook it briefly.

'Nice to see you, too, Miss. See you around some other time, maybe.' He threw her a smile. 'Cheerio,' he called and drew out into the heavy traffic.

David took her arm and led her towards the restaurant. 'Seems like a pleasant fellow,' he said.

'Yes; he is.'

'The only person you've ever admitted to knowing in the whole of London.'

'It's a big city,' she retorted. 'It's full of strangers.'

They were shown to a booth at the far end of the restaurant where the lighting was dim. The unexpected meeting with Curly had thrown Barbie off-balance and her hands were trembling.

'Coincidence there being two Curlys,' he said.

She laid down the menu on the table so that David should not detect the tremor in her hands but she knew only too well that she had failed.

'The same name as your father.'

'My father's name was Ken.'

'Oh; I thought you said it was Curly.'

She flushed in the darkness and he reached out to take her hand. 'Do you love me, Barbie?'

'You know I do.'

'But not enough to tell me a single thing about your life since the age of ten.'

She pulled away from him. 'Surely we're not going to start that conversation all over again.' She felt trapped here on the inner seat of the confined booth. 'I thought I'd made myself quite clear.'

'You've made it quite clear that you don't want to share it with me.'

'So why do you keep asking questions?'

'Because it's not good for you to keep something locked away inside yourself. Sooner or later you're going to have to trust someone not to let you down. I'd like it to be me.'

'I don't know why you have to be so interested in knowing all about my past.'

He took her hand again and held it tight. 'Look, Barbie; what you did before you came to me is none of my concern. I'm not asking out of curiosity. But it's all tied up with your fears and insecurity; I think you ought to share it.'

She turned on him harshly. 'Look, David; you're always asking me these questions. Sooner or later you're going to find out something which is going to stop you loving me. Is that what you want?'

'You silly girl.' He stroked his thumb across her wrist. 'What on earth could you tell me that would stop me loving you?'

'Plenty.'

'Am I that shallow?'

'I'm just telling you that if you knew everything about me, you wouldn't want me any more.'

'Nothing's that bad.'

'Isn't it?'

'Then trust me to find out.'

She sat for a long time staring at the table. 'All right,' she said at last. 'You've asked for it. But, afterwards, don't say I didn't warn you.'

'I'll take that chance.'

She told him of the circumstances of Gran's death and of her life with Ken and Mary.

'I understand now,' he said, 'the reasons for the insecurity.'

She told him, too, that she had run away from Wansdyke Avenue, omitting only the circumstances which determined her rapid departure.

'And what did you do when you came to London?'

'I worked for Curly.' Her words sank to a whisper.

'Doing what?'

He moved his face closer to catch her indistinct words but, instead, she turned to him and spoke clearly and deliberately. 'I was a whore,' she said. 'A floozy . . . a high-class, dressed-up tart . . . or anything else you might like to call me.'

She waited for his reaction and it came with a strange sound from the back of his throat. For a brief moment his hand tightened across her own and then went slack. He drew away from her.

'I didn't know. I thought . . .'

'David . . . ?' She reached out for him but, even as she touched him, he stood up and strode out of the restaurant.

For a long time she sat staring after him and it was not until the waiter came for their order that she became aware of her surroundings. She stammered out an excuse and stumbled to the door.

Her throat was tight and sore, and her eyes were dry but as she stepped out onto the street, the tears began to fall. She walked home, street after street, oblivious to the stares of passers-by. The

251

streets were crowded and she was jostled and pushed, colliding first with one person and then another, pushing them roughly aside with her elbows and her hands – for none of them was David.

The house was deserted except for Sam who bounded to greet her as she opened the door. For the first time ever she knocked him aside, locking him in the kitchen where he lay behind the door, whimpering.

She wandered round the house and eventually threw herself into an armchair in the library, crying until she gasped for breath. Then, exhausted, she let her mind go blank, staring unseeingly at rows of books, feeling, seeing, thinking nothing – the safety valve of oblivion.

When, at last, her mind began once more to focus, she realised that she was cold, shivering with the feeling of ice in her veins. She got up and wandered about the house, touching things which were his, picking up his jacket from the back of a chair and carrying it with her to their bed, where she flung herself down into the pillow which bore his scent.

She climbed into bed for warmth but got up again when she heard a sound downstairs. It was only Sam scratching at the door and she went once more into the library, automatically setting a match to the fire which lay prepared in the grate. The flames licked upwards, gradually giving out warmth, and she crouched before it was on the hearthrug, still hugging David's jacket, her head resting on the seat of the armchair.

A door slammed and she looked up with a start. David was striding through the house, opening first one door and then another, calling her name. She went to the library door and he saw her there.

'Oh, Barbie. I'm sorry.' He ran towards her and kissed her so that she could not speak. 'I'm so very sorry.'

Both tried to speak but neither listened, each stopping the other with their kisses; each wishing more to kiss than to be kissed in return.

At last he took her across the room and sat in the armchair, drawing her down upon his lap. It had been raining and his coat was wet. She removed it from his shoulders and flung it across the floor.

'I'm sorry, Barbie,' he said. 'I told you one thing, and I did another.'

She shook her head. 'I shouldn't have told you.'

'It was the shock. I hadn't guessed.'

'I didn't think that you'd come back.' She hugged him tightly about the neck.

'I love you, darling,' he said. 'It was a terrible thing for me to do.'

'I shouldn't have told you.'

'Of course you should. It was I who was at fault.'

'No.' She kissed him again.

'I told you that your past didn't matter to me; then, suddenly, I discovered that it did.'

She drew away. 'I told you things would never be the same.'

He sat looking at her and she turned her face away from him. 'You'll tell me that you love me,' she said. 'But every time you look at me you'll . . .'

'Yes,' he said. 'I shan't forget. I can't pretend to forget a thing like that. But it will be a different kind of love; accepting one another for what we are, not just for what we want each other to be.'

She was not convinced. She drew away and made to stand. 'It will only be a matter of time.'

But he caught her hand and drew her back upon her knee. 'Don't you see, Barbie, it was I who was wrong. If I loved you this morning, what difference can it make what you did last year? The difference is in the knowledge, not in my love.'

'It was enough to make you walk away.'

'It was the shock. Look, Barbie; I'll tell you what I thought. I thought, right from the moment when I first met you, that you were reeling from some unhappy love affair. I thought that some man had hurt you so badly that he had destroyed your trust. When I found out . . .' His voice cracked. 'Somehow, for that moment, it was all too much. I couldn't take the thought of you with all those . . .'

'Don't.' She stopped his lips.

'I'm sorry, Barbie. Whatever you did, you must have had a reason for it.'

'The reasons don't sound very convincing any more.'

He pulled her against his shoulder and began to stroke her hair, twisting his fingers through the strands, while, with his other hand, he massaged the small of her back. She closed her eyes

253

and thought of the porter who had stroked her back on the evening when Gran had died.

'I'm sorry,' he said. 'Please forgive me.'

It seemed incongruous that he should be asking forgiveness of her. She began to cry and realised at the same moment, that he, too, was crying.

'Happy birthday,' he said and wiped her tears with the ball of his thumb.

'I'd forgotten that it was my birthday.'

'I'll take you out tomorrow and buy your painting.'

'I don't care about any stupid old painting.' She flung her arms about his neck and kissed him. 'I only want you.'

He slid her down from the chair towards the floor. There, on the hearthrug before the fire, he undressed her; then slowly, tenderly, and finally in a frenzy of insatiable passion, they kissed, and bit, and drank each other dry.

In December, David was to visit Stanford University in California, so that he might see at first hand a number of research projects which were currently making good headway. He booked passage for himself and Barbie and it was arranged that, after he had been to Stanford, they would spend Christmas together in Los Angeles. Barbie was excited at the prospect of her first visit to America but on the morning of departure she awoke with a sore throat and a high temperature; her limbs ached and it was evident that she was suffering from influenza.

David made immediately for the telephone in order to cancel their flight but Barbie stopped him.

'You go, David,' she said. 'Your appointments have all been arranged.'

'But I can't leave you.'

'Of course you can.' She forced an appearance of shaky confidence. 'I'll follow on in a few days' time when I'm feeling better.'

'But who's going to look after you?'

'I shall be all right. I'll make up a bed in the library. I'm not so ill that I can't walk into the kitchen to make myself a glass of hot lemon.'

David was irresolute to the last moment, reluctant to leave her, and when at last she heard the taxi pulling away from the front door, she regretted her insistence that he should go, for suddenly the house was empty and she became all the more aware of the pains in her limbs.

For two days she lay in bed while Sam slouched about the house, missing his exercise but sensing that all was not well with Barbie.

By the third day she was much improved and she got up and dressed, trying out her unsteady legs by walking in the garden. It was a bright, mild day for mid-December and she decided that she would take Sam to Battersea Park so that he might have the freedom of a large open space in which to run.

She was on her way to fetch his leash when she heard the sound of a car on the drive and stopped to look out of the stained glass window beside the front door. The car drew up before the steps and she could see two women inside, their faces distorted through the patterned glass.

She was about to open the door to them but something held her back and she stood instead, watching as the woman in the driving seat got out and walked round to the passenger door. She opened it but the passenger made no move to get out. Instead, the driver opened the rear door and removed a folded wheelchair which she opened and manoeuvred into position beside the passenger seat. Barbie's stomach dropped.

She heard conversation, which she could not decipher. The passenger slid herself into the chair and, as soon as she was seated, the driver made towards the steps. Barbie opened the door before she reached it and the woman held back, startled, while over her shoulder Barbie saw upon the face of the other a fleeting look of surprise which was instantly extinguished.

'Oh, good,' she said. 'There's someone in. All right, Mrs Leach; you may go and attend to those errands, then come back for me here.'

The driver smiled politely at Barbie. 'Good afternoon,' she said and turned to get into the car.

Barbie walked down the steps but, before she reached the wheelchair, the woman had already swung herself towards the side entrance. She moved off quickly, leaving Barbie standing.

'I'll have to go round to the side door,' she said. 'I can't cope with those steps.'

She manoeuvred the chair efficiently, stopping only at the small step beside the side door, waiting without comment for Barbie to help her across it.

Immediately she was clear of the obstacle she was away, independent, making for the kitchen. It was not until she was on the opposite side of the room that she turned and introduced herself: but Barbie had no need of introductions.

'I'm Diana FitzGibbon,' she said. 'I'd like to see my husband.'

Chapter Thirteen

Diana FitzGibbon sat looking about her, taking in every item in the room.

'I see that David is still as untidy as ever,' she said.

She was a strikingly elegant woman, with dark hair sweeping in casual waves across a flawless complexion. Even in the confines of the chair, the cut of her cream-coloured suit was evident for the way in which it fitted perfectly across the shoulders and flattered the slim, still youthful figure. She had a way of using her hands, fluttering long, slim fingers, causing a large diamond solitaire to catch the light.

Beside her, Barbie felt suddenly aware of her own tender years – almost gauche.

'Where is my husband?'

She explained David's absence and Diana clicked her tongue.

Barbie did not know how to respond but it was soon evident that Diana was not expecting response. She swung her chair and made towards the hall.

'I see that David has had the decorators in,' she said. 'Who on earth is responsible for this ghastly colour scheme?'

'I . . .' stammered Barbie but Diana swung round towards the library door.

'I see they've been in the library too. The place has gone to rack and ruin since I was here last.'

'The whole house is being re-decorated,' said Barbie. 'David has agreed to all the rooms being done.'

Diana looked at her sharply, almost as if she resented Barbie's familiarity in using David's name. 'It will cost him a small fortune,' she said curtly.

'Would you like some coffee? I have some hot in the kitchen.'

Diana gave a fluttering gesture with her hand. 'Black,' she said. 'No sugar.' And went off to inspect the other ground-floor rooms.

From the kitchen Barbie could hear the sound of the wheelchair moving about and, when she returned with the coffee, found Diana in the study. She set down the tray upon the desk.

'What on earth is David doing with these plants?' Diana waved her hands towards the equipment to which they were attached.

'It's a recording equipment,' said Barbie, not wanting to be more explicit.

'Good Lord! It's about time he stopped all this frivolous nonsense. The magazines may be prepared to pay for it, but it's hardly the sort of thing his talent warrants.' She shook her head and sighed and, for a moment, her attitude seemed to change, become more approachable. 'He had the most marvellous career before him, you know,' she said. 'There were no limits to the heights he could have reached.'

'He seems to be doing very well now.'

But immediately Diana reverted to how she had been before. 'I understand that it's something to do with life after death; some sort of spiritualistic nonsense.'

'I hardly think that David would refer to himself as a Spiritualist,' said Barbie.

She was immediately quashed by a look from Diana.

'Shall I pour the coffee?' she asked.

Diana gave a gesture which Barbie interpreted as assent.

'I take it that you're David's mistress.'

Barbie was taken aback by the remark.

'I've heard rumours, of course.'

'I . . .'

'It's a pity David couldn't have told me for himself.'

'It wasn't David.' Barbie sprang to his defence. 'I didn't . . .'

'But I must admit I wasn't expecting someone quite so young.'

Barbie was totally put down by this woman. With every moment she was losing what remained of her self-confidence.

'I think it's only fair to inform you,' said Diana, 'that I intend to return.'

Barbie, already weakened by her illness, raised a hand to her head and Diana waved her to a nearby chair.

'I think it will be sometime in about February,' she went on. 'Or maybe March. I need to have time to have the work done in here.' She looked about her and spoke aloud her thoughts. 'I haven't

258

decided yet whether to convert the ground-floor rooms or whether I shall have a lift installed on the stairs.'

Barbie stood, her mouth open, trying to regain some measure of composure.

'Forgive me for being so forthright,' said Diana. 'But I believe that when there's something to be said, one should come right out and say it.' She looked across at Barbie for confirmation. 'Don't you agree?'

'Oh, yes,' said Barbie lamely.

'It's all happened in something of a rush. My sister is marrying shortly and going to the States. She'll have to sell up her house.'

'Oh, I see.'

'It seems the obvious thing for me to come back home.' She seemed in some obscure way to be asking for Barbie's approval. 'Perhaps my husband told you about my sister's marriage?'

'He didn't mention marriage.'

'No, of course not. I didn't know myself until last week.'

'Oh.'

'You do know that this house is mine?'

'Yours?'

'Technically speaking; it was a wedding gift from my father.'

Again Barbie was robbed of speech. This house, which she loved so much, belonged, not to David, but to Diana.

'How long have you been here?'

Barbie counted the months since May. 'Eight months,' she said, and Diana raised her eyebrows in a gesture which she could not read.

'And my husband's away, you say. When do you expect him back?'

'We hope to be home some time in the New Year.' She had let slip the 'we'. It reasserted some small measure of confidence.

'And do you have his address at the hotel?'

'No,' she lied. 'I'm waiting for him to contact me.'

'Very well. Perhaps you'd inform him of the situation when he next contacts you, and tell him that I shall be in touch immediately after his return.'

'I'll tell him,' said Barbie. 'I'll see what he says.'

Diana looked at her. 'I think I mentioned that the house is mine.'

'Yes, you did.'

'I'll have to get the work started in here as soon as possible.

259

Workmen take an age to carry out the simplest tasks these days, and it's imperative that I'm out of my sister's house before the end of March.'

'I'll tell him', said Barbie again.

'Thank you.' Diana looked about the study. 'I've always liked this room,' she said, and her tone was almost chatty. 'It will suit me quite well. Do you think David would prefer to work in the library, or shall I have one of the rooms made into a study upstairs?'

Barbie thought of David's habitual use of this room for his work.

'Perhaps you'd ask him when he telephones,' said Diana. 'Then he can give the matter some thought and let me know.'

Perhaps if Barbie had been more sure of herself she would have been able to stand up against Diana FitzGibbon. But, instead, she was aware of her relationship with David slipping away. She felt like a child at the end of a glorious outing being told that it is time to put away the bucket and spade; the treat is over.

Diana registered something of her emotion and spoke for the first time as if with some concern for her. 'I trust you'll be able to find yourself somewhere suitable by February?'

Barbie did not reply but said instead, 'I love him . . . very much.'

'I'm sure you do.'

'And he loves me.'

Diana gave a small, sardonic laugh. 'I doubt it,' she said. 'Unless he's undergone a radical change. David has always been far too tied up with his work to love anyone.'

'He loves me.'

It appeared to find some chink in Diana's veneer. She took a sip of coffee, which had so far been left untouched. 'I don't believe you gave me your name,' she said.

'You didn't ask. But it's Barbie.'

She ignored the response. 'Well, Barbie, I don't know what my husband has told you but I, too, am very fond of him.'

Barbie looked at her, unimpressed.

'He hurt me, you know – very badly.'

'I'm sorry. He told me about the accident.'

'I was not referring to the accident.'

'Oh.'

'We all have needs, Barbie.' Barbie looked across at Diana and

260

for a fleeting moment caught a glimpse of a frightened, lonely woman. 'And I need David.'

'I need him too,' said Barbie.

'But not as much as I.'

'I don't know how we measure need.'

Diana gave an impatient gesture. 'This is all rather . . .' But then she relaxed and turned more quietly to Barbie. 'Be reasonable, Barbie,' she said. 'You're very young; and you're not unattractive. You've got the ability to go out there and make a whole new life for yourself.'

'But I need David.'

'God damn it, child. What on earth can you know about need?' Her voice rose but as Barbie looked across at her she brought it under control. 'What do you know about being stuck in this damned chair, dependent upon other people, not able to do a damned thing for yourself without calling on someone for help.'

'I'm sorry.'

'You can have no idea.'

Barbie fought for inspiration. 'Perhaps you could have the house,' she said. 'And David could find someone to come in and look after you.'

'I don't want "someone",' snapped Diana. 'If I wanted "someone" I should make do with Mrs Leach.'

'But David . . .'

'David is my husband. And I need him. For the last time – *I need him.*'

An awkward silence grew between them and it was almost a relief when the doorbell sounded.

Immediately, Diana's veneer snapped back into place. 'That will be Mrs Leach,' she said. 'Go and let her in, will you. And fetch my bag; I left it in the kitchen.'

Barbie performed both tasks, glad of some activity, and mechanically went through the procedure of seeing Diana out to her car.

Mrs Leach settled her into the passenger seat.

'Tell my husband to contact me the moment he gets back from the States,' said Diana. 'I'll endeavour to get the workmen to come in during the second week in January; though Heaven knows if one can get anything done on time these days.'

Barbie closed the car door beside her.

'I'm so glad to have met you,' said Diana.

'Yes,' said Barbie and watched as the car drove away.

She walked back into the house, conscious of the symptoms of delayed shock. She went upstairs to the room which was hers and David's and sat for a long time upon their bed.

She knew that she would not stand against Diana FitzGibbon, but would admit defeat without a blow being dealt. She made no attempt to analyse her feelings; the conviction was too deeply ingrained. Long ago fate had decreed that she was not entitled to lasting happiness. Such luxuries were the right of others, but not of herself. It was not for her to question it.

She sat for a while, her mind half-blank, half-reflective, then eventually got up and went to a drawer in the chest beside the bed. From it she removed a pack of contraceptive pills which she turned for a moment in her hands before dropping them deliberately into the wastepaper bin.

She would walk away; but this time she would not go entirely alone.

She went downstairs to make arrangements for Sam's care and for the night flight to California.

For three weeks Barbie exhibited a facade of gaiety. She gave no hint to David of her encounter with Diana. She declared delight at the sights of Hollywood, of Long Beach, the Sierra Nevada, while inside she was in turmoil. David noticed the change in her but attributed it to the after-effects of illness. She kept up an insatiable demand for love and with each ejaculation willed the stirring of life within her.

While each day held its own agony, she begged the weeks to tarry; but they paid no heed and, before she knew it, she was sitting in the aeroplane beside David heading back to London.

'Happy?' he asked.

She nodded, feigning joy at the thought of returning home.

'You look a bit pale.'

She swallowed. 'I feel a little sick.'

As she said it her stomach fluttered. She guessed that the sickness was caused by tension and by fear, but the knowledge that there could be some other cause threw her into turmoil.

'I'll get you something,' he said and called to the stewardess.

When they arrived at Bishops Walk she went through the routine of inspecting the house, touching familiar objects, but this time it had a double significance for each touch registered both greeting and farewell. She went into the garden and found Christmas roses on the terrace and, in a sheltered corner, one polyanthus brazening the mild winter weather, impatient for spring.

She found herself listening for the telephone and, when it did ring, she let out a startled cry which brought a look of surprise from David. It was the kennels confirming that they would be returning Sam within the hour.

She knew that she must leave the house without delay. If Diana should ring, David would learn of her imminent departure and, while she did not know how she would find the strength to leave, she was quite certain that she would never find the strength to say goodbye.

That night they went to bed early but Barbie did not sleep. She lay, watching the silhouette of David's face in the darkness and listening to the night creakings of the house, until a pale dawn broke and David opened his eyes beside her.

'Good morning,' he greeted her. 'What shall we do today?'

She forced a tone of normality into her voice. 'You've got to work. You promised before you went away that you'd have an article ready for tomorrow.'

He shook his head at her and smiled. 'You're the greatest slave driver I ever met.'

'It's for your own good.'

He took her in his arms. 'You're the only thing that's good for me.'

She kissed him, knowing that it would be the last kiss.

She waited until he went into his study and she could hear the steady tap-tapping of the typewriter keys; then she went upstairs and packed her bags. Upon his pillow she left a simple note, then went to the window and gazed out across the garden.

It was drab and colourless in the damp January air but she saw it as in all the splendour of June. She stood staring with a fixed expression which would lock the memory within her mind. Then, calling softly to Sam, she walked down the stairs, pausing for a moment as the tapping of the typewriter keys echoed across the hall, and let herself out of the front door.

As her feet scrunched across the gravel drive, she counted the number of times she had walked away from other chapters of her life – from the cottage, from Wansdyke Avenue, from Clapham, and now from Bishops Walk. Another compartment of her life had slammed shut; but this time it was not going to be so easy to seal it and forget.

She booked into a small back-street hotel in Islington, considering that she had put sufficient distance between herself and Chelsea to avoid the risk of running into former acquaintances. The receptionist asked how long she would be staying but she was unable to give any definite reply. She did not know how long it would take her to find a flat and a job.

She knew, however, that she must search with frantic intensity, filling every second of her time, for in every moment of unguarded idleness there came the overwhelming desire to return to David. Repeatedly, her mind was besieged with the thought, the sight, the scent of him, seeing his face a hundred times mirrored upon the faces of strangers in the street, feeling his presence behind her, his breath upon the nape of her neck, about to slip his arms about her waist.

She wondered how he would take the parting but, after all, he had known well enough that the end had been inevitable. She had told him often enough. Yet, even now, she knew that she had not. She had found no way of adequately telling him that everything she treasured must ultimately crumble into dust, as surely as the flakes of grey ash which had lain within the urn.

She half-toyed with the possibility that long ago she had committed some unforgivable sin which she could no longer remember but for which she must forever be punished by some savage, inexorable hand. It was an unthinkably terrifying prospect which robbed her of the ability to think beyond this moment, the present urgent need to find work, to find a roof, to fill every moment in order that she might not think of David.

She remembered vividly her experience of three years ago when she had searched for a home and a job; but now she bolstered her courage with the assurance that she had the benefit of added maturity, a knowledge of the city, and a sum of money in her bank account. It was not a large amount, for the ready flow of cash which she had received at Clapham had not been conducive to habits of thrift, but she had a little put aside from the allowance she had received from David. She knew it would not be sufficient to sustain her for any length of time without the security of a job.

She did not know what job she could do. At sixteen she had been totally without experience. At nineteen, she smiled bitterly to herself to realise that she must declare herself qualified as 'housekeeper' and 'whore'.

Although she searched for a flat and a job with equal urgency, she found the job first. By grossly stretching an account of the one day she had spent in the coffee bar on her arrival in London, she secured for herself a position as waitress in a small restaurant in Hampstead. It is unlikely that the manageress was fully taken in by Barbie's fabrication but she had an eye for all that would enhance her establishment and she had little difficulty in picturing Barbie, with her natural charm and her red-gold hair, dressed in the little black dress uniform, with its white frilled apron. It was arranged that she should commence work on the following Monday, which suited Barbie well for it would give her a chance to search for a flat not too distant from the restaurant.

With one half of her dual task complete, her longing for David increased with even greater intensity. Repeatedly, as she moved about the city, her heart would stand still for there, in the middle of a crowd, she would see the back of his head and would stand transfixed, torn between the desire to run towards it and the need to run away. But then the head would turn to reveal the face of a stranger and her heart would jerk, half from a sense of relief and half from the bitter disappointment that it was not the face she had longed to see.

She fought an ever-present desire to go to Bishops Walk, to conceal herself somewhere just to see him pass, just to see his head through the window of the car as it swept from the drive; to see the door of the house beyond which he might be moving, passing from room to room, sitting at his typewriter, lying upon his bed – their bed, touching plates from which she had eaten, forgetting to wash up, forgetting to iron his shirts.

But perhaps Diana would already be there, supervising the workmen. Mrs Leach would be washing up, preparing meals, moving furniture to suit Diana's taste and to allow free passage of the wheelchair.

Barbie's mind closed in upon itself. She must not think of anything but the need to find a flat.

She visited many apartment blocks, each one more expensive than the last, and on each occasion was presented with the same recurring problem. In each lease there was a clause – 'no children, no pets'. The former restriction gave her some reason for disquiet but that was a matter to which she could temporarily turn a blind eye; the latter was all too evident. Sam stood beside her, large, boisterous, and impossible to conceal.

Eventually she was forced to take the ground floor of a house in Camden Town at a rental far beyond her means but it was the only one to which she could take Sam. She knew that, even with a weekly wage from the restaurant, she would still have need to eat into her savings in order to pay her way. She signed the lease for three months, hoping that in the meantime she would find somewhere less expensive.

It was a pleasant, comfortable apartment, consisting of three rooms with a kitchen and a bathroom. French windows opened onto a small area of patchy turf which was described as a garden and across which was stretched a clothes-line for each of the three floors of the house. It was an area hardly large enough for Sam to bound three steps but it was at least a space of sorts. Barbie was not over-concerned by its lack of size for, within easy walking distance, lay Regents Park with space enough for Sam to run.

On the morning of the Monday upon which Barbie was to commence work, she awoke early, intending to take Sam for a long walk. She was free until eleven-thirty for she had arranged to work from noon until ten o'clock in the evening, with an hour's break between tea and dinner. The hours were long but she had been particularly compliant with the suggestion that she should work regular overtime, partly as a means of earning extra money but mainly as a means of filling her time.

She made toast and a pot of coffee; but when she sat down to eat it, she found that she could not face the thought of food. She had a feeling of nausea which sprang upon her suddenly, without warning, and quite unlike any feelings of nausea she had experienced before.

She rushed to the bathroom in no doubt as to its cause and, when she returned, announced to Sam, 'I've got morning sickness, Sam.'

It set up a mixture of emotion which threw her mind into a whirl. Her first reaction was one of elation that here, as she had planned, was David's child; but the emotion was quickly joined by another – a feeling of panic. She was alone and pregnant.

The feeling of nausea passed as quickly as it had appeared and she resumed her breakfast. As she ate, her mind continued to fluctuate between elation and fear, with elation taking the upper hand, only to be joined by another – a deep longing for David in preference to his child.

It was bitterly cold when they set out to walk, with a raw east wind and the feeling of snow in the air. People hurried past in the street, huddled inside overcoats with expressions upon their faces which underlined the fact that it was January and a Monday morning.

There were few people in Regents Park, apart from spartan nannies with well-wrapped charges in expensive perambulators. Barbie looked at the infants with new-found interest, finding it impossible to envisage that within a few short months it would be she who would be wheeling a perambulator. She tried to imagine the face of the child, knowing that it was David's child.

She did a little mental arithmetic and arrived at the month of September which did something to calm her nerves for it seemed a long time ahead. She looked up at the bare branches of the plane trees and calculated that first winter must pass, followed by spring and summer which, in turn, would give way to autumn. It was a long time to wait.

She took Sam home and travelled by Tube to Hampstead, where she donned her black dress and white frilled apron and worked until late evening. It was tiring work and although she was used to walking long distances with Sam, she felt the strain upon her legs and back; but the manageress was pleased with her work and her pockets jingled with the tips of satisfied customers.

It was almost eleven o'clock when she arrived home. The cold east wind of the morning had intensified and flakes of snow stung her face as they were whipped along the street. She was exhausted and bitterly cold but Sam had been locked within the confines of the flat for over eleven hours and she knew that he must be walked before she could give any thought to her own comfort.

Sam fell upon her with pathetic exuberance and she felt guilty that she had left him so long unattended. She took him out into the cold night air but even Sam was reluctant to go far in the teeth of such a wind and very soon they returned.

Barbie was so tired, she flung herself fully-clothed upon the bed, intending that in a moment or two she would get up and make herself a mug of hot chocolate before preparing for sleep. The next thing she knew, was waking up shivering with cold, knowing that she had slept for several hours, her only comfort

Sam's body curled beside her on the bed. She crawled beneath the blankets but found now that she could not sleep, so passed the hours mechanically running through routines which were designed to encourage sleep but which drove it ever further away. All the time her mind was filled with but one thought, that she wanted David, that she needed him here beside her in the darkness of the night.

When she did eventually sleep it was only to fall into the clutches of a nightmare in which she was running, she knew not where – whether to a goal or away from danger she could not tell – only that her feet were weighted so that they could not be lifted, could only be dragged inch by inch in a desperate effort to run. And when the scene miraculously changed, it was to find herself within a tunnel which was growing ever smaller so that she was forced to squeeze until her head was trapped and only a pinpoint of light lay ahead.

She awoke with a feeling of exhaustion and a thumping in her temples, to find that she had overslept. It was almost ten o'clock. She jumped up, too quickly, causing her head to spin and, as the blackness cleared, the feeling of nausea swept over her again. She went to the bathroom guessing that this was to become the regular routine of each morning.

The nausea took longer to clear than the previous day and when she was finally able to take Sam out there was little time left to walk. In the streets the snow had turned to dirty slush, splashing up from the wheels of passing traffic, but in the park it lay white and crisp upon the grass, its surface criss-crossed by the footprints of earlier walkers.

Sam frollicked inquisitively in an unfamiliar environment, racing back and forth across the snow, stopping only to snort into the white carpet, causing an eruption of particles which temporarily blinded him and caused him to sneeze. He was enjoying himself immensely and when, all too soon, it was time for Barbie to call him back, he was reluctant to come to heel.

She was forced to shout at him several times and even then he teased her, coming almost within touching distance and then dashing away. It was not until she raised her voice in anger that he came to her, shamefaced, and submitted himself to the leash. His shame added to her guilt for she knew that he had had insufficient exercise and that she would have gladly let him run had she not been short of time.

Back at the flat he looked at her with doleful eyes for he knew that he was to be locked up again. 'I'm sorry, Sam.' She went down on her knees and hugged him. 'But things are different now. This is how it has to be.' He turned and licked her face but she imagined a measure of accusation in his response.

That night when she returned there was an unpleasant smell and a stain across the carpet just inside the door. She could not be angry with Sam, for he would not have soiled the carpet unless in desperation, and she took it upon herself with an even greater sense of guilt. When she discovered that, in boredom, he had chewed his way through the leg of a small occasional table, her dismay was even greater. The table tottered, threatening to collapse. She scolded Sam harshly, as much in response to her own personal disquietude as in chastisement of him, and turned the table towards the wall, knowing that she would have to replace it at the termination of the lease.

Next day she left the French window open so that he might have access to the garden but when she returned at night the room was icy cold. It had been snowing heavily and the snow had drifted in through the open window, causing yet another stain across the carpet. Sam lay shivering behind a chair in the farthest corner and hardly seemed inclined to rise to his feet in order to greet her. When he did get up she saw that he was limping. Pushed beneath the door was a note written in violet ink.

'*Your dog this afternoon forced its way through the hedge bounding my property and attacked my child . . .*' 'Attack' was a ridiculous word. Sam had obviously been in the mood for play. '*. . . I was forced to throw a stone at it. Please keep it under proper control in future or I shall have no alternative but to inform the police. Yours . . .*'

There was a scrawled signature which Barbie could not read.

'Oh, Sam.' She sank to her knees in the corner beside him. 'What am I going to do with you?' Sam pushed his nose beneath her arm, huddling close for reassurance and for warmth.

She determined that in future she would go back to the flat during her late-afternoon break but, even so, this gave her only twenty minutes before she must rush to the Tube station and back to work. It meant also, that she had no opportunity to rest during the long hours spent on her feet and no time to eat a proper meal.

The tiredness and the irregular eating habits built up into a feeling of general indisposition, combined with increasing bouts of nausea, which now were no longer confined to the morning but reappeared at frequent intervals throughout the day. They came upon her with little warning and at moments of least convenience so that she had need to rush to the staffroom of the restaurant at moments when her duties were most pressing. It was a practice which brought comments of disapproval from the manageress to which Barbie was unable to offer any word of explanation.

The morning bouts of nausea grew more prolonged, so that the time available for walking Sam grew less and less. He developed an air of listlessness which matched her own. He went off his food and gradually, across his coat, and across his eyes, there spread a dullness and an apathy which worried her greatly. It was early March and Barbie clung to the vain hope that in a month or so, with the coming of spring, the situation would somehow improve but the grip of winter showed no inclination to ease and the final blow came with a letter from the landlord. She opened it and read it twice before the full impact of the words sank into her brain.

'Dear Miss Harding,

I have received repeated complaints about your dog which can be heard whining for long hours each day. You will appreciate that not only is this disturbing to your neighbours, it is also highly distressing to them. I must inform you that you must take measures to give proper care to this animal or I shall have no alternative but to report the matter to the RSPCA . . .'

The thought that she could be accused of cruelty to Sam was unbelievably shocking to Barbie. She re-read the letter several times, then held Sam in her arms. 'Sam, have I been unkind?' Sam roused himself and for a moment the old sparkle flashed across his eye but then he gave out a long, quivering sigh and dropped down his muzzle across his lanky forepaws; Barbie stood indicted.

There was only one thing that she could think to do. She put on her coat and calling Sam, took him across London to the familiar streets of Chelsea.

'I'll take you to David,' she choked. 'He'll take care of you.'

As she approached Bishops Walk her heart began to pound in her chest and Sam, too, became more alert, sniffing the air, straining at the leash. A few yards from the entrance to number five he took to his heels and would have dragged Barbie behind him had she not let fall the leash and allowed him to run away from her, dragging it behind him.

'Find David,' she called softly. 'Go on, boy; find him.'

She moved cautiously towards the gate, shielded from view behind an overhanging laurel, and saw two cars parked upon the drive. To Barbie there seemed a sense of intimacy in the way in which Diana's car was parked side by side with David's, and she bit her lip at the sight of it.

At the same moment there came a sudden burst of confusion from within the house – a paroxysm of barking from Sam – a shout from Diana – 'Get out!' – and a cry from David, *'Sam!'*

Barbie turned on her heel and ran, blundering her way down the road, and round the corner into the anonymity of crowded streets.

As she turned the corner, David ran down the drive, calling her name but Barbie did not hear for his voice was drowned in the noise of the traffic.

By the time David had cleared the obstruction of the laurel bushes, she was out of sight, and by the time he reached the corner, she was lost within the crowd. He hurtled along busy streets, still calling her name, and when he reached a junction he hesitated, not knowing which way to turn. He turned left, finding no trace of her, for Barbie had turned right: had he but taken a few steps in that direction he might have caught sight of her as she stumbled on to a slow-moving bus.

At last, giving up hope of finding her, he came to the conclusion that Sam had run away while being walked. He had, after all, returned home dragging his leash. Something must have frightened him and caused him to run off: he might well have been walking the streets for hours trying to find his way home.

David ran to fetch his car, making first in the direction of Battersea Park, then Hyde Park and Kensington Gardens, cruising, searching, getting out to walk round areas inaccessible to the car, certain that somewhere he would find Barbie frantically searching for Sam.

As each hour passed he grew more despondent and eventually, as darkness fell, he returned to Bishops Walk.

As he let himself in at the side entrance he heard Diana's voice raised in irritation.

271

'Get out of here, you damned great brute. For goodness sake, Mrs Leach, lock him up somewhere out of the way.'

As David walked into the room she turned on him. 'David! What on earth am I supposed to do with this damned dog? Wherever I turn he's in the way of my chair. I can't move without running into him.'

David called to Sam and made a fuss of him. 'Where's Barbie, Sam? Where did you leave her?'

'Really, David! It's just a dog. How do you know it's her dog? The owner's probably out there somewhere searching for it, while you've got it locked up in here.'

'It's Sam.' He stroked his hand along Sam's coat and immediately Sam responded to him. 'I'd know him anywhere.'

'Any dog would make a fuss of you if it thought it was going to get fed.'

David did not continue the conversation but took Sam into the library, which now contained his desk.

Diana followed and sat in the open doorway. 'David,' she said. 'That girl has been gone for over two months. Yet still you do nothing but sit mooning around in here, or walking the streets in some vain hope of bumping into her.'

David did not look up.

'Isn't it time that you started to face facts?' Her voice softened slightly. 'She's left you, David. She's gone. She isn't coming back.'

David closed his eyes. 'She hasn't left me,' he said. 'She's run away.'

'Well, really, darling; I can't personally see the difference.'

He turned on her sharply. 'You're in no position to do so.'

She was hurt by that. 'Well, all I do know, darling, is that if the girl had really cared for you, she wouldn't have gone off like that.'

He turned his back on her. 'Look, Diana; I'm not going to discuss it with you. You don't know Barbie; and there's no way that you could understand.'

'You blame me, don't you.'

'What the hell am I supposed to do? Thank you for coming in here and frightening her away?'

'I didn't frighten her away.'

'I should dearly like to know exactly what did go on here that day,' he said.

272

'I swear to you, David; I've told you a thousand times, I did nothing but tell her that I planned to come back home after Angela's wedding. She didn't even raise any objections.'

'No,' he said. 'She wouldn't.'

'Then I really don't see your argument. If the girl had really cared for you, she would have told you where she had gone.'

'She needn't have gone at all if you hadn't come in here and interfered.'

'I didn't interfere. How was I to know she'd be here all alone when I called?'

'And how were you to know she would go when you threw her out!'

'I didn't throw her out. I asked her to leave.'

'Yes; I bet you did.'

'Well; what did you expect me to do? Invite her to remain here as a threesome?'

'Don't be obtuse, Diana; you know darned well there's no question of that.'

She deliberately misunderstood him. 'Yes,' she said. 'It would be a bit bizarre.'

'You know very well that I would have gone with her.'

She swallowed and looked away. 'Then why don't you go now?'

'Because,' he said, brutally, 'I want to be here when she comes back.'

She turned her chair and sat with her back towards him.

'Look; I'm sorry, Diana.' He softened his voice. 'I don't mean to be so brutal, but you keep forcing me into it. You know very well that there's no question concerning my feeling for Barbie. You can have the house, and I'll make ample provision for you; but the moment that Barbie returns, you know what I must do.'

Diana made a sound which was halfway between a sob and a bitter laugh. 'It seems to me,' she said, 'that I'm the one who loses out every time.'

'I'm sorry,' he said quietly. 'Heaven knows, I don't want to hurt you. But things have altered.'

'You always were a selfish pig, David,' she said. 'You haven't changed.'

She propelled the chair out into the hall and back to her room. He watched her go, then dropped his head down upon the desk, across his folded arms.

273

Sam pushed his nose to rest upon his knee and let out a low, soft whine.

Barbie returned to Camden Town, fell into bed, and remained there for two days, alternately crying, or sleeping, or lying staring at the wall. She forgot to eat and she forgot to go to work.

When she did eventually take up the threads of her life once more, she returned, palefaced, to the restaurant and reported that she had been ill.

The manageress looked at her, suspicious. 'You seem to be unwell most of the time, Barbie. Is there anything seriously wrong?'

Barbie shook her head without looking at her. 'I seem to have had a stomach infection. It's over now.'

'This is a restaurant, Barbie; and we have a very high standard of hygiene. If there's any question of a serious infection you should obtain medical advice.'

Barbie determined that, in future, she would endeavour to be more discreet in her visits to the staffroom. 'I've got an appointment to see the doctor tomorrow,' she said. This statement was correct for she intended to submit herself to medical supervision for the duration of her pregnancy.

'Good. You don't look at all well to me.'

Barbie duly attended the doctor's surgery the following morning. He examined her and, as she dressed, washed his hands.

'I can certainly confirm the pregnancy,' he said. 'From what you tell me, I should say that it should be about the last week in September, or the first in October.'

'My birthday's on the eighth of October,' said Barbie inconsequentially.

He looked at her and smiled. 'Are you pleased? Or may I be forgiven for asking whether you find yourself in a bit of a fix?'

The question took her aback. When faced with it, she was almost forced to admit to herself that she no longer knew what her feelings were concerning the baby. 'It's what I planned,' she said simply.

'Oh. I'm more used to young girls coming in here telling me that they've made a mistake.'

'Well, I didn't.'

He looked at her closely. 'It's not easy coping with a pregnancy when you're on your own,' he said. 'Most need a little guidance and support.'

'I shall manage. I'm used to coping on my own.'

'All the same, I think I'll get my health visitor to keep in touch.'

Barbie tasted panic. 'No,' she said. 'I'd rather not.' She recalled the social workers of her childhood. Not that any had been anything but kind to her, but the very thought of social workers held unhappy connotations.

'Just as you wish.' The doctor's tone seemed unconcerned but he looked at her with a hint of curiosity. 'But I can do something about the nausea.' He wrote out a prescription and passed it to her across the desk. 'Here,' he said. 'Have this made up by the dispenser and I think you'll find that you'll be able to cope with things a little more easily.'

He gave her details of the antenatal clinic to which he was referring her and, as she was leaving, looked up at her and smiled. 'What would you like it to be – a girl, or a boy?'

'A boy,' she said without hesitation. She had given no thought to bearing a female child.

Barbie took the tablets prescribed by the doctor but the nausea did not ease. The attacks continued to plague her three or four times each day and she felt thoroughly sick and miserable. Now that she no longer had Sam for company, she took to sleeping until late morning so that the days became one long drudgery of work and sleep, with any small gap between lying in wait as a trap for loneliness and longing.

There was still a month to run on the lease of her flat. She knew that soon she must start to search for something less expensive but found that she had neither the energy nor the inclination to make much effort.

As March gave way to April, and the deadline loomed ever nearer, the nausea ceased as suddenly as it had appeared. It was a release which did much to raise her spirits and immediately she set about her search. She had hardly begun before trouble struck from another direction.

The manageress of the restaurant had been watching Barbie's abdomen and now the tell-tale distension could just be discerned. She challenged Barbie with her suspicion one morning as Barbie was squeezing into her tight, black dress uniform. It was useless to deny the allegation, for soon enough it would be apparent to all.

'I feel that you've been less than honest with me, Barbie. You must have known that you were pregnant when you applied for the job.'

Barbie saw no point in explaining that, at the time, the knowledge had been little more than hope.

'It's not the pregnancy I object to,' said the manageress. 'But the fact that you hid it from me.'

Barbie felt that this was something of a catch twenty-two. If the manageress had known of her pregnancy, she would doubtless have refused to employ her.

'You realise that you can't stay here much longer. It would hardly be fitting to wait at table in that condition and, in any case, it's very unwise for you to be on your feet all day when you're carrying a baby. I suggest that you take a month to find yourself something more suitable.'

Barbie nodded dispassionately. Once again she was without a home or work but it was a problem now too familiar to raise the original sense of alarm. She would just have to find another job.

This time her predicament was a direct result of her pregnancy but she viewed the fact as calmly as she had viewed her dismissal. At no time had she become consciously aware of regretting the deliberate conception of the child, but her attitude towards it was changing. No longer was it a part of David. The longing for him had been consistently beaten down until it was suppressed into a nagging ache, which frequently rose to screaming pain, and, little by little, the foetus had become disassociated from him. It had become merely something with which she must cope, without question, and without thought. She had set in motion an act of nature and now she had no choice but to see it through to its conclusion. There had been no stirring of the maternal instinct which she had anticipated; merely a knowledge that she must adapt her life to a growing multiplicity of cells.

There were still brief periods when the elation could be found. It flashed upon her at odd, unguarded moments, but it was ever more quickly subdued by the stronger feelings of loneliness; and the growing awareness that a foetus was no substitute for David.

She began her search without delay, strengthened by the improvement in her health now that she was no longer laid low by the bouts of nausea, but she was in her fourth month of pregnancy and knew that she would have considerable difficulty in finding anyone who would employ her, or who would offer accommodation.

276

Her financial resources had been overstretched by the expense of the Camden Town apartment and her savings were seriously depleted. She knew there was little chance of finding another flat in such pleasant surroundings, and the clause 'no children, no pets' was a constant feature in the lease of such rooms as she could afford.

At times, the desire to return to the comfort of Bishops Walk was almost overwhelming, but it was also totally unthinkable. The bridge had been irreparably burned and there was no going back. On one occasion she took the Tube to Clapham and sat for a while upon the Common. She knew that she could seek shelter with Curly but to return to him was equally unthinkable. She had only to think of David to know that she could never turn for help to Curly.

Had she but known it, David had already considered such a possibility. By a series of discreet enquiries he had located the flat in Clapham and had succeeded in tracking down Curly.

'Mr . . . ?' David hesitated, for he did not know Curly's name.

'Just call me Curly, mate. Everyone does.' Curly had a reliable memory for faces. He had recognised David immediately.

David nodded his acknowledgment. 'Forgive me, Curly,' he said. 'But I've come to seek your help.'

'Sure, mate. Anything I can do.'

'It's about Barbie. Have you seen her?'

Curly shook his head. 'Not since that day I saw her with you. Where is she?'

'That's the problem. I don't know. She's run away.'

'Run away?' Curly looked surprised. 'Why should she want to do a think like that?'

'I don't know. That's something I shall have to ask Barbie. But my estranged wife might have had something to do with it.'

'Oh,' said Curly knowingly. 'I see.'

David swallowed down all his personal feelings concerning Curly. 'Curly,' he said. 'I know that Barbie was very fond of you. If she's in trouble she may come to you.'

'If she's in trouble, mate, I hope she will. But there's no reason to suppose that she is in trouble. She's probably managing perfectly well out there somewhere.' Curly waved his hand towards the city outside the window. 'She knows her way about London and there's no reason why she shouldn't be able to look after herself.' He paused and looked across at David. 'And if she's

277

not in trouble, mate, I'd rather she made a life for herself somewhere else than here.'

David inclined his head. 'Thanks for that, anyway, Curly.'

'How long has she been gone?'

'Four months.'

'Four months.' Curly whistled through his teeth. 'She'll be well settled by now. Or far away in some other part of the country.'

'I've looked everywhere, Curly. I don't know where to turn.'

'And you've got no clues?'

'None. When Sam found his way home I did hope that she would realise he'd come to me, and that she would come looking for him. But she didn't.' He shook his head despairingly. 'I just want to see her, Curly; just to speak to her, sort something out.'

'She was fond of that dog,' said Curly. 'She's going to be pretty cut up about losing him.'

'I know. She's out there somewhere, all alone.'

Curly sat looking at him for a moment. 'You're pretty cut up about it yourself, mate.'

'I love her, Curly. I just want her to come home.'

'Well, I'll tell you what I'll do, mate. I'll keep an eye open for her when I'm out in my cab; but there's no guarantee that I'll find her. There are eight million people out there in that city. I could drive through her area a hundred times and never even see her. But I'll do my best, mate. How about that?'

'Thank you, Curly.' David stood up and held out his hand. 'I'm very grateful to you.'

Curly took the hand in a firm grasp. 'If I do see her,' he said, 'I'll tell her what you've said. It's up to her whether or not she comes back.'

'Of course. I can't ask for more than that.'

Curly clapped a hand to David's shoulder. 'She's a good girl, young Barbie. She deserves to be happy.'

David nodded, too choked for words. 'She's very special.'

'I'll go out now, mate, and start looking straight away.'

Curly cruised about Fulham, Hammersmith, Chiswick, Camberwell, Peckham, Lewisham, Deptford, keeping his eyes open and watching the faces of the crowd, looking for a flash of red-gold hair, but it was an almost impossible task. He had no idea where to concentrate his search and he realised that he could be passing her door, her place of work, without catching sight of her.

278

He went on through Holborn and the West End, Paddington, Wembley, and Golders Green. He even passed the restaurant in Hampstead, but, had he stopped and looked inside, he would not have found her, for it was Barbie's day off and she was on her way to a café in King's Cross to answer an advertisment for a cook.

Chapter Fourteen

Bert Fabrozzi was a tall man, with a large belly and a drooping moustache.

'Can you cook chips?' he asked.

Barbie indicated that she could.

'Good. That's all you'll need here. My customers know what they like. Egg and chips, sausage and chips, beefburger and chips. They don't go in for anything fancy.'

He was cooking as he spoke, conducting the interview as he prepared meals for a steady stream of customers. 'I've got another place over in Victoria,' he said. 'I'm usually over there; but the girl walked out on me here last week. I'm losing money all the time I'm trying to be in two places at once.'

He slapped two sausages, an egg, and a pile of greasy chips onto a plate, added a hunk of bread, and poured tea into a half-pint mug, spilling a good measure of it into the slop tray beneath. He whistled to a customer sitting near the window who came to the counter, collected the meal, and returned with it to a tea-stained table.

'When could you start?' He threw another egg and two rashers of streaky bacon into the pan.

'I'm due to leave my present job at the end of the month but I could probably arrange to start straight away if I have another job to go to.'

'Good. I can't hang about waiting for someone. I'm losing money all the time I'm here instead of in Victoria.'

Barbie would have preferred some other place of work than this dingy back-street café, but she had attended many interviews and, being obliged to declare her pregnancy, had secured none of them. She took a deep breath and made the statement which she believed would terminate the interview. 'I feel I ought to tell you,' she said, 'that I'm four months pregnant.'

He looked down at her abdomen. 'I don't care if you're giving birth to a chimpanzee,' he said coarsely. 'So long as you do your work. The moment you don't come up to scratch, then you're out on your neck.'

'I'm normally very strong and healthy.' She held her fingers crossed behind her back and prayed that the nausea would not return.

He shrugged. 'Do you want the job, or not?'

'Yes, please.' Barbie felt that she had no alternative. It would at least give her a source of income while she looked around for something better.

'Good. The hours are eight-thirty till six.' He scraped the contents of the frying pan onto a plate and added an untidy pile of chips. 'Where do you live?'

Barbie took the plate from him and carried it to the customer's table.

'I'm living in Camden Town,' she said as she returned. 'But I'm looking for somewhere a bit smaller and cheaper.'

Fabrozzi nodded his head towards the customer whom she had just served. 'You don't want to wait on 'em,' he said. 'They've got legs to walk up here to the counter and fetch it for themselves.'

'Sorry,' said Barbie. 'I was just trying to be helpful.'

He pointed with a spatula towards the ceiling above them. 'I own this block,' he said. 'There's a flat empty on the third floor.' Barbie turned to him, immediately interested. 'It would be handy for me,' he went on. 'You could keep an eye on the place. We get more than our share of vandals.'

Barbie had no more desire to live in this squalid, run-down neighbourhood than she had to work here but her reasons were the same. It was the only place which had so far been made available to her.

Fabrozzi nodded his head towards a pile of unwashed plates. 'If you'll give me a hand,' he said, 'I'll take you up there later when we get a quiet spell in here.'

She fell to at the sink, washing the plates, then made an urn of fresh tea, and cooked a batch of chips. By mid-afternoon there were fewer customers, and when only one old man remained drinking a mug of tea, Fabrozzi unceremoniously told him to 'drink up and get out'. He locked the door and led Barbie out of the back entrance into a yard filled with dustbins.

He took her through another door and up three flights of stairs. The light was so dim that several times Barbie stumbled and had to reach out to steady herself against the wall. The walls had long ago been painted a dull, chocolate brown, adding to the dimness, and had since been daubed with graffiti.

'It's rather dark in here,' commented Barbie.

'That's not my fault.' Fabrozzi staggered up the stairs before her, the seat of his baggy trousers reminding her of the rear view of an elephant. 'Fast as I fit light bulbs, someone comes and rips 'em off.'

'Someone could get hurt on these stairs.'

'Tell that to the bloke who rips off the light bulbs.' He was out of breath and wheezing heavily. 'The flat's just over here.' Barbie followed him across the third floor landing and stood behind him as he fumbled a key into the lock.

The flat was no more than a bedsitter, with a curtained recess into which had been installed a sink, an electric hotplate, and an ancient refrigerator. The previous tenant had added touches to brighten the dim interior of the room, mainly by way of posters depicting voluptuous females in varying stages of undress, but there was also a print of Monet's 'Poppies'.

'As you see, it's fully furnished,' said Fabrozzi, alluding to an iron bedstead, a chair, a gate-legged table, and a wardrobe, its door wedged shut with a strip of folded card. 'And the bathroom's at the end of the landing. There's one to each floor.'

'How many people share it?' asked Barbie, alarmed.

'Not many on this floor. A young bloke and his wife and two families.'

'I hope they're not large families,' she responded quietly.

She crossed to the window and looked out onto the walls of an identical tenement block beyond a back alleyway and, beneath her, the yard with the dustbins through which she had picked her way before climbing the stairs.

Fabrozzi looked at the expression on her face. 'It's not Buckingham Palace,' he said. 'But it's handy if you're going to work downstairs. And there's plenty more who'll take it if you don't want it.'

She took heart from the Monet and decided that, with a little imagination, there was a good deal that could be done to improve the room. 'I'll take it,' she said. 'But if you want me to keep an eye on the café I shall expect a reduction in the rent.'

He looked at her for a moment and then shrugged his heavy shoulders. 'It's a deal. I need three weeks' rent in advance.'

He was anxious to re-open the café before losing business and the formalities were quickly concluded. He handed Barbie the key and left her alone while he went downstairs.

She sat on the bed trying, unsuccessfully, to avoid comparing her surroundings with the house at Bishops Walk. She tried to suppress her thoughts but the need was overwhelming and she gave in to them, allowing them free rein to meander their way through the rooms of the house. The memory was so clear that she could recall every inch of the interior. She did not think of David; only of the rooms and of the garden.

It was almost exactly a year since she had first seen the garden. The seasons had turned full circle and the magnolia would be coming into bloom, hyacinths would be scenting the air beneath the study window and there would be drifts of narcissi and tulips. With the coming of spring, David had planned to call in a firm of professional decorators to paint the exterior of the house. She wondered if they were there now and whether they would take care not to damage the magnolia.

After months of sustained work on re-decorating the interior of the house, she had completed all but two rooms and had been cheated of the satisfaction in achieving her self-appointed goal. She wondered now if Diana had already begun to change the colour scheme. It was this latter thought which finally brought the tears. She laid down her head against the thin mattress and sobbed.

As she lay there, Curly drove up to the mainline railway station at King's Cross, less than half a mile away. He set down his passengers and engaged another fare. Over the following months he regularly plied the route but at no time did he actually see Barbie. He had no call to drive down the back street in which the café was situated, and Barbie spent little time in other streets. Had she walked to work each day there would have been some possibility that their paths would cross but she had merely to descend the stairs and cross the yard. After work each day she was always tired. She had no friends to visit and nowhere she wished to go, so she spend most of her free time within her room. The only time she ventured out onto the streets was in order to shop for provisions. She did not know of Curly's movements and Curly did not know of hers. There was a strong chance that at some time they would find themselves in the same place at the same time. But fate was no friend of Barbie's so that as she made her way to the supermarket, Curly drove along some other street, sometimes far away in some other part of the city, sometimes just a block away, but never close enough to catch a glimpse of red-gold hair.

On two occasions, David himself had need to catch a train from King's Cross. He was so close to Barbie that one could almost imagine that he would have sensed her presence, but no such sensation occurred and on each occasion he boarded the train for Yorkshire, mechanically carrying out an assignment without any of his previous zest and flair, for the heart had gone out of his work.

Barbie settled well into the routine of the café. In the evening, after closing time, she spent long hours cleaning and scrubbing until she introduced a homely sparkle which pleased the regular customers and attracted others. When not thus engaged, she occupied herself with much the same task in her own room and soon she had achieved a measure of comfort, whereby she could climb the dingy tenement stairs and lock herself away from the world in a place which she had made her own. The work was tiring but it filled her hours so that there was little time for anything but toil and sleep. The ever constant danger of dwelling upon her loneliness and longing must always be avoided.

To her customers she exhibited a facade of lightheartedness and a natural charm which quickly endeared her to them. It brought her a constant flow of social invitations but she refused them all. She had no interest in building new relationships and, as the outward signs of her pregnancy increased, the invitations became less numerous.

As month followed month, her ambivalent attitude towards her pregnancy gradually crystallised. In conversation she referred to the foetus as her baby, but she did not think of it as such. Even after she became aware of movement within her, the sudden jerk of a kick against the wall of her abdomen, she hardly altered her impersonal, detached attitude towards it. She preferred to restrict her thoughts to the superficial problems of work, and of adapting her routine to an increasingly cumbersome burden. But, as August gave way to September, she began to adjust her thoughts to the fact that the problems of pregnancy must shortly give way to the problems of caring for an animate object.

At the antenatal clinic she had been strongly advised to quit work by the seventh month of her pregnancy but she had made a niche for herself at the café, however inglorious, and she had no wish to abandon it for the uncertainty of some other life, coupled with the possible loss of her room. Bert Fabrozzi was an astute businessman. He was aware of Barbie's value to him and of the increased income from the café since she had taken over. He had no wish to terminate her employment but, at the same time, he was not a generous man and the extent of his forebearance was limited to two weeks' unpaid leave following the birth.

There was a need to plan for the care of the child during her working hours and into this breach stepped Mrs Purvis. Mrs Purvis was the wife of a retired British Rail ticket collector – they occupied a room on the ground floor of the tenement block. Being a woman of outgoing nature, and with time on her hands, she had taken to waylaying Barbie in the entrance hall.

At first Barbie had withstood her attentions but Mrs Purvis was as kind-hearted as she was persistent and, little by little, Barbie had become accustomed to accepting invitations to 'a cup of tea and a natter'. The invitation invariably led to the tea being partaken in Barbie's room, for Mrs Purvis was at all times ready to grasp any opportunity to escape from the one room which she shared with her husband.

'He's a miserable old bugger,' she frequently informed Barbie. Barbie had seen little of Mr Purvis beyond the back of his head as he sat watching the large television screen which dominated their cramped and overfurnished room. He appeared rarely to move except for the purpose of making quick sorties to the betting office whenever the television could be tuned to horse racing, greyhound racing, boxing, or any other form of activity upon which he could place a bet.

'He's the laziest old bugger I ever met,' said Mrs Purvis one day. She came into Barbie's room and settled herself in the armchair. 'I have to lift his feet for him if I want to sweep the floor.' Barbie brewed tea and smiled without comment, for she was used to Mrs Purvis airing her grievances concerning her husband.

Barbie was now heavily pregnant and tired following the long hours at work. She wanted nothing more than to rest but she did not object to Mrs Purvis' presence, for she did not stand on ceremony and knew that Mrs Purvis would not object if she drank her tea while lying on her bed.

'Here, give me that teapot,' said Mrs Purvis, suddenly realising that she was sitting down while Barbie was still on her feet. 'Sit down on that bed and put your feet up. You'll be having that baby before your time if you go on standing on your feet all day the way you're doing.'

Barbie sank gratefully onto the bed and closed her eyes as Mrs Purvis clanked cups and saucers onto the table. There was something comforting about the sound of boiling water being poured onto tealeaves and Barbie felt herself relaxing.

'You should have given up work weeks ago,' said Mrs Purvis. 'Old Fabrozzi will work you into the ground given half a chance.'

'Oh, he's not so bad,' said Barbie lazily.

'Right old skinflint. Talk about getting his pound of flesh. Ought to be called Hemlock, if you ask me,' said Mrs Purvis, who had never mastered Shakespeare. 'He ought to know you're not fit to stand on your feet all day.'

'I'll be all right. I just get a bit tired by the end of the day.' Barbie eased herself into a more comfortable position. 'And, anyway, he can't be expected to close the café just because I'm having a baby. He's been good enough to keep me on and agree to take me back after the baby's born.'

'Lord love us.' Mrs Purvis banged down the teapot beside the cups and saucers. 'You're not thinking of going back there once you've got a little nipper on your hands?'

'Of course.' Barbie opened her eyes. 'I've got to work. How else am I going to live?'

'I thought you'd go on the "club", dear.'

'I couldn't do that.'

Mrs Purvis went to the refrigerator for milk. 'Why not? Everybody else lives off the State.'

'Not me. If I can't earn my money I'd rather starve.'

Mrs Purvis looked at her as though a determination for self-sufficiency was a novel idea. 'You got any biscuits?'

Barbie pointed to her shopping basket in the corner of the room. 'I haven't unpacked them yet.'

Mrs Purvis rifled the shopping basket and spent some time deciding between rich tea fingers and custard creams. She

286

weighed the two packets in either hand, before plumping for the custard creams.

'Funny you not wanting to draw Social Security,' she said. 'That old bugger down there . . .' nodding her head in the general direction of her own room '. . . spent half his life on the dole or out on strike. Even when he got the job with the railway he spent half his time on the "sick". Oh, he's a lazy old sod.' She shook her head and sat, as if contemplating the fact for the first time. 'Spent half his life getting under my feet and now he wears out the backside of his trousers on the seat of that chair. Knowing him, he'll see me into the grave without ever having had a bit of peace from him. Never does nothing to wear himself out.'

Barbie closed her eyes and drifted off into a half-doze while Mrs Purvis conducted her diatribe for the benefit of her own ears.

'What's wrong with being on the "club" anyway? You're entitled to Social Security, same as anyone else.'

Barbie shook her head, her eyes still closed. 'I'm too much like my Gran. I can't abide taking something for nothing.'

Mrs Purvis' eyes flashed with a new-found interest. 'You never told me about your Gran.' Barbie bit on her lip. She had spent many hours with Mrs Purvis but the conversation had never strayed beyond the most superficial topics. 'Come to think of it, you've never mentioned nothing about your family.'

'The trouble is,' said Barbie, hastily steering the conversation back on course, 'how do I cope with the baby while I'm working?'

'Lord bless you, that's no problem. Give him to me. I'll look after him for you.'

Barbie snapped open her eyes. 'Do you really mean it?'

'Wouldn't say it if I didn't, would I.' Mrs Purvis handed her a cup of tea. 'It'll give me something to do instead of sitting looking at the back of that old bugger's neck.'

'What about Mr Purvis? Wouldn't he mind?'

Mrs Purvis dunked a custard cream into her tea and waved it towards the wall. 'I bet you,' she said, 'he wouldn't even notice. So long as I put his dinner in his hand at half past twelve every day, he wouldn't even notice if I'd taken up training a troupe of sea-lions. Do you know, last year I took up basket-weaving and guess what he did . . .'

'It would be a marvellous arrangement,' Barbie interrupted. 'I'd pay you, of course.'

'Wouldn't dream of it, dear.' Mrs Purvis spread her hands as though the thought of payment had been farthest from her mind. 'Mrs Tindall gets paid by the hour but I have heard that some get paid by the week.'

Barbie kept a small half-smile to herself. 'I'd have to insist on paying you.'

'Oh, well dear, if you insist. I'll pop round later and ask Mrs Tindall what she charges.'

Barbie closed her eyes again and settled back into the pillows. She was pleased that a major problem was to have such a simple solution. Her affairs seemed to be sorting themselves out into an orderly and satisfactory routine.

'Do you want another cup of tea, dear?' Barbie shook her head and allowed Mrs Purvis to remove the empty cup from her hand, her eyes still closed. She drifted and dozed, listening abstractedly to the rustling of cellophane as Mrs Purvis munched her way through half a pack of custard creams, and started suddenly at the sound of Mr Purvis' voice from the ground-floor echoing up the well of the stairs.

'Cissie!'

'Give me strength!' Mrs Purvis hauled herself from the chair. 'Can't a body sit down for five minutes without having him yelling his bloody head off.'

As Mr Purvis rarely used his voice except to shout for his wife when she absented herself for long intervals, Barbie suppressed another smile.

'He wants his tea. Too bloody lazy to get out of that chair and boil himself a kettle. Just you wait. One of these days I'm not going to be around when he shouts. He's going to shout himself hoarse and there won't be anybody there to run round after him. He'll wonder what's hit him . . .'

Mrs Purvis went off, still muttering to herself, and Barbie lay listening to the voice as it continued along the landing and down the stairs, rose in pitch as it headed towards the presence of Mr Purvis, and died away. In the distance a door slammed and there was silence.

She must have slept, for she opened her eyes with the feeling that time had passed. She consulted the clock beside her bed, toying with the thought that she ought to find the energy to prepare a meal. Had she wished, she could have eaten in the café but, after cooking chips all day, Barbie had no stomach for eating them. She preferred to eat in her room but as she was also apathetic about cooking for herself, she lived mainly upon salads, fruit, and cans of soup. She closed her eyes again and decided that she was too tired to eat.

It was hot and stuffy in the room. The weather throughout the summer had been cool, with more than the usual rainfall, but with the coming of September it had thrown itself into a final fling of rising temperature. The window was opened wide but the close proximity of other tenement buildings allowed little circulation of air and Barbie felt uncomfortable in the hot, stale atmosphere. She got off the bed and removed her clothing, wrapping herself in her lilac-coloured silk negligée.

She still possessed many of the garments from her more affluent days and they seemed strangely out of place in her present surroundings. They had evoked many probing questions from Mrs Purvis which Barbie had studiously learned to sidestep.

She examined the contents of the teapot but Mrs Purvis had drained all but the dregs, which were cold and stewed. She helped herself instead to milk and lay on the bed sipping it from her teacup.

She felt a fluttering in her abdomen and eased herself into a more comfortable position, watching the rippling movement across the distended skin with a resigned, almost disinterested, casualness. Suddenly, the flesh peaked with the unmistakable inner thrust of a tiny leg or fist. It caught her attention and she gazed fascinated as the movement came again. She opened her negligée wider and lifted herself up onto one elbow. She had many times seen such movement but, all at once, it was as if she saw it for the first time and became aware that this moving thing within her was a child who had taken shape with arms and legs, toes and fingers. For the first time since the early days of her pregnancy she allowed herself to visualise his features, the colour of his hair, his eyes. It was as if, by some new revelation, she realised that here within her was a little boy who looked like David.

The suppressed longing for David overflowed and she asked herself, bemusedly, why she had not realised before that she carried his child. She folded her arms across the bare flesh of her abdomen and, from that moment, set her sights upon the moment of birth.

It was a moment which appeared reluctant to arrive. September went out in a blaze of Indian summer and October took over with a rich mellowness of warmth which lifted even the drabness of back street King's Cross. Barbie's birthday passed without anyone aware of its significance. She wondered for a fleeting moment whether David had remembered and the thought swept her down into an abyss from which it took her several days to escape. By the tenth of October the birth was overdue by a week and Bert Fabrozzi was growing impatient that Barbie could not organise her personal affairs with more accuracy.

'That little fellow's got his head screwed on, if you ask me,' said Mrs Purvis. 'With the state of this bloody world, I wouldn't be in any hurry to get born either.' She looked around the walls of Barbie's room and raised her teacup in a toast. 'Here's hoping he finishes up in some other bloody hole than this.'

Barbie smiled and raised her own teacup. 'Here's to a future millionaire.' But the remark had touched her deeply. Mrs Purvis had meant it kindly but Barbie realised that his future lay within her own fragile hands and the burden of responsibility rested heavily upon her.

'Now my Eric,' said Mrs Purvis. 'He was in such a bleeding hurry he couldn't even wait till the nurse arrived. All of a rush he came. Mr Purvis had to cope.' The unlikely circumstance of Mr Purvis acting as midwife caught Barbie's attention, which had been straying. 'Only useful thing the old bugger's ever done in his life.'

'How many children did you have?'

'Five, dear. Three of 'em was killed by a buzz-bomb in the blitz and the fourth bunged off to Australia soon as he was old enough to get into the Merchant Navy.' She said it in a matter-of-fact way as if the pain of bereavement had been borne by some alien being having no connection with herself. Barbie wondered if she should offer sympathy but Mrs Purvis was not asking for any.

'What about the fifth?'

'I see him sometimes, dear. He doesn't come round here much.'

'You must miss him.'

'Well, I ask you, dear. Who'd want to come in this bloody hole and stare at the back of that old bugger's neck. Not exactly something to put yourself out for, is it.'

'Life's hard, Mrs P.,' said Barbie with feeling.

290

'Is it, dear? I hadn't really noticed.'

On the fourteenth of October arrangements were made for Barbie to be admitted to hospital for the birth to be induced.

'Now, do you want me to come with you, dear?' Mrs Purvis snapped shut the suitcase which Barbie had packed. 'You could do with a bit of company at a time like this.'

'No, thanks, Mrs P. It's not as if I'm in labour.'

'You would have been last week if you'd taken that castor oil I gave you.'

'No thanks. I didn't fancy it.'

'Well, let me walk you to the taxi.' Mrs Purvis lifted the suitcase from the bed. 'I can carry your case.'

'I'm all right, Mrs P.,' insisted Barbie. 'I can manage by myself. I'm as strong as a horse – or haven't you noticed!'

'I've noticed,' said Mrs Purvis. 'And as stubborn.'

Barbie smiled and brushed a rare kiss across Mrs Purvis' cheek. 'I'll see you in a few days' time.'

'Good luck, dear.' Mrs Purvis walked with her down the stairs. 'I'll be thinking of you.'

Barbie walked towards the taxi rank at King's Cross Station but, as she turned the corner, she saw a bus heading in the direction of the hospital. She joined the queue waiting to board it and decided to save the taxi fare. At the same moment Curly drove towards the station. As Barbie stepped onto the bus he thought for a fleeting second that he had caught sight of her but his eye was diverted by heavy traffic. When he looked again she had gone. For five months he had scoured the city, his eyes attuned to scan the passing crowds, but, as he watched the bus draw away from the kerb, he decided that once again he had been mistaken.

At the hospital Barbie walked onto the ward and thought immediately of Gran. She had not been inside a hospital since the day of Gran's death but memories came flooding back. She was put to bed and a drip inserted into her arm, which reminded her all the more of Gran. She lay staring at the pot-bellied bag hanging from the stand beside the bed, as the colourless fluid dripped down the clear plastic tube into her arm.

'Oh, Gran.' It was almost as if she could touch her there. The feel of warm, pliant flesh, the smell of gin, the sparse grey strands of hair. 'I need you, Gran.' It was a long time since she had voiced the need. It brought back David's words of reassurance,

'Wherever she is, you can bet she's happy.' 'But you're not here, are you, you silly old bleeder. Not where you're needed.'

After all these years the sense of injustice had still not completely faded. It caught her out at moments like this and left her feeling foolish.

'Are you comfortable, Mrs Harding?' The ward sister came into the room and checked the chart at the foot of Barbie's bed.

'Miss Harding,' Barbie corrected.

Sister Minton smiled. 'We call everyone Mrs. It saves embarrassment. Would you prefer your Christian name?'

'Yes, please. It's Barbie.'

'Short for Barbara?'

'Yes, but no one ever uses it.'

'And what are you going to call your baby?'

The question caught Barbie by surprise. After nine months of pregnancy she had not given a moment's thought to the name of her child. 'I don't know. I haven't thought about it.'

Sister Minton raised her eyebrows. 'Well, you'd better start to give it some thought now. You haven't much time.'

Barbie realised that the omission must appear odd. 'I've had such a lot of other things to think about.'

'Well, lie there and think about it now. It will give you something to do while you're waiting.' Sister Minton checked the drip and walked out of the room. 'I'll pop back later but ring the bell if you feel anything happening.'

Barbie lay back against the pillows and looked out of the window beside her bed. The Indian summer was holding out and the patch of sky above the rooftops was a deep azure blue. The obvious name for her child must surely be David, but that could not be. David had already lost his Davie and her child was not a substitute. So, it must be John. David's second name was John. After nine months, the decision called for but a moment's contemplation.

'John Harding.' She toyed with the name and felt a thrill at its discovery. 'John FitzGibbon Harding.' No; she dismissed it immediately. It was too pretentious; she had no claim to it. 'Johnny Harding' rested more comfortably upon her.

She pictured a little boy with dark hair and David's eyes; and settled back once more into the pillows to await the moment of birth.

It came shortly after four o'clock the following morning, the fifteenth of October. 'Push, Barbie. Push.' Barbie gave out one last supreme effort and felt her body give up its charge. She fell back dazed and exhausted, and almost immediately heard the highpitched wail of the newborn infant.

'All over,' said the midwife. 'It's a girl. And just look at that hair.'

She laid the baby into Barbie's arms and Barbie drew back, appalled. If fate had been unkind to her in the past, then this must surely be the most brutal blow of all. For lying beside her was a female child with a shock of red-gold hair, standing up in wet spikes upon her head. The pale white skin looked sickly, blotched with red from the exertion of birth and from the exertion of crying, for the thin wail had become a scream.

'She's gorgeous,' said the midwife. 'Isn't she lovely?'

'Yes,' said Barbie thinly. She turned her head and removed her arm from about the baby.

The midwife exchanged glances with the pupil nurse beside her. 'We'll take Baby to the nursery and you can catch up with some of the sleep you missed last night.'

Barbie closed her eyes and realised that she was very tired. She had expended a great deal of energy. She had done her part. She had given birth to the child and now she wished that this could be an end of it. She paid little attention to what was happening about her. She was aware of being taken back to the ward but she did not hear the conversation which took place between the midwife and the ward sister, nor did she see the expression of concern upon their faces. She wanted only to sleep and fell immediately into a state of deep oblivion from which she was reluctantly awoken a few hours later.

'Here's your baby, Barbie.' Sister Minton stood beside the bed. 'Are you going to feed her?'

Barbie drew back, feeling her body physically shrinking from the child. Despite the apparent numbness of her brain, it worked quickly and she surprised herself with the swiftness with which she found an excuse. 'I can't,' she said. 'It's got to be looked after by someone else while I'm at work. It will have to be put on a bottle.'

'In time, maybe.' Sister Minton placed the baby against Barbie's breast. 'But let's give her a good start in life. Let her have the comfort of you, even if it's only for a few days.' When Barbie showed no signs of response she leaned over and gently rearranged Barbie's clothing in order to expose the breast. The baby's mouth gaped and searched until it found the nipple. Sister Minton moved Barbie's arm until it rested more comfortably about the baby, stood watching for a few moments, and then moved off. From across the room, while engaged in other duties, she unobtrusively kept watch.

Barbie lay in the position in which she had been placed, her eyes turned towards the ceiling and not to the baby. The sucking sensation was strange to her but, apart from this, she felt nothing; no emotion, no thoughts – just the total blankness of bitter disappointment. In due course she passively allowed Sister Minton to remove the baby and place it in a cot at the foot of the bed.

'She's a beautiful little girl,' said Sister Minton. 'She's the image of you.'

Barbie shrugged. What possible merit could be claimed for producing a replica of herself. Sister Minton looked at her searchingly then, with a slight shake of her head, left the room.

Barbie had been placed in a four-bedded ward. The other three occupants had been there longer than she and chatted amicably amongst themselves. They made some attempt to include Barbie in their conversation but she merely smiled and refused to be drawn. Instead she got out of bed and walked over to the window, staring out across the rooftops of the city. Eventually her companions wandered off down the corridor, leaving her alone, and she was glad of the solitude. The baby began to cry – a strident, high-pitched wail which jangled her nerves.

'Your baby's crying, Barbie.' Sister Mintion stood behind her. 'Aren't you going to pick her up?'

Barbie had been aware of the cry but it had not occurred to her that she should do anything about it. Now she turned from the window and went to do what was expected of her. She lifted the baby awkwardly and held it against her shoulder. It was stiff and rigid, struggling against her hold with none of the malleability she would have expected.

Sister Minton remained in the room, busying herself with tidying an already tidy locker. 'I see from your notes that you planned your baby,' she said conversationally.

Barbie looked at her blankly. The doctor whom she had seen in the early weeks of her pregnancy must have seen fit to record the fact in her notes. It seemed such a long time ago.

The baby had stopped crying as soon as it was lifted. Barbie replaced it in the cot.

'So you've always been quite sure in your mind about keeping her? There was no question . . . ?'

'Of course not.' Barbie was genuinely shocked.

'I just thought you might have had a slight change of heart. You seem a little uncertain of yourself.'

'No.' Her voice faltered. 'Why should you think that?'

The baby began to cry again. Sister Minton looked at her, and then at Barbie, and Barbie obediently picked her up. Immediately the crying ceased but this time she did not put the baby down again.

'Did you decide on a name?'

'John,' said Barbie.

Sister Minton looked at her with a curious expression. 'That would have been nice if she had been a boy. What did you decide for a girl?'

'I don't know. I didn't get round to it.'

'Did it mean a great deal to you to have a boy, Barbie?'

Barbie shrugged her shoulders, feigning indifference.

'Would you like to tell me why?'

Barbie had no wish to discuss something which she would find impossible to explain to a stranger. 'I hadn't thought about it.'

Sister Minton threw out a faded carnation from a vase and rearranged the remaining display. 'You couldn't wish to have a prettier little girl,' she said. 'She's going to grow up to be beautiful – just like you.'

Barbie had never been impressed by reference to her own beauty; at this moment it became an insult.

'How about giving some thought to a name now?'

'I don't think I'm in the mood at the moment.'

'It always helps when a baby has a name,' said Sister Minton. 'It makes her more of a person in her own right.'

Barbie shook her head disinterestedly. 'I can't think of anything suitable at the moment.'

'How about your mother's name, or your grandmother's? Some of the old names are coming back.'

'Gran's name was Gertie.'

'Well, perhaps not Gertie. But there are lots of other pretty names to choose from.' She started at the first letter of the alphabet and began to work her way through. 'Alison . . . Anne

'. . . Audrey . . . Alice . . . Bernadette . . . Catherine . . . Debbie . . .'

Barbie thought of Debbie and Sue and wondered what they would be doing now. She looked at the clock on the wall and knew they would be sleeping.

'. . . Emily . . . Fiona . . . "G" . . .' She was stuck for a 'G'. 'Grace . . . Gloria . . .'

Gloria Beckworth. Dear Miss Beckworth.

'. . . Helen . . . Imogen . . . Jackie . . . Kathleen . . .' She continued through to Zoe.

'I knew someone once called Gloria.' Barbie said it apathetically.

'It's a pretty name.'

Barbie did not respond.

'How about Glory? With that hair she could carry a name like Glory. It makes me think of sunshine and happiness.'

For the first time a spark of interest glimmered. There was a certain ring about the name which appealed to Barbie. Gloria Beckworth had a habit of flitting in and out of her mind at unexpected moments.

'Glory's as good as any,' she said, but with no hint of the spark.

'Glory Harding.' Sister Minton walked over and touched the baby's hand. 'Welcome, Glory Harding.' The baby squirmed against Barbie's shoulder.

'Can I put it down now?'

'Don't you want to hold her for a while?'

Barbie was aware that she ought to say the correct thing. 'I thought it ought to be sleeping.'

'Probably. But it's just as important to cuddle her. It's a way for you both to get to know one another.' Barbie perched on the edge of the bed and continued to hold Glory against her shoulder.

'Barbie, do you mind if I say something?'

'What?'

'It may sound like something from the script of some awful "B" movie, but it's true and it's important nonetheless.' Barbie wondered what she was about to say. 'Glory didn't ask to be born. And it isn't her fault that she's a girl.'

'Of course not. Who said it was?'

'It's just sometimes a good thing to state the facts and actually hear the words.'

The statement had more effect upon Barbie than Sister Minton realised. It was not Glory's fault that she had been born. It was Barbie who had conceived her, Barbie who had given birth.

'And it's not your fault either.' Sister Minton appeared to have read her thoughts. 'To be perfectly correct, one would have to say that it's the father's chromosomes which determine the sex of the child . . .'

Barbie fought against the need to think of David.

'. . . But it would be better to look at it from the point of view that every child is born as an individual, and we should accept them in their own right.'

Barbie could not cope with thoughts of David at this moment. Almost imperceptibly, she tightened her hold about Glory and stroked her thumb across the tiny hand on her shoulder but, outwardly, she gave no indication of response and she did not alter the apathetic expression upon her face.

Sister Minton looked at her for a moment and stifled a sigh. 'Are you expecting any visitors this afternoon, Barbie?'

Barbie shook her head. The only person who would have any interest in visiting her would be Mrs Purvis and she had told her not to bother.

'What about your parents? Do they know about the baby?'

'No.'

'Perhaps they'd like to know they have a grand-daughter.'

'I doubt it.'

'Most parents do rally round once they know they have a grandchild. No matter what difficulties might have preceded it.'

'I haven't got any parents.' She said it sharply.

'I'm very sorry. Are they dead?'

'No. My father's around; and my mother ran off to London years ago.'

'You must have missed her terribly.'

'No I didn't. I never knew her.'

Barbie had never given much thought to the fact that, having run away to London, she had followed in her mother's footsteps. It occurred to her now and she found it an intriguing thought which occupied her for several moments.

'Would you like me to contact your father, Barbie? He may be able to give you some support.'

'No,' said Barbie, with such conviction that Sister Minton did not pursue the subject further.

'What about friends? Good friends can be invaluable at times like this.'

Barbie did not like being faced with direct questions; they forced her to confront reality when it had always been more comfortable to skirt around it. She thought now about friends, ticking off acquaintances who had passed through her life, people who had temporarily been of importance to her; but she failed to come up with the name of one permanent friend.

'I know what you're thinking,' she said testily. 'That I brought it on myself.'

'No, Barbie. I didn't say that. Is that what you think?'

'You may not have said it,' she retorted. 'But it's what you think.'

'I wouldn't be so foolish as to generalise, Barbie. There are lots of reasons why people find themselves alone. But it is also true that some people do have a way of holding others off.'

'Well; do you know what I think?' Barbie dumped Glory into her cot, causing her to let out a high-pitched squeal of fright. 'I think you ask too many bloody stupid questions.'

She marched to the door and slammed it behind her, so hard that the glass pane rattled and the noise reverberated along the corridor. 'It's none of your bloody business what I think; or what I do.'

She collided with a white-coated figure standing in her way and pushed him aside, making for the only haven of privacy she could find – the bathroom. Tears of anger were streaming down her face – at least, she supposed them to be tears of anger.

Sister Minton watched her go then walked over to lift Glory from her cot. She held her gently to soothe the cries. She had worked on the maternity unit for many years. Nothing upset her more than the knowledge that, occasionally, a child could be placed at a disadvantage from the moment of birth.

A short time later Barbie crept back to the room. She lifted Glory and held her close. This time the tiny body seemed more pliant, moulding itself against her own.

'I'm sorry, Glory,' she said. 'I'm very, very sorry.'

The red-gold hair grew in downy tufts upon the pale skin of the scalp, reminding Barbie of the head of a newly-hatched bird. Glory opened her mouth, groping with her lips against Barbie's breast. Barbie sat on the edge of the bed and fed her, even though she knew that it was not feeding time.

In the meantime, Sister Minton sat in her office making notes in Barbie's file. At a time when non-accidental injury to children was an increasingly prevalent problem in society, all hospital staff were trained to recognise the breeding grounds for possible abuse. A network had been carefully structured to minimise the risk, to maintain constant scrutiny and, above all, to give support. Barbie's name must be referred to the Community Physician; the health visitor must be alerted, and the general practitioner warned to keep watch for any hint of trouble.

As she wrote, Sister Minton lifted the telephone and asked for the social work department. The hospital social worker must become involved and, on discharge, would refer the case to her colleagues in the community.

As Barbie sat nursing her baby she was unaware of the wheels which were being set in motion. Before leaving the hospital her name was to become known to a number of people whom she was yet to meet.

Chapter Fifteen

Barbie called a taxi to take her home from the hospital. As she sat waiting for it to arrive, she turned in her mind the possibility that it might be Curly who would call to collect her. It stirred conflicting emotions, not least of which was how she would explain to him the presence of Glory. It was not Curly who came, but a pleasant young man who took pity on Barbie as she carried both baby and suitcase. He helped her up the stairs to her room.

She had not unlocked the door before Mrs Purvis came hurrying up the stairs behind her. 'How are you, dear? I thought you might be home today.' It was good to see Mrs Purvis. 'Here, give him to me. Let me have a look at him.' She took the bundle from Barbie's arms and pulled aside the shawl.

'She's a girl.'

'A girl!' exclaimed Mrs Purvis. 'And you so certain it would be a boy.' She placed her finger beneath Glory's chin, talking to her with sounds quite unintelligible to Barbie but the universal language of all who talk to babies. 'To tell the truth, dear, I always wanted a little girl. I only had one and she wasn't much bigger than this when the buzz-bomb . . .'

'I'm sorry, Mrs P. It must have been terrible.'

'It was then, dear, but it was a long time ago. What are you going to call her?'

'Glory.'

'Glory,' mused Mrs Purvis. 'Can't say as I've ever heard of it before.'

'I knew someone once named Gloria.'

Mrs Purvis repeated the name several times to herself. 'It sort of grows on you,' she decided. 'Glory, what?'

'I don't know. What was your baby's name?'

300

'Jean. Why?'

'Then it's Glory Jean.'

Mrs Purvis' face moved with a flush of deep emotion. 'Thank you, dear,' she said softly. 'That's very kind of you.'

Barbie became embarrassed to be found standing on the bridge which she had built between herself and Mrs Purvis. 'Would you like a cup of tea?' She busied herself with the kettle.

'No, thank you, dear. To tell the truth, I'm glad you came home when you did. I thought I'd miss you. I've got to take the old bugger to the hospital.'

'Hospital,' echoed Barbie. 'Is he ill?'

'Says he's got pains in his chest.' Mrs Purvis tutted with her tongue against her palate. 'Too many bloody cigarettes, if you ask me, and not enough exercise. Says he's got pains in his arm as well.' She laughed and poked Barbie's shoulder. 'You know what that is. Strain of lifting it to switch channels on the telly.'

'I hope he'll be all right.'

'He's only got to go for tests. Old bugger's not going to like it when they tell him to give up smoking. By the way, I popped in here while you were away and got a few things ready.'

Barbie turned and saw the cot standing, ready made up with blankets. 'Thanks, Mrs P. I don't know what I'd do without you.'

'Welcome home, dear.' She turned as she was leaving the room. 'I missed you while you were away.'

Barbie returned the smile. 'It's good to be home.'

She placed Glory in the cot and tucked the blankets around her. As she folded back the blue-ribboned edge and overlaid it with a quilt of deeper blue, she told herself that convention would have to be ignored. She could not afford to replace items of blue with others of pink.

She lay down on her own bed and drank her tea. She was very tired. The months of pregnancy, followed by the confinement and the emotional strain, had taken their toll and now she felt exhausted. In the hospital she had become accustomed to taking an afternoon nap and she stretched out her limbs, badly in need of sleep.

She had barely closed her eyes before Glory began to cry. Barbie groaned and half-lifted herself on one elbow. 'Go to sleep, Glory,' she said. 'There are more people to be considered than you. I want to sleep even if you don't.' She flopped back onto her bed hoping that if she left her for a while, Glory might settle. She did not. The cries rose to an ear-splitting shriek and Barbie reluctantly capitulated that she must do something to stem the noise.

She was about to rise from the bed when another noise caught her completely by surprise. A heavy hammering thundered through the wall beside her ear, so loud and so unexpected, that she let out a small cry of alarm. A voice accompanied the hammering. 'Shut that bleeding row!'

Barbie had had little contact with the family who lived in the two rooms adjacent to her own. She had never spoken to them but on many occasions she had heard the husband coming home late at night, the worse for drink. She had heard the quarrels, the crashing of furniture, and knew him to be a violent man. The hammering came again. 'Shut that bleeding row!'

Barbie got off the bed quickly and snatched Glory from her cot but the sudden movement startled her and increased the volume of the noise. She walked up and down the room holding her against her shoulder, patting her in an effort to soothe the cries.

'If you don't shut that bleeding row, I'll come in there and do it for you!'

Barbie was angry but she was also afraid. Fowler was a big brute of a man and his voice was slurred with drink. She had no wish to cross swords with him. 'Please, Glory. Please don't cry.' She smothered the noise, as best she could, with a shawl and held Glory close against her shoulder. The high-pitched wail soothed to a whimper, but only so long as Barbie paced the floor. She knew that the moment she stopped, the cries would erupt again.

For half an hour she walked the floor. Each time she stopped, Glory cried, and each time Glory cried, Fowler hammered on the wall.

Barbie was tired. She wanted only to rest but she knew that she had no alternative but to take Glory out of the room and out of earshot of Fowler. There was nowhere to take her but out, onto the streets.

She looked about her. 'Good old Mrs P.,' she said wearily. 'She's got the pram ready too.' Barbie had left the chassis of the perambulator still in its cardboard packing but Mrs Purvis had unpacked it and left it leaning against the wall. Barbie kept Glory balanced against her shoulder with one hand while, with the other, she lifted it from the corner.

The cot doubled as a body for the perambulator. It formed a

light-weight, collapsible unit, but it had to be carried down three flights of stairs. She could not carry the body and the chassis in one journey, so she had a choice between carrying Glory in the cot, and leaving her unattended beside the dustbins in the yard whilst she returned for the chassis, or leaving her to scream in the room. Barbie was fearful enough of Fowler to choose the former and she panted down the dim staircase, stumbling beneath the unaccustomed weight and size, then ran back for the chassis. She grazed her shin and cursed to think that this procedure must be repeated every time she wished to leave the building.

The Indian summer had broken while she was in hospital and the afternoon was overcast with a sharp autumnal chill in the air. The streets were drab and grey after weeks of mellow sunshine and dark clouds were strewn like tattered garments across the floor of the sky. Barbie shivered and lifted her collar as she set out in the direction of Regents Park. She had not been to the park since the days when she had walked with Sam and the sight of grass and trees stirred strong memories which she fought to quell. The fallen leaves lay thick upon the ground and made soft swishing sounds as the wheels of the pram passed over them.

She saw a large red dog, not at all like Sam but sufficient to cause her to change direction, heading off along another path where a small boy squatted on his heels, examining the shape, the smell, the texture of a fallen leaf. Nearby a nanny slowed her pace and called repeatedly that it was time to hurry home for tea. As Barbie approached he stood up and handed her the leaf as if it were a precious gift. 'Pretty,' he said and ran off to his nanny. 'Thank you,' said Barbie and watched him go.

It was on this very path that she had seen other nannies, with other charges, upon the day when she had first been certain of her own pregnancy. She had wondered then how it would feel to hold David's baby. She had not known then what she knew today – that it was not David's baby which she carried, but merely her own. Her emotions then had been ambivalent and they were no less ambivalent today. The stab of bitter disappointment swung to guilt, remorse, the knowledge that she must not lay the blame on Glory.

It began to rain – a steady, uncomfortable drizzle which found its way inside her collar and soaked into the fibres of her sweater. The chill was all the greater because she was overtired and it was a long walk back to King's Cross. Glory had been sleeping peacefully from the moment Barbie had started out, for the movement had lulled her into deep slumber. Barbie was tempted to return immediately but she thought of Fowler and decided that it was wiser to remain until dusk. She returned eventually at six o'clock, the dim twilight already replaced by the harsher light of street lamps. Glory would shortly be demanding food and, although Barbie was more than pleased to retrace her steps, she balked at the knowledge that henceforth her life must be sub-divided into rigid four-hourly demands at two, six, ten, and two o'clock.

Glory did not wake. Even when Barbie jostled the perambulator up the stairs, she did not stir. Barbie set her down in the corner of the room and moved about quietly. She had no desire to rouse her, even though it was almost half past six. She removed her wet coat and shivered, setting a match to the gas fire in an effort to drive the chill from the room. She stooped before it rubbing her hands but it only served to increase the bout of shivering.

The only way to completely remove the chill from her bones was to have a hot bath. She looked doubtfully at Glory and then decided that she would take a chance. If she were very quick she could have a bath and return before Glory woke. She gathered up the items she would need and hurried along the landing to the bathroom. By good fortune, it was vacant and she quickly cleaned the bathtub which bore the greasy ring left by its previous occupant. She lowered herself down beneath the surface of the hot water, submerging all but her head, and felt her skin prickle as the temperature rose.

She had hardly closed her eyes and released a sigh of satisfaction when she heard the sound of Glory's cries. She shot up – 'Oh, Lord . . .' and almost immediately heard heavy footsteps on the landing. The sound of hammering on the door of her room was followed by an unrecognised voice – 'She's in the bathroom' – and the footsteps thundered down the landing towards her, followed by a hammering on the bathroom door. 'How many times have I told you to shut that bleeding row in your room.'

'I'm coming.' Barbie jumped out of the bath and, without bothering to dry herself, wrapped her robe hastily about her body. She unlocked the door and brushed past Fowler as he lurched across the landing.

'I'll shut that brat myself if I get my hands on it.'

Barbie's protective instincts rose and she almost turned on him.

'D'you wanna make something of it?' he drawled and squared up to her.'

'No.' She turned and went instead to her room. She blamed herself for leaving Glory, but now she herself was wet and colder still. With one hand she held Glory whilst attempting to dress herself with the other, but it was a difficult task and Glory's cries rose to a shriek.

'I'm cold, Glory. Can't you please shut up.' She held her hand to Glory's mouth and the tiny body contorted itself with even greater vigour.

There was no peace until she fed her. Only then did silence fall, broken by the sounds of urgent sucking. Barbie was sitting on the floor before the gas fire. She leaned back against the leg of the table, closed her eyes, and drifted off into a shivering half-doze of exhaustion. Glory, too, having satisfied her hunger, sank into sleep against her.

'Are you there, Miss Harding?' There came another knock at the door, not the thunderous banging of Fowler but nonetheless insistent. 'Would you mind removing your things from the bathroom.' It was a woman's voice. 'You've left a tub full of water and your belongings scattered all over the floor. I want to bath my children.'

'Sorry.' She jumped up again and, still holding Glory, went back along the landing to clear the room. Her nerves were frayed and now her head began to ache with the steady thumping of exhaustion. She returned to her own room and, still holding Glory, fell upon her bed.

Again, a tapping on the door. 'Oh, please. Not again.'

This time it was Mrs Purvis calling out, 'It's only me.'

'Come in, Mrs P.'

Mrs Purvis opened the door. 'Are you all right, dear? I'm just going off to Bingo.'

'Yes, thank you.' Barbie did not rise from the bed. 'Have a good time.'

'Are you all right, dear? You're looking tired.'

Barbie dragged out a reluctant smile. 'It's been one of those days.'

'Has Glory been playing you up?'

'She cries a lot.'

Mrs Purvis walked over and took Glory from Barbie's arms. 'You can't expect a baby not to cry, dear. Wouldn't be natural.'

Barbie was glad of the relief and stretched her cramped muscles. 'I know. But I'm afraid of Mr Fowler. He's been complaining.'

Mrs Purvis' face registered immediate alarm. 'You watch him, Barbie. He's a vicious bugger, that one.'

'I know.'

'Been in trouble for it with the Law, more than once. Hits out first, then thinks about it later.'

The reiteration of what Barbie already knew, only increased her own anxiety. 'I don't know what I can do.'

'You'll have to try and keep her quiet. He'll get used to it in a day or two.'

'I hope so. I can't carry her around and walk the streets for ever.'

Mrs Purvis began to unbutton her coat. 'I won't go to Bingo tonight, dear. I'll stay and keep you company instead.'

'No, please.' Barbie had no wish to impose upon Mrs Purvis. 'You go. I'll be all right. Look, she's fast asleep.'

'Are you sure, dear?'

'Of course I'm sure. I could do with some sleep myself. You go and enjoy yourself at Bingo.'

'Well, if you say so, dear. I'll go and let you get some rest. I'll look in when I get back about eleven.' Mrs Purvis handed Glory back to Barbie and went to the door.

'How's Mr P.?'

Mrs Purvis turned. 'You know what hospitals are, dear. Don't tell you nothing. Just says he's got to have more tests.'

Barbie sensed a measure of concern beneath the bluff exterior. 'I do hope he'll be all right.'

'He'll be all right. Nothing's going to kill that old bugger off.' She laughed and closed the door behind her.

Glory stirred and began to whimper. Barbie was afraid to move her in order to place her in her cot. Instead she took her into her own bed and together they lay on the narrow mattress. Glory slept, but Barbie found herself unable to rest. She was afraid that in her sleep she might turn and smother her. Repeatedly, she felt her eyelids drooping, followed by the sensation of sleep descending like a rush of water, only to jerk into wakefulness, listening for the sound of breathing at her side. The inability to succumb to sleep was almost worse than the initial unfulfilled desire for rest, and the throbbing in her temples finally made sleep impossible. She got up and made herself a cup of coffee.

She drank it crouched before the gas fire. She was still cold. It seemed that she had been cold all day and there was no way in which she could warm herself. She pulled another sweater on top of the thick one she already wore but the chill came from within herself and there seemed no way in which she could banish it.

Glory was still sleeping peacefully but Barbie was afraid to disturb her. Through the thin walls of her room she could hear the voice of Fowler raised in anger against his wife. She had no wish to transfer it upon herself. She stretched out on the cold, uncarpeted floor but sleep continued to elude her and slipped ever further away. At last she switched on the television, drowning the sound of Fowler's voice, and sat on the small square of threadbare hearthrug, glazedly watching the screen until Glory awoke for her ten o'clock feed.

By half past ten Glory was once more asleep. Barbie gingerly placed her into her cot and stood there, hardly daring to breathe, afraid to remove her hands for fear of waking her. She did not stir.

Barbie crept away and fell fully clothed into her bed. She was too cold to get undressed and too tired to bother. She fell at once into a kind of sleep, but not the kind of sleep to bring her rest. She plunged into a jumbled patchwork of vivid dreams and night-mares which tossed her through space and time, so that she knew not where she was, except to recognise it as a realm of panic and anxiety. She wheeled a perambulator through rank vegetation, making no progress, her charge not a baby but a dog – a large, red dog. But then the perambulator changed into a car, and Sam was the driver – driving fast, out of control, so that she lurched with sickening speed, clutching out at objects which were smeared with slime. David was there. She saw him flash before her, almost there but never close enough to touch. She screamed out to him for help but the sound of the scream sucked him up and carried him away, vibrating through a sky of glaucous jelly.

Mrs Purvis returned from her Bingo session. She tapped on the door, and obtaining no reply, tiptoed away.

The tapping on the door transferred itself in Barbie's dream to hammering upon the wall. Fowler was tearing through bricks and mortar as if through a fragile membrane – flecks of blood in slippery, elasticated film. He was tearing through to get at her, as

she shielded herself with hands and arms, waiting for the blows –
blows which rained down, not from Fowler, but from Ken. 'You
little slut! You dirty little slut!' She slipped and fell, falling, falling,
down through space, and knew that she would land on Glory.
Glory was beneath her, smothered.

She snapped to wakefulness with a painful jerk and felt for
Glory. She was not in the bed but in her cot. It had been nothing
but a foolish nightmare.

She was still cold but bathed in perspiration, aching and tired.
She had never before been so tired. She pulled the blankets
tighter round her throat and shoulders, curled herself into a ball,
and fell immediately into the clutches of yet another dream.

She slept and woke, woke and slept, until, at one o'clock, she
fell into a deep black pit of dreamless oblivion. It seemed but for a
moment.

The cries came to her as if from a great distance. She heard them
and drifted back to sleep, roused again, and drifted. Little by little
it registered in her mind that the cries were close at hand. She did
not want to hear. She needed sleep and Glory summoned her,
demanding to be fed.

Suddenly, the hammering came again. 'Shut that bleeding
row! It's the middle of the bleeding night.'

She shot from bed and everything turned black, a sickening
lurch, as she groped her way towards the cot, feeling sick, her feet
not knowing where to find the floor.

'Shut up.' This time the voice was hers. 'For God's sake, shut
up!'

She found the lamp beside the cot and switched it on, focusing
her eyes upon the tiny face contorted with screams. She felt
ashamed. 'I'm sorry, Glory,' she said and picked her up. 'But I'm
tired. I'm very, very tired.'

The clock beside her bed indicated two o'clock. The cot was
wet, sheets and blankets saturated. She ignored it, fed Glory
quickly, and put her back into the damp cot; but immediately she
was consumed with guilt. The bedding must be changed.

She laid Glory on her own bed and the cries began again.
'Shhh!' she hissed, and cocked her ear for sounds from the
adjoining room.

The clean bedding was not immediately to hand. It was packed
at the bottom of one of several boxes stacked in the corner of the
room; and Barbie could not remember which. She searched

through the contents, throwing them across the floor, as the last dregs of patience ebbed away in grunts of stifled tears. All the time Glory whimpered, soft mewling sounds, interspersed with louder wails.

'Shut up, Glory. Just shut up!'

At last she found the bedding, changed the cot, and tucked Glory back beneath the blankets. For a moment she lay there, and then she began to cry.

'Oh, for God's sake; can't you just shut up and go to sleep!'

The cries increased: tiny, curled-up fists punched the air. Barbie picked her up and carried her about the room. The air was cold. She had left the gas fire burning when she went to bed but it was controlled by a meter and the supply had run out. She went to her purse and slotted more coins into the meter, squatting down before the fire with Glory in her arms.

Glory lay there, content now that she was held, working her mouth and punching her fists and her feet with abrupt stabbing movements; then lay quietly, her unfocused eyes latching upon the bright multicolour of Barbie's sweater.

Barbie's chin dropped down on her chest, engulfed in swirls of sleep, then snapped backwards, paining her neck, as she lost balance and slumped sideways towards the floor.

She saw Glory lying contentedly in her arms and put her back into her cot. Immediately the cries began again.

'Please, Glory.' Her voice was tight with exasperation. 'I can't carry you round all night. I've got to sleep.' She picked her up again and walked about the room.

She heard footsteps outside and held her breath but they moved off along the landing in the direction of the bathroom. She lifted the shawl to cover Glory's mouth. 'Be quiet,' she whispered, 'Before he hears you.'

But Glory did not stop. 'Oh, for God's sake; what can I do to shut you up!' Her voice rose.

Glory's fair skin was mottled, blotched with red, her body rigid. Barbie's head throbbed and her body shook with uncontrolled shivering. 'You're going to get us both into trouble in a minute,' she threatened. 'He's going to hear you.'

It was not long before the hammering came. 'Shut that bleeding row,' he shouted. 'There are people in here trying to get a bleeding night's kip.'

'There you are,' she said. 'I told you he would hear.' She

squashed Glory roughly against her chest trying to stifle the sound.

'Shut that bleeding row!' The hammering echoed through Barbie's head.

'Glory, if you don't shut up, I'm going to . . .' Her voice was little more than a whisper but harsh, pushed out between white lips drawn tight.

She heard footsteps outside and turned to see the door-handle move. She held her breath.

'Open this bleeding door!'

She stood, hardly daring to move.

'If you don't do something about that row, I'll break this door down and stop that brat myself.' She heard the shuffling of movement as he leaned against the door; but the lock withstood the pressure.

Barbie felt trapped. There was no way in which she could remove Glory from Fowler's presence as she had done during that afternoon. There was nowhere to take her; and she could not walk the streets at such an hour.

She battled with a sense of unreality, half born of exhaustion and half by an awareness of the hour. At two-thirty in the morning, the world has a way of taking on a new dimension as if, by drawing breath ready for the new day, it sucks down into the vacuum all positive thought. She was overwhelmed by the knowledge that she was out of her depth and could not cope.

'Shut up, Glory.' Her voice rose. 'Shut UP. SHUT UP!'

She held Glory out at arms' length, unaware that her fingers were digging into the soft flesh of the upper arms and shoulders. 'Would you please SHUT UP!'

Fowler gave up and, with a final threat, went back to his room.

The shock of being held suspended caused Glory to scream afresh.

'You're nothing but trouble; and I wish that I'd never set eyes upon you – you squawling little BRAT!' She shook her; and threw her across the room into the cot.

There was complete silence – louder than the cries – and then a single, piercing scream of fright.

'Oh, Glory; I'm sorry.' She fell to her knees beside the cot. 'I'm sorry; I'm sorry; I'm sorry.'

She picked her up, cradling the tiny, trembling body against her breast. 'I'm sorry, Glory. I'm very, very sorry.'

She bent her head and touched the face with her lips. For the first time, she became aware of the scent of the new-born – an undefinable sweetness. She kissed her and pulled up her sweater to offer her breast; but Glory was too overwrought to accept it. Gently, she pushed the nipple inside the mouth, wanting to offer herself to ease the cries.

Slowly, little by little, Glory responded until the trembling eased and the cries were replaced by sobs and mewling sounds, which petered out into a calmer snuffling against the breast. Barbie sat on the bed and held her, all thought of exhaustion swept away by the onrush of remorse.

Even when Glory drifted into sleep, she did not release her but continued to watch over her, marvelling at the shape and size of tiny fingers, the features of the face, the ears, eyelashes one shade lighter than the hair. She sat on the bed and held her until morning.

Dawn broke with a weak sun piercing its way through a gap between tenement buildings. It fell directly upon the mirror above the sink and reflected back, splashing the walls with light. It was like a new beginning.

From the room next door she heard voices, followed by the slamming of the door, and Fowler stomped down the stairs and out of the building. A sense of relief fell upon her and her spirits rose.

She bathed Glory, handling her gently, smiling down into eyes which were at present of pale, indifferent colour but which showed signs of grey. She examined them more closely. She had not noticed before that they would likely turn to grey.

Mrs Purvis called. 'How are you, dear? You're looking tired.'

'I was, Mrs P. – but I'm better now.'

'Here, I've got some news. Old Fowler's gone away.'

'Gone away?'

'I was talking to his wife. He's got a job up North.'

Barbie's spirits rose further. 'I heard him going off this morning.'

'He's gone up North to a building site. She reckons he'll be gone for weeks. The longer the better for her, poor soul.'

'The better for everyone,' breathed Barbie. 'We'll all get a lot more peace when he's not around.'

'I thought you'd be pleased.' Mrs Purvis went to lift the chassis of the perambulator which was leaning against the wall. 'You get

311

your head down for a while and have a sleep. I'll take Glory off your hands.'

Barbie was almost reluctant to release Glory from her charge but Mrs Purvis bustled efficiently with the perambulator. 'Help me down the stairs, dear. I'll walk her to the shops and keep her happy for an hour or two. It's a long time since I walked a baby in a pram.'

It was easier to manoeuvre the perambulator down the stairs when there were two to share the load. Barbie stood beside the dustbins and watched Mrs Purvis walk away with Glory; then she went upstairs, took a hot bath, and slept soundly until they returned. By the time she awoke, she had eclipsed from her mind all memory of the events of the previous night.

It was three o'clock when the health visitor called. She announced herself as Barbie opened the door. 'Hello, Barbie. I'm Enid Neville, health visitor.'

Barbie was immediately on guard. 'I didn't expect . . .'

'I've just popped in to see how you're getting on.'

'I'm fine, thanks.' She wanted to close the door.

'We always drop in on new Mums shortly after they arrive home. Just to see how they're coping.'

'Everything's fine. There's no need . . .'

Mrs Neville was a pleasant, motherly woman in late middle age. There was a comfortable roundness about her and a casual, easygoing air. 'May I come in?' she asked, and, reluctantly, Barbie stepped to one side.

'What a nice little room.' She walked across to the armchair and looked about her.

'It's not much; but I do my best.'

'You've done wonders with it.' Mrs Neville looked at the chair. 'Do you mind if I sit down? My feet are killing me.'

'Help yourself.'

She eased herself down and, with a grimace, released the heel of one shoe with the toe of the other. Barbie found herself warming to her.

'Would you like a cup of tea?'

'I'd love one, dear. I've been on the go since six this morning. It's been one of those days.'

Barbie brewed tea and they chatted with an easy casualness. Mrs Neville hardly mentioned Glory and, when she did come round to speak of her, it was to offer practical, down-to-earth

312

suggestions, born of many years' experience. Barbie accepted them gratefully and without resentment. She felt none of the hostility she would have expected.

'May I take a look at her?' Mrs Neville hoisted herself from the chair and went to the cot where Glory lay awake, but quiet.

She lifted the clothing and, with skilful hands, examined the limbs. 'Barbie, dear. There are bruises on Glory's arms and shoulders.' It was said with observation, not accusation. Barbie froze. 'Would you like to tell me about it.'

Barbie averted her eyes and stood for a long time wondering why Mrs Neville did nothing to break the silence.

'I'm here to help you, Barbie.'

'It was nothing.' Her voice felt tight in her throat. 'It was an accident.'

'Do you often lose your temper?'

'No; I do not. And what else are you going to accuse me of?'

'Barbie,' said Mrs Neville quietly. 'I had three children of my own; and eight grandchildren. I've spent too many sleepless nights with crying babies to accuse any young mother of anything.'

'Then why say I did?'

'Because it's important to find out how she got the bruises.'

'I told you it was nothing.' Barbie picked up Glory and held her.

'She doesn't get bruised by doing nothing, dear.'

'So; she was crying.'

'And . . . ?'

'And what?'

'Go on.'

'She wouldn't stop.'

'Yes; I see.'

'No, you don't. I didn't do anything . . . really.'

Mrs Neville said nothing but looked at her with a kindly expression, which was almost worse than accusation.

'Well – don't just stand there! What are you going to do about it?' demanded Barbie.

'The first thing I'm going to do is to help you ensure that it doesn't happen again.' She waited until Barbie raised her eyes and looked at her. 'But I do have to report it, Barbie. You realise that, don't you.'

Things were happening to Barbie's mouth. She was having

313

difficulty in controlling her lower lip. 'Please . . .' she begged. 'It won't ever happen again.'

'I've got to, Barbie. I have no choice.'

Barbie clutched her arms tightly about Glory and felt her stomach run cold. 'They'll take her away from me.'

'Barbie . . .' Mrs Neville came to her and placed a hand on her shoulder; but Barbie shook it off and turned her back, standing between Mrs Neville and Glory.

'The Authorities don't remove babies from their parents unless there's very good cause. They do it only when it is in the interest of the child. And the interests of most children lie with the parents.'

Barbie gained some slight reassurance from this statement, until she analysed it and realised that Mrs Neville had promised nothing.

'They're not having her.'

'It's our job to help people look after their children. Not take them away.'

'I bet!'

'I'm going to come and visit you often. And I'm going to tell you how you can contact me. I want you to get in touch with me the moment you find things building up and getting out of hand.'

'You're not going to take her away?'

'Come and sit down, dear.' Mrs Neville took Barbie's arm and this time she reluctantly allowed herself to be led to the bed. They sat down side by side, Barbie still holding Glory close against her.

She looked at Mrs Neville and knew instinctively that she could trust her; yet she was afraid.

'Now listen to me . . .' Mrs Neville sat and talked to her for a long time, explaining in detail the ways in which she intended to offer friendship and support.

At last she stood up. 'Is everything clear?'

'But you're still going to report me?'

'I have to, dear. I have no choice.'

'And supposing they decide to take her away?'

'Then we must face it in the best way we can. The final decision is not mine but my opinion is always taken into account, and I am here to help you look after her as best I can.'

'I'm scared.'

Mrs Neville smiled. 'There's nothing to be afraid of, dear. We'll see it through.'

'You see, I can't lose her; I just can't.'

'Then we'll have to see that you get all the support you need to look after her.'

'I'm sorry. It's not your fault.'

'It's no one's fault, dear. These things happen.'

'She's the only thing I've got left.'

'Now, you say this man Fowler has gone away?'

'He's got a job up North.'

'So you won't be under quite so much pressure to keep Glory quiet. And if you follow the little tips I gave you, I think you'll find that she'll settle down.'

'I'll do my best.'

'And I'll come back first thing tomorrow morning to see how you are.'

Barbie saw her to the door. 'Couldn't you forget to report it?' she asked. 'Just this once?'

Mrs Neville held her head on one side and smiled without saying anything.

'I know. You can't.'

'Don't worry, dear. It will all work out; you'll see.'

Barbie closed the door behind her and leaned heavily against it. The memory of the previous night was hazy and the whole affair had blown up out of proportion. She looked down at Glory, whom she was still holding in her arms. 'This is crazy. I wouldn't hurt you, Glory; you know that, don't you.'

It was less than an hour later when the social worker arrived. The door was ajar, for Barbie was expecting Mrs Purvis. She tapped on the door. 'Good afternoon. I'm Marion Trotman, social worker.'

'The liar!' exclaimed Barbie. She swung round and slammed the door in Miss Trotman's face. 'The stinking liar!' Mrs Neville, for all her sweet talk, had lost no time in sending the Authorities. She shot the bolt and leaned her weight against the door.

Miss Trotman tapped lightly. 'I only want to introduce myself,' she called. 'There's no need for alarm.'

'My God,' sneered Barbie. 'The stinking liar.'

'Barbie, dear. Open this door.' It was Mrs Purvis' voice. She had been climbing the stairs and had heard the altercation. 'Open this door and let me in.'

'I can't.'

'Why not, dear? What's going on?'

315

'She's come to take her away.'

'Barbie.' It was Miss Trotman's voice. 'I have no idea what you are talking about.'

'Oh, no? The health visitor sent her.'

'I haven't spoken to Mrs Neville all day. I've been out of my office. I merely came here to meet you.'

'Open the door, dear.' It was Mrs Purvis again. 'We can't talk like this. Let us in and we can sort something out.' Reluctantly, Barbie opened the door.

'Now; what's all this about?' Mrs Purvis made straight for the teapot and kettle, filling it at the sink. Miss Trotman followed her in and closed the door behind her.

'It's her arm,' said Barbie, nodding dumbly towards the cot.

'Her arm?' Mrs Purvis looked puzzled and went over to Glory, lifting her clothing. 'Oh; Barbie, dear. The poor little soul. And it's all my fault.' She was speaking to Barbie, but she was addressing herself to Miss Trotman. 'I knew I shouldn't have gone off last night and left you.'

Miss Trotman was looking equally puzzled. 'I think there's been a slight misunderstanding,' she said and she, too, went over to the cot. 'It is true that Mrs Neville will liaise with me; but we haven't spoken yet. As I said, I've been out of the office all day.' She examined Glory's arms and shoulders. 'This was merely a routine visit. I only came to introduce myself.'

'Well, now you've seen it for yourself,' said Barbie defiantly.

'Yes; I have.'

'So what are you going to do about it?'

'I don't know yet. I suggest we both sit down and talk about it.' She turned to Mrs Purvis, who was arranging cups and saucers on the table. 'Mrs Purvis,' she said. 'Would you mind if I had a word with Barbie – alone?'

'Of course, dear.' Mrs Purvis poured boiling water into the teapot and set it down beside the cups. 'Have yourself a cup of tea. Barbie could do with it.'

She touched Barbie lightly on the arm as she passed. 'I'll pop back later, dear, to see how you are.'

'Thanks, Mrs P.' Barbie turned to her with a thin smile. Mrs Purvis had not voiced one word of condemnation.

Marion Trotman watched Mrs Purvis leave. 'Would you like me to pour the tea for you?' she asked and Barbie nodded. She sat on the edge of the bed, frozen into inaction.

Miss Trotman poured two cups and handed one to Barbie. 'We had better start by you telling me something about yourself,' she said. 'Where would you like to begin?'

Barbie made no move to respond.

Miss Trotman looked at her for a moment and then sat quietly drinking her tea. She was about thirty, tall and plain, but with a warmth in her pale, hazel eyes.

'Do you find it difficult to talk about yourself?'

Barbie stared blankly at the cup before her. One tealeaf floated on the surface, swirling in a dance of decreasing circles.

'I understand that you're just turned twenty; you've lived in London for several years and you haven't been in touch with your family for some considerable time. Am I correct so far?'

Barbie shrugged indifferently.

'Let's go on from there.'

Barbie had no wish to be questioned. She closed her mind and continued to stare at the teacup.

'It's very important for you to try,' encouraged Miss Trotman. 'You're obviously in need of some support, and there's no way I can help you without your cooperation.'

Barbie raised her eyes slightly and looked at her.

'I want to help you, Barbie; really, I do. But you have to help me, too. You owe it to Glory. The only way I can help Glory is with your cooperation.'

Barbie nodded slowly. 'What do you want to know?'

'I need to know something about you. I know it's difficult for you, Barbie, but start at the beginning and tell me something about your parents.'

Barbie swallowed.'

'Take your time.'

'I didn't have any real parents,' she began. 'I lived with my Gran.' She told her story, leaving out nothing, and when she had finished she slumped her shoulders, feeling drained.

'Thank you,' said Miss Trotman. 'I know that wasn't easy.'

'And now I suppose you're going to say that I've made a real mess of things.'

'No. I was going to say that I've heard it all before.'

Barbie looked at her sharply.

'I've heard the same kind of life-story many times, Barbie – hundreds of times in the course of my career. Not exactly the same as yours; but all a variation on the same theme. We call it the cycle of deprivation.'

'The cycle of what?'

'Deprivation.'

'Well, at least it's only a mess like everyone else's,' she said sarcastically.

'Not at all; just because it's a widespread misfortune, it doesn't lessen the problems of the individual; nor the anguish it causes.'

'I suppose you're going to give me some clap-trap about my being a bad mother because I was illegitimate.'

'No. But you were deprived of love.'

'I had my Gran.'

'Yes; you had love in plenty from Gran. But it was taken away from you, suddenly, when you weren't expecting it; and it was never replaced.'

Barbie felt the prick of tears behind her eyes.

'And you have had difficulty ever since in forming new relationships.'

'I didn't need them,' said Barbie. She closed her eyes in danger of allowing the tears to escape.

'We all need them, Barbie. But, after you lost Gran, you found it impossible to form them.'

Barbie nodded.

'That's how the cycle begins. It usually occurs when people are deprived of love as babies. They experience this difficulty in forming relationships: then one day they grow up and have babies of their own. They have trouble forming a bond with the baby, and the cycle is complete: the baby is trapped in the same cycle. It can go on for generation after generation.'

'It doesn't seem fair.'

'It isn't. But, then, life is never dished out in fair measures. It's a lot easier to cope with it when you learn that there's no point in sitting back waiting for life to be fair.'

'So I just have to sit back, instead, and accept that I'm trapped,' said Barbie. 'That's a big help. Thank you very much.'

'That's not what I said.'

'No; but it's what it all amounts to. I lost my Gran; so now I knock my baby about and the Authorities come and try to take her away from me.'

'You start from the point of understanding. You recognise that you're caught up in a vicious circle from which it's very difficult to

318

escape. Once you understand the problem, you can begin to work towards a way of coping with it.'

'What did you call it again?'

'The cycle of deprivation.'

Barbie twisted her mouth. 'I suppose in the case of Barbie Harding, you could call it a "barbed circle".'

She returned the bitter smile with one more gentle. 'A barbed circle would describe it rather well,' she said.

Barbie sat and thought on it for a while. 'David once told me that life was a spiral,' she said. 'Now, you come along and tell me that it's a circle.'

'It does sound rather paradoxical when you put it that way.'

'And he said the spiral is always carrying you onwards and upwards. Now you say that the circle is dragging me down. How the hell is anyone supposed to go onwards and upwards, when they're trapped in a bloody circle which is dragging them down?'

'I've read several of David FitzGibbon's books.' Marion Trotman reached out and straightened the spoon in her saucer. 'I can't say that I agree with everything he says; but he does certainly force one to stop and think.'

Barbie looked up in surprise. Miss Trotman had opened up a new measure of communication between them. 'I never did get round to reading them,' she said. 'David did try to explain it to me; but I never did get round to actually reading the books.'

Marion Trotman smiled. 'You must be one of the few people who haven't. They're very popular.'

'You must think me awful.'

'Not at all. You had the author. The rest of us only have his books.'

There rose a sudden, almost uncontrollable, surge of grief. Barbie swallowed on it.

Marion Trotman noticed but chose not to comment upon it. 'I agree with him that life is an ongoing thing,' she said. 'It's nothing unless we keep looking forward. And it should also be uplifting.' She looked at Barbie and smiled. 'Life's wonderful, Barbie; it's meant to be enjoyed.'

Barbie closed her eyes. 'That's a pretty easy thing to say when you're not the one who's trapped.'

'We're all trapped in one way or another.'

'Except that it's easier for some to survive, than for others.'

'We all have to find our own way out. You owe it to yourself to

319

try. And you also owe it to Glory. Don't forget that Glory is caught up in the same trap.'

Barbie sighed and dug her teeth into her lower lip. 'If it's that difficult, I really don't see what I can do to try.'

'You start by making a conscious effort to build up a stable, loving relationship with Glory; and then you go on from there.'

Barbie turned, defensive. 'There's nothing wrong with my relationship with Glory.'

'Good. Let's cement that bond; then go on to others.'

'I don't need any others.'

'We all need other people, Barbie. You're not the exception to that rule.'

Barbie wondered if Miss Trotman could have any real understanding of rejection. 'You don't know,' she said, 'how it hurts . . .'

'Why did you leave David?'

The question caught Barbie by surprise.

'You left the best, most stable relationship you ever had.'

'I told you why.'

'You told me that you left him. You didn't tell me why.'

'Yes I did.'

'No; you didn't.'

'I told you that I didn't have any choice.'

'But you did.'

'No. I didn't. I had to.' She felt the muscles of her stomach contracting.

'Did he ask you to leave?'

'I've already told you,' she shouted. 'I had no choice.'

'Don't you think that he had the right to be consulted?'

The tears which had been threatening to fall, began to slide down the side of Barbie's nose. 'You don't understand.'

'Then tell me.'

'How can I? It just *hurts*.'

'But this time you hurt yourself.'

She spread the tears across her face with the flat of her hand.

'And, what's more, you hurt David.'

'No, I didn't. I only hurt myself.'

'You don't really believe that, Barbie.'

'He knew I had to go.'

'Do you really think that you could just walk out on him, without hurting him?'

320

Barbie did not want to hear this. 'I didn't hurt him,' she shouted, and raised her hands to her ears. 'I didn't.'

Marion Trotman lowered her voice to extreme gentleness. 'You did, Barbie. And you know it.'

'I didn't mean to. I honestly didn't mean to.'

'Don't you think he has a right now to know that he has a daughter?' Barbie looked up at her again. 'And hasn't Glory the right to know her father?'

'What do you mean?'

'Go back to him, Barbie. Go back and speak to him.'

'I can't.'

'You can, Barbie. You had the makings of a good relationship. It's worth re-building.'

'I can't go back.'

'Why?'

'I'd just die if he didn't want me any more.'

'That's a chance you'll have to take. But surely it's worth the risk?'

Barbie shook her head. 'Anyway, he's already got a wife.'

'I should have thought that he'd made his choice quite plain to you concerning his wife.' She paused for a moment and then went on. 'But now, after this lapse of time, you've got to go back and find out whether he's changed his mind.'

'He'd be so angry.'

'He has a right to be angry.'

'I couldn't bear him to be angry with me.'

'I think you'll find that, in the long run, love's a lot stronger than anger.'

Barbie shook her head. 'I couldn't,' she said. 'You don't know what you're asking.'

'I know very well. It's immensely difficult to you. But anything worth having, is worth taking a risk for.'

Barbie sat for a long time, saying nothing.

'There's another way of looking at it, Barbie. You owe it to David, to give him the chance. You owe it to David; you owe it to Glory; and you owe it to yourself.'

'Why can't I just go on with my own life, without opening up old wounds?'

'Would you like me to go with you?'

'No.' Barbie shook her head again and sighed. She felt physically drained. She leaned back and closed her eyes. She knew

321

now that she must return to Bishops Walk but the danger of David's rejection was too painful even to contemplate. 'I'll go by myself. I guess I owe him an apology.'

'Good.' Marion Trotman smiled at her across the table. 'I suggest you go as soon as possible. The longer you put it off, the more difficult it will become.'

Barbie nodded, her eyes still closed. 'Just give me a few days to build up my courage. I don't think I could make it right now.'

Marion Trotman smiled again and changed the subject. 'How do you get on with Mrs Purvis? She seems a very kind woman.'

'She is.'

'And fond of you?'

'Yes, I suppose she is.'

'I was thinking that she could be a great help to you.'

'She's going to look after Glory for me when I go back to work.'

'I know. It's just the kind of practical help that you need. But she could do more than that. Mrs Neville and I will give you all the support we can, but Mrs Purvis is on hand all the time. And she seems a very sensible woman.'

Barbie nodded. 'She took Glory out this morning so that I could sleep.'

'Would you like me to have a word with her, put her in the picture?'

Barbie looked uncertain. 'I wouldn't want . . .'

'It's not for me to tell her of your personal affairs, Barbie. Everything that you've told me has been accepted in confidence. But I could ask her to give you that extra bit of help with Glory.'

Barbie nodded. 'She's been very good to me.'

'Would you like me to have a word with her?'

'Yes,' said Barbie. 'I think I would.'

Mrs Purvis was asked to join them; she climbed the stairs still declaring that the incident of the previous night had been entirely due to her own failure, rather than to any fault on Barbie's part.

'Lord, bless you, dear,' she said. 'Of course I'll give you a hand. There's no need to ask. It'll give me something to do.'

'Thanks, Mrs P.'

'And when old Fowler comes back, you just bring her down to me all the time. Keep her out of the rotten bugger's way.'

'What about Mr Purvis? Won't he mind?'

'Don't you worry about him, dear. Just leave him to me. Give

322

him his telly, and his can of beer, and he won't give us any trouble.'

'But he's already got to put up with her all day while I'm at work.'

'I've already told you.' Mrs Purvis lowered her voice and tapped the side of her nose. 'Don't worry. To tell the truth, dear, he's got a soft spot for kids. Feels kind of cheated 'cause he had five of his own and no grandchildren. I reckon he'll take to having a little nipper about the place.' She laughed and poked Barbie on the arm. 'Might even get him up out of that chair.'

Marion Trotman joined the conversation. 'Thank you, Mrs Purvis. I'm most grateful to you.'

'Lord love us, dear. What are friends for, if we can't lend a hand.'

Barbie smiled ruefully. 'Only a few days ago I told someone that I didn't have any.'

'Give people a chance, Barbie,' said Marion Trotman. 'If you can just trust them, most will repay in equal measure.'

'Do they?' she asked doubtfully. She thought of David. 'I just hope they can all be equally forgiving.'

Chapter Sixteen

Barbie meandered her way through the streets of Chelsea, stopping to look in shop windows, turning off down side streets for no other purpose than to relive memories. Outwardly, she appeared relaxed but her eyes darted from place to place and her fingers were restless, touching her hair, her clothes, items on display in the stores through which she wandered, then returning to Glory whom she carried in a sling strapped about her shoulders and her waist. One part of her wanted to run headlong through the streets towards her destination but the other held back, afraid, for the fear of David's rejection overshadowed all. It was four weeks since her first conversation with Marion Trotman and still she had not yet summoned sufficient courage to approach him.

Strange contractions were taking place in the pit of her stomach, fluttering movements which robbed her of breath so that she had need to concentrate upon the act of breathing in order to restore the rhythm. There was a feeling of light-headedness and unsureness of foot, with the tingle of pins and needles, as though the blood supply, needing to converge upon her stomach and her lungs, had neglected the extremities.

Glory moved. In sleep she turned her head so that unsupported by the sling, it rolled back forcing her face upwards towards the sky. Barbie gently returned her to the support of the sling and, in addition, folded her arms across her body. Glory felt warm against her and she enfolded her more closely.

The past few weeks had been amongst the most constructive in Barbie's young life. She had been surrounded by help and guidance and she had responded to it, tenuously putting out the first feelers of trust. She had weaned Glory onto the feeding bottle and had gone back to work where she benefited from the return to a routine which was more familiar to her. Each morning, as she went down to open the café, she stopped off on the ground floor and handed Glory to Mrs Purvis. There was a feeling of relief in being able to off-load the sense of heavy responsibility but, at times when business was slack, Mrs Purvis would find her way into the café and would sit at a table drinking tea while Glory lay in her pram where Barbie could see her each time she passed.

Mrs Purvis had a way of handling Glory with a calm competence born of experience and this, by example, she passed to Barbie. Fowler had returned to the tenement only occasionally at weekends and at these times Mrs Purvis had kept an open door, day and night, wherein Barbie could seek refuge.

Mr Purvis, too, responded surprisingly well to the change in his routine. At first he ignored Glory and did no more than grunt at Barbie but, within a week, she was amused and delighted to catch him unawares dandling the baby upon his knee. 'There you are,' laughed Mrs Purvis. 'Told you the old bugger was soft with nippers.' Mr Purvis looked sheepish and handed Glory back to his wife but the next time Barbie called he was rocking her to sleep with a bawdy song about railway trains and milkmaids.

Mrs Neville visited frequently, offering Barbie much practical advice, teaching her to talk to Glory and to cuddle her. Little by little the bond of love was growing stronger.

Only one burden weighed down her lightened load and that was the struggle which she fought within herself concerning David. Each day she longed to go to him but each day she tarried, making excuses, then regretting them. She had not allowed herself to build up any hope of renewing the relationship, for to have hoped and failed would have been unendurable. It would have been like a gambler staking his life, except that Barbie would be forced to live on with the pain. Instead, she thought only of the need to speak to him, and to apologise, for the need to make amends lay heavily upon her.

Now, the thought of standing in his presence robbed her once again of breath. She sucked in air, feeling the strange contractions of her stomach. The uneven movement disturbed Glory, who worked her jaw in sucking movements as she slept.

Over the past four weeks she had started several times towards the streets of Chelsea; but never as close as this. Now, she stood on the corner of Bishops Walk and her courage threatened once more to desert her. She stood there for a long time; then, as if by some force in which she had no part, she began to move towards the gate.

The laurels had been cut back, giving an impression of greatly-increased space, and, in the centre of the lawn, the roses had been pruned. The house was newly-painted, standing white against the grey of the dull November day, the window frames outlined in black, and the shutters a shade of olive green. The virginia creeper had been pruned back and the remaining branches clung starkly bare against the newly-painted wall. Barbie stopped and looked up at the house, tasting the bitterness of jealousy because it was not she who had adorned it.

There were no cars on the drive. She half-convinced herself that David was not at home, and almost turned to leave, but her feet carried her on across the gravel drive and up the steps to the front door.

The sound of the doorbell reverberated through the interior of the house. Barbie heard movement and her mind flew into a panic. She should have prepared herself for what she was about to say. She could not string the simplest sentence through her brain.

Mrs Leach opened the door, her face simultaneously register-ing both recognition and surprise. 'Good afternoon, Miss.'

Barbie floundered. Her thoughts had been of David, not of Mrs Leach.

'Is there something I can do for you?'

She realised that she had been standing too long speechless. 'May I speak to David?'

'I'm afraid Mr FitzGibbon is no longer here, Miss.' Mrs Leach passed her tongue across her teeth and looked uncomfortable.

'Not here?'

'No, Miss. He moved away some time ago.'

Barbie reached out towards the wall. 'Do you know where?'

'I'm afraid I couldn't say, Miss. Would you like to speak to Mrs FitzGibbon?'

'No.' She turned to go.

'What is it, Mrs Leach?' The voice transfixed her.

'It's the young lady, Madam. The one who was staying here.'

Barbie heard the reaction. It was silent, yet it carried across the distance between them. She stood and listened to the sound of the wheelchair approaching across the tiled floor.

326

'It's all right, Mrs Leach.' Diana stopped as she reached the hall and sat for a moment, her eyes on Barbie. 'I'll deal with it.'

Mrs Leach glanced at Barbie then moved off towards the kitchen.

Diana said nothing as she propelled herself across the hall and remained silent still as she manoeuvred herself before the front door. 'What can I do for you?'

'I came to see David.'

'He isn't here.'

'I know.'

'Then what was it that you wanted?'

'It doesn't matter. I only . . .' She paused, then asked more directly, 'Can you tell me where he's gone?'

Diana shook her head several times from side to side. 'You've got a damned nerve,' she said at last.

'I only want to speak to him.'

'I bet you do.'

They remained looking at one another for a long time and Barbie noticed again the colour of Diana's eyes – a curious shade of violet blue.

'You have the nerve to come here,' said Diana, 'standing on my doorstep, complete with baby slung around your neck, and tell me that you wish to speak to my husband?'

'Yes,' said Barbie.

'Then you've got a damned nerve,' she said again.

Barbie stood looking at her, not knowing what to say.

'I suppose you walked straight out of here and got yourself into trouble with some other man.'

'No . . .'

'Was he married, too? How many more homes have you wrecked?'

Barbie winced.

'And, now, I suppose, you want David to bail you out?'

'I only wanted to speak to him.'

'I bet you did. But I'm afraid you're out of luck. It so happens that David has no wish to speak to you.'

It was the sharpest stone of all. 'I thought . . .'

'He's forgotten you, my dear. He's gone off on some other wild-goose chase.'

Barbie turned and began to walk down the steps.

'I'd like you to know . . .' said Diana, and Barbie stopped, with one foot on the lower step. Her voice had lowered but it was embedded with the same ice which glinted in her eyes. 'I'd like you to know that you destroyed more lives than one when you walked out of this house.'

'I never meant to hurt him.'

'Don't play the innocent with me.'

'I never meant to hurt anyone.'

'But you did, didn't you. You came here, playing games; and when you had had enough, you ran off to play them with someone else.'

'No.'

'At first I thought it was nothing more than we could expect. If David was weak enough to get himself caught up with a young girl of half his age, then we must expect her to behave like an irresponsible child.' She paused and levelled Barbie with the icy stare. 'But it was more than that, wasn't it; it was a deliberate ploy.'

'Deliberate?'

'Yes; deliberate. You deliberately set out to rob me of my husband.'

'No!'

'I loved David; and you robbed me.'

'You bleeding liar.' Shock and tension revealed itself in a sudden burst of explosive anger.

'I beg your pardon?'

'I said: you are a bleeding liar.'

Diana drew back slightly and Barbie noticed her fingers, long and slender, clamped white on the arms of the wheelchair.

'You,' went on Barbie, 'don't even know what love is.'

'My God! You have the nerve to stand there . . . ?'

'Yes,' said Barbie. 'Yes, I do. You have no idea what love is all about.'

'I suppose it's about walking in here – taking everything you can get from my husband – then walking out, without even a word of thanks.'

'You bleeding hypocrite.'

'I beg your pardon?'

'Who left him and went to Sussex? Who left him when he was grieving for his son?'

'*Our* son.'

'It was his son, too.'

328

'You impertinent little . . .'

'You only came back because your sister didn't want you any more. She had better things to do than look after a selfish, self-centred, bitch like you.'

'How dare you!'

Barbie flinched backwards, sensing that, if Diana had been standing, she would have struck her.

'Get out of here.'

'Not until you tell me where he is.'

'Over my dead body.' The words were levelled down to a savage, controlled rage which frightened Barbie more than unleashed anger.

'I need to know.'

'And I have no intention of telling you.'

'Please.'

'I will tell you just one thing.' She sat for a brief moment, her eyes biting into Barbie's. 'I will tell you, right now, to leave my house. If I ever catch you again within half a mile of this door, I promise you that I shan't answer for the consequences.'

'Just tell me . . .'

She thrust her chair backwards to clear the doorway. 'Goodbye,' she said, and slammed the heavy door in Barbie's face.

The noise woke Glory. The tiny body jerked against Barbie and screamed. Barbie's hands moved instinctively to comfort her, cradling her as she turned and walked away. The muscles of her legs had turned to pulp and it was as if she had to issue verbal instructions to steer them towards the gate.

There was a total sense of unreality about her surroundings. David had gone. She knew now that all the time she had thought of him at Bishops Walk, he had been accessible; now he had gone. It was like losing Gran all over again, without a grave, and with nowhere to pinpoint her thoughts.

She stumbled her way back across the city to King's Cross, automatically going through the motions of travel but paying no heed to the means of transport. She wanted to get back to her room, to close the door, like an animal running for its lair.

In the hall of the tenement block Mrs Purvis was standing, white-faced. Several other residents stood about, looking uncomfortable.

'He's dead, Barbie.'

'I know.' How could Mrs Purvis know?

'I just went in and found him lying there.'

Through the mist of Barbie's mind it slowly permeated that Mrs Purvis was referring to her husband. 'Oh God, Mrs P. No!'

'The old bugger's dead. He's on the floor.'

Barbie looked through the open door. Mr Purvis was on the floor, lying awkwardly in death. 'Come away, Mrs P.'

'No, dear. I can't. I've got to go and pick him up.'

Barbie shook her head. 'I'll call an ambulance.'

'He's dead.'

'They'll know what to do.'

'I just walked in and found him there.'

'The ambulance people will know what to do.'

'They're on their way.' Another resident stepped in and interrupted.

'Oh, yes, dear. I forgot. I've got to go in there and pick him up.'

'You can't do any good in there.' The neighbour leaned forward and closed the door.

'I've got to, dear. I can't just leave him lying there.'

Things moved quickly. The ambulance came and carried Mr Purvis away. Barbie watched it, stunned, one state of shock overlaid by another.

'Come up to my room and have a cup of tea,' she said.

'I can't, dear. I can't go off and leave him.'

'He's gone now. They've taken him away.'

'I can't go off and leave him, dear.'

She refused to be drawn upstairs, but neither would she go into her own room. Barbie, too, had no wish to enter and they stood, instead, in the dingy hall. Someone fetched a chair for Mrs Purvis and set it down beside an old bicycle leaning against the wall.

'We've sent for her son.'

'Her son?'

'I told them, dear.'

'She gave us a number and asked us to ring.'

'He's a good boy, dear. He said that he'd come.'

'He'll be here soon.' A neighbour brought out a mug of tea and handed it to Mrs Purvis.

'Oh, Barbie. The old bugger's dead.'

'Yes, Mrs P.'

'I should never have said all those things about him.'

'Shh . . .'

'And now he's gone and I can't even say I'm sorry.'

330

'Don't talk like that.'

'He wasn't such a bad old bugger.'

'Don't, Mrs P.'

'I loved him, you know.'

'He loved you, too.'

'Do you think he did?'

'I'm sure he did.'

'But I didn't even say I'm sorry.'

Mrs Purvis' son appeared as if from nowhere and took his mother to one side, leaving Barbie standing alone. She went upstairs to her room. There seemed a strange silence hanging about the place and Barbie, feeling numbed, found herself going through the routine of feeding Glory and tidying the room as though nothing untoward had happened.

Later, Mrs Purvis tapped on the door. 'Come in, Mrs P.'

Mrs Purvis was pale, with small red veins standing out on her cheeks, and her movements were jerky as if with enforced control. 'Did you see my son?'

'Yes,' said Barbie. 'I met him downstairs.'

'He's a good boy. He came when they sent for him.'

'Yes,' said Barbie, lost for the words she needed.

'He's going to take me back to Ilford, dear. I can't go back in that room downstairs. I just can't.'

Barbie nodded her understanding. 'You'll be better with your son.'

'He's got his own place over in Ilford.'

'You'll be better there.'

'He asked me to go and stay there for a while. Maybe go and live if his wife agrees. She works for the Gas Board, you know.'

'Oh,' said Barbie lamely.

'I haven't seen much of him lately. He didn't get on with his Dad.'

'Yes. You told me.'

'Oh, did I, dear?'

'Yes,' said Barbie again.

Mrs Purvis was folding and re-folding her hands in her lap. 'He was a good boy to come when they sent for him.'

'When are you going to Ilford?'

'Now, dear. He's waiting downstairs.' Mrs Purvis rose from the chair, a glazed expression across her eyes. 'I didn't want to leave you when you need me, dear.'

331

'Don't be silly, Mrs P. You have to go.'

'I'd better ring Miss Trotman and tell her.'

'No.' A sharp arrow of fear zinged its way through the numbness of Barbie's mind. 'No,' she said. 'I'll tell her.'

'Are you sure, dear? Tell her I'm sorry. Tell her I didn't want to let you down.'

'Oh, Mrs P.' Barbie wrapped her arms about the limp figure of Mrs Purvis. 'I love you, Mrs P.'

'Do you, dear? I'm sorry. It's the shock.'

Mrs Purvis' son came to the door and led his mother away by the arm. 'Come on, Mum,' he said. 'I'll take you home.'

'Will you, dear?' she said. 'That's nice.'

The door closed behind them and Barbie was alone once more. The silence was heavy and slowly, particle by particle, the knowledge settled upon her that Mrs Purvis had gone away. The sense of loss was unacceptable at that moment. Her mind would not tolerate the additional load and she transferred it mechanically into practicalities. Without Mrs Purvis there was no one to look after Glory and, without anyone to look after Glory, there was always the possibility that she would be taken away. This was Saturday evening. She need not work tomorrow but by Monday morning she must find another baby-minder.

Mrs Purvis had spoken of a Mrs Tindall. Barbie sought her out and went to see her.

'I'm sorry, dear,' said Mrs Tindall. 'I've got my quota. They're very hot about overcrowding. I'd lose my licence.'

Barbie's heart sank. Mrs Tindall stood at her open front door, two of her own toddlers clinging to her skirt.

'I already take two babies and three other little tots. That's all I'm allowed.'

'Oh, I see,' said Barbie. 'Do you know of anyone else?'

'There's a Mrs Fisher in Wendell Street; or Mrs O'Rourke. I did hear that Mrs Jankowska had a vacancy last week; but I expect it will be gone by now.'

Barbie followed up these suggestions, then spent the greater part of Sunday making other enquiries; but she was unable to come to any satisfactory arrangement for the care of Glory. By Monday morning she knew that she had no alternative but to take her with her when she went to work.

She ought to have notified Miss Trotman of her change of circumstances, but she had no intention of doing so. Either she or

Mrs Neville might have been able to assist in finding another baby-minder. But, how could she be sure? After weeks of sustained work in building up a sense of trust, that trust had been undermined in a single day.

She wheeled the perambulator into the café and parked it in the corner close to the counter where she could keep a constant watch on Glory. Business was slack but by midday the lunchtime trade was building up. She knew that Glory was about to wake for her twelve o'clock feed but a steady stream of customers were threading their way through the tables and her hands were more than full.

When the moment came, she was summoned first by whimpers which grew in intensity until they rose to a scream. The customers made light of the situation, joking about the noise, but Barbie's nerves were frayed, feeling herself torn between two equally demanding rôles. She found herself fumbling, lacking her usual competence, and swore distractedly as she dropped the fried egg she was sliding from the pan.

In the midst of the confusion, Bert Fabrozzi appeared. 'What's going on in here?' It was unusual for Fabrozzi to put in an appearance and fate had decreed that it must be at a moment of least convenience.

Barbie explained her difficulty but he was not impressed.

'I told you when you came here what would happen if you couldn't do the work,' he said. 'You'd better find someone quick.'

'I can't,' said Barbie. 'There isn't anyone who can look after her.'

'Well, you can't bring her in here. I'm not having my customers frightened away by squalling kids.'

'I'm sorry, but I had no choice.'

'What d'you think this place is – a flaming nursery?'

'Look, I'm trying. But it's going to take time.'

'You haven't got much time. If you can't do the job, I can always find someone else who can.'

Barbie held her tongue and slapped a portion of chips onto a plate.

'What's she bawling for, anyway?'

'She's hungry. It's time for her feed.'

Fabrozzi snatched the pan from Barbie's hands. 'Well, go and give it to her, for Gawd's sake, and shut her up.'

Barbie relinquished the pan and hurriedly took Glory into the back room where she fed her and returned with all possible speed. 'I'll take over now,' she said. 'She ought to be quiet.'

'I hope you're right.' Fabrozzi was doing nothing to disguise his annoyance. 'When I call in here tomorrow I want to see this place back in some sort of order.'

Barbie was no less annoyed but, as she watched him leave the café, she knew that she must do something quickly. Her job and her home depended upon it.

Glory did not settle in her pram. She grizzled, demanding attention. Eventually, in desperation, Barbie slipped to her room to fetch the sling. She strapped Glory across her chest then, realising the danger from the splashing oil of the pan, reversed the sling so that she carried her upon her back. She carried her there all afternoon and, by six o'clock, her back was aching.

She went home to her room and eased the sling from her shoulders, setting Glory down upon the bed. Immediately, she began to cry.

'Oh, for goodness sake, Glory; can't I have just a few minutes' peace?'

She fed her. Barbie had not eaten all day but there was no time for her to think of food. Darkness had already fallen and she must go out into the mist-laden November night. She hitched the sling once more about her shoulders, transferring the weight this time to her chest: her muscles went into a spasm of cramp.

It was a thick, miserable night with mist hanging listlessly at rooftop level, collecting in droplets to fall from overhanging awnings, or swirling in eddies down back-alleyways like the breath of some disgruntled ogre.

She passed two women in the street and overheard snatches of conversation. '. . . Taking a baby out on a night like this . . .' She hitched Glory more snugly into the sling and trudged on.

She travelled widely, moving from one unlikely lead to another, but at ten o'clock she returned, having achieved nothing. She was cold, tired, and dispirited, and when she heard voices from the room next door her spirits dropped to an all-time low. Fowler was back.

'Oh God,' she breathed. It was half-way between a curse and a supplication. 'What have I done to deserve it?'

She put Glory to bed then switched on the television while she heated a can of soup. The television was showing a situation comedy programme with dubbed audience laughter which irritated her.

She switched channels to a discussion programme – sombre, intellectual voices discussing some obscure subject not immediately apparent to her. She left it switched on for the sound of voices to drown the silence of her own room and of Fowler's conversation from the next. She paid no heed until another voice joined the discussion.

'David . . . ?'

She sucked in her breath and held it. Her back was turned to the screen and she stood motionless, staring at the wall, until it came again. It was David.

She turned and, as she did so, he looked towards the camera as if meeting her eye.

'*David . . . !*'

She went down on her knees before the screen, pressing her hands against the flat, unyielding surface which sought to repel her with a tingling sensation through her fingers.

Trauma and unresolved grief seethed to the surface and overflowed in tears which fell hot and stung her cheeks. She was crying full and hard so that she fought for breath.

Glory began to whimper. At first Barbie ignored her, then rose mechanically and went to fetch her from the cot, returning to sit upon the floor before the television set, endeavouring to see, but blinded by her own tears.

David was sitting on the edge of the group, at the far end of the table. Glory's cries smothered the sound of his voice and she reached out to increase the volume.

'Shh, Glory,' she said and rocked her, but it was more a shake.

The camera tracked away and fell upon another face. She did not want to see. It was not David. Where was David?

Glory clawed the air and screamed afresh. 'Shut up, Glory. I'm trying to hear.'

The camera tracked again, this time to David; but he did not look at her.

'David – I'm here.'

The tears were falling still, blinding her, coursing down her cheeks to fall salty into her mouth. The need for David filled her until she felt inflated like some grotesque balloon, seeping salty tears.

'I'm here, David. David, I'm here.'

She discarded Glory to the floor beside her and went again to touch the screen. Glory showed her objection by increasing the intensity of her cries.

'SHUT UP!'

It brought a banging upon the wall. 'Shut that bleeding row in there!'

'Shut up yourself,' retorted Barbie.

David was speaking again. She tried to hear, endeavouring to draw down into herself the sound of his voice; but Glory's cries were drowning it.

'SHUT UP!' she shouted and increased the volume of the set to maximum. 'SHUT UP!'

'What the bleeding hell is going on in there?' Fowler's voice thundered above the noise.

She turned on Glory. 'SHUT UP! Shut up – or I'll . . .'

Glory's face had turned a deep crimson colour, clashing with the red-gold hair. She looked ugly. 'It's all your fault!' Barbie thought only to stop the noise, to break the intrusion upon her need for David. 'You ugly, squawling, leeching, little . . .' She raised her fist.

Glory seemed to sense the danger and flinched into a rigid spasm of fright. But, even as she did so, Barbie let her hand fall limp.

Music was coming from the television screen and captions were rolling. The camera was on the chairman, not on David, and as he spoke the picture faded. The screen flashed white then produced a nubile figure advertising toothpaste. David was gone.

'Oh, God, what have I done?' She had done nothing; but the intention had been there.

She was still sobbing, but now with dry eyes which stung and smarted. She forced the sobs, beating herself with the pain. She realised now the futility of it all. It was only a matter of time before, eventually, she would give the Authorities cause to condemn her. It was as inevitable as all the other inevitabilities which stretched behind her like tombstones.

She wanted to run away and hide, to crawl into a hole and pull in the world on top of herself. She wanted David – but David had faded from the screen. She wanted Gran. Above all, she wanted a place where she could go and hide.

The solution came to her without effort, as if it, too, were inevitable. She wrapped Glory into a thick blanket and strapped her once more into the sling. Then she threw a number of items into a bag and set out across the mist-laden city to catch a train.

It was in the early hours of the morning when she alighted at an almost-deserted station. There were no buses running at this hour and she struck out towards country lanes.

The mist of London had settled here to a thick fog, and her footsteps echoed eerily through a silence heightened by the grey blanket. Glory slept, jolting against her as she walked. Apart from a few brief periods of respite, she had carried her since midday. Her back, which had been aching, had now taken on a numbness which posed no questions but toiled on, obeying an equal numbness of mind.

There were no footpaths on country lanes. She walked on tarmac, her footsteps ringing out towards hedges and trees which could not be seen, rebounding back against the obstruction of fog. Occasionally, she was forced to take refuge upon the grass verge as vehicles nosed their way, headlights probing the night like sensors, looming as if from nowhere and fading with a muffled roar of protest into the fog. The grass was wet, collecting the moisture, droplet by droplet, to hang pendulous upon the blades, before trickling down to soak her feet.

Objects loomed, took shape, and receded – gate-posts, bushes, boundary walls. A pheasant, disturbed from its resting place, took flight across her path, clacking the night to shreds. She jumped at the unexpected noise but the numbness of her mind was not stimulated to fright. She watched the grey shape swoop and disappear with a clatter as it hit the field on the opposite side of the lane.

She made her way onwards, more by instinct than by conscious effort, until she passed objects more familiar and came at last to the edge of the village. She passed buildings, hardly recognisable in the gloom – the lychgate standing before the solid mass of the church, the low thatch of the village store, the Post Office where she used to draw Gran's pension, and on, until she reached the cottage.

There was something different about the cottage but, in the fog, she could not make out what it was. The outline was the same, hardly distinguishable, but familiar. It was something about the atmosphere, as though others had recently trodden the path. She tripped over something and cursed. It was a plank of wood. She made her way along its length, guiding her way with her fingers against the wall. There were other objects lying about, odd shapes which she could not make out in the murky darkness.

The door was standing slightly ajar and, timorously, she pushed her way inside, remembering that the way had been barred when last she had visited with David. All was in total darkness. Her footsteps echoed on the stone floor with a strange, ringing, hollow sound and it was not until she felt about her, reaching out into the darkness with her fingers and with her feet, that she discovered the reason. She searched around for the table but it was not there. The room was completely empty. All the fittings had been removed.

She felt her way through the hall and up the stairs, the same clattering echo of emptiness pervading the whole cottage. In the bedroom she felt for the bed. It was not there. Questions circulated through a brain fuddled by trauma and by need of sleep, but she could not come to grips with them.

She found her way to the corner of the bedroom and slid down the wall until she was crouched upon the floor. There, she unstrapped Glory, stretching her shoulder muscles with a wince of pain, and settled her across her lap. From the bottom of her bag she felt for a feeding bottle filled with milk. It was unheated and at first Glory complained, alternately sucking and spitting out the teat, but hunger overcame objection and eventually she settled down to drink, breaking the empty silence with the snuffling sounds of contentment.

Barbie remembered that the last time she had been in the cottage there had been a hole in the roof above this room. She looked up towards the ceiling, expecting to see a faint glow through the darkness, but over all there was the same uniform blackness, except that from the blackness there came a slight sound, a soft, soughing whisper which she could not identify.

She did not try to guess its origin for she had no wish to answer questions. She had no idea what the morrow would bring, only that tonight she had come home. She had come to Gran and she needed sleep. She laid back her head against the wall and drifted into a state of semi-consciousness.

It was still dark when Glory awoke for her six o'clock feed. Barbie took another bottle from her bag then went to the window but she could see nothing through the dust-encrusted glass and returned to the corner. She was cold and, holding Glory close to her, she curled up on the floor and dozed again, waiting for the dawn.

It was almost eight o'clock when a pale light filtered across the room. She stood up, moving Glory gently to one side and rearranging the blanket about her. It was cold and Barbie's limbs were aching; her back and shoulders were stiff, and the calf muscles of her legs were taut with cramp. She stretched painfully and went over to the window. She would go downstairs and find wood to build a fire. Then she would go into the village for provisions. She had no more milk with which to feed Glory and she herself had not eaten since the previous morning.

She still could not see through the grime on the window, so she opened it, forcing it when it resisted her pressure, scraping it outwards on rusty hinges. Daybreak had brought a stirring of wind which was shredding the fog and she could see almost halfway to the village.

But it was not the distant view which attracted her attention; it was the strip of garden immediately below the window. There, she saw the plank of wood over which she had tripped the previous night and knew now that it had slipped from a pile of sawn timber stacked beneath the hedge. Nearby there were piles of bricks, arranged neatly, row upon row.

She looked quickly upwards towards the ceiling and knew at once the origin of the sound she had heard from the roof, for it was covered with tarpaulin. Someone was re-building the cottage, invading its privacy. At any moment workmen would arrive and order her away.

There was no haven left to her now. She had been irresponsible to come here on a whim, bringing with her a young baby for whom she had no adequate care. It would go against her with the Authorities.

'I'm a fool, Glory.' She picked up the sleeping infant and held her. 'I've played right into their hands.'

Glory stirred and re-settled herself against the warmth of Barbie's body. 'I've given them an open invitation to walk right in and take you from me.' She drew her tightly against her chest and Glory struggled against the hold.

She thought she heard movement outside and went nervously to the window but there was no one there. She went back to the corner and laid Glory on the floor, covering her again with the blanket.

'I'll just take a look around and then we'll be on our way,' she said. 'There's no place left here for us now.' She knew that she had little time before the workmen came but, with shoulders slumped, she left the room and went to say goodbye.

At the landing window she paused – as she had always paused – and gazed out across the garden. The fog was lifting quickly, allowing a weak sun to break through onto the sodden landscape. Everywhere was damp, water dripping from guttering, from trees, from hedges, and from the sheets of white plastic draped across the pile of timber.

She watched a droplet grow and plop as the sun fell upon it and sparked a rainbow. Beneath her the overgrown vegetation was laid flat, beaten down by heavy rain, submitting itself to the oncoming decay of winter. The walnut tree, its one broken bough still hanging limp, stood denuded of leaves, and the elders pointed bare twigs, like gnarled fingers, towards the sky. Beyond the hedge, the barley field had been ploughed, lying in rich, dark furrows which stretched towards the copse, still partly hidden by the mist.

Barbie looked out across the scene and saw, not damp desolation, but the playground of her childhood – aching, bittersweet memories which carried her away until once again she was the child looking out upon the morning. She searched for birds and, as her eyes became attuned, saw a robin upon the roof of the privy, its sharp eyes cocked. In the walnut tree a blackbird set up the 'pink . . . pink . . . pink' of warning. A dog barked. Lost in her daydream, she thought for a moment that it was Bess. It came again and she smiled at its familiar sound.

Familiar? She snapped back to the present and listened again. There was silence but still the blackbird pinked the warning of approach. She strained her ears and eyes, searching for evidence of what she knew she had heard but which she could not believe.

She craned her neck and saw a flash of red – a large red dog bounding through the undergrowth.

'Sam!' she screamed but the sound caught in her throat and emerged as a high-pitched squeal.

She leaned further, desperate to see the lane but the lane was on the opposite side of the cottage. She turned and ran, blundering her way across the landing, tripping over her feet with a clatter which resounded through the empty shell. She ran across the bare floorboards of the bedroom and flung wide the window, leaning out in her frantic effort to see who might be approaching.

David saw her at the same moment that she saw him, the same look of incredulity upon his face, and she saw him mouth her name.

She ran, clattering down the stairs and, as she crossed the kitchen, heard footsteps running down the path towards her. They met at the door and fused in a tangle of grasping arms, feeling her fingers clawing into the flesh of his neck as he caught her to him.

Both tried to talk; each stopped the other with their kisses.

'I thought I'd never find you.'

Her fingers were probing the contours of his face, finding again the shape of his ears, the feel of the soft hair on the back of his neck.

'I've searched for you,' he said. 'I've searched the whole of London; and half of England.'

'I went to Bishops Walk and they told me that you'd gone away.'

He tore himself away, just long enough to say, 'I waited for you, Barbie. I waited for months but you didn't come.'

'I asked your wife but she wouldn't tell me.'

'Didn't she tell you that I was here?'

She shook her head. 'I asked her but she wouldn't say.'

'Damned bitch.' He tightened his hold until it hurt. 'I might have known what she would do.'

'I'm sorry, David,' she said. 'I'm so very sorry.'

He drew back and looked at her, holding her out at arms' length. 'Oh, Barbie. I've asked myself a thousand times what I'd do at this moment. Now, I don't know whether to kiss you, or to hug you, or just to spank you.' She bit her lip. 'I think I might very well spank you.'

'Are you angry with me?'

'I'm angry; I'm happy; I'm confused; I love you. God, but I love you.' He pulled her back towards him and kissed her roughly. 'If you ever run off like that again I swear that I'll kill you.'

'You are angry.'

'No; I'm not angry. I just thought that I'd die.'

'I never meant to hurt you.'

'Where have you been? You've no idea how far I've searched for you.'

'I never realised that you'd go and look for me.'

'Damn it, Barbie; of course I looked for you.'

'I'm sorry,' she said again.

He kissed her, tenderly this time. 'You're here now, and that's all that matters.'

'What are you doing here, David?'

He held her away from him so that he could see the expression upon her face and a grin spread across his own face until she laughed through her incredulity. 'I bought the cottage,' he said.

'You did what?'

'I bought the cottage.' He picked her up and swung her round in a mad, twirling dance.

'I can't believe . . .' She worked her mouth and fought to find the words as he laughed at her bewilderment.

'Now you've come home,' he said.

Tears of relief welled up with the left-over tears of grief and loneliness which had need to be washed away.

'You're home, Barbie,' he said again. 'Welcome home.'

He led her to the pile of timber stacked beneath the hedge and sat her down upon it, both of them crying and laughing at the same time.

'I'm going to wake up in a minute and find that I'm dreaming.'

He took out his handkerchief, dabbing the tears from her face. 'I found an old chap named Bateson and told him I wanted to buy it.'

'I remember Mr Bateson. He used to come for the rent.'

'He was quite happy to part a fool from his money.'

'You should have heard the things Gran used to say about him.'

'He must be ninety now, if he's a day. Heaven only knows why he never bothered to have the place repaired.'

'Gran used to say he was loaded. Perhaps he didn't need the money.'

'Then it's a pity the old skinflint didn't do something about it while you were still living here.'

Barbie shook her head. 'No,' she said. 'Then someone else would have moved in and the cottage wouldn't have waited.'

He smiled at her.

'Oh, David; whatever gave you the idea of buying it?'

'I don't know,' he said. 'It just came to me one day when I was desperate. It just seemed the logical thing to do. It was the one place where I could be near you – in spirit, if not in person.'

He sat fingering her hair and letting it run through his hands. 'I've been staying at the pub in the village waiting for the workmen to get under way.'

'All that time you were here; and I didn't know.'

'I stayed at Bishops Walk until it was obvious that you weren't coming back. Then I stayed at a number of places but I could never settle.'

'I'm sorry, David. I never meant to hurt you.'

He changed his tone before she could slip once more into tears. 'What shall we do with the cottage?' he asked. 'I've cleared the furniture but I've kept it all in store in case there's anything you need.'

'I'd like the table,' she said. 'We could scrub it and put it back in the kitchen. And the clock from the hall.'

'You can have anything you like,' he said. 'So long as you promise that you'll never go off like that and leave me again.'

'We'll have some old, some new.'

'And there's your garden.'

'Just as it always was; with wild flowers and honeysuckle.'

'Of course,' he said. 'We must preserve our honeysuckle bower.'

She met his eyes and met such a depth of love that she caught her breath. 'I love you,' she whispered and, placing her fingers upon his jaw, she kissed him.

'Come on; we'll go to my room at the pub.'

She glanced towards the bedroom window. 'There's something I have to tell you first.'

'Tell me later,' he said. He called for Sam. 'There'll be time for everything later.'

Sam had been running on the far side of the field. In response to the call he broke through the hedge but then he stopped, hesitated a moment, one paw suspended as if testing the air; then, with one great whooping bark of recognition, he fell upon Barbie, toppling her backwards onto the timber. 'Oh, Sam. You remember me.' He trampled her and lapped his tongue about her ears, giving out soft yelps of delight.

'Of course he remembers you. Did you think that he'd forget?'

Sam gave one last lick of welcome and ran off to fetch a stick. He brought it to her feet and cocked his head, waiting. She took it from him and threw it far into the dense undergrowth. 'Go on, boy. Find it.' He let out a loud retort and bounded through the sodden vegetation, setting up a loud clammering din which echoed across the misty landscape. Suddenly, above the noise, there came the sound of Glory's cries.

David stopped in his tracks and looked aghast.

'I was going to tell you,' she said. There was a dreadful expression of doubt upon his face. 'It's my baby. She's upstairs.'

He shook his head in disbelief. 'I don't believe . . .'

'Her name's Glory.'

'Oh, Barbie, *no*. Don't tell me that . . .'

'Your baby,' she corrected hesitantly.

He stopped abruptly and looked at her again.

'Our baby.'

'*Our* baby?'

'Yes; ours.'

'But you weren't . . .'

'Remember California?'

With one bound he had turned and was making for the stairs. By the time she caught up with him he was in the bedroom holding Glory in his arms. 'Oh Barbie, how could you?'

'I'm sorry, David.'

'How could you stay away with our child?'

'I didn't know you'd feel like that.'

'How else am I supposed to feel? It must have been dreadful for you. How on earth did you cope?'

'I'm sorry, David.'

'You were all on your own.'

'I didn't do very well. I'm not much of a mother, David.'

'Then why didn't you come to me?'

'I guess I was afraid.'

'Afraid? God, Barbie; what does anyone have to do to convince you?' He reached out for her, holding her against his shoulder, with Glory still crooked in his other arm. 'How could you be afraid of me?'

'Miss Trotman told me to come back.'

'Who's Miss Trotman?'

'I'll tell you later.' She buried her face against his shoulder. 'I made a terrible mess of things.'

'What do you expect, trying to cope without support?'

'I'm not a very good mother, David. You'd never believe . . .'

344

'She's beautiful, Barbie,' he said. 'She's just like you.'

'I know; I'm sorry.'

'Why sorry?'

'I wanted you.'

He shook his head at her. 'It's a damned lucky bastard who loses one red-haired beauty, and then finds two.'

She laughed. 'She'll keep you awake all night.'

'I don't care.' He looked at her and there was the old familiar glint in his eye. 'I doubt that I shall be sleeping much, anyway.'

'I love you too,' she smiled.

'We'll have our bed right here, close to the window, where you can see the sun. And come to think of it, we'll need to build on an extra room. I wasn't planning on accommodating a family.'

They were standing before the window. Outside, Sam was racing through the garden, stopping every now and then to spin in circles. 'Look at that dog,' he said. 'He's gone mad just because you're home.'

'He's as crazy as ever.'

He sped off again and there came a loud, snapping report. Barbie raised her head and listened.

'It was the sound of a dead branch snapping. Sam must have jumped on it in the undergrowth.'

'No,' said Barbie. 'You've just heard the sound of a barbed circle breaking.'

Glory Jean FitzGibbon opened her eyes and blinked at the morning. Outside, a blackbird was fluting his song from the topmost branch of the walnut tree; the housemartins were twittering in their nest beneath the sill, and, far away in the village, a dog barked, echoing through the still morning air. She threw back the covers and padded, barefoot, to the open window. At ten years old the world holds too many promises to lie in bed.

In the corner Sam stirred and came to greet her. He was an old dog now, turned grey about the muzzle, no longer boisterous. 'Lazy old thing,' she said. 'Want some breakfast?' He licked her hand and led the way downstairs.

As she passed her brother's room she looked inside and snorted at the sight of dark auburn curls immobile upon the pillow. 'Lazy thing,' she said. 'He's lazier than you.' She picked up the faded, dishevelled, toy gorilla which had fallen to the floor and tossed it carelessly upon the bed. Two steps further she peeped into her parents' room, limbs entwined one within the other, as they always were in sleep. She smiled and tiptoed away. She would go downstairs and make them tea. At ten, she was old enough to creep downstairs and make them tea.

At the landing window she paused – as she always paused – and gazed out across the garden, to a profusion of wild raspberries and rosebay willowherb, while, at its boundary, bindweed and old man's beard still fought for prominence amid the giant saucers of elderflower which frothed and bobbed. She sighed with a feeling of love and belonging which was almost pain. This had been her home for all but the first few weeks of her life and she would never wish to be anywhere else.

A rabbit ran across the grass and she followed it with her eye. Glory knew every inch of this garden for she shared its secrets with her mother. She knew of the moist green hidey-hole beneath the elder hedge where hop vines spread their curtain; where she could sit and watch the rabbits at play; could see the flash of the goldfinch's wings as he feasted upon the seed-heads of the thistle; and listen to the hoarse, cracked squeal of the pheasant as he strutted through the barley field. She was a friend to the ants which lived at the foot of the walnut tree and of the beetles which hid beneath the stones. She knew the joy of running through scabious, foxglove and golden rod, of playing hide-and-seek in shoulder-high cow parsley, and daydreaming in a great perfumed sea of honeysuckle.

Sam pushed his nose against her hand and she turned to follow him down the stairs. In the kitchen she brewed tea, poured a good measure into a bowl for Sam, and filled two mugs for David and Barbie.

The lower stairs were in shadow. She counted them as she climbed, carrying the two mugs of hot, strong tea in her hand. 'One, two, three, four, five . . .'

Upon the eighth stair the landing window spilled its light – a cascade of June morning, splashing, bubbling, dribbling its way down the honey-coloured carpet of the staircase. She reached for it with her toe, '. . . nine, ten, eleven, twelve . . .' until, at the fourteenth stair, she stood on the landing and lifted her face to the full warmth of the sun.